Joshua Rutherford

PEACEFALL

BOOK TWO OF THE FOURPOINTE CHRONICLES

PEACEFALL | *Book Two of The Fourpointe Chronicles*

Published 2021

ISBN-13: 978-1737129011

Published by:
Falcon Compass Press
Austin, TX

For my North Star, Elisa
For my Falcon, David
For my Compass, Nathaniel

Acknowledgments

So much of myself went into this novel. And so much more happened in my personal life to remind me of the blessings God has granted me, especially some major life changes over the past few years. I could not have gotten through the many obstacles I encountered – including the completion of this book – had it not been for the love and support of many. First, I would like to thank my family, starting with my parents and my sister, whose jokes, conversations, and love have provided me relief, even as the miles still separate us. Then there are my friends – both those back home in San Diego and my newfound ones here in Austin – who have cheered me on to complete this latest installment. As with my last novel, a special acknowledgment to my brothers from high school and college – Greg Gibsen, Danny Hawn, Visva Huynh, Tom Buaas, and Jesse York. I also want to thank those friends I have made through Toastmasters and the Young Hispanic Professional Association of Austin (YHPAA), whose queries, feedback, and encouragement have driven me to be a better writer and a better person. Finally, there are my wife and two boys, who are my North Star, my Falcon, and my Compass. Together, they are the light through my darkness, the beacon that leads me from the storm of my mind to safe harbor and calm waters... They are my journey and my destination.

Prologue

"Your Majesty."

Audemar nearly strode on before he realized that the salutation was meant for him, not his father. "Yes?" he asked.

"The courier has arrived in the War Tent."

My brothers can wait. Audemar made an abrupt turn to his right, as did his Right Captain and guards. They sloshed through a narrow path that took them directly to the center of the camp. Mud as thick as paste clung to their boots, hampering their speed as they came upon a red three-peaked pavilion. From within, the hard voices of dozens slammed against one another, each baron inside speaking over the other. Warnings and rebukes turned to cries and shouts. The tumult spilled forth to meet Audemar as a guard opened the tent flap for him.

With his entrance, the crowd hushed. Audemar squinted as his sight adjusted to the dimness of the pavilion, lit by the roaring blazes of half a dozen braziers.

"Your Majesty," said the huddled voices of Marlish barons, nearly all at once, though a few trailed the initial volley. The mass bowed as every nobleman made a fist that they then placed over their hearts.

Audemar returned the gesture. "Mar be good." He scanned the crowd. Every Marlish nobleman who had accompanied him to the continent seemed to be present. His newly-appointed treasurer, Baron Thybalt, of Har-Kin Giscard. Baron Gale of Har-Kin Mallory, his family's most ardent supporters. Then there were the lords of Har-Kin Boivin, along with those of Hamage, Nevishold, Droigg, and many others.

Too many. Such numbers never coalesced so quickly and stilled so swiftly due to good news.

"Now, what news have we received?" he asked nonetheless.

The barons near the front exchanged anxious glances while those behind turned to the rear. In the back, the crowd parted to make way for a lone courier, a slender Marlishman with a mop of sandy hair and a freckled face. No more than sixteen, the lad stepped forward, albeit hesitantly as every baron along with the King watched him approach.

"Your Grace," the courier said nervously.

"Your Majesty," Audemar's Right Captain corrected him. The knight fell in line beside the King, glaring at the young man until he lowered his gaze.

Audemar raised his hand. "Sir Lijart, please. Dismiss with the formalities." The King nodded to the courier. "Your news?"

"Sire, the Tarshade Forest... the army there... the one you sent. It fell."

Murmurs and chatter erupted. Baron Rayvenn of Har-Kin Warci, as portly as he was raucous, shouted over the clamor. "You told us that already. What do you mean 'fell'? Details. Give us the details."

The courier sighed, clearly distraught at the concept of speaking about the incident. "They, whoever they were, surrounded us last night. From nowhere they came. Then everywhere. They overwhelmed the sentries on duty before swarming through the camp. They lit the tents on fire. We retreated to a set of hillocks on the other side of the stream. That's when my lord, Baron Marvynn, sent me here to give word..."

He paused to inhale, gripping his side as he did so. Only then, his sight having adjusted to the low light, did the King note the ash and grime on the lad's face along with his disheveled clothing. *He fought to come here.* "Grab a seat for him," Audemar commanded. At once, an attendant appeared with a wooden stool for the courier, who gladly sat. Another servant, anticipating the King's next request, produced a cup of wine for the man, who drank thirstily.

"Did anyone else make it out of the camp?" Audemar asked.

The courier gulped the last of his wine. He looked up to his sovereign. He need not shake his head. His look – both of mourning and shame – confirmed all.

Audemar straightened, his gaze never leaving the young man.

"The Tarshade Forest is not more than two days' ride from here," Baron Thybalt said. "We must mobilize our defenses and get you to safety."

"Bah," Baron Gale chimed. "His Majesty is a Saliswater. Battle-hardened since birth."

"Is it true?" Baron Oweyn asked of the courier. "Your encampment, was it only a ride of two days?"

"I suppose so, my lord. Though it's hard saying, as we were attacked at night–"

"How many?" Oweyn pressed further. "The enemy?

Tell us their numbers."

"And their sigil?" cried another baron.

"Did they have heavy infantry?" asked a third.

"Quiet!" Audemar bellowed.

His voice nearly shook the pavilion canopy and flaps, startling the audience of barons to silence. Their attention fell upon their king as he strode right up to the courier to grip him by the shoulders.

"Go directly to my pavilion across from here, the one with the golden canopy. There, give a full account of the Battle of the Tarshade Forest to my scribes." Audemar patted the courier on the back as he left before addressing the assembly of barons. "You will have an account of what befell our countrymen in due time."

That promise did little to satisfy the curiosity of the audience, who chattered amongst themselves. Their words, both the explicit and indistinct, carried the tone of the disgruntled, which only fueled Audemar's frustration.

The King leaned into his Right Captain. "Clear this room, save my War Counsel."

"Go! Leave!" Lijart shouted. "Make ready your soldiers and guards. Word will be sent to you via our generals once countermeasures have been made."

The barons grumbled but complied. They filed from the pavilion, leaving only Audemar, Lijart, and the King's generals: Baron Conandus, Baron Alec, and Baron Philkin.

Once the tent cleared, Audemar took a seat on the courier's stool, resting his elbows on his knees. "How many?" Audemar asked, referring to those encamped in the Tarshade Forest.

Baron Conandus paced among his peers. "Nearly eight

hundred. A tenth of our fighting force. A sizeable loss, especially if Baron Marvynn was killed rather than captured."

"Psst, Baron Marvynn, captured?" Alec said. "That old bull would rather eat a morningstar than surrender and be held for ransom."

"Aye, stubborn he was. But one of our best commanders," Philkin added, placing his right fist over his heart. "Har-Kin Rorkke won't be pleased with the loss of their favorite son."

"None of us are pleased," Audemar said as he rubbed the bridge of his nose between his fingertips.

"Sire," Conandus began. "As troubling as this news is, I beg of you, consider your safety. With you and your main army so close to the battle lines, we should pull back–"

"No, never."

"Your Majesty–"

"I thank you for your concern, Baron Conandus. It is not misplaced. And I am not unaware of the dangers. However, the safety of one – even a monarch – is of little importance right now. What matters now is survival. *Our* survival."

Audemar rose from the stool to approach the oaken table at the rear of the pavilion. There, the primary map of northwestern Colinne laid, with wooden pieces strewn about to mark the forces – both allies and enemies – situated throughout the terrain. Audemar leaned over the map as his subordinates collected beside him.

"The courier will provide what details he remembers, but his mind is battle-scarred, so information on how many – or even who – attacked his camp will be scant, at best. The only facts we know for certain are twofold. One, we must consider the information we have gathered to date on the terrain."

"And two?" Conandus asked.

"We know ourselves. Our army. Our forces here."

Audemar turned back to the map. "Baron Marvynn, may Mar bless him, took his position in the Tarshade Forest to gather intelligence on the eastern front, to be closest to the fields of battle should our conflict move to that area. Well, they did, and the lord of Har-Kin Rorkke paid the price for it. But not before he provided his reports." Audemar grabbed the scrolls, six in total, piled on the left edge of the table. "His scribes recorded in abundance on the waterways, land, and trees of the Tarshade and beyond. Little stands before our enemy and the Tarshade Forest save for a few streams and hills. They will make their way here with little to stop them. But beyond the Tarshade, even further east of its woods..."

Audemar's fingers slid over to the edge of the map, where the painted image of trees ended. He grabbed one of the scrolls to his left, of beige vellum, which he promptly unfurled. The painting within, consisting of broad strokes and jagged lines, illustrated a fractured landscape of ravines and gullies.

"... lies shattered ground," Audemar continued. "Whatever force made its way to Marvynn's encampment did so only after traversing rough ground, pockmarked by Mar Himself. Such an army who defeated Rorkke suffers from the pride of victory. They will not require reinforcements, and even if accomplices try to send support, they will need to cross the serrated earth bordering the Tarshade.

"Our camp would take half a day to pack should we

order a retreat. The land to the north we know to be laden with mountain kin loyal to no one, while that to the south and west presents rocky and narrow forces that would constrict our forces and render what numerical advantage we have useless. Yes, we can stand our ground. Deepen our trenches. Lay more spikes. Or we can do that which they will not suspect."

The last thought sat uneasily with those listening. Even Sir Lijart, always the King's optimist, shifted his weight from one leg to another.

"A bold move," Philkin conceded. "And unexpected. An ambush for an ambush."

"We will send our best into the woods, in a bull-and-horns formation, towards the Tarshade to meet the enemy head-on. The rest of us will be only a step back, hidden in every depression, outcropping, and grove to provide support as needed. The hell Marvynn suffered came from the woods. Let us hide there and flush it out, send it back."

Hesitantly, the four nodded.

"You'll need your brother's men for the onset of this assault," Alec advised. "His army took position in this area first. He has the battle-hardened, the tested, of this area."

Audemar needn't be told which brother his general referred to, the one they all preferred. "Aye," the King said. "Osgar can lead the vanguard, while Wilfred can command the reserves." *If the barons will allow my latter brother the honor.* "Make preparations."

"Bloody fool." *Still, I pity him.*

Audemar clipped his heels into his mount, sending the steed deeper into the canopied forest. From a low angle, dappled sunlight fell upon him. *The hour is late. The sun will set soon.*

As will our hopes.

Hours had passed since Audemar had given the command to counterstrike the assailants with an excursion toward the Tarshade Forest. With haste, his three generals at hand had mobilized a formidable force of light cavalry to enter the woods first with a second wave of pavisers and pole-men to support them. The troops set, he had awaited word on his sibling. And waited. Prince Wilfred, his youngest brother, had arrived shortly after being summoned. In Osgar's unexplained absence – which stretched into hours – Audemar momentarily considered sending Wilfred to lead the vanguard. Logic prevailed over haste, though. *Wilfred has not the grit. Nor the instincts. If he enters the forest first, he will fall. We all will.*

Three hours had passed since Audemar's command. And with it, restlessness. The King sent out couriers and squires to inquire, albeit gingerly, on the Prince's whereabouts. A quick search of the grounds revealed not only the departure of the King's brother but of his personal guard. A more in-depth investigation, carried out by Sir Lijart himself, finally revealed the reason for Osgar's absence.

That same reason now spurred the King onward.

The canopy became thicker. More branches and leaves above melded into one another, shielding the woods below from the sanctity of light. Dimness and shadows concealed a root here and a stone there, making the journey more fraught with the peril of being tripped or thrown. Nonetheless, Audemar quickened his ride, slapping the heels of his boots into the side of his steed with little concern for the safety of his horse or himself.

I must find him. I must...

"Your Majesty! Over here!"

The horse nearly threw him as Audemar yanked on the reins. The destrier shot up to his hind legs and whinnied. Remarkably, Audemar remained in his saddle, settling back in it with a thud as his horse returned to all fours. Undaunted, the King looked over his shoulder to find his Right Captain ushering him to the right. Audemar pulled the reins in that direction as Lijart rode to catch up to him, his voice growing hushed as he came close.

"Sire, the Prince, I saw him."

"Then lead me –"

"I will... up to a point. Then I shall stand aside. To allow you two a moment."

Audemar straightened. The last thing his Right Captain would ever consider proposing is to leave his side, even when the King was among other royals.

"He needs you, Your Majesty."

Sir Lijart extended his hand, motioning the King forward. Audemar complied.

He spotted his rich golden mane first. Parted down the middle, the hair fell to his shoulders. Then his brow came into view. Followed by his eyes.

At that, Audemar dismounted.

Handing the reins to Lijart, Audemar continued without him. He passed his brother's personal guard, who held the Prince within their sights but respectfully kept their distance. They turned their gaze to their sovereign and bowed, though their peripheral vision remained focused on Osgar.

Audemar waved them off. They did as commanded,

their stoicism fractured as each face held tones both somber and dark.

Within a few steps, Audemar saw why.

Osgar sat on a squat boulder, hunched over. His battle-axe laid with its butt to the ground, the blades sheathed as they leaned against his chest. He touched it not as his elbows dug into his thighs. In one hand, he held a dirk, the blade of which gleamed in the single shaft of light that fell upon the Prince. His other hand stayed still, open, as Osgar ran the tip over his palm and down his exposed wrist, which bled.

"Brother!"

Osgar glanced at Audemar before returning his attention to the blade.

"I saw the news you received..."

Audemar's voice faded so as to allow Osgar the chance to respond. The Prince neither offered a word nor a look in reply.

The King recalled the little he had read in haste upon one of the squires discovering the letter Osgar had received from Marland. The set of homing doves the mages had trained on the front returned earlier that morning with announcements from the island. Most of the correspondences were of a military nature, though on occasion, they brought word of the events of Court.

Such was the case with one letter addressed directly to Prince Osgar, as it told of the passing of his stillborn child and his wife.

Osgar dug the point of his dirk deeper into his flesh, sending a river of blood dripping down the length of his forearm.

"Osgar, please!"

Audemar reached for the dirk. Osgar met his eyes. His free hand rotated directly beneath the sharpened tip of his blade. Audemar halted.

"Do not try me, Brother."

"I'm sorry. So sorry."

"It was a son. The lad my love bore."

"I know."

"She was so happy when she gave me the news. That night before we sailed. She glowed, she did. Proud to be carrying my son. My son."

Osgar hung his head. Eyes unseen, Audemar nonetheless noted his tears as they fell to the earth.

Audemar kneeled, lowering himself to look upon Osgar's pained face.

"Let's go home," he said.

Osgar lifted his head at once. The dirk sank from his meaty paw to clatter against the boulder. He fell to his knees before his brother, allowing his battleaxe to fall to his side.

"What?" he asked.

"Marland. Let us return. It has been almost seven months. We are overdue."

"But... What of the front? We are at the forest's edge, within reach of, of –"

"We are in a stalemate, Osgar. Every fool and attendant in our midst knows it, let alone our soldiers and commanders. We lost the Tarshade Forest. Again. Sure, Conandus and the others will retake it. Perhaps this time, we can even take the lands beyond the ravines if Mar blesses our assault. Then what? Our supply lines will grow thin and more susceptible to attack. To traverse the land, trails will need to be widened, bridges and watchtowers built, then manned. Such events will take time, something this bloody war seems to drag out. And as that happens, more conflicts will arise, whether here or in greater Colinne, or Volkmar, or Ibia…"

Dear Mar, Audemar thought as he once again considered the staggering weight of the conflict, *will it ever end?*

A firm hand came to rest on Audemar's shoulder. The King looked up to find Osgar staring back at him.

"You would endure the damnation of the barons, the risk of the Conclave usurping your Throne, *our dynasty,* so that I may grieve?"

"Only if you will it."

Osgar sighed. Whether he relented to the offer or rejected it, Audemar could not say. However, for all the ambiguity of the reaction, the King knew the gesture had appeased his brother. For the moment.

Before the warrior returned.

Osgar the Fierce – eyes keen, instincts focused – gripped the shaft of his battleaxe. In one fell motion, he unsheathed both the blades of its head. He pivoted on the balls of his feet to look behind and scour the thick brush.

"Four songbirds," he whispered, his words barely audible to Audemar. "They were singing when I arrived. Back and forth, chirping in the distance. Now they're silent. Gone."

Audemar, remaining on one knee, slowly unsheathed his sword, careful not to let the slide of steel against leather make a sound. Not that it mattered.

For the attack had begun.

Bolts sliced through the silence, the whizzing of their arrowheads and shafts like wasps on the offensive. Audemar spotted one as it zipped past his left eye – a shot too close – before a second broke through his breastplate.

"Brother!"

Osgar tackled Audemar. He lay atop to shield him from the next onslaught of projectiles that flew overhead.

Blinking, Audemar wedged his left arm out from under his brother to paw at the bolt. It protruded from the upper-right section of his armor, just below the leather strap fitted over his shoulder. The tip had come in at an angle – not as a direct shot – and now poked up from his flesh. Audemar wrapped his fingers around the shaft and massaged it free from his plate. He allowed himself a sigh, knowing the danger was far from over.

With the last projectile sailing past, Osgar rolled off Audemar. He yanked his warhorn from his belt and blew.

Oooo... Oooo... Aaaaa-Ooooo...

Two short blasts followed by a long one. The distress call of Marland.

Those guards of Osgar's and the ones who accompanied Sir Lijart need not another signal nor command to know what to do. From behind the trees and bushes, they appeared, a tide of Marlish courage and discipline only the finest training could forge. Audemar managed to hear the quick clanks in the hidden forest beyond, surmising that the enemy worked desperately to reload their crossbows. A few more bolts flew, but nothing like the wave they had witnessed. In the Marlish blitz, the guards had closed the gap between themselves and their assailants. The time of hand-to-hand combat had come.

Arming swords unsheathed. Twigs and short branches snapped. Men grunted. Then yelled. All noises quick and instinctual stumbled over one another, the sharp chords of battle.

Audemar, hardly conscious of his own efforts, found himself on his feet, rushing toward the chaos. Before him, steps ahead, raced Osgar.

The man strode with his battleaxe, possessed. He held his weapon in his right hand. Most soldiers would have needed two hands to do so. But not Osgar. The Fierce had rightly earned his reputation as a proven, unapologetic warrior. Now, as ever, he would show their enemies the reason for his namesake.

Osgar spotted the first combatants in range, two assailants fighting one of Audemar's guards. The guard had suffered a wound to his right leg, barely able to deflect the blows that landed upon him. Osgar cut diagonally from the trail, heading directly for the two. They scarcely noticed the Prince before he cleaved through their armor, cutting clean the arm of one and hacking the neck of the other. As the blood gushed from the freshly slain, he raced to the next opportunity, a crossbowman who held the Prince in his sights. Undeterred by the threat, Osgar belted out a war cry to inject the fear of Mar into the man. Whether it worked or not, the bolt missed, rushing past the head of Osgar's battleaxe as it rose, then fell, straight down into the man, splitting his clavicle and the ribs below.

That last attack slowed the Fierce, as the axe head became stuck in the attacker's broken bones and mangled flesh. Osgar kicked and kicked at the corpse until it fell free from his weapon to slump to the ferns below. Catching his breath, the Prince glanced at his brother, who also paused.

"Are you well, Audemar?"

The King nodded. He surveyed the scene around them. In the blink of an eye, Sir Lijart and the guards had succeeded in their counterassault. The one-on-one skirmishes between the attackers and the guards had all ended, with the Marlish emerging victorious. Only a few of the enemy managed to retreat into the woods, with a handful of guards in pursuit.

"We were fortunate," Audemar chimed.

"Bah! You can keep your fortune. This is my fate." Osgar held up his axehead, admiring it.

That is what I'm afraid of. With your family gone, what do you have to live for?

"I am here for you, Brother," Audemar said, as if in response to his own question.

"I see that," Osgar replied.

"Will you continue to fight by my side?"

Osgar hesitated, the weight of the morning's news suddenly returning to him. He groped for the sheath of his dirk, which remained empty, the blade lost in the commotion. Noting its absence brought a curl to his lips, a hint of a smirk.

"Aye, my liege and my kin. I will fight. For you."

In the distance, from the direction of the Marlish encampment, the rumble of hooves echoed. Reinforcements. Audemar, relieved, lowered the tip of his sword.

"We should –"

Whack!

Blood splattered his breastplate. He fell into a defensive stance before realizing the droplets had come from the neck of the enemy corpse before them, a neck bearing the slashed ends of sinew and tissue. Osgar, with blood dripping from the edges of his axehead, stared down at the fleshy, red brawn. Then he shifted his attention to the severed head beside his foot. He lifted it by the hair before turning to his brother.

"What are you doing?" Audemar asked.

"Whatever it takes." Osgar raised the head to inspect it. The face had all the distinctive features of the Volkmar: dark hair, rough stubble, a crooked nose, and fair skin. Osgar, seemingly unimpressed, grunted. "It'll make a fine trophy for the piked fence around our perimeter. When I return to camp, I'll issue the order to all those under my command: No quarter for those Volkmar caught or injured. All will be beheaded, their tops placed on the piked posts for their brethren to see."

Audemar clenched his jaw, breathing through his teeth. The Volkmar often did the same to imprisoned soldiers as a way to intimidate their enemies. In the early years of the Century War, the Marlish had returned the favor in kind until the Saliswater monarch King Aethelrik banned the practice midway through the conflict.

Now, a prince of Marland – not its king – would reinstate the barbaric act of retribution.

Osgar, perhaps sensing Audemar's coming protest, strode up to him. Audemar, disturbed by the head he so casually carried, fought the urge to step back.

"You asked that I fight for you. So let me fight for you," Osgar said. "I learned today I lost a wife and child. My legacy – not the Saliswater one, but mine – is at an end. Wilfred, Mar bless him, is a runt unable to sire a halfling, let alone an heir. Synnova is barren. That leaves you – our King – the only hope for the Saliswater dynasty to live on. And live on it will."

Osgar raised the head. He pointed at it with his axe. "He would have done the same to you. But so long as I'm alive, I will not let that happen. We will win this war, brother, by any means. We will scare them pale as ghosts. They will shit themselves. We will crush their spirits. Drink their blood if we have to. All so that you may emerge from this bloody fight victorious, to return home and have sons. Marlish sons, who will grow to become men of Kin Saliswater."

Finding no gesture or word of objection from his brother, Osgar moved past. He lifted the head high enough for his remaining guards to see. Like Audemar, they froze, shocked at the brutality of the deed. Entertained by their disgust, Osgar chuckled as he glanced back at the King.

"Remember," the Fierce began. "Whatever it takes."

Audemar turned to the decapitated corpse, which sat leaning against a tree. He looked to his blade, which still ran scarlet from the battle. He knelt to wipe his sword on the grass before he sheathed it, moving slower than necessary. For the words of his brother – never more prescient – rang through his head.

We will win this war.

Men of Kin Saliswater.

Remember.

Whatever it takes.

Chapter 1

Mar, forgive me.

The image of his hands wrapped around his brother's neck overwhelmed his mind. He knew that such thoughts would not serve him well to control his temper. Nonetheless, the fantasy, the daydream, persisted.

"Stupid, stupid."

He is worse than that.

He is reckless.

At least stupid can be forgiven.

Dawkin's foot sank. He paused. Looking down at his boot, he noticed a track in the mud carved out by a wagon. In that same depression, a horse had shat.

"Honestly? For the love of..."

Dawkin bit his lip. The two Voiceless knights behind him stepped back, neither one wanting to be in close proximity when their king unleashed his wrath.

No wrath came. Though his nostrils flared, Dawkin resisted the urge to allow his fury to get the better of him.

Not now, not now. Later.

Dawkin lifted his soiled boot from the muck. He shook his leg vigorously. A few clumps of excrement fell loose. Dawkin took a few steps to his left, where the ground was drier, and dug the sole of his boot into dirt.

"Stupid, stupid, stupid," he muttered as he wiped his boot.

Upon finishing, Dawkin looked around. The fecal matter he had encountered reflected the better qualities of the town. Dank and grimy, every building – from the homes to the tavern to the church – bore shades of black or brownish-green, no doubt from the mold and moss that sprouted in every nook and crevice. Unlike Arcporte, the roads sported not a single brick nor cobblestone as all were but dirt or mud paths. The townspeople that traversed them looked no better, with every face sullen and bitter, as though the souls within had endured a lifetime of debt and depression.

Dawkin wondered why his brother, even in his most unstable states, would seek out such a pit. But after glancing at the two Voiceless in tow - who donned simple wool shirts, trousers, and coats of indistinct colors to blend in – he recalled his regal duty, and instead asked himself:

How can such a place exist in my kingdom?

He resisted the urge to inquire with the citizens and investigate their plight further. He refocused his efforts on the task at hand, which involved finding his fool of a brother.

He noted the sign at the end of the curved street, which had no letters. Instead, crudely engraved in its wooden panel Dawkin saw what he could only assume to be a stein crowned by foam.

"Of course he'd be there," Dawkin said to himself. Ely would brave a tempest on the high seas for a drop of ale.

Dawkin marched toward the tavern, the interior of which rang with the raucous sounds of the morally corrupt. From every open window and cracked shutter crept moans, shouts - nay, threats - and more cries.

He came to the door, just about to extend his hand, when it burst open. The King jumped aside as two brawny men spilled into the mud of the street with a half dozen spectators chasing after them.

"Kill the bastard!" one screamed.

"The ribs! The ribs!" yelled a second.

On it went, with the spectators forming a ring around the brawlers. Uninterested in the outcome, Dawkin wedged past the onlookers who crowded the doorway to enter the establishment.

Inside, the haze of cheap tobacco hung steady, as did the pitch of every conversation. Dozens of voices clamored over themselves, much like those who uttered them. Dawkin could scarcely stride a foot without having to shove through a small gathering to make more headway. By the time he reached the bar at the far end of the tavern, he felt like he had trudged through a bog.

"Pardon!" He had to yell at the barmaid to garner her attention. She glanced his way yet made no move to approach him. Knowing the game he had to play, Dawkin retrieved a bronze coin from the satchel within his vest. He flashed it at the woman. She stared at the coin for a moment. Still, she didn't move.

Bloody, bloody thieves. Dawkin reached into his satchel again, this time drawing a larger coin, one of silver. This time, the barmaid came before him.

"Look at you in your fancy duds," spat the craggily-toothed woman. She may have been in her thirties even though she could pass for twenty years her senior. "What brings a lordling like you to a squalor like this?"

Dawkin frowned. His garb was as simple as they came,

with both his trousers and coat a dark gray while his white shirt was one of simple, unembroidered cloth. All his clothes, however, stood out as clean and spotless in a sea of stains and spills, which probably gave him away.

"I need to find another lord," Dawkin said, dropping the pretense of trying to fit in. "My brother."

"Ain't been another that looks like you," replied the wench.

Disguises, Dawkin thought. *Of course. But which one?* "He's my half-brother," he lied. "I haven't seen him since my youth. He would be my height, though. And with coin, I might add."

"You not seeking to rob the poor chap, are you?"

Before Dawkin could answer, the barmaid leaned in, lowering her voice. "Because if that be the case, I'll allow it. My portion for such an act being half of whatever you take, of course."

Dawkin pulled back, mostly due to the stank of her breath, but also to take in the room. The majority of the patrons ignored the disguised King save for a few unscrupulous-looking characters. Dawkin had spotted them when he entered, men who tried a little too hard to remain inconspicuous. However, as he approached the bar, the potential thieves – five within his sight – had abandoned their positions and casually snaked through the crowd toward him.

The barmaid, perhaps sensing Dawkin's suspicion, glanced to her left and right. She returned her gaze to Dawkin, who held hers.

He reached inside his vest.

She stretched her hand beneath the bar.

A tall, stocky bald man from among the five moved in

first. He rushed in on Dawkin, coming within three paces of him. The two Voiceless who had accompanied Dawkin inside closed in on the brute, one from each side. But before they had the chance to lay a hand on him, Dawkin drew a tiny vial of violet liquid from his vest to throw it in the man's face. The glass container shattered against the bridge of his nose, dousing his eyes, cheeks, and mouth with the fluid. Steam from the melting of his flesh joined the haze of the tavern.

"Ahhh!" the man shrieked. The others in the tavern hushed as they watched him collapse to the floor, gripping his broiled face. "Mar! Oh, Mar!"

The barmaid behind the counter stood with a long, rusty kitchen knife drawn. She turned to Dawkin, her mouth agape. "You..." She thrust her blade at him. "Get him! Go on, you fools, slit his bloody throat!"

Initially, no one moved. Suddenly, the remaining four Dawkin spotted earlier – plus another three he had not – charged.

The Voiceless fell in to protect their king, with one on each side, arming swords and daggers drawn. For his part, Dawkin had but time to retrieve only one more vial. He reached for the longest one he carried: a slender flask filled with dark green liquid speckled with flakes. He uncorked it and, in a single motion, unleashed its contents in a wide arc.

The curve of potion that sprayed the floor erupted in emerald flames so bright they blinded the lot. The attackers stumbled back, afraid to catch fire, while everyone else stampeded towards the exits.

Though he instinctively shielded his eyes, Dawkin

remained calm. He lowered his arm and neared the fire, fearless. He crossed through the green brightness with ease, much like a child does when stepping over a puddle. The Voiceless, also undeterred, did the same.

The assailant nearest to him laid on the floor, eyes wide in shock. He wriggled backward on his elbows as Dawkin and his Voiceless knights advanced.

"You, you devil!" he shouted and pointed. "Witchcraft, I say. Witchcraft!"

"No, you idiot. It's just some purified alcohol with crystals of Dywar's Tears mixed in." Dawkin tossed the empty vial to the floor, where it shattered into a thousand bits. That scared him and the other attackers further. With their fear peaked, Dawkin nodded to his Voiceless, signaling the real start to the hostilities.

The knights were a vision of flailing cloth and leather jerkins, of calloused hands and gleaming steel. In such close quarters, arming swords would have proven a liability, not an advantage, so the Voiceless donned daggers. Each of the two Voiceless wielded one straight blade and one curved, to stab or pierce and hack or cut, respectively. Their strikes were so precise, especially given the ensuing chaos provoked by the flames, that the Voiceless had nary to defend themselves. The blades found their mark every time. No matter the target, flesh and blood soon came to the dim light of the tavern.

Though the Voiceless would have preferred their liege abstain from the conflict, Dawkin was not one to remain idle. He took to the one he considered the mightiest target: an intimidating fellow with sinewed muscle throughout his body and dark gray hair that hung to his shoulders.

Seeing him approach, the man drew a rusty dirk. Dawkin paused, pulling from his waistband a short mace with brass studs.

"What's that?" the muscular thief said, a grin growing on his lips. "You going to grind some flour for me morning bread, are you?"

Dawkin furrowed his brow. He glanced at his weapon, noting it didn't look particularly intimidating in the dim light.

Oh well. So long as it worked.

He charged toward the thief. The foe, in return, slashed at Dawkin's face. Dawkin quickly swooped aside and landed the head of his mace against the man's wrist. He heard a crack of tiny bones fracturing. Then a thud as the man fingers let loosed the dirk, which fell to the floor.

"Ergggg..."

The man had nary a moment to grip his wounded hand when Dawkin landed another blow, this one to his nether regions. The foe cupped his crouch and scowled before the king struck his left temple.

The muscular thief crashed to the floorboards, unconscious. Dawkin, still in the fighting spirit, swung around, ready for the next challenge. Only there wasn't any. The Voiceless had managed to disarm and defeat every other crook who threatened them, with the conquered writhing on the ground or leaning against the walls. Dawkin nodded once to them before he and the Voiceless turned back to the bar.

The rusty knife tumbled from the barmaid's fingers. In shock, she had remained as she was for the entirety of the bout, which was mere seconds. Now, confronted by

Dawkin and his guards, she peddled back until she hit the wall behind her. She raised her hand to her bosom as Dawkin hopped over the bar to approach and place his short mace before her face.

"My brother... Which room is he in?"

"Room?" she squeaked.

"Yes! Upstairs or downstairs? I know you've seen him."

"I have. At least, I think I did. But he's in no room. He took two of my girls out back."

"Back?"

"In the barn. There's a small one in the rear."

Dawkin needn't any more confirmation of his brother's whereabouts than that. He tucked his short mace into his waistband and hopped back over the bar to exit.

The barn was little more than a thatched roof and a wooden frame. Stenches from all corners of the village flowed freely through the dwelling, doing nothing to deter the three on the straw heap from frolicking in their delights.

"Uhh-hmm," Dawkin uttered, clearing his throat.

From under stalks of straw, Ely peeked his head up. The women on each side of him rolled off, covering their breasts as they moved. Ely dusted himself clean as he attempted to straighten.

"Brother!" Ely exclaimed with a broad smile. "You're here."

"Your powers of observation serve you well," Dawkin said, his arms still crossed. He and the Voiceless had stood nearly half a minute before the pile of straw without Ely nor the two girls noticing.

"Well, I am a king. Aren't I, girls?" He tickled one, then

the other, with both blushing as they fought to suppress their giggles.

"Leave us!" Dawkin boomed. The two women jumped from their spots to hurry out of the barn.

"Well, that hardly seemed necessary." Ely buttoned his shirt as his face soured with the girls' departure.

What were you thinking? How could you? Do you want to be robbed and murdered? Those questions and others raced through Dawkin's thoughts as he glared down at his brother. He gave breath to none of them, though. For after all, what was the point?

Instead, he looked over his shoulder to the Voiceless at his right. "Gather his horse. It should be nearby."

"Actually," Ely said. "I lost it in a wager."

King Fool! "Then take mine. I'll buy another in this forsaken town."

"Embarrassed to be seen riding the same mount with your brother?"

"We *can't* be seen together, you idiot. Sir Everitt and half of Har-Kin Furde are looking for you, seeing as you left your Right Captain with no word of your destination. I only guessed at it when Everitt alerted Saliswater Manor of his search."

"A little excessive, wasn't he? I mean, this isn't the first time I have ascended and skipped out –"

"But never as king. 'Tis his duty to watch over you."

"I know *that*, brother."

"Well, *brother*, you should also know that our Right Captain has been stricken with worry over his father. Baron Ralf has fallen ill with fever and coughing. Your stunt took him away from Furde Manor at a time when he should be with his family." Dawkin glared at Ely, his face conveying he had no room within his heart for his excuses nor quips. "Grow up for once in your life and act like a king!"

"Fine." Ely rose, now thoroughly perturbed. "Far be it for me to have a little fun."

Ely brushed past Dawkin, bumping his shoulder as he did.

Reckless, reckless.

Dawkin and his two guards escorted Ely to the grove outside of town, where another Voiceless waited with their horses. Ely took one, while the two Voiceless to accompany them shared a mount. Dawkin watched the three ride off until they disappeared behind the bend of the road.

Annoyed but also content that his task was complete, Dawkin mounted his destrier as the other remaining Voiceless took to his. He and the knight began to ride when Dawkin slowed his horse to look over his shoulder.

Behind them, the woods – darkened and empty – met his gaze. He peered at them in search of something he swore was there, looking back.

A breeze ruffled the leaves of the trees, which otherwise stood solemnly, always on guard. Moonlight shone on the heights of the canopy, while beneath the void hung, desolate. Within the black, not a creature nor soul moved. Still, Dawkin swore he felt something – or someone – looking at him. Nay, *studying* him...

He shook the thought from his mind. *Tis nothing.*

Nothing.

Chapter 2

"Brothers... Kings..."

Gerry scarcely heeded the rest of his brother's words. His concentration ebbed and flowed like the tide beneath Siren's Cavern. Now and then, he caught an expression of interest before returning to his original thought. That is until Dawkin uttered the one mention to capture his full attention.

"Princess..."

Gerry perked just as Ely slammed his hand on the table.

"Why not me?" Ely insisted. "I drew the longest straw. It should be me!"

"The straws were not for that..." Dawkin replied.

That? What was 'that'?

"But I –" Ely said.

"They were for who among us goes on to Ibia for the royal wedding. You three chose the longest straws, while I selected the shortest, so I will stay. The matter of who stands in for the wedding and the wedding night will fall to another drawing entirely."

The wedding night?!

"Aye," Symon chimed. He shifted in his seat to focus on Ely. "You know this, Ely. On all the voyages we took with Father in our youth, we always chose straws for who would go. And then we always did another drawing for who would represent the Prince in important matters. Like for banquets, royal tournaments, and the like."

"But this is different," Ely continued. "Or so it should."

"Why is that?" Dawkin asked.

"Because I won."

Dawkin and Symon shared a look, smirking. Even Gerry could not help but to respond with a sly grin.

"Need we put it to a vote?" Dawkin asked.

"No, no," Ely responded, throwing his hands up, exasperated. "I know how the lot of you will decide."

"Very well. Then it shall be. The one to attend the wedding will be determined by another vote, the time and place of which I will leave to you three."

Gerry's heart fluttered. *I still have a chance. To stand in as King Jameson for the entire length of the ceremony. To say the vows before the High Bishop, to be toasted and congratulated. To see her to the wedding chamber for –*

His breath caught in his throat. He nearly choked as the blood drained from his face. His pulse fluctuated, becoming erratic.

Her... I...

He came to, returning from his anxiety to the present moment. Only then did he notice his brothers staring at him, with even Ely expressing a look of concern.

"Are you well, Geremias?" Ely asked.

Am I? "I, I just considered, that, when one of us is with Taresa, Princess Taresa, after the ceremony, that night, when all the festivities, the toasts, everything, have concluded–"

"Oh, for the love of Mar!" Ely interrupted, his impatience returning. "Out with it!"

"I just wonder if Taresa will take notice of us."

The other three looked at each other, confused.

"Us?" Symon asked.

"I mean, when we... lay... with her. The first of us. Then... another... Then the other two of us. I presume she will notice a difference with our bodies –"

At that last word, Gerry blushed. He had hoped his brothers would fill in the gaps before he spelled out the extent of his thoughts. They hadn't, so he found himself laying open the concept of which they never spoke, that is, the sharing of a woman.

The three looked at each other again. This time not out of confusion but consideration. While each of them – even Gerry – had been with women, the situation of all four being with the same woman had never happened. Princess Taresa was assumed to be a virgin, pure from the day of her birth until the night of her wedding. With no experience per se, she would have no prior exposure to intimacy. That would translate to an advantage in the first few encounters, Gerry thought. However, as the brothers rotated from one ascension to another, the lifelong secret to their true identities would be put to the test, putting themselves at risk. Along with Taresa.

The moment of his embarrassment subsiding, Gerry turned to his siblings for guidance and support. To his amazement, Dawkin and Symon seemed equally flustered. Neither offered a reply, leaving Ely to pipe up in typical fashion.

"So what's the problem? We have our truth sessions. We will simply go about this issue like all the others so that we as brothers will know what the other has done."

Symon stroked his chin, obviously less than satisfied

with Ely's assurance. "Gerry has a point. Our differences will be so much more obvious in the flesh."

"Oh, so now you boast of your *long* sword?" Ely quipped.

Symon's face went flush. Not from embarrassment. From anger. "My *sword* is none of your concern."

"I beg to differ, thanks to the musings of our younger brother."

"I only –" Gerry started.

"Yes, yes, you were thinking with your sword – long or otherwise – that is very, very clear."

"Ely!" Symon shouted.

"Symon!" Ely jested back.

"Everyone!" Dawkin roared, pounding his fist on the table as he did. "That is quite enough, don't you agree?" He sighed. "Though it pains me to say this, I agree with Ely. Our truth sessions are designed to recall the details of events which, should they turn problematic, we can then discuss to come to a joint resolution. In regards to the Princess Taresa, should she note then voice anything about our... distinctive qualities, imagined or otherwise... we can then comprise a plan of action to deal with her."

"Do tell, Dawkin." An impish grin bent on Ely's lips. He clearly enjoyed where this conversation had taken them.

"Well, we can give her some fading potion–"

"No!" Gerry erupted.

"Pardon?"

"She is not a soldier or a whore you can just, just inebriate at will. She is to be my wife."

Even Symon raised a brow at that one. He shifted, leaning forward. "Gerry, calm yourself. Dawkin meant no slight. Remember, she is to be a wife to King Jameson. Which means the four of us."

"This is outrageous!" Dawkin said. "Listen, if it becomes a problem, we will find a solution. Fading potion. Ale. Salve. Hell, I don't care. We are ruling a kingdom, for Mar's sake. Let us return to the *important* matters of state at hand. Yes?"

The three nodded, with Symon and Ely seeming at ease of letting go of the discussion. Gerry's thoughts, though, persisted with the topic long after Dawkin had droned on and on before adjourning their meeting.

The topic of Taresa - or rather, that of the royal wedding – soon resurfaced, however, when Artus descended to tell the boys the Sovereign Fleet was nearly set for departure.

His brothers at the ready, Gerry found himself scrambling. He had retired to his chamber in Terran to daydream about the wedding. In doing so, he had forgotten all about the preparations he was to take for the voyage. With Ely chosen as the one to represent them as King Jameson, Symon and Gerry were to don the garb of the Voiceless to escort their brother undetected. Symon could always slip into a breastplate, jerkin, or other armor with ease, making his robing effortless. Gerry, on the other hand, always struggled with the straps and clasps. No matter the tailoring or cut, no bit of armor ever fit him right.

In haste, Gerry tossed the knightly armor on his bed, all the while the voice of his approaching grandfather ringing through the halls, growing more boisterous. Both his tasset and pauldron were askew by the time Artus checked in on him.

"My boy," Artus said. "What is going on with you? Why

aren't you ready?"

"I... forgot," Gerry admitted.

Artus placed his hands on his hips, more perplexed than frustrated. From behind, Ely came.

"Why the delay, Grandfather?" Ely peeked over Artus' shoulder. "Seriously? After Dawkin's far-too-long speech this morning, you keep us waiting?"

"I'm sorry." Gerry lowered his head, making a show of quickening his pace when, in fact, he was trying to hide his shame.

"You're nowhere close to being finished," Ely snorted. "It's one thing if I make us look like King Fool. But, Gerry, for you to do this –"

"Ely," Artus said.

"He can't possibly put on his armor in time for outgoing tide now."

"You've said your piece," Artus chided.

"Very well." Ely studied Gerry for a moment. Then, he raised a brow. "At least allow me to propose a quick solution."

Artus looked from Ely to Gerry, curious. "As you wish."

Within the hour, Gerry stood on the flagship's deck, the salt air smacking his cheeks. Such gusts often bothered him, though in this case, he wished for them to strike more forcefully. Or for the sea below to rise as a rogue wave to wash him bare. Or for any force, natural or otherwise, to swipe the moles and prosthetic nose from his face.

He felt like an idiot, as surely as Ely had intended. He bore the garb of a lesser Har-Kin – Kutte, Yves, or some sort – though his cape had the insignia of the King's Treasurer, to mark him as an attendant or aide of some sort, that no one may question his presence. Still, as if the embarrassment of being lowered to the status of a servant weren't enough, the arrangement of his disguise made his self-consciousness even worse. Ely had fitted him with the most hideous of snouts: a slender nose with a goosebump in the center. So profuse was it in length he knew it garnered attention rather than deflect it. To further add to his façade, Ely had adorned Gerry with all manner of moles. Small ones. Large ones. Round moles. Those of intricate shapes and patterns. Gerry, having seen himself in the mirror once Ely finished, shuddered at the idea of what others thought. *They think me a leper, I suppose.*

Symon, in the full armor of the Voiceless, strode up to Gerry. Though he had lowered his visor, Gerry still caught the whiffs of muffled chuckling.

"Laugh all you want," Gerry said. "I'm sure behind closed doors, everyone else is."

"Serves you right. Being undressed before the most important voyage of our lives."

"Glad to have your support, Symon."

Between them sauntered Ely. He slapped a hand on each of their shoulders. "Cheerful! Come on, be cheerful, chaps!" He glanced at Gerry, clearly pleased at his work. "No one suspects a thing."

"I hope a storm rocks this ship so much that you spew your guts," Gerry said.

"Bold words from a servant." Ely slapped him on the back. "Away with you!" Ely said loud enough for all those within earshot to hear. "Fetch me a skin of wine, you lowly peasant. Your king requires drink before our long seafaring adventure."

Utterly humiliated, Gerry slinked away to fetch for his brother. He descended the forecastle to the main deck, about to go below, when the Royal Admiral shouted from the quarter deck.

"Prepare to set sail!"

In his moping, Gerry had not noticed the planks connecting the ship to the dock had been cleared, the ropes at the cleats untied, and the sails lowered. All took place with remarkable efficiency, at least in Gerry's eyes. Within a minute of the Admiral's command, Gerry felt the deck below his feet shift as the flagship made its way from the dock pilings.

Forgetting his ridiculous persona, Gerry moved to the rail, where many of the sailors had gathered to wave at their families on the dock. The commoners, separated from the nobles and royals by a line of guards, stood at the far end of the pier, waving back. At the near end of the pilings, relatives of the upper caste offered their salutes to their departing loved ones, which expressed much less affection and far more formality.

And there, at the very end of the dock, Artus offered a hand.

In the absence of King Jameson due to the royal wedding, the Conclave of Barons – at the King's urging – had appointed Baron Ralf of Har-Kin Furde as Steward of the Throne. That resolution was issued weeks before. Since then, the Furde baron had contracted an unexplained illness, rendering him unable to tend to his noble duties, let alone his newly-appointed regal ones. Every other lord the Saliswaters could trust had committed to attending the royal wedding in Arinn, while those who couldn't appeared suspiciously too eager to step in and tend to the Throne. Not wanting to witness such infighting, Artus stepped in at the last moment to serve as Steward. The barons of the Conclave – seeing the former king chose duty to his country over the chance to see his grandson wed – conceded to the change.

Around Artus, several Voiceless and personal guards to the Saliswater stood. Gerry paid them little attention save one, the Voiceless knight closest to Grandfather.

The lowered visor on his helm prevented Gerry from seeing his face. Nonetheless, he knew the posture, the disposition, of the man too well.

Dawkin, in the armor of a Voiceless, stared at the flagship with Artus. Unlike his grandfather, he raised no hand, made no gesture that could be interpreted as affection. He kept up the ruse of a knight on duty. As the one who had drawn the short straw in the Fourpointe Chamber, he knew that was his charge. And so he committed to it.

The Sovereign Fleet eased from Arc Harbor with nary an incident. Once again, meandering in his own thoughts, Gerry had lost sense of time. Only a few hundred paces from the wharf, a current carried the first of the fleet into the vast ocean beyond, toward Ibia and the beginning of a new chapter in Marlish history.

The flagship entered the current last. Though far from the mouth of the harbor, Gerry could still make out the shapes of his grandfather and brother on the dock.

He knew not if they could see him. Still, coming out from the confines of his mind into the present, he knew he should say goodbye. Thus, he offered them a wave.

The next time I see them, he thought, *I will be a different man than I am now. I will have seen the continent for the first time since we were crowned. I will have visited the courts of lands beyond my own. I will be a king proper — one with a wife.*

My very own queen.

Chapter 3

"My dear."

Taresa sighed. "Yes, Mother?"

"What of this design?"

The Princess glanced over her shoulder, turning her sights away from the sea. To her left, her mother sat with her sister, Ermesinda, with a length of peach-colored chiffon stretched over their laps. Beside them, a tailor waited, with a roll of the fabric and three others of different hues in his arms.

"The tone will complement your skin. As will the texture," Queen Belitta added.

"You mean dry and coarse?" Ermesinda cracked.

"Young lady!" Belitta slapped her leg, the smack ringing through the cavernous room.

"Owww!" Ermesinda whined. In the far corner, Nataliya, who was being fitted by another tailor, giggled.

"Don't *you* start." Belitta shot a sharp look in Nataliya's direction. "The both of you behave. This is no time for your antics. This is for your sister."

Taresa sighed, turning back to the sea. *It doesn't* feel *like it's for me.*

"Taresa, I said what do you –"

"It's fine. I saw it. The one on your lap is fine."

Belitta, seemingly please by her daughter's decision, folded the length in her hands and returned it to the tailor.

"Very well. That takes care of the banquet gown. Now as for the dress for the ballroom dance –"

Taresa fought back another sigh. *I can't bear another moment of this.* "Mother?"

"Yes, Resa?"

"All this fitting has me famished. I would hate to go on with these important decisions while being hungry. Shall we have our high tea early?"

The Queen paused, considering. "I am a bit hollow myself. Very well, then." She raised her index finger, beckoning a servant forward. "Tea, with small plates, at once." The servant, an elderly fellow with black hair save for the gray at his sides, nodded before clapping to the three subservants behind him. They scurried through the side door to Taresa's bedchamber into the hallway beyond.

The tea will take a moment to brew. "I will take in the air outside while we wait."

"Very well, Dear." The Queen motioned for Ermesinda and Nataliya to join their sister.

No, I want to be alone! "No need for company," Taresa blurted. "I mean, they should stay, pick out the next spools to go over and such. I could use their help in such matters."

"As you wish." Belitta nodded to her middle daughter by her side. "Ermesinda, you and your sister pick the next fabric to examine. Then the one after that. Plus, a third, my Lovely."

Ermesinda sighed, then nodded. She moved to rise and join her youngest sibling, but not before shooting a hostile glance at her eldest.

Taresa, in response to her jealously, only smiled. She retreated to the rear door, which led to the portico and the small opportunity of freedom beyond.

The air smelled especially sweet for autumn. The dryness of the coming winter remained absent, replaced by the warm embrace of the lingering summer. Though usually not one for any hint of humidity, on this occasion, Taresa welcomed it. The sensation reminded her of simpler days, of a time when she did not have to think of events of regal responsibility, such as her upcoming marriage.

Taresa strolled across the marble walkway until it gave way to a set of stairs that descended to the tree-lined avenue below. The pedestrian street, one of many which stretched through the palace grounds, teemed with patrons this particular afternoon. The scene stemmed partly from her upcoming nuptials but also because her father was rumored to be in a generous mood. In truth, Taresa had never known her father to be as hard a man as people said. He simply allowed such musings to percolate for the advantage of his reputation.

As the princess went on her way, those she passed paused and bowed, offering courteous glances and smiles. A few even asked her about her pending nuptials, idle banter Taresa endured so long as she could inch forward slowly to indicate her haste. All gathered the gist she meant to imply — all except Xain.

The Grand Duke of Almata stood on the southern knoll bordering the avenue, which boasted covered decks of Ibian cedar. He and his companions – Ibian generals, Taresa gathered, judging by their uniforms – conversed until Xain caught sight of Taresa.

So much for my chance at solitude. The Grand Duke excused himself from the audience to make his way from the deck to the avenue below. He soon appeared past the trees onto the brick boulevard, his steps somehow quick yet not anxious. Taresa considered retreating to her room or perhaps initiating a more thoughtful discussion with one of the nobles within her reach. Alas, Xain came upon her before she had a chance at either.

"Your Highness," Xain said as he stopped before her to bow.

"Your Grace," Taresa tilted her head and curtsied.

"May I borrow your ear for a moment?"

This should be a laugh. "As you wish."

He extended the crook of his arm, which she obligingly took. The pair continued down the avenue, unencumbered by interruptions from nobles nor servants. Now that she had a man on her arm, out of respect, all others kept their polite distance. Alone, as a woman, she could be approached by any beggar or bishop who wanted a moment of her time.

Foolish tradition. Taresa and Xain strolled together, neither looking at the other.

"Your wedding is the talk of every circle and table in Arinn," Xain said, breaking the silence.

"Only Arinn? Why, cousin, surely you can try harder to flatter me? Why not our entire country? Or the whole of Afari?"

Xain smirked. "Or I could have said that your betrothal has shattered the hearts and souls of every bachelor in Ibia, thereby rendering our borders defenseless and our ships unmanned."

"What do you want?" she blurted.

Xain raised a brow. "You abandon your pretense so

easily?"

"I want to know the truth of your motives. The generals and nobles here at Castle Arinn may tolerate your games of the mind and your feeble attempt at wit. I, on the other hand, tire of such niceties."

They had come upon a path leading to a recess – a small side garden – adjacent to the avenue. Spotting an opportunity for greater privacy, Xain led her to the secluded area.

The garden harbored various flowers native to Arin and the surrounding foothills, including silk-petal gardenias from the Capiwaan Valley, blood-orange blossoms from the Greynaida Shores, and wildflowers from the marshlands of the Jokarre River. However, the most prized flora of the beds was the Arinnese sunroses. From ancient times, the blossoms had been known to be medicinal while also offering stunning petals of violet, red, and gold. The colors often intermixed in patterns, from swirls to freckles, although the rarest of blooms were those of pure gold, unblemished by any other hue.

Such a beauty – of eight large gold petals – captured Taresa's focus as they entered. Though the bear-like grip on her upper arm soon broke her concentration.

"What in the name –"

"Careful," Xain insisted. "Low voice now." His fingers remained clenched.

"Off of me. Now!"

The last word, though hushed, threatened to rise higher. Xain, his eyes never leaving Taresa's, loosened his clamp around her arm. Taresa snapped free of his grasp; her look one of dirks and daggers. At that, Xain's lips twisted into a sinister grin.

"Tsk, tsk, sweet princess. Such rebellion is unchaste, far from what is expected of a young lady."

"And your... desires. The whole of your behavior." Taresa paused to look her cousin up and down. "Xain, you disgrace Kin Garsea."

The last comment struck a nerve with the Grand Duke. Not one noted by a twitch, nor a sneer, nor by a wise retort. No. Xain's displeasure, marked by silence, echoed volumes.

Not seeing him react – a rarity for him in such moments – sent a shudder through Taresa. Though she dared not to show it. Wanting to abandon the entire encounter altogether, she turned to march toward the south end of the garden, where she hoped for a footpath to lead out of the area.

"Don't you want to know?"

Taresa, instinctively, glanced over her shoulder. She slowed, not wishing to stop.

"Why I desired to speak to you?"

"Not particularly –"

"It's about your Promised."

Taresa paused. *Jameson?* "What in Mar's name are you talking about?"

The grin, partial though not wholly, returned. "Your focus these last few weeks has been on your nuptials, as it should be. But make no error, your union to Prince – pardon me, *King* Jameson – is not without judgment."

"*Whose* judgment? Those generals I saw you with?"

"For a start, yes."

"Why should our military oppose my marriage to the King?"

"He is, shall we say, untested by the experience of battle."

Taresa, unsuccessfully, tried to suppress a laugh. "You're mad. The Marlish king has as much training in combat as any of our best soldiers. Not to mention the successful campaigns he has led on his island."

"Precisely. His island. It has been invaded twice in the past year. His defense of his homeland has been minimal at best, with the last hardly a success, at least by Ibian standards. He allowed one warlord to float away down a river while another escaped his prison! Then there was the small matter of his barons nearly removing him from the throne. The whole of arrangement stinks even worse than your promise to Prince Denisot."

At the mention of her last Promised, her face burned. Taresa forged ahead to Xain. She halted before his visage, intent on letting him see the full intensity of hers.

"My promise to Jameson is nothing like what I had with Denisot. Nothing. I never even met the prince of Colinne. My betrothal to him was the result of an archaic tradition, one that tied our kin to another. Believe me, I breathed a sigh of relief when the Devout dissolved the arrangement. And unlike that promise, the one with King Jameson is fitting, as I agreed to it, on my terms."

"But your father –"

"Proposed it, yes. A treaty hinged on it, yes. In addition to the hopes of many wanting to see Ibia aligned with another power once again." Taresa glanced at the roses to her right. She sidestepped to them, deftly plucking two: one with a swirl of red and gold, while the other bore the robust gold petals she admired earlier. With a rose in each hand, she turned back to Xain.

"I saw the prospect of what could be. However, I also knew my next promise would have to be appropriate, a match between two souls not simply bound by regal or church tradition."

"You speak of love?"

"The prospect of love. Love takes time. Time is a resource we royals have little of, for all of our wealth, power, and prestige. Nonetheless, love can happen if the arrangement is between two who have similarities in goals and interests."

"What could you possibly have in common with the Marlish king?"

Taresa's eyes locked with his. "We both fight to secure the Throne, to protect it from the likes of which we never want to see rise to sovereignty. You know of whom I speak. The warlords from afar. The corrupt nobles. Even the foxes within our own families."

Now, the embers of anger and hate flared on Xain's face, threatening to consume his very person.

Taresa, in response, offered an innocent grin. "Tis hard work, putting faith in a royal one knows little of, especially one from across the Vortriac Ocean. Yet, in the sparse time I had to acquaint myself with the King, I discovered him to be kind, humble, and pure of heart."

"What if you're wrong?"

"Then I shall just go about busying my days as my mother does. Only I won't bug my daughters so much. Not bad, considering there are worse fates. Or suitors."

At that last slight, the flames within Xain blazed to become an inferno. He opened his mouth to retort. At the ready, Taresa tossed him the rose from her hand.

Absentmindedly, he caught it: thorns and all. A rather large one pricked his index finger, causing him to yelp and drop the blossom.

The game done, Taresa pivoted. She headed down a small footpath leading beyond the garden back to the avenue, all the while smelling the solid-colored golden rose in her hand.

Still smitten, she scarcely arrived at the top of the staircase leading to her portico when Nataliya came running up to her. "Resa! Come, come!" She took her older sister by the hand.

"What? What is it?"

"You must see."

They made haste to Taresa's bedchamber, where Ermesinda and their mother stood waiting impatiently.

"The air outside? Honestly, Taresa, I half thought you ran to the docks to escape on a merchant vessel."

If only. "What is this news that has Nataliya so excited?"

Her mother nodded to the tea cart beside the dining table. On it lay a folded letter, the seal broken.

"It wasn't me," Ermesinda said. "Mother opened it."

"As is my right."

Taresa approached the cart, noting the top half of the seal. The impression in the wax, though ripped, clearly showed the three points of a compass.

"A flyboat brought it to our royal dock not long ago," Queen Belitta said, "having sped ahead of the Marlish fleet. Blessed be the winds of Mar, your Promised will be arriving early, nearly a full week ahead of schedule."

Taresa nearly gasped as her gut fluttered. "Here?

Early?"

"Why, yes, Child. That's what I said."

A week less of preparation. Of going over dresses and other details of the wedding. Fewer moments to contemplate the nuptials. Robbed of days to enjoy the waning solitude. To hold on to her maidenhood. Her innocence.

The accelerated timeline left Taresa aghast. "Well, well..."

"Yes, Child?"

"Whatever shall we do?"

Belitta smirked. She motioned to the tailor, who had been standing nearby obediently, a spool of finely woven fabric in each hand. "We do what we've been doing. We go over the finer points. We fashion the entirety of your royal ceremony. Above all, we enjoy ourselves while doing it."

The Queen sauntered up to the tea cart. Taresa expected her mother to embrace her. Instead, she reached for one of the frosted tea cakes on the dessert tray, a wedge coated with a pink spread. She plucked it into her mouth, smiling.

Good Mar, she thought. *Let us be done with this wedding.*

Chapter 4

"Bloody bloody bloody bloody bloody hell," Ely muttered under his breath. "Some just have all the luck."

Around Ely, barons and baronesses clapped and nodded in approval, a stark contrast to the glare imprinted on his face. He cared not. Not when Mar and the whole world had wronged him as they did.

From behind, a gentle nudge from a patron put Ely off balance. As did a brush from his left side. Both the product of guests clamoring to catch a better glimpse of the newly-married royals before them.

They appeared at the top of a marble staircase, which fanned out to the ballroom below. On the ground level waited a string quintet ready to serenade the couple for their first dance as husband and wife. The guests surrounded the square dancefloor. Though of royal and noble blood, the attendees clustered around the open space like children clamoring for sweets on Harvest Day. Their present enthusiasm, along with the general euphoria that followed the ceremony, was enough to nauseate Ely to no end.

Dear Mar, he thought, *I am going to drink myself into a stupor the likes of which none of these patrons have seen before.*

Ely's stomach churned, and his anger mounted, as Symon took Taresa by her hand to guide her down the stairs. Steady applause accompanied each of their steps and continued until they paused in the center of the ballroom. Even Sir Everitt, who ringed the dance space with a retinue of Marlish and Ibian guards, broke with his tradition of service to offer a clap to the newly married.

The quintet adjusted their bows as Symon slipped his left hand into Taresa's while his right slid to the small of her back.

Get me a drink! Ely nearly screamed as he shoved his way from the dance floor. The quintet loosed their strings, giving rise to a soft melody, which only spurred Ely on more. He arrived at the nearest bar to the additional accompaniment of ohhhs and ahhhs.

"You!" Ely said in Ibian. He shoved a finger at the barkeep behind the counter. "An ale. Your strongest."

The barkeep, a sturdy man built like a bull with a coarse mat of black hair, replied with a raised brow and wry look. "We aren't serving such drink tonight. By the Throne's orders, the menu tonight is of sparkling ambrosia and vintage wines."

"Mar damn it!" Ely exclaimed far too loudly in Marlish. Those directly around him cast a judgmental glance in his direction, while all the others paid no notice. "Very well," he went on in Ibian. "Give me a goblet of whatever. With another every minute thereafter. I'll need it."

Having not shed his stern demeanor, the barkeep leaned in, his gaze set on Ely. "My lord, I know not from where you hail, but in this land, we show some respect during our ceremonies — especially royal ones. No one drinks until the new king and queen finish their first dance. No one."

"Not even King Felix?" Ely retorted.

"If you were to sprout a crown on your head and grow a face as presentable as His Majesty's – rather than the rat's nest you have now – not even then."

Ely fumed. Instinctively, his hand went to the dagger hidden inside of his shirt. However, another hand – firm and steady – caught him before his fingers found their mark.

He glanced up to find a Voiceless, in the garb of a noble, staring him down. Then he felt the hot breath of another silent knight as he too leaned in on the opposite side to offer his scowl.

Their directives for the ceremony had been clear. Symon had made sure of that. Neither brother – especially Ely – were to make a scene. If either sibling dared to fall out of line, then the Voiceless had the authority to subdue and remove that brother by any means necessary.

Ely, his actions subdued though his temper continued to burn, looked the two guards of his up and down. His gaze traveled the length of them, resting to the free hand of the one who caught him first.

"I don't want to hurt you," the Voiceless signed, his fingers flexing just under the lip of the bar so Ely could see and no other.

"Then let go of me," Ely responded in taut Marlish words he ground through his teeth.

"Behave."

Ely glanced at each knight, then nodded. The Voiceless eased his grip. Ely pulled away.

"Seems your men-at-arms saved you some embarrassment," the barkeep said.

Ely opened his mouth to offer a curt retort only to be

cut off by a barrage of applause. He swung around to find the first royal dance between King and Queen had ended. The guests broke from their lines around the dance floor to approach the couple. Guards immediately swooped in to keep the eager attendees at a respectable distance and arrange them in an orderly fashion.

Ely turned to order his drink finally. Before he could, the barkeep slid a goblet of mint green wine across to him.

"Every minute thereafter, I know," said the barkeep. "So long as you keep that boorish trap of yours shut and behave."

A curse and an insult crossed Ely's mind. Several, in fact. For once, he thought better of it, as he was just glad to have a draught in all the boredom.

Three goblets and several minutes later, Ely's demeanor softened in a way he did not expect. No stranger to intoxication, he studied the glass in his possession, which carried his fourth round of spirits.

"Pardon me," he called to the barkeep.

The bull in britches, at the far end of the bar serving another, paid him no mind. Still curious, Ely tapped the patron closest to him.

"Kind sir," he said in his rough Ibian. "These spirits, do they seem off to you?"

"You one of Jameson's subjects?" the man replied in Marlish.

Though with the classic olive complexion of an Ibian, the gentleman spoke Ely's native tongue without the hint of an accent. Ely paused, surprised.

"Tis from King Felix's private vintage," the man went on, not waiting for Ely to reply. "Predates the Century War, as do most of the spirits served tonight. They say the wine aged so well it gives, well, not drunkenness... But, how do you Marlishmen say... A good time? A good time?"

"Euphoria," chimed the woman next to him.

"Aha! Yes, euphoria. Your mood changes and your senses dull; however, you don't get drunk the same way you would off of ale."

"Oh," Ely replied. "Why, I thank you for the information."

"Yes, well, that's me. Always offerings, always offering... In fact –"

His companion tugged at his sleeve to usher him toward another couple. The man, sensing her hint, bowed and returned to his companion. Ely returned his attention to the goblet in hand.

Euphoria? he mused. *Interesting.*

He glanced around him. Suddenly, the affair throughout the ballroom changed. No longer did it seem the haughty gathering of earlier. Part of that clung to the air while something grander, more opportunistic, presented itself.

Euphoria.

Ely eyed the crowd. His focus narrowed on the familiar — the supple, soft flesh of maidenhood.

It spilled forth not just from the constricted bosoms of corsets and gowns but also powdered cheeks and rosy lips. It beckoned him from every exposed female orifice, whether sensual or not. From clasped hands. From under the cuffs of wrists. From necklines. Earlobes.

Yes, the receptacles of words both bitter and sweet.

Ely glanced at the dance floor. Symon remained at the

center, with Taresa at his arm, as the two bowed and curtsied to their guests. They then proceeded to make idle chitchat, nodding politely and smiling as though on cue. Behind those they engaged waited a line of many more patrons, each eager to have their moment of association.

"Dreadful," Ely said aloud to no one. He chugged the contents of his goblet. He extended it to the Voiceless closest to him. The knight instinctively reached for the glass. But Ely, obviously not caring, released it prematurely, allowing the goblet to shatter into a thousand pieces.

Both knights glared at their sovereign, who did not even bother to turn. Those attendees around him, also in their own worlds, barely shot a glance at the glass bits on the floor.

"Well then, gents," Ely said to the Voiceless, still not meeting their eyes. "If my brother shall win the bride, then I will turn my sights to the other spoils."

So began the dance. Ely, at his finest – or worst – slipped between man and matron to chase every maiden. His approach started as delicate. His look, kind. His words, subtle. At first. Until they weren't. Within moments, he unleashed his flattery with language and gestures oozing all of his charms. He elicited a giggle or smile at first before he fished for a name, then a kin, followed by a story. He soon excused himself when a fairer maiden caught his attention out of the corner of his eye, offering the hollow promise of returning.

On and on this went, first with one brunette, followed by two black-haired beauties, and after that, a maiden of golden locks. The latter responded with a kiss to the cheek before Ely coaxed her to the servant's hall, where he proceeded to discover the lass was far removed from her maidenhood.

Ely repeated his hunt, the chase and conquest, two more times before returning to the bar to catch his breath. The Voiceless, who he had purposefully lost on his second tryst, were nowhere in sight, allowing Ely to settle back with another goblet in hand.

Euphoria.

Conversations swirled around him like breezes on an open plain. Though the bulk were in Ibian, languages from a dozen lands fluttered upon his ears, as butterflies do on spring petals. Soft, welcoming. Even seductive.

"Hail to the King! The Queen!" said one.

"May they live a thousand years!" cried another.

"Here, here."

"What say you? Another stein. And a goblet?"

"Is this vintage new? I've never tasted such, such... wet, good drink."

"Oh, my lord. Do go on."

Ely chanced – nay, interjected –half a dozen more times, not caring for the judgmental glances and inquisitive stares he received. He was simply too drunk on the atmosphere to experience any level of shame.

The swell of attendees softened the brusqueness of Ely's antics. Since the end of Symon and Taresa's dance, the ballroom had absorbed several hundred more so that now the patrons stood packed elbow to elbow. The influx represented the lower caste of nobility invited to the royal ceremony, those high enough in rank to have some lineage to the barons present but not so refined as to have the coin or mannerisms that came with a more sophisticated upbringing. Ely, always on the prowl despite his self-inflicted stupor, could spot just such marks of the attendees that bordered on being of the common folk — stitching on clothes tailored by the less-skilled, often crooked, or of mismatched thread. Hair braided or combed though not recently washed so that it bore the sheen of grease. Then there were the scents. Or rather, the stenches. Of course, the masses tried to bury their odiferous bodily secretions with garlands of wild roses or hearty applications of musk oil and perfumes. Such attempts merely added to instead of replacing the stink that accompanied the growing crowd.

Still, Ely did not mind. He welcomed the less affluent, knowing they brought with them maidens less accustomed to refinement, those more gullible, more likely to be seduced by his charms. Such prey – two fair-skinned women fresh from the outer hall – came within his sights. Ely snaked through the crowd and their mingled voices, edging toward his subsequent victory.

"My, my, aren't you a sassy lass?" said one baron a tad too loud.

"My ship, you really should visit my ship. I brought the finest wool," said another.

"Dear, freshen up my goblet."

"Charmed."

"May the royal couple live forever!"

"Death to the King."

Ely nearly missed the last one. It struck his ears, though he took another step before he considered the totality of what had been uttered. The words were in Marlish, in an unfamiliar accent. He paused and turned, scanning the throng.

"That Marlish monarch will not last. His reign will suffer –"

Who said that?

" – within a fortnight. Or sooner –"

Where is he?

Ely could feel the breath of the man speaking those foul words. However, he struggled to *see* him. The ballroom was packed beyond capacity, with each patron brushing up against five others. Ely, perturbed, shoved his way toward where he thought the voice originated.

"You seem so sure," replied another man, his Marlish heavily accented.

"Of that I am," the voice continued. "Jameson is not half the ruler his father was, which isn't saying much."

That mangy fox.

"Truthfully, I'm surprised what will happen to him didn't occur sooner."

"Oh, and what *will* happen?"

Ely spun. The two were nowhere in sight. He twisted. Nothing other than raucous banter. He craned his head. He turned again.

And he saw them.

A tall, commanding man with a stiff, round beard paused to take a swig from his stein. With him stood a shorter, slender man, clean-shaven and pale. There was a clear juxtaposition between the two, yet they spoke to one another with ease and familiarity.

The taller one gulped before resuming his thought. "He will be exposed, as wanting. With every challenge and obstacle presented, he will lose face. First, here in Ibia. Then in Marland."

The smaller man turned his nose, unconvinced. "You speak with such certainty. Have you not forgotten the victories he has pulled off as of late? Routing the Lewmarians while convincing their Conclave of Barons to extend their rule, all while somehow their castle withstood a surprise attack."

"Fancy tales and fabrications. No one man can do such things. No. Not one."

The bearded one continued to stare at his companion, though he paused a moment too long.

Ely ducked. He spun around. *No, he couldn't have. I was careful.* At least three guests stood and mingled between Ely and the two subjects of his interest, with others all around. As he always did when trying to blend into a crowd inconspicuously, Ely trod carefully, doing nothing to attract attention to himself. Yet he swore he saw the commanding one look at Ely from the corner of his eye.

"Perhaps you're right," Ely managed to hear the shorter one say. "Ah, Your Grace. Venidoze."

Venidoze? Ely glanced back in their direction. He spotted a third man approach the two. The newcomer had the classic look of an Ibian, with olive skin and dark hair and medium height. He responded to the shorter one in what Ely assumed was his mother tongue. In response, the small man continued the conversation in Ibian, as did the taller one.

As native speakers do, they spoke rapidly, so much so that Ely had difficulty understanding anything other than a few words or phrases. *King? The marriage? Disowned. No? Disavowed. Disrupted.*

One of the maidens Ely had courted earlier, a brunette, ambled up to him. Clearly of a kin of country barons, Ely hadn't thought much of their conversation though her bust had inspired him to compliment her nonetheless.

"Fancy seeing you again, my lord," the maiden – if she was one – said with a grin.

"Oh, piss off. I'm busy."

"Well, I – I never."

"Never is right."

The maiden launched into a tirade of insults, Marlish interspersed with Ibian. Ely perked.

"Wait, you speak Ibian?" he asked. He pulled her closer as he inched toward the three. The crowd had bulged in their immediate vicinity, threatening to turn the safe distance Ely had kept into a buffer that would prevent him from hearing more.

"Why, let go of me!"

"Shhh!" he pleaded. He fished a bracelet from his pocket. He always carried jewelry should he need it to sweeten his seduction. "Here. It's yours."

"Really?" the maiden asked.

"There's more if you help me."

"Well, if you'd like –"

"Translate. Help me translate."

The maiden, as if insulted by the refusal of her near-offer, paused. She considered, though, and shrugged. "Very well, my lord."

"Good." Taking her hand, Ely wedged through the crowd toward the three men of interest. Approaching them without drawing attention proved difficult. However, when a pair of couples gravitated in behind the gentlemen,

Ely saw his chance. He pulled the maiden close to him as he neared his targets.

"What are they saying?"

The maiden craned her head. "The Ibian, there, in-between the sizes of the other two, he's talking about the king from Colinne."

"Colinne? Here?" Ely asked before realizing she was referring to Taresa's former betrothed. "You mean King Jameson?"

"That's what I said."

Ely rolled his eyes. *This girl is only good for one thing. Well, maybe two things.* "What else?"

"He's saying the king's pulses, wait, impulses, can be predicted. Whatever that means. They can be predicted if he is presented with the right catalyst. What's a catalyst?"

"It's a type of farm cat. Now what?"

"I agree, gentlemen..."

Ely straightened. The last portion he understood, as it was in Marlish. Ely fixated on the speaker of his native tongue, who was once again the tall man. He continued speaking in Marlish as the three went on to reply in Ibian.

"We should not be so bold as to speak in public," translated the maiden. She cocked her head. "Oh, now that I can't understand."

Ely, hiding behind the maiden, focused his hearing. Undoubtedly, the words assaulting his ears –

Wait? Tosilian? Volkmar? Colinnese?

Yes. The men switched languages with ease, speaking all three.

Ely, obsessed, pushed the maiden aside as curiosity overtook him.

"Hey–" the maiden yelped.

Ignoring her, though still using the pair of couples as a buffer, Ely listened.

"Then it is settled," the tall one said, returning to Marlish. "We will bait the king. He will respond as he always does. Like a hero. Then, with the trap set, we will strike. And the downfall of the Marlish will begin."

His two companions nodded.

"Let us delve into the details, then. In private."

The two shorter men turned to the servant's hall to leave. The taller of them made a motion to follow them. Not before he paused, however, to look about him.

Ely averted his eyes. No sooner did he when an open palm came across his face.

"This is the one, Father!" the maiden shouted. "He's been teasing me all night, he has."

"How dare you, Sir. Have you no decency?"

Stunned, Ely stood slack-jawed. He tried to shift his attention back to the three men of interest when the maiden delivered another slap, this time to his other cheek.

"Come now! *That* one was uncalled for."

"Serves you right. Thinking you can ignore me. Now, Father – Hey!"

Ely ducked behind the pair of couples who had been shielding him. He darted to and fro to make his way to the servant's hall. His reflexes served him well, for within seconds, the dimness of the corridor cloaked him.

As his sight adjusted to the low light, Ely scanned the vestibule. The area offered some degree of room, as two servants shoulder-to-shoulder could take to the hallway at any given time. Waiters and cooks took advantage of the space, moving about with their wares and dishes, all while ignoring Ely. The hubbub distracted Ely nearly to the point of him losing his target. Until the flash of the tall, bearded man as he rounded the corner down the hall summoned his attention. Without hesitation, Ely chased after him.

Ely needn't hurry after the mark too long before the echo of his boisterous chords came into range. He turned the corner to discover the hall curved at random points, so he couldn't see any person – including the three he chased – more than a dozen paces ahead.

"Following the raid tonight, send word to our compatriots. Have them buy flour by the barrelful. Then the molasses. The fervor will be mild at first, then grow as the taverns and pubs find it harder to feed the masses that have swelled the streets and docks of Arinn for the royal wedding. The Throne... Nay, the Thrones, will both release an edict calling for calm and voluntary rationing. When that happens, our agents will take to the –"

Abruptly, the words which had been strong and clear stopped.

Ely, disregarding all concern as a sleuth, bolted. The lit sconces he passed became a blur of streaked orange as he zigzagged the corridor. The walls seemed to close in as the path narrowed to a width not much more than shoulders width. Then without warning, the hall ended.

"What in Mar's name..." Ely panted. Exasperated, he placed his palms on the wall before him. He pushed. He shoved. He clawed at the grooves and indentations of the cut stones, hoping in vain one would shift loose and thereby reveal a secret passage.

The wall did not pivot. Nor did any stone move. Ely

rambled back whence he came, repeating his efforts against the walls to each side of him. Again, the stone facades stayed in their place, resistant to his acts of frustration and desperation.

Soon, he came upon the rush of the servants in their hallway again, then after he arrived back in the grand ballroom. He hardly considered his trek due to the unease which overtook him. By the time he reached the bar, his trance was complete.

"Are you well, sire?" asked the gloved hand of a Voiceless.

The motion snapped Ely from his daze. He snapped his head to find himself flanked once again by his two guards.

"Why... I'm... Wait, where were you? The one time I could have used your help, and you were nowhere to be found."

The Voiceless looked to each other, befuddled.

"We were looking for *you*!" the Voiceless to his left emphasized the last word with a sharp gesture to vent his frustration. "You slipped away from us. Intentionally."

"Oh, you knights and your malarkey. Never mind your excuses. We have work to do. Come."

Ely forged ahead across the ballroom, heeding no protest from the pairings of guests he cut through or interrupted. For the briskness of night could not come to him soon enough.

He pressed on by way of the balconies and stairwells, which took him down the storied terraces of Castle Arinn. Only a handful of guests here and there populated the stairs, and the guards he passed paid him no attention as he came upon level footing to approach the lower gardens.

"Dear Mar!" Ely exclaimed as he tromped through the gardens. "How much longer do we have to walk?" Though Arcporte Castle was the crown jewel of Marland, by contrast, it stood as a hovel compared to the expanse of the grounds and size of the edifices that made for Castle Arinn. Ely glanced back over his shoulder to confirm the Voiceless still trailed him, and in doing so, caught sight of the seven terraces leading up to the ballroom.

"What is this about?" signed one of the knights.

Ely, noting not a soul within earshot, paused. "The King is in trouble. I think."

Both knights raised their brows, unsure of what to make of Ely's statement.

"Oh, don't give me those looks. I know what I heard."

"What was that?" asked the other.

What was it? The absence of commotion and revelry allowed Ely to reconsider all that had happened. Such reflection shifted his thoughts, stirred his emotions, so he began to doubt the tone and truth of what he heard.

"I need a drink," Ely began.

Both of the knights cleared their throats. Ely stopped. It was the closest thing they could offer as a vocal protest.

"Please," urged one. "Tell us."

"Very well." Ely paced before the Voiceless, his head down as he stared at the ground, attempting to gather himself. "Two men inside, I caught them speaking ill of the, you know, my brother. It was while all the rest were offering congratulations. It caught my attention. So I listened. They spoke of King Jameson falling, his reign ending. They said it would happen soon, very soon.

"I've heard such critiques of my kin before. I'm not an

idiot. I know being a royal attracts its share of hate, whether deserved or not. But this was different. They were so *sure* of Jameson's failure. They predicted it. With a degree of certainty that would only come from them... planning it."

The revelation jolted Ely. His head rang. A weight formed in the pit of his stomach. All while a sense of dread – not unlike the mania he had known from birth – came over him.

"Those men... Those bastards..." Ely's breath quickened, as did his pacing. His mind raced. His fear mounted. "They spoke in all manner of tongues. They were versed in every language of the continent. Perhaps more. So why speak in Ibian for all the guests to hear?"

He glanced at the Voiceless. They offered no response save for the sharp narrowing of their eyes.

"Why speak Marlish? At the exact moment I was there?"

It dawned on his guards. Never less than stoic, no expression of panic overtook them. Not truly. Their unsettled nature manifested itself as they shifted their weight from one leg to another, in how their hands inched closer to – but never touched – their sidearms. It bore on them, their silence now matching their tone, their degree of consideration, of dread.

I was meant to hear those words. The threats. The plans. Ely's mind went on, not waiting for his Voiceless to digest the exposed conspiracy. *Despite my disguise, they knew I was Marlish. They spoke so I understood. My coyness meant nothing to them. They fed me bits. I ate them. They mentioned my brother...*

My brother, my brother, my brother.

"We need to warn him," one of the knights said with his hand.

His compatriot nodded. They pivoted to march back up the steps.

"No. Don't."

Both Voiceless halted to turn to Ely, confusion protruding from their faces.

"They know. About us four. My brothers."

Ely said no words. The spoken word was too dangerous now, lest the leaves and stems, statues and stones, have ears to betray their privacy. Instead, he resorted to the dialect of his guardians.

"Are you sure?" asked one of the knights.

"Yes," Ely signed.

"Then why not tell Symon?"

"We need more. More details. Key information on all that is unusual. All that appears out of sorts." Ely couldn't chance being wrong about this. His suspicion had to be on point this time. Moreover, he needed proof – and quickly – to bring to his brothers so they could prevent the malaise in store for their kin.

"At least let us warn Everitt. He could extend the watches, raise more guards."

"No. I fear it's too late for that. If the enemies know the secret of me and my brothers, then the foxes in this hellhole will notice such a change, no matter how discreet we are."

"Then this information you say you need... Do you have a plan?"

"Something like that." Ely jingled the coins in his pouch.

Not enough. What a time to be bloody poor. "How many free knights do I have at my disposal? Those not assigned to Symon or Gerry?"

"Four."

"Four?!"

"Symon needs a grander detail, now that he has the Princess to protect."

Of course. Some buffoons have all the luck. "No matter. Four will do. It's not like the lot of you can act like regular folk, what with your tongues cut out and all."

Though used to Ely's jabs, both knights still replied with glares.

"Oh, I didn't mean it," Ely insisted. "Now listen, you two gather the four and return with as much coin as you can carry without looking conspicuous –"

"Conspicuous?"

"Obvious. No large satchels weighing you down. And get your hands on all the fading potion you can find. Vials upon vials of the stuff, if you can manage. Oh, and bring me a fresh disguise. This one has certainly done little to hide me tonight."

Ely ripped the prosthetic nose from his face, along with the false mustache and long, curved eyebrows.

"One of us should stay," offered the knight to his right. "For your protection."

"Mark my words, I am in no sort of danger. Yet. If those vermin wanted to slay me, I would be dead already. No, they want me alive. They crave it, to witness whatever it is they have in store. Just go. When you're ready, meet me at the *Cabiiyo Duraldo* tavern." Knowing he would be on his own while his brothers took their turns as Jameson, Ely had memorized the locations and names of the finest – and seediest – taverns and inns in Arinn. "Don't worry; I won't attract attention as I wait for you. I promise I'll be fine."

Whether absorbing his paranoia, doubting his commitment to behave, or just uneasy with the thought of leaving their detail, the knights hesitated.

"I command you to leave and follow my orders," Ely barked louder than necessary. Agitated, though offering no act or word of protest, the Voiceless turned.

Ely watched after them until they reached the steps of the first terrace before going about in the opposite direction, toward the nearest barbican leading into the city.

The mood of the citizenry should have brightened Ely. Even the most common of folk reveled in the royal wedding. All about, shouts of glee and bursts of laughter rang. Couples strolled arm in arm. Children chased each other through the streets. Even the beggars smiled more, no doubt helped by the extra coin their upended caps and open palms received.

Rather than celebrate with the city, which had risen to the occasion, Ely sank into the gutter of his mind. The jubilation did nothing to pull him from the depths of his despair. It only served to emphasize all that he – and the subjects of two nations – had to lose.

Don't become King Fool, not now. Too many depend on you. You need to stay strong. You need to focus –

Ely's foot sank into a divot left by a loose cobblestone. He fell forward, scraping his knee as his hands braced the ground.

"Are you well?" asked a random citizen in Ibian, a slender man in an elegant doublet, as he broke from the circle of his family to tend to Ely.

"Yes, yes." Ely waved the man off. Then he glanced down to find his right pant leg torn. Lifting his knee, Ely winced as a sharp pain shot up to his thigh.

Hobbled, Ely pressed onward. He made it another four doors down the block before coming to lean on a hitching post. There, in the shadow of an unlit building, he allowed himself a moment. His mania, subdued ever since he left the servant's hall in the ballroom, spilled forth.

Why this, Mar? Why this? He prayed through the tears. *Have we not suffered enough tragedy? Enough betrayal? Did we survive, conquer, only to face another plot away from our land? Will we not see an end to the foxes in their dens and the knives in our hearts? Will it ever end?*

A chill swept through Ely, not unlike the one which visited him at Terran. The one on the night his father died.

He turned to the palace on the hill. Massive. Radiant. Bathed in the light of ten-thousand candles, sconces, and torches, within and outside, highlighting the glory of Castle Arinn.

My brother. My brothers...

Ely shoved off the hitching post. Another stab of agony came over his leg. Still, he limped.

"Symon..." he said aloud though only to himself, low enough to avoid attracting attention.

"Dawkin..."

He paused.

"Gerry..."

He continued.

"Symon... Dawkin... Gerry..." His limp fell into a pattern. He hopped on his left leg every fifth step to alleviate his right, if only for a time.

"Symon... Dawkin... Gerry... Symon... Dawkin... Gerry... Symon... Dawkin... Gerry."

Chapter 5

Never before had Symon felt less sure of what to do.

Hesitation wasn't unfamiliar to him. In battle, he paused, whether he forced himself to stop and formulate an immediate plan or because the situation called for him to lie in wait. In court, even when matters of law or diplomacy catapulted over his head to escape him, he managed to sit and look regal. Then there were the moments of sure death. Not his demise. His subjects. For as king, he now presided over executions of the high-ranking, duties he could not pass on nor ignore. Even in such scenarios, both straightforward and trying, he always knew to do *something*.

Now, though, he did nothing. Save for standing before the closed door like an idiot, as the most stunning woman in the world waited behind him.

"Your ... Majesty?"

Symon sighed, opening his eyes. He turned away from the door to face Taresa.

"You can stop calling me that. We are married."

"Ever since your coronation, I've grown so used to your title I never thought to address you otherwise. Yes, I suppose we should try to be more... familiar. How do your acquaintances address you?"

"Your Majesty."

"Your family?"

"Your Majesty."

"Even your grandfather?"

"Son. He calls me Son."

"Well, that'll never do. For me, at least."

Symon smirked. "My Right Captain, Everitt. Sometimes he calls me James."

"I like that. James."

Symon gazed at Taresa. Hearing his name – well, what she thought was his name – ignited a passion within him, one he had never experienced. In all his years, with all the women he had known, none had stirred him as she did right then, in the fire of the moment.

Still, he stayed by the closed door.

What is wrong with me?

"Everitt, stop staring."

His Right Captain hardly ever broke from his knightly demeanor. It felt odd having to correct him, especially in such a public ceremony.

"My apologies, James. By Mar, a thousand apologies."

"Don't appear out of sorts, is all."

"I'm not. It's not as though anyone is looking at *me*. Even the High Bishop is agape."

He wasn't wrong. Though sworn to celibacy, His Grace Lunes Sanzo had a façade that betrayed his vows. Then again, his stare was not unlike those of everyone else in the cathedral. Whether sparked by attraction, stirred by curiosity, or enamored by the sight of pristine beauty, all the guests in attendance studied the Jewel of Ibia as if for the first and last time.

Only Symon glanced away. Not that he wanted to avert his focus. He longed to gaze upon Taresa, who had been kept from his sight since he landed. No sooner had he set foot on the royal dock in Arinn when he found himself ushered away to attend pressing matters of state. First, he met with the High Bishop of Arinn, who blessed him and offered prayers to Mar in thanks for Jameson's safe journey. Then Symon paid a visit to the Concidaad, the Ibian royal order of barons consecrated by both the King and High Bishop to protect the Throne. Little more than the extended family of Kin Garsea, Symon nonetheless had to convene with each baron, a true exercise of patience measured by tiresome, uninspiring conversations. Lastly, Symon gathered with King Felix himself for a modest dinner, which marked the start of his *selabatto*, an Ibian tradition in which the groom spent the three days before the wedding avoiding his bride.

Such absence from Taresa had built up the anticipation of this moment. A little too much.

Symon's palms turned clammy. His focus blurred. His throat became parched.

What is happening?

His first intimate moment with a woman had caused no such reaction. At least not in him. True, the girl had been two years his senior and confessed to being experienced. Still, she had blushed when he first rolled on top of her. In fact, every girl – whether maiden or not – had expressed some shyness when Symon had taken them. Even before such affection blossomed, all his past lovers showed some degree of intimidation.

Not Taresa.

In a gown of overlapping layers of white lace and chiffon, she looked like a rose, her petals perfectly blossomed.

Her hair, styled in overlapping braids, matched the flawlessness of her dress. Smooth, pure, her face exuded a soft radiance. Not the product of any cosmetic or potion, her glow came from within. Her long stroll down the aisle displayed her perfect gait, the result of a lifetime of unspoiled confidence and charisma.

Arriving at the first step of the alter, Taresa paused. The High Bishop raised his hands toward the heavens, signaling the audience to bow their heads.

At that, Taresa looked up at Symon.

Had he been riding, he would have fallen from his horse. If in the middle of chewing, he would have choked on his food. If speaking, his words would have turned to mumbles and gibberish. Thank Mar, he was only standing, though that proved less than easy as his knees began to buckle.

"Easy, James," Everitt whispered, noting his loss of balance.

Come on, you fool. Even Gerry could do better than this.

Symon straightened. He lifted his chin. He breathed deeply. *By Mar, all the eyes of two kingdoms are on me. I need to act the part. I need to be Jameson. I* will *be King Jameson.*

I must.

That strength of nerve lasted well through the night. With renewed determination, his composure returned, allowing him to partake in the ceremony without any further hindrance. When Taresa approached the altar, Symon bowed. He kneeled with the Princess as the High Bishop officiated the ceremony. When their union had been sealed, Symon led Taresa down the aisle before the raucous audience. His composure went on from the carriage ride to the ballroom and well after the last toast. Only when King Felix and Queen Belitta bid goodnight did Symon's collectedness falter. Not wanting his new bride to feel his suddenly clammy hands, he guided her up the steps of their tower with a gentle touch to the small of her back. In the spirit of Ibian tradition, he allowed her to enter first as he bent to one knee to offer a prayer of gratitude to Mar. Then he followed after her before closing the door.

"James?"

Symon jerked his head. Taresa had closed the gap between them. *When did that happen?* Her hand hovered over his forearm as she stared into his eyes.

"I..." Symon sputtered.

Taresa placed her hand on his forearm. "Would you care for me to –"

She glanced at the folding screens in the corner.

Symon, understanding her implication, nodded. In turn, she smiled.

"Why don't you pour us some mead?"

Without waiting for an answer, Taresa glided to the screens. Symon, by contrast, shuffled like a lame horse over to the end table by their canopied bed. There a servant had laid out a platter with a carafe of mead and two crystal goblets etched with the seals of Kin Saliswater and Kin Garsea.

Wonderful. Another reminder of what is at stake.

Dutifully, Symon poured each of them a glass. Holding them, he turned.

Taresa had her back to him as she undid clasp after clasp, button after button. She stretched and reached, working with remarkable efficiency. Soon, her neck and shoulders laid bare above the rim of the screens as she flung her gown over the edge of one. The goblet from his right hand nearly slipped from his grasp as she raised her bare arms to unbraid her hair.

"Uhhh..." he muttered as mead splashed the floorboards.

"Did you say something, Your – James?"

"No... How do you like to be called?"

She stooped beneath the rim of the screens. "I just became a queen, *your* queen. I haven't had the title of a sovereign nearly as long as you have. 'Your Majesty' is fine until it feels worn out. Or 'My Queen' if you prefer."

"Oh, very well, My, Your –"

Taresa snapped back up and peered over the edge of a screen. "James."

"Yes?"

"That was a jest."

"Oh... Good one, I might add."

Taresa winked. Symon blushed. He realized the thin straps of a lace nightgown now stretched over her shoulders. With deft fingers, Taresa tussled her unbraided hair, allowing her dark brown strands to stream down. She came out from around the screens, revealing a single white bed dress which stretched from her bosom to her ankles. She wore no other ornament. No jewelry adorned her neck nor wrists. She had wiped off her modest cosmetics, revealing a purer form of beauty than what all the wedding guests had witnessed. With feet bare, she crossed the room to approach Symon, taking a goblet from his hand.

"One last drink before –"

"Yes," Symon's voice cracked. "To, um, uh... The kingdoms of Ibia and Marland."

"How about 'to us'?"

"A finer choice. Us." Symon clanked his goblet against Taresa's. She finished his mead before she even had a chance to sip hers. Grinning, Taresa tipped her glass to return the gesture in kind. She took the empty goblet from his hand and set both on the platter.

"Do you want to change?"

Symon followed her gaze. In his stupor, he had forgotten to disrobe.

"Why, I, I think so." *Bloody hell, I'm an embarrassment.*

He went around her to retreat behind his own set of folding screens. He found several nightshirts and trousers, all either white or light blue, with wispy ties and frilly collars. Symon scoffed. None would make him look the least bit appealing. He supposed that was the point, as the clothing served to cover him only until he retreated under the covers with his wife. Nonetheless, the absence of decent garb only set his mood fowler.

He chose instead to disrobe down to his undertrousers. Though clean and white, he felt the fool as he emerged from the screens half-naked. *She wears lace while I don the same garment as a peasant.*

Taresa, having settled under the sheets, perked upon seeing Symon bare-chested. Suddenly, her unfettered confidence dissipated as a rush of scarlet flooded her cheeks. In turn, Symon – considering that maybe he had revealed too much of himself too soon – blushed as well.

Dawdling to the canopied bed, Symon arrived at its edge. He sat down, his back half turned to Taresa, not wanting to offend her yet unsure what to say. With the sheets firmly planted under her arms, Taresa shied away from his glance.

Is this her first time? Symon dared not ask.

"I, I thought the ceremony was nice," he said.

"So did I."

"Your family has been such gracious hosts."

"They're your family too, as of today."

"Hmmm..."

"James?"

"Yes."

"Can we just lay down? Before... we begin?"

"I would like that."

Symon pushed himself onto the bed, where with some awkwardness, he burrowed under the comforter. He shifted to his side, as did Taresa, so the two came face-to-face.

"I appreciate you allowing me the time to adjust."

"Tis no effort, really."

"This is my –"

"Not to worry."

"And you?"

"Me?"

"Have you... Never mind."

Taresa cast her eyes down. Whether out of timidity or disappointment, Symon could not gather.

"My parents," he started. "Their Promise lasted all of three months."

"Three months? Why so short?"

"War. They knew it was only a matter of time before my father would be called back to the front in Afari, so with the blessing of the High Bishop, they married soon after the announcement of their Promise. At least that was the official account.

"My grandfather once told me such talk errored to mention both my father and mother had fallen madly in love at first glance. It was summer, and my father had just returned from his seventh campaign, his third as king. My grandfather worried his heir would fall in battle without siring a son, so with each homecoming, he arranged for barons to present their most eligible daughters, the fairest maidens Marland has ever seen.

"However, at each ball or banquet where these young ladies appeared, my father came away wanting. He grew tired of the formalities, the false mechanisms of beauty, with the corsets, wigs, girdles, and whatever else your... well, what most ladies wear. One evening, after attending yet another stuffy dinner, he went on a ride through the countryside. When he and his entourage came to a stream to water their horses, they chanced upon a huntress dressed in forest green and sporting a long quiver packed with hunting javelins. She was mid-hunt, in pursuit of a stag, when her javelin missed its mark and nearly impaled my father!"

"Oh! That's quite the impression."

"Certainly. The Right Captain and his guards drew their swords and made to arrest my mother on the spot. My father roared for them to withdraw so he could approach the mysterious woman in green –"

"And?"

"My day of birth came nine months later."

Taresa's mouth dropped. Symon grinned. Not sure if

the tale was tall or true, she swatted him on the forearm as he playfully recoiled.

"You're horrible!" she said.

"I tell no lies!"

"Really? Well then, King Honesty, were you so enamored with me when I first arrived in Arcporte? And don't just say 'yes.' Paint a scene for me. What I wore. No. The hue and style of my dress. The fruits of the perfume I had applied. The words I said. How I uttered them. Tell me, James. Tell me a real story."

She looked at him longingly, waiting for a response.

Symon paused. Though Gerry had recited every detail he could fathom of that encounter, Symon, for all the memory tea he had consumed to remember, failed to recount a shred of it. It was as though a mischievous elf had mixed the most concentrated fading potion into his mead.

Do something, you fool!

He didn't. She did.

Her lips, like rose petals, found his. Her hand, its caress as comforting as a warm cloak in winter, drifted to his side. Then to his chest. Which she then kissed twice before returning to his mouth.

Astonished, Symon's eyes kept on her for a moment before he allowed himself to surrender. He slid into her arms, she in his. His fingers spread over the length of her bed dress, where her warmth radiated from underneath. Eager, they gravitated to the straps that held her clothing in place, and with a nimble touch he didn't think he possessed, they unloosed them.

His skin then met hers. He shifted. As did she. Atop her, he opened his eyes to find her looking into his.

The texture of the sheets. The dimness of the dying candles. The strands of her hair as they laid over his skin. Symon knew not anything that came before, nor did he want to consider anything after. He longed to imprint this moment – and only this moment – into his memory for as long as he lived.

He wanted all of it. The innocence in her eyes. The comfort of her embrace. The scent she carried. Of pear blossoms. Of a gentle dew. Of incense. And ash.

Symon narrowed his eyes. *Ash.*

"James?"

He rose off of her. He strode toward the shuttered window. Through the slit, he spotted a glow.

Throwing open the shutters, the inferno on the horizon bathed the room in fiery light. Symon shielded his eyes as his sight adjusted to the brilliance. An explosion, though far, startled him back as Taresa rushed up from behind.

"What is happening?" Taresa asked, panicked.

Symon focused on the blaze. White at its center, orange at the periphery, it gleamed unlike any fire he had ever witnessed. Its tongues of flame whipped and flailed, each seeming to dodge and nip like wild dogs in a crowded kennel. Likewise, the roar emanating from the combustion brought to mind a pack snarling and howling in the night.

Taresa placed her hand on Symon's shoulder. Symon broke off his stare at the brilliance to look down at the grounds. Though no yard directly below their window, Symon spotted groupings of attendants emerging from the servants' entrance, no doubt curious about the uproar. They assembled before the edge of a small ravine, which gave way to a dense forest beyond. Their presence aside, he saw no royalty nor nobles nor knights.

"Where are we?" he asked.

"In the newlywed chamber."

"Yes, I know, but where is it? What part of the castle?"

"The northeast corner, facing away from the harbor."

Northeast corner. Northeast. The city lies full of wedding guests and their retinues. High royalty inhabits the spare chambers of the castle. By the King's order, all the rest – the Ibian army, my soldiers – set up camp on the city's perimeter.

Desperate, Symon peered again at the blaze, trying to gather his bearings. *Could it be? There? My countrymen?*

In answer, the white core of the inferno bulged, overtaking the orange tips. It blasted up and outward, the sheer heat from the explosion shocking Symon and Taresa back.

In its wake, no dogs of fury roared. Replaced a thousand-fold came the screams of men.

I have to know.

Symon took Taresa by the arms to guide her back to the bed.

"Do you have arms here?"

"Arms?"

"Weapons. Daggers. Swords."

"Why, no."

Symon withdrew to his folding screens. In haste, he dressed pulled on a pair of loose trousers and an undershirt. In his rush, he cast aside his wedding attire. *Clank!* He swung around to find his ornamental sword, a gift from the King, having clattered on the floor. Bejeweled and overlaid with gold leaf, Symon had not even inspected its edge for sharpness.

He grabbed the faux weapon – bejeweled and overlaid

with gold leaf - and handed it to Taresa.

"This'll do."

"James –"

"Taresa, my... Listen, you need to stay put. Lock the door behind me and do not open it for anyone – *anyone* – until I return. Do you understand?"

"You don't have to do this. Stay."

As though thunder atop of thunder, a second clap blasted through the window, its brightness and heat stronger than the one before. Symon, eyes shut, felt its warmth upon his skin.

"I must," he said after the heat and light subsided. He made haste to the door. "Remember. No one enters."

Outside, madness ensued. Panicked servants collided with one another. The guards fared little better as their commanders blasted war horns and barked overlapping orders. From one level to the next, Symon dodged them all until he came to the main bailey. There, the frenzy swelled exponentially as the lingering wedding guests added to the chaos. Fancy coats and feathered hats swirled with the matted hair of the peasantry. They collided and trampled each other with nary a thought to rank, as instinct tromped privilege. Having neither the time nor the resources to quell the turmoil, Symon shoved past the mob. Arriving at the first row of stables, he discovered the horses in as much disorder as the citizenry. He managed to find one, saddled and bridled, nearly ready to stomp the stableboy holding its reins.

"Give me!" he sputtered. Though still naked from the waist up, Symon retained his regal presence. The stableboy obliged, stepping back as Symon mounted the courser naturally. With a clip of his heels, Symon bolted.

The night air greeted him first. Then the screams of the masses. Those faded quickly enough, as did the torchlight from the castle grounds. Soon, only the hoofbeats of his mount accompanied him, along with the canopied darkness of the forest. Symon thought himself lost.

On the spur of the moment, another blast lit up the forest, paving the way ahead.

The brilliant line he had glimpsed from the tower glowed in every latticed opening allowed by branch and bush. Those small segmented lights converged and enlarged as he pressed onward. With the illuminance, the shouts that had first assaulted his ears at the castle heightened. By contrast, mere whispers before, now they boomed. Hollers. Shrieks. Pleas. All manner of agonies.

Emerging onto a meadow, Symon faced the blaze in all its glory. The thread of orange and white now stood as a mighty wall, nay, a range of foothills before him. The swelter from its face proved almost too much to bear, as beads of sweat burst forth on Symon's brow while he shielded his eyes.

"James!"

Symon turned around. Sir Everitt, with three Voiceless in tow, approached. From whence he came and how long he had been in chase, Symon could not say.

"Are you bloody mad?! Don't you ever take off like that again!" his Right Captain fumed, not caring if his conduct violated protocol.

"I'm sorry," Symon offered. A Voiceless rode up to Symon, offering him his belt with a sheathed broad sword. Symon looked down at his mount, noting his saddle had not been holstered with a weapon. Embarrassed by his oversight, he humbly accepted the sidearm.

With that receipt, the brilliance behind him died.

Stunned, the five directed their attention to the now smoldering ruins of whatever remained. Symon, apprehensive of the answer to come, nonetheless begged the question to his Right Captain.

"Everitt, that camp... Ours?"

Nothing followed. Symon pivoted as if to pose the prompt again. This time, his Right Captain replied with a nod.

Dear Mar.

Duty followed. Symon felt the beat of each hoof beneath him, as though the horse he rode stomped not on the ground but on him. The shock echoed through the endless cavern of his soul, intensifying as the earth gave way to charcoal and embers. The ruins of the fire had blackened to a hue darker than a starless night. In addition to its lifeless color, the terrain offered the occasional snap and crunch of whatever the inferno had consumed, be it structure or beast, weapon or its owner. Symon feared more of the latter, as no soul appeared before him. Save one.

A squire, perhaps no older than his tenth year, stumbled through the smoldering remains. His eyes, reddened no doubt by smoke and heat, stood apart from the soot which caked his body. Seeing his King and the guards, the boy reached out. He attempted to hurry, though his legs did not respond in kind. His right appeared misaligned, moving at a clip behind his left. Not privy to his injury, the squire fell forward. Everitt hopped from his mount to rush to the boy's side, with Symon close behind.

"Young master," Everitt began, cradling the squire in

his arms. "What happened?"

The boy, the light behind his eyes fading, blinked.

"Stay with us, please," Everitt begged.

"Brave one," Symon started. "Give us a word. Anything."

The boy, sparked by duty, uttered. "Fire. And fox." He pointed.

Symon and Everitt followed his gesture. On the crest of a nearby hill, amongst the smoldering remnants, stood a single cross. The banners of Kin Foleppi flapped from the crossbar, one on each side of the pole.

Beyond the banners, barely visible yet making no attempt to stay hidden, rested the silhouettes of four men atop coursers. Thanks to a steady breeze, one curtain of smoke after another drifted before them, accompanied by the occasional ember.

"Hey!" Symon yelled as he rose. "You!"

In response, the horseman farthest from Symon pulled at his reins, guiding his mount down the other side of the hill, away. Another rider followed suit, disappearing beneath the crest.

"Your Majesty," Everitt urged. However, his plea came too late. Symon, unsheathing the sword the Voiceless had given him, marched up toward the hill.

"Mar damn your fire!" Symon cursed.

The third rider on the crest rode away. However, the fourth – and the last – remained, looking down upon Symon as he approached.

"You dare to attack my men?!"

"My King!" Everitt raced on after him. "James! James!"

"Come face me! Fight me! Damn you! Fight!"

Symon cocked his arm as he raised his sword, ready to storm the last rider. Only then did Everitt close in on him, as did the Voiceless in his retinue. They enveloped Symon, their gauntleted hands and plated arms wrapping around his body.

"Who are you?!" Symon screamed. "Who are you who dare to do this?!"

Symon thought he saw the last silhouette raise and drop his shoulders as if to shrug. The moment passed as soon as it came, for with another drift of smoke, the rider vanished.

Let me go!" Symon commanded as he tried to break free of his guards. "Let me –"

Another fire roared, this one as frightening and sudden as those that came before. Only it didn't erupt on what remained of the encampment –

It came from behind. From Castle Arinn.

Symon and his men froze. They peered over their shoulders, each wary of what they might find. On the ridge holding the ancient seat of Kin Garsea, one of the southeast towers exploded in light, like the wick of a candle suddenly catching a spark to combust into an open flame. And burn it did, the kindle sending volumes of blazes and fumes to pollute the stars above.

Symon pulled free from his shocked men. "Taresa..."

A second blast erupted from the base of the burning tower. It engulfed the rest of the edifice, its inferno rising upward, turning the wick into a candle in flames. The crack of the blast sent shock waves into the forested region below. With the sound, the branches and leaves bent away, trampled by the unseen force. The horses – as battle-ready as any – nonetheless became spooked by the booming chaos. They scattered in all directions. The Voiceless, seeing their coursers panic, went on after them, leaving Everitt with Symon.

The two, still stricken, never took their eyes from Castle Arinn. They watched as the tower, cracked and burnt, surrendered to its many inflictions.

The tower collapsed first. The weight of its split roof sent the top section down, followed by the middle before the base crumbled into a mess of scattered stones.

Symon scarcely saw the last stones topple. For his legs, burning just like the fires he witnessed, pressed long and hard as he cleared past tree after tree in the forest.

Twigs snapped under the constant pounding of his feet, as did the branches that clawed at his face. And the leaves he tore from their hosts.

The air beat his face so that it could have easily bruised his skin. Yet his lungs could not consume enough, so hard they worked to breathe as he raced. Only when a wall of troops appeared before him did he halt, his momentum sending him into a mass of polished steel and aged wood.

"Let me through!" he raged. "Let me pass!"

A shaft slammed into his gut. Symon keeled over, gasping. Dropping to one knee, he fumed as he looked up to the visor of a helmed Realeza.

"Do you know who I am?" Symon demanded.

The Ibian guard responded by placing the butt of his halberd on the ground.

Symon rose to his feet. Intermixed with the regular troops stood Realeza, no doubt the nearest officers who dispersed orders to secure the grounds in the wake of the castle assault. All the personal guards of the Ibian royal family wore their helms with the visors down, obscuring the identity of each individual, preventing Symon from imprinting the image of their faces into his memory. The wall of soldiers that had blocked his path donned no such masks, as their headgear covered only their skulls, ears, and the bridges of their noses. In the absence of such concealment, those same troops carried a nervousness about them. Whether due to the recent attack or the masses still lingering after the festivities or the possibility they had restrained a king, the Ibian men-at-arms threw glances and shifted their weight far too much for warriors. Symon, seeing the fear and doubt only a commander knew, straightened.

"Allow me to pass," he said to the Realeza who had struck him, "and I shall forgive your slight."

Symon stepped forward. The Realeza extended his halberd, as did the other guards. Warily, the Ibian soldiers held the line.

"Defy me," Symon reassured, "and I will see every one of you hung."

That threat sent a chill through the line. Even the Realeza loosened their defensive stances, save for the one who had dealt a blow to Symon.

Very well, Symon thought. *We'll continue this ruse.* "And as for you," he addressed the indifferent guard. "I will make you watch, one by one, as the men you have served with perish."

The guard burnished the shaft of his halberd with his gauntleted hands, biding his time. Whether to consider letting Symon pass or wanting to plow his weapon into Symon's gut, only Mar and the man could say.

The cascade of hooves approaching interrupted the

impending threat. Having recovered their coursers, Sir Everitt and the three Voiceless rode up to the line, which had grown considerably with spectators. The Right Captain dismounted to march up beside Symon.

"Move back!" Everitt barked. Seeing the Right Captain and the Voiceless in armor, which validated their authority, sent the troops scurrying. Gaps formed in the line, offering Symon passage.

"I was just about to convince them to let me pass," Symon insisted.

"Not looking like a washerwoman, you weren't."

Symon glanced down at his clothes. Now stained with sweat and grime, he did give the aura of an unkempt peasant.

"No matter," he said, casting aside his foolishness. He strode through the mass of troops and onlookers, nearly making his way past the horde.

"Your Majesty!"

Symon paused, as did Everitt and the Voiceless at their sides.

The Realeza who had challenged Symon released his halberd, letting it fall. He stepped forward to raise his visor.

Grand Duke Xain.

"Your Grace?" Symon inquired, puzzled.

"Don't look so surprised, cousin." The Grand Duke softened his soldierly posture, strolling up to the king as though in a pair of comfortable riding breeches. "You'll often find me in the guise of my uncle's personal guard."

"To what end?"

"To serve, Your Majesty. You see, unlike some kin, we do not put on airs about doing our duty. We actually consider all responsibilities related to protection – be it a battle, standing watch, even shoeing horses – to be a great honor in defense of the Throne."

"And you consider denying my king entry back into his bedchamber a noble act?" The Right Captain came face to face with the Grand Duke as he laid his hand upon the pommel of his sword.

"Everitt," Symon directed. "Stand down."

"As you wish." Though Everitt's hand never left his pommel.

"I only sought to keep the Princess – actually, now, the Queen – from harm. You see, it never occurred to me that King Jameson would leave his newlywed wife on the night of their ceremony. Even further from my mind was the thought he would abandon her, fleeing his love to chase a bonfire while my family's ancient house burned. Quite contrary to the expected norms and behaviors of a monarch, much less a Marlish one. Some would go so far as to point out the deed as cowardly."

Sir Everitt inched his sword from its sheath.

"Everitt!" Symon yelled.

"Command or not, I will not stand for anyone disgracing my king."

"Disgrace? I was merely mentioning –"

Everitt unsheathed the full length of his sword. In response, the Realeza tipped their halberds. The Ibian soldiers bent their blades as well. That prompted the Voiceless, though outnumbered, to bear their arms.

"Sir Everitt!" Symon roared.

Everitt pivoted. "Your Majesty. I will march ahead and clear your path. That you may rejoin your queen."

Everitt waited for Symon to consent. Symon nodded.

His Right Captain marched past, but not before offering a glare to Xain.

"A spirited fellow, wouldn't you say?" Xain quipped.

"Everitt is a better man you could ever hope to be," Symon declared.

"I'm sure. Though better isn't always advantageous. You're my better, and yet before you lies an army with nothing more than contempt for your reign, seeing as how you threatened them with hanging."

Symon stewed. With every fiber of every muscle, he restrained himself from making an example of the Grand Duke.

"Your Majesty!" Everitt called from the small door of the rampart. "Your Queen awaits."

Symon turned. As he marched, he clenched his fists almost as hard as his jaw. He caught up to his Right Captain, who fell to his side, silently allowing the King his anger. Together, with the Voiceless, they proceeded through throngs of frightened servants and nobles. As Symon came to the main bailey, remnants of the collapsed tower lay blackened, strewn as though cast aside by giants. Knights of the highest rank, from kin both Marlish and Ibian, inspected the damage. Some reported back to their barons. A large cluster gathered before King Felix, who listened patiently as his family – including Taresa – stood at his side.

"James!" Taresa broke from the crowd. She ran to him, shattering all pretense of refinement for his comfort. Before Symon had a chance to cry back, she fell into his arms.

"I didn't know... Where did you go? Who did you find?"

Indeed, who? Symon thought as he recalled the silhouettes of the riders on the burnt hill. *Who?*

Chapter 6

When plagues and wars besiege us, in their wake, what is left?

Songs of old sing of victors who emerge. The great. The bold. The legends. But what of the rest of us? Those broken by seeing the carnage of our kin, left to bury the departed and mourn until the black of our days. We become ghosts, haunted more by our memories than by the slain. We return home as warhorses, expected to relish in the safety of our pastures. Yet the darkness remains.

Our daily routines hide our anguish. We toil in the fields. We tend to the stables. We eat. We sleep. We rise. On occasion, whether prompted by a curious lad or caught in a moment of silence, we return to the disturbance. Yea, we boast of surviving. Yea, we tell of the win. We even smile.

But the true words of the soul are never spoken. The psalms of our loss never chanted. Even when we emerge from our nightmares and scream, we never give life to the horrors that plague us.

For all, for always, the suffering never ends.

Dawkin closed the book. He stared out the grimy window to the street and harbor beyond.

"Drivel," he said to himself. "No sense of verse or pace. Poorly-written prose. Dreadful."

He plopped the volume on the pile by the window sill. *Musings on the Century War* by Sir Keith of Kin Hadleigh had all the promise of a rousing narrative based on the first few pages Dawkin perused. As a knight fighting during the onset of the conflict, Sir Keith had battled in no fewer than two dozen engagements, possibly as many as fifty. The reason the Hadleigh veteran could not recall the exact number stemmed from the fits of madness he endured, with each one seeming to rob him a little more of his memory. *Musings* appeared to be written throughout the knight's life, in chronological order, so that chapter one must have been penned upon his return from the war, chapter two a few years after that, and so on. By the fifth chapter, the knight managed to muse very little on the actual fighting, choosing instead to rant about his thoughts. Dawkin, noting he had not yet completed a quarter of the book, decided against finishing his read by a knight who no doubt had descended into madness.

"Poor chap," Dawkin concluded before reaching for another book from the pile beside him. His next volume, bound in soft leather dyed forest green, held promises of being more soothing: *Dreams from the Woodlands* by Master Allan Colgatt.

"That one's misleading."

Dawkin perked. The woman's voice had roused him from his peace. Aside from the shopkeeper, no one ever bothered to give him a second glance whilst he visited Sir Nygell's Books, let alone speak to him. He leaned over the left arm of his plush chair to stare down the aisle, finding nary a soul.

"Uh-hmm."

In clearing her throat, Dawkin sensed she had moved closer. But where? He looked up and down the aisle again before his gaze began to gravitate toward the bookshelf before him. There, between the gaps of the manuscripts of various widths and lengths, he spotted a pair of eyes staring back at him from the other side.

"Can I help you?" he asked.

"If you can lift a finger, I'm sure you can," she retorted. "I think you mean, 'May I help you?'"

Dawkin scowled. His servants at Arcporte Castle never addressed him in that manner. But in disguise, amongst the commoners, he commanded no such respect. *The price I must pay for any moment of solace.*

Let's try this again. "Perhaps I could determine if I may or can assist you if I knew *why* you interrupted me."

"It started as, how do they say, small talk." Her eyes disappeared as she shifted from behind the shelf. "Then I noticed you have a book I've been searching for in that tall stack you're hoarding."

Dawkin glanced at the pile of books to his right. Indeed, it had grown to an impressive height, encompassing some fifteen volumes. "Which book interests you?"

She paused as she rounded from the other side of the shelf, disappearing momentarily, before presenting herself. "That one," she said, pointing.

Dawkin noted her finger, yet not the manuscript she identified. Rather than follow her gesture, he set his sights on her golden curls, her porcelain skin, and her soft green eyes. The dark blue and white velvet of her dress further painted her as a patron unlike any other who frequented Sir Nygell's, for rarely had he seen a woman in the bookstore who wasn't a Maiden of Mar, let alone one of such stark beauty.

“May I?” she asked as she leaned over to reach for the book.

“Oh, uh, yes. I’m sorry I stashed so many. Please, take as many as you want.”

“Just the one.” She grabbed *Musings* and pivoted to stroll away.

“Why?” Dawkin blurted.

The golden-haired woman turned.

“Why did you say this was misleading?” He held up *Dreams from the Woodlands.*

“You know it sold well when it was first published, don’t you?”

“So I’ve heard.”

“Do you know why?”

Dawkin shook his head.

“Upon its release, those in the cities – Arcporte, Kandin, Yore – believed the tales Master Colgatt told to be true. He had spun the yarn about how he traveled the highways and back roads of mainland Afari, documenting the folktales of the villages he encountered. His accounts of the quaint woodland hamlets and their simple peoples captured the imagination of the Marlish, who often romanticize the continent as having a special charm not found on our rock in the sea.”

“And from your implication, am I right to suppose that isn’t the case.”

The maiden smiled. “You catch on quickly, my lord.”

Dawkin blushed. “Oh, I’m not –”

“A baron? Or the son of a baron?”

More like the baron of barons. “Yes, my father is a lord. Therefore, I am not. I am simply a gentleman, a ‘Sir,’ if you will."

"Sir…?"

"Jameson."

"Oh, like the King."

Drat! Though he had an alias for his excursions from Terran, he scarcely used it, for he hardly interacted with the public. His constant role as Jameson had been ingrained into his senses, so he naturally identified as the monarch, even when he wasn't.

"Why, yes, my parents are staunch supporters of His Majesty and Kin Saliswater. So when the King was born, my father and mother never thought twice about naming me anything other than the royal moniker."

"Well, for your sake, I'm glad His Majesty did not turn out to be Her Majesty." She smirked, brushing back a strand of curls as she did.

"Yes, well, I too am grateful. For the honor, that is, of being associated with him. Pardon, of being named after him. The Prince. I mean, the King."

"Yes, well, you bear a small resemblance to him. I suppose it's your frame. Alas, the similarity stops there. Perhaps if your eyes were darker, your hair lighter. Then there are your freckles –"

The disguise he bore nearly escaped Dawkin's mind. He ran his fingers through his hair, slick from the oily dye Ely had lent him to color it black. His brother had also granted him an inkwell of semi-permanent face paint, allowing him to apply the freckles with the tip of a dull quill. As for the eyes – relief overcame him upon hearing of their continued light hue. The potion he used earlier in the morning, applied by splashing right into his eyes, sometimes proved unreliable. Not that it didn't work at reducing his irises to a light blue tone. Rather, the length of its efficacy proved inconsistent. Sometimes the effects lasted days. At others, a mere hour.

Dawkin, suddenly realizing his lack of manners, hopped from the chair. He bowed his head. "Sir Jameson of Har-Kin Tavnest. And who do I have the honor of addressing?"

"I am Lady Cora, of Har-Kin Glennish."

"Glennish?" Dawkin thought he knew of all the kins and har-kins on the island. He had undoubtedly invested enough time as a youth to believe so, as the genealogy of his people had become a hobby of his.

"We are a dying har-kin, with as little as a dozen who still carry the name. Most of my relatives, through marriage and other acts of alliance, adopted the handles of other, larger families in the Anders Foothills."

"I see. Well, Lady Cora, I thank you for saving me from a wasted afternoon." He glanced at the volume of *Dreams* still in his hand. "Though I am curious to know if Master Colgatt didn't record the stories from the country villages of greater Afari, why would the Marlish citizens in our cities fall for such a ruse while our countryfolk – with which I assume you associate – caught on to his lie?"

"It was as clear as the light of day to us 'countryfolk' Colgatt had never set foot on the mainland. For his supposed observations revealed his complete ignorance of rural life. May I?" She extended her hand to *Dreams.* Dawkin, stricken by her confidence and boldness, obliged. She took the vellum-bound volume in her hand and opened it, flipping through its pages. "Notice as early as page four; he refers to a millstone as a millwheel. On page eight, a butter churn as a butter mixer. And then, on page twenty-seven, he calls a scythe a 'wheat cutter.' Honestly, who on earth would not catch on to that?"

Dawkin, his mind peripherally focused on the book and her argument while her visage attracted the larger share of his attention, shook himself from his daze. "Well, they sound like plausible-enough definitions from a man touring the countryside for the first time."

She smirked. "You're innocent." She caressed his forearm with her index finger. "I like that."

Who is this woman? A warming sensation flooded Dawkin's cheeks. At once, he realized he was blushing. "Um, well, I would never suppose that. But honestly, why do you insist this author is a fraud?"

"Well, I must confess, maybe not *all* those from the country believe Master Colgatt is a liar. The truth is, while his account was well-received on the coastal cities, we hardly heard of him inland. Still, his lies are as clear as day to me. He's my kin."

"I thought you said your har-kin –"

"Yes, I said Glennish. Though remember, I also said my kin had taken on the names of other families, reducing my circle to a mere speck."

"So, he didn't travel to Afari?"

"Oh, he did. His declared intention was to visit the lands Har-Kin Colgatt had been granted in the aftermath of the Century War. Only when he arrived, he went on to spend his time in every tavern and brothel he could stumble into. He scarcely saw the country, except when he went from one inn to the next, and he never interviewed anyone on their country folktales, unless you count questions about the choicest ale as research."

Dawkin chuckled. "Well, then, I suppose I can just consider his book a work of fiction."

"If you must. Though I prefer to invest my time in good reading."

"Well then, *that* won't satisfy you," Dawkin said, nodding to the *Musings* still in her hand.

"You read it?"

"Tried to. I couldn't stand it."

"Why?"

"It was just... awful."

"Come now. You can do better than that."

Damn it. I can. Dawkin opened his mouth to regurgitate his mutterings and internal critique of Sir Keith's memoir. Then he stopped himself. In a minuscule moment of reflection, it occurred to Dawkin his thoughts on the book sounded like petty, pompous observations. Hardly the fare to impress a woman, much less a learned one.

"Sir Jameson?"

"It was bleak," he found himself blurting. "Depressing."

"Certainly, a manuscript depressing in tone can still be worthy of a read?"

"Yes. However..."

"Was it poorly written?"

"Well, I suppose. Though not that badly."

"Was it boring?"

"No."

"Then what did you not appreciate about it?"

"I expected a triumph. Instead, I got defeat. The Century War was a long, bloody affair. But we won. Against all the odds, Marland won. We didn't lose our kingdom like Colinne, nor did we slink back to our fjords like the Lewmarians. After a centennial period of sacrifice, we emerged a power to be reckoned with. And so many great works – from written accounts to paintings to songs – confirm the same.

"But Sir Keith did anything other than celebrate our collective victory. He lamented so damn much. About the losses, the absence of soldiers from their families, of the lives never to thrive. Rather than honor the war and their noble dead, he spoke against it as though it should have never happened. How dare he speak ill of our conquest. He, he, he turned out to be a bit of a bastard about the whole thing."

Dawkin paused. He had never had such passionate thoughts about a book manifest themselves. Nor had he ever dared to consider sharing such beliefs with any soul. Especially a maiden. A maiden he hardly knew.

"My apologies, my lady." Dawkin, resuming his stately composure, bowed his head. "Such crass language has no place in a shop nor the presence of a maiden."

"Oh, posh!" she said, waving her hand. "Formality conceals truth. The barons use it to hide their small minds. Hard to believe the nobles can hold on to their britches, let alone their lands."

Dawkin smiled. "I believe myself mistaken. You may enjoy *Musings* after all."

"I look forward to it."

"As I may have tainted your enjoyment of the book, I must insist on gifting you a copy." Dawkin dug his fingers into the satchel at his waist.

"Oh, no. By all means, don't trouble yourself."

"Tis no trouble."

"No, really. If my, I meant to say, it's a tradition with my kind not to accept the charity of strangers."

"Oh, yes, from strangers. Forgive me."

"I meant nothing by it."

"Of course not."

"My un – my father, his allowance grants me enough to indulge in such luxuries. I couldn't let you buy me this knowing he has already given me coin for the same purpose."

"You needn't explain."

"It just so happens I should be going. Good evening to you, Sir Jameson." Lady Cora offered an awkward curtsy, followed by a smile, more earnest than any Dawkin could remember. He watched her stroll down the aisle toward the front of the store, where she proceeded to engage the shopkeeper in idle conversation.

Stupid, stupid, overeducated louse! Dawkin had half a mind to knock over his stack of books, and would have, if not for the ruckus to follow. Instead, he grabbed his coat from the back of the chair and hurried for the rear door.

Spilling into the alleyway, he met the blank stare of a Voiceless. The mute guard, who bore the disguise of a craftsman, could hardly be mistaken for a skilled soldier considering his drab garb. Even the apparent musculature peeking out of the sleeves could be attributed not to combative training but to work as a sailor or smith. Dawkin, like his brothers, knew the nuances of their experience much better. The steps of a Voiceless – always seeking sure footing – were too purposeful. Their stares, which even when not direct, constantly sought out details in their surroundings. The most apparent signs though, at least to Dawkin, had to be their hands. They never strayed too far from their persons, with at least one hovering near the waistband or a cuff, ready to draw a blade at the first hint of a threat.

The Voiceless before Dawkin nearly made such a move. Upon recognizing His Majesty, however, he whistled. Moments later, his companion - another Voiceless - rounded the corner of the bookshop to join them.

Dawkin sighed. As heirs to the Throne, they had enjoyed a feint sense of freedom, which allowed them opportunities to experience the joys of the city or country. So long as the brothers traveled in disguise, the Voiceless remained behind in Terran, content on protecting the long halls and caverns until they returned. Hell, without the watch of his chaperones, Ely had spoiled half the maidens in Marland with his sly tongue and false fronts. While Dawkin had never been so bold nor reckless, often choosing the comfort of books to the taste of women, he still relished in the fact that he *could* commit such sins with impunity.

All that changed with the coronation of King Jameson. His experiences now, mere reflections of that bygone princely era, seemed hollow by comparison. With every rotation from the castle to Terran, he found himself stifled all the bit more. Even when sufficiently disguised, the Voiceless insisted on accompanying him, just as they did with his brothers. Never mind the promises to stay out of harm's way or the commands to the knights that they should stay put. They never listened. And who could blame them? For above all else, they had sworn to protect the King against every danger, including himself.

Flanked by his protectors – who at least had agreed to stay outside while he read – Dawkin considered withdrawing to the shop once more to rejoin Lady Cora in discussion. He had the time, for with his three kin away in Ibia, his rotation to the Throne could not resume until they returned. Furthermore, he had the motivation. Not only due to the lady's beauty, which in his mind spanned infinity, but because she had challenged him with earnest conversation the likes of which he had never experienced.

And yet, he hesitated. Why?

A tap on the forearm distracted Dawkin from himself. The Voiceless to his left, with a face slightly freckled and a head of auburn hair, signed. "The fog. She rolls in."

Dawkin looked down the alleyway, which dipped with the hill. A blanker of mist consumed the seaward half of Arcporte Harbor, threatening to overwhelm the other half and city at its shores. Knowing he had hours at most to fulfill his declared intention, Dawkin turned from the water to take on the incline with his entourage.

Less than half an hour later, the three arrived at Mar-by-the-Sea Cathedral. Though leisurely, the stroll left Dawkin a tad winded. He dared not to show his guards his vulnerability, lest they admonish him with the language of hands for not practicing his drills as of late.

At its peak, during the middle of the Century War, rumors told of soldiers' widows flooding Mar-by-the-Sea, to the point they lined the street outside to wait their turn to enter and pray. Those days had long passed, and save for the occasional wedding or funeral, the sanctuary saw only a handful of parishioners every ten days when the High Bishop held services.

Where have all the faithful gone? Dawkin asked himself as he entered the cemetery through a bent, wrought-iron gate. *Surely Mar means something to my countrymen?* In ruminating on that question, Dawkin became sheepish, the irony of his rank as sovereign weighing on him. Growing up the figurehead of the kingdom named after their god, he and his brothers had learned every detail of their faith. While the history and legends fascinated him, he never took any for its intention. Sure, he spoke the prayers before the beginning of a banquet; he bowed his head when in public service. Yet such displays of faith rang hollow, with no meaning attached.

In reverence, while Dawkin's mind flailed, the mourners stood still. The headstones, weathered and worn, at one time coarse yet now smooth. The trees, none full of leaves or life, their trunks and branches having shed with the onset of autumn. The stalks of grass, sprouting from the earth and the cracks of stones, small but vibrant amongst their taller, duller neighbors.

Each object played its part. They held in place. They prevailed against time. In the quiet. In the storms. They remained above while their companions lay below. No matter the seasons, the weather, or the petty wars of men, they revered the deceased.

Including the one Dawkin sought.

The footfalls behind him, of the two Voiceless, paused. His silent knights knew without being prompted to grant their monarch his space. Dawkin weaved through more substantial markers of kings and queens long since passed, before arriving at the more modest ones of his parents.

Side by side, their headstones rested, identical in width and height. The starkest difference between the two was the relief of each; Audemar, his carving reflecting his fine beard and square face, while Ellenora's features revealed a softer touch. As they had on the day he first saw them together, the markers seemed slight, inconsequential. To the day, a full year had passed since then...

A full year.

Dawkin bent to one knee. He removed his glove to stretch out his hand. His fingers, clean and bare, dug into the earth before him. They clawed the green blades from the dirt, wanting not to touch the flora nor the soil. No, they yearned to connect to the souls beneath.

One year. Dawkin's rotation had allowed him to partake in the funeral that fateful day. He had stood over his father's casket, in the presence of a kingdom, and said the farewell. He had been chosen to be the rock in the merciless storm, the island amidst an unforgiving sea. His grandfather, in grief, had leaned on him. The High Bishop had extended his condolences to him. Taresa had offered her funerary token to him.

Symon, Ely, and Gerry had failed to come that day, not even in disguise. No, it was Dawkin, the sole son in attendance. He alone. On that day of mourning. As well as a year later. He had returned. He. Alone.

I wonder if they even realize what day it is. What it truly means. For the first time, a squall stirred in the depths of Dawkin's bowels at the thought of his brothers abandoning him. *The straws were drawn, the rotation set. I became the chosen. Then, on the day of the funeral. And now, for the royal wedding. Twas fair to stay behind. Us four all must do it. By the Law of Terran, we are sworn to rise and descend when our turn comes. Still...*

The resentment. The anger. The regret. Of his lot in life. The sum of it, mounted, remained.

And to think they have Taresa on top of it as well. The Princess. Nay, the Queen! The one who comforted me, not them, a year ago. They will lay with her, as we agreed. Perhaps more times I can count. She will experience them, not me, long before she returns to Marland with those three. My brothers, the three kings to our one queen.

How dare they!

Dawkin rose. He longed to be back in the bailey with the bows and blades for the opportunity to slash or hit something. He departed his parents' plots, moving a straight line for the cemetery's edge. His Voiceless shuffled to follow though they stopped at Dawkin's wave, albeit hesitantly.

Dawkin came to the edge of the burial grounds, where the hill sloped gently toward the sanctuary quarters below. He paused, considering his next move before haste and indifference propelled him forward. He cared not who he encountered nor offended. Though his true self laid concealed, he was nonetheless of a king – and a man – entitled to mourn as he pleased if nothing else.

With the leveling of the incline, he stomped through the gardens and vineyard bordering the monastery, muttering to himself as mud-caked his boots. By the time he arrived on the tiled walkway, his monologue had become a full discourse on the ruins of his life.

"What is that racket?" a portly monk asked with

irritation as he swept into the walkway. He cut off Dawkin from his march, looking him up and down. “May I help you?”

“Doubtful.”

“Are you lost?”

“Hardly.”

“What is your business here?!”

“Here. Not a damn thing –”

“Mind your tongue.”

“I-How dare you! Do you know who I am?”

“I don’t.”

“I’m, I’m...”

“Out with it, boy.”

Dawkin sighed. He couldn’t speak the truth, not even to a man of faith. His lifelong secret – the one he shared with his brothers – was all he had. For over two decades, it had kept him and his brothers safe. It allowed Kin Saliswater to recover its bloodline from the throes of war and assassination. It provided hope to his father all those years, the ones following the death of his mother, giving him comfort that a part of her would endure.

The lie had granted a Saliswater the Throne. The ones for his brothers.

My Throne.

“Are you ill, lad?”

Dawkin met the monk’s gaze, which had softened from one of anger to one of concern.

“I am. Not. I am not, I mean. Forgive my lack of manners. You see, I am, I, found myself visiting the grave of my father –”

The monk waved his palm. “Ah, say no more. Tis

understood, young master. Grief can rob goodness from the best of us. Even one as noble as you."

Mar, does he know? "You think me of nobility?"

"Undoubtedly. Your father must have been a great man, to be buried up there, amongst heroes and kings."

Dawkin grinned. *You have no idea.* "How kind. Thank you."

He turned to retreat up the hill, where he saw the Voiceless atop, waiting.

"Young sir."

Dawkin glanced over his shoulder.

"Would you care to join us?" the monk inquired. "We were just in the middle of our supper."

"Oh, thank you, no. I wouldn't want to intrude."

"Tis no bother. We would welcome the company. Honest."

Dawkin looked back to the Voiceless. With his hand by his thigh, out of sight of the monk, he signed to them. *It's safe; stay there.*

He looked to the monk. "Lead the way."

The dining hall, built of white oak, stood sparsely furnished with long tables and benches for the brethren. A few peeked at Dawkin as he passed, though most gave him nary a thought, focusing instead on bowls of stew. Dawkin could hardly fault them for the aroma of braised lamb, carrots, potatoes, and a hint of turmeric wafted thickly through the air, reminding him of the time since his last meal. The monk led him to a table in the northwest corner, where two other monks sat.

"Brother Clayton and Brother Marleigh, this is..."

Might as well continue with today's ruse. "Sir Jameson

of Har-Kin Tavnest. My father named me in honor of our sovereign."

"A fine name." The portly monk extended his hand. "I beg your forgiveness. I forgot to introduce myself earlier. I am Brother Dawkin."

You have to be joshing me. "Named after Sir Dawkin? Of Har-Kin Ylou?"

"'Twas my great uncle, on my mother's side. How do you know of him?"

"I've read his manuscript, *Histories of Our Kin.* Twice."

Brother Dawkin grunted. "That makes one of us. I couldn't get through half the bloody book, dull as it was. I've never been much of a reader."

This will be a merry meal. "Well, your kin had a way with words. As you do with hospitality."

The monk, smitten by the compliment, motioned to the open bench space across from him. Dawkin grinned, taking his seat while a cook swooped in to set a bowl of steaming stew before him.

"Tell us, Sir Jameson," Brother Clayton began. "What brings you to Our Lady of Arc Monastery?"

"I chanced upon it."

"How does one chance upon a sanctuary of Marlish brothers upon a hill?"

"Sir Jameson, my brothers," Brother Dawkin interjected. "Was atop the cemetery, paying his respects to his kin. In his… grief… he found his way unto our walkway, by accident I suppose, where I accosted him until I discovered his true purpose here."

"Oh," Brother Clayton said. "My apologies for being so brusque. My curiosity sometimes prompts me to abandon my manners."

"There is no need for redress, brothers," Dawkin replied. "It is I who erred, I who invaded your holy space. The fault lies with me."

"A humble man," Brother Marleigh concluded, his gaze not leaving his bowl. "A most welcome one. You would be surprised how many souls say they 'chance' upon us before their true intentions show. They offer a lie, a woeful tale. Then they prance on our sympathies for any morsel, board, or coin they feel entitled to, leaving with nary an acknowledgment of our hospitality."

"Brother, the poor we've been called to help include the depraved and corrupt."

"The poor? Those in our midst are certainly depraved and corrupt but not impoverished." Brother Marleigh shot a look across the room. Dawkin glanced in that same direction, catching sight of a table ringed by brothers in white. Actually, off-white, for stains of grime, dirt, and ash had soiled their once pristine robes.

"Who are they?" Dawkin asked.

"The spoiled of our kingdom."

"Brother Marleigh!" Brother Marleigh chastised.

"Really, in front of our guest?" Brother Clayton asked.

"Bah!" Marleigh waved. "Guests are like gophers in our garden. With one come more."

"They are sons sent by their kin and har-kin," Brother Clayton explained, ignoring his cantankerous counterpart. "Or those from such manors who come to us of their own accord. The Lost Souls. Their guilt is beyond the aid of prayers to Mar alone, so they arrive to atone."

"They serve your monastery?" Dawkin asked. "Like

attendants?" He had heard of barons sending their males to abbeys and monasteries. He had even read of it. But he always figured such mentions were embellishments, for all the young nobles he had known over the years had not once uttered a word of such punishments. "Is this common?"

"'Twas at one point, I remember. In the final years of the Century War, plus the years following. We saw many a young lad come to us. Some crawled in on hands and knees, stricken by shame for not having served in the conflict."

"Bloody cowards," Marleigh grumbled. "Even I swung a sword in battle before taking my vows."

"The less courageous came here, yes," Clayton continued. "Though some simply felt guilty for not being sent to serve before the war ended. Many had even just completed training before word of the Final Peace spread.

"Whatever their reason, we accepted them into our fold. Many paid the penance and left. Quite a few stayed, though, going on to serve us still, some so dedicated they committed themselves to long vows of prayer, asceticism, or silence.

"Then after that uptick, we saw only a trickle come to 'atone in service,' as we say. That is until recently. Now, the ranks of such temporary recruits have swelled for reasons aplenty."

"Such as?" Dawkin inquired.

"Debauchery," Brother Marleigh replied. "Drunkenness. Gambling. You name it. Like I said, spoiled."

"It is not for us to judge those Jeselthorne has seduced," Brother Clayton said.

Marleigh scoffed but returned to his stew. Brother

Dawkin, wanting to turn the tide, set his sights again on his guest. "What say you of the stew?"

"Wonderful," Dawkin replied, glad the conversation had shifted and the mood of the table had quelled.

The brother nodded. Their group sat in silence for the several minutes that followed, mirroring the rest of the brethren in the hall.

The absence of conversation - what would have been considered awkward in court – turned out to be most welcome to Dawkin. His meals above in Arcporte Castle always involved a set of eyes upon him, whether of barons, visiting dignitaries, or servants. Below, in Terran, the opposite occurred, with Dawkin most often finding solitude in his room at mealtime. This, the camaraderie of a community so pious and devoted to Mar, fell somewhere in between, allowing Dawkin the comfort of his mind at rest and a good meal to rejuvenate him.

Clang!

The single vibration of a bell prompted all the brothers to release their spoons and rise. Dawkin, proceeding in suit with his hosts, lifted himself from his spot.

"Oh, please. Do finish," Brother Dawkin urged.

"I'm quite full," Dawkin insisted. "Really, it was satisfying."

"Good."

"Well," Marleigh said, wiping his mouth with a kerchief. "He sat through a meal without trying to con us. A polite guest, I suppose, if nothing else."

"Brother Marleigh, your acceptance knows no bounds," Brother Dawkin chided.

"All I'm saying is that if we had more like him and less

like *them*, our coffers would be the better for it, instead of us toiling like mounts and having to beg for support from the King."

Though he had no familiarity with the brethren or their monastery at first, it suddenly dawned on Dawkin where and when he initially encountered their kind. "You mean to say you regularly present yourselves to His Majesty, before his Court."

"Aye," Brother Clayton confirmed. "The Throne always manages to grant us an audience, especially the kin of the current dynasty, may Mar bless them."

"When our alms become scarce, the Saliswaters step in to replenish," Brother Dawkin added.

"Though it would be a kinder act of respect if His Majesty would consider our pleas for better seeds," Brother Marleigh argued. "If our crop fails, such bowls will find themselves empty."

"Fail?" Dawkin responded, puzzled. He had heard as of late from the west and south of the island of farmers whose fields laid barren, their staples floundering to sprout. He did not realize the condition had spread to the more populated eastern half of their kingdom.

"Yes," Brother Dawkin said. "That garden you passed, it usually displays remnants of its bounty by now. It just so happens we finished collecting from it in half the time it regularly takes, as the yield wound up so poorly this season."

"First time since the Century War concluded in which we collected so little. A drought then resulted in that loss. This season, though, well, I don't know what happened in the past year to account for such a pitiful harvest." Brother

Marleigh scratched his head at the thought.

The rains fell, the sun shone. The only point of difference for Marland is we took the Throne.

"May I see?" Dawkin blurted. "The garden again? Or lack thereof?"

"You want to see empty rows of black soil?" Brother Marleigh prodded.

"Horticulture is a bit of a hobby of mine."

"Very well," Brother Marleigh waved. "Brother Dawkin, you discovered the lad. You give him the tour."

"I would be delighted," Brother Dawkin said, ignoring the slight. "Come, Sir Jameson. Let me show you the grounds."

The monk directed Dawkin to a side door as brothers bearing aprons made their rounds to the tables to collect the bowls and other wares. The exit led out to a narrow hall lined with various tridents enveloped by hands. Dawkin admired the craftsmanship of each as he strolled ahead of the brother, who ushered him forward.

The pair toured the whole of the sacred grounds. First, they passed through the barracks, which housed the newer recruits, and some of the small bedrooms afforded to the eldest brethren. From those spartan quarters, they continued to the spring, the miniature mill, the winepress, and then the cellar, the latter of which held an impressive array of rare vintages. Finally, they approached the grotto, an area of greater Arcporte that Dawkin was embarrassed to admit he had never known of before.

A small crack in the cavern's roof provided a beacon of light that guided Dawkin and his companion to the reception area. There, the brother lit a candle to illuminate the walls with a soft glow.

Stunning.

Dawkin gazed upon the frescoes spread out over the walls. The assortment of scenes and paintings shifted and swayed with the flickering flame in the brother's hand, providing the sensation of animation. Though faded by time and moisture, the artistry of the pieces remained. From an angler wrestling with his line to a rider galloping through a meadow to an archer releasing his bow – every depiction offered a performance, a blend of illumination and pigment come together.

"This is... beyond what I expected," the King admitted.

"I know," Brother Dawkin replied. "Most visitors have a similar reaction, though not one so profound and awestruck as yours."

"Where did, I mean, how long... Why this must have taken centuries."

"Perhaps more. You see, this monastery was founded near the spring I showed you, so we'd have a source of freshwater. But in digging the cellar we passed through, the brethren discovered this here grotto, the paintings having already shown the effects of time."

Dawkin reached back into the recesses of his memory. "But the beginnings of this monastery predate Kin Anglisk and the building of Arcporte Castle."

"You know your history, lad. Most young nobles don't."

Damn it, stop thinking like a king. "I read quite a bit of history when I was younger. Some facts just stick."

"Yet you knew nothing of the paintings you see here before us."

"This, I profess, cannot be found in any book."

"Well, then, you're in for more of a surprise."

The monk set down his chamberstick on the ground, where he picked up a few pebbles. He looked to the area ahead of them, a smooth expanse of black stone, as he cocked his arm and released the rocks.

Rather than skid across the floor, the pebbles pierced the black canvas to create ripples, revealing the spring-fed pool. As the gravel sunk, tiny bulbs with short quivering tails scattered, casting brilliant green light onto their surroundings.

"Now, you may stand impressed," the brother beamed as his blue eyes shone with the radiance cast upon them.

The bioluminescence created a second coming on the murals. The collection Dawkin previously admired now stood in stark contrast to the plethora of compositions that awakened around them. Every spot or space empty moments before blazed with tendrils and strokes of glowing life. The angler wrestling with his catch bore new meaning as a storm threatened on the horizon. The sole rider galloping through the meadow found himself joined by a hunting party, all of whom pursued a golden stag suspended midleap over a meandering stream. As for the archer, his released arrow pierced the chaos of a battle in full outbreak, with the field of fallen and victors oblivious to the projectile.

Amid every setting, accompanying the men either in the foreground or the back, stood a woman. Though a different character in every scene, the motif of the woman remained constant: Strong, confident, a pillar of determination – the intensity of conviction painted on each female face – and ready to take hold of any situation. In fact, in some of the scenes, she did. In one, she rushed into the head of a hunt. In another, she handled an attack with the ease of a child at play.

Never one to overlook such glaring details, Dawkin glanced at his companion. “The paintings with the women, why were they concealed?”

Brother Dawkin smirked, settling down on a stone ledge by the pool, which still shimmered from the school of fish beneath the surface. “Tis a mystery, my lad. As I said, this grotto was discovered with the paintings having been finished sometime before. No one knows why any of it was formed, let alone the inspiration behind the hidden compositions. I suspect the random characters give some of the story.” The monk pointed to the periphery of a scene that glowed with lettering unlike Dawkin had ever seen.

“Atyian?” Dawkin guessed, believing it to be the relic of the peoples who inhabited Marland at the First Dawn. Until a few hundred years ago, the ancient language was thought to exist only in the fringes of Afari, still used in secret by ones who kept to traditions long banished by the Church of Mar.

“Mayhaps. Tis anyone’s guess. I venture the explanation lies closer to home, one we encounter to this day.”

“Meaning?”

“You’ve read *The Papyr*, have you?”

Dawkin nodded.

“A little cryptic, isn’t it?”

Dawkin raised his eyes at the touch of blasphemy. “I’m surprised to hear a man like you say that.”

“We all think about it. The vow of silence most of my brethren take at the start of our brotherhood conditions us to keep such musings to ourselves. Still, they percolate. But I stray from my point. You noted the women. How often are women mentioned in the Works of Mar?"

Dawkin considered. The Conclave of Ages had a fair share of women, from warriors to mothers and even thieves, though such references to them had been restricted to the First and Second Volumes of *The Papyr*. Beyond them, only one female was mentioned in what remained of the other volumes.

"You speak of the Lady of Mar."

"A good guess. And the correct one. Yes, my brothers and I believe the men you see in each painting, the central figure, stands in for our god, Mar. The women, one for each protagonist, well, we assume she's the Lady.

"Consider how she stands at the ready, always by his right side, much as the Lady of Mar did for our Lord when faced with every obstacle and war imaginable. Whenever he took on a challenge, she buttressed him, held him up, fed him an energy that ensured his survival. Some of the cults which split from the Church even put her on equal footing with the Lord himself, though such a supposition still stands as a reach.

"Still, as that unnamed companion at his side, she captures the public imagination, with all us Marlish having heard of the strength to Mar's commands. We've known her since birth, as the nurturing presence til our death. Is it any wonder, having heard the tale of Mar and his Lady, that we long for the companionship of others? Well, maybe not my fellow monks and I; we're more of a sordid bunch. I mean lads like you who seek the love of a good maiden. Yes, the truth of our needs was apparent in ancient times, as you've borne witness to here, just as it remains to this day."

The monk quieted, the string of his consciousness seemingly run dry. He gazed upon the fullness of the scenes, which began to fade as the fish in the pool settled, subduing their brilliance.

The Lady of Mar. The mysterious woman who, according to The Papyr, *miraculously appeared before Mar and his siblings one day. Without origin or name, she lived among them. She enchanted all the gods, even Mar himself. Then the war between them began. The Great Battle for Power. Mar defeated his siblings one by one. Though she never fought, the Lady of Mar never strayed too far from her beloved. Some cults within the church even suggest she hid weapons for him in the earth, including the Oreflare Halberd, which he pulled from the ground and used to finish his last brother, Dywar.*

A loyal companion. A good maiden. His one true love.

The concept percolated in the eye of Dawkin's mind, as did the image of golden curls above green eyes.

Dawkin straightened. He withdrew to the entrance of the grotto.

"I think the hour of my leave has come."

The brother, lost in his musing, rustled from his trance. "Yes, yes. I did not mean to keep you so long from your day. Forgive the ramblings of an old, tired monk."

"There need nothing to forgive." Dawkin fished a gold coin from his satchel. "Alms for your hospitality."

Brother Dawkin waved his hand.

"But your fellow in the hall went on and on about groveling before the sovereign for support."

"Oh, that old windbag. He has made such complaints since entering the brotherhood. Do not worry about our finances. Mar will provide, as he does with everything."

Dawkin nodded as the brother rose from his seat to show him back through the monastery. He took Dawkin back to the corridor bordering the garden, where he bowed. Dawkin thought it a touch over the top until he turned.

"Treat her well, Sir Jameson. She'll make a king of you yet."

Dawkin perked, twisting around to the monk. "What do you mean?"

"Many a young man come here to meditate on love. Oh, I'm sure you came to pay your respects to your kin, I do not doubt. Though I believe I have the right of it when I say a woman has also been on your mind."

Dawkin, pausing, offered a single nod.

"And judging from the guards who came with you – whether they be kin by blood or hired hands – I would further venture you come from a grand family, one who may not approve of your affection?"

Dawkin, not knowing how to respond, remained agape.

"I overstepped my bounds. Still, if I may be so bold: It will work out, somehow."

The monk turned to take his leave. Dawkin, relieved the *entirety* of his secrets had not been exposed, sighed. He turned to take to the hill, where he found the two knights dutifully fighting boredom as they waited.

In the eyes of the Church and two kingdoms, I am married. I have a queen. She may even be with child as we speak. She will produce my heirs. She will live the whole of her life in my castle. Dawkin strolled to his parents' gravestones, his sights firmly on the pair. *And when I pass, I will be laid by her side: I, King Jameson.*

Only today, I am not King Jameson.

Before his mother and father, he pondered asking them for their forgiveness for abandoning his royal duties, even in secret. His intended behavior was more in line with his brother, Ely, not his own disposition.

Instead, he pivoted to descend the hill.

The stroll back to Sir Nygell's Books took half as long as his ascent, in part due to Dawkin's haste. His knights, who had almost bested him in their earlier climb, now struggled to keep pace.

"Stay behind," Dawkin commanded his guards. "I won't be long."

Dawkin skipped up the steps two at a time to enter the bookshop out of breath. To his surprise, he found the shopkeeper still there, his apprentice having not relieved him.

"Sir Evenon," the shopkeeper, Master Franque, said. "Fancy you coming here twice in one day."

The salutation reminded Dawkin of the moniker he used within the confines of Sir Nygell's. He approached the counter behind which Franque stood, his voice low as he leaned. "Ummm, yes, I only returned to inquire –"

"On the young lady I saw you speaking with earlier." Master Franque removed his spectacles as his look became more earnest. "A beauty who caught your eye, isn't that right?"

Dawkin fought to suppress the blush rising to his cheeks. *Seriously, what is the matter with me?* "Why, I suppose. I mean... am I that obvious?"

"Certainly. I can only surmise your companion had the right of it as well. For she left you this." Master Franque bent down to retrieve a hearty manuscript, one bound by stiff leather with pages browned by age and moisture.

"For me?" Dawkin asked absentmindedly while his fingers outlined the impressed lettering of its title, *The Adumbration*. The last book of *The Papyr* had never held so much intrigue and mystery for Dawkin than in that moment, even though he had heard it read by the High Bishop dozens of times.

"'Tis what I said." Master Franque left Dawkin to his gift as he tended to a patron wanting a volume from a high shelf.

Dawkin thumbed through the book's pages before noting it had a thin ribbon bookmark within. As though cradling a babe, he held *The Adumbration* in his left hand while opening the text with his right. Hefty his new prize was, for the last entry of *The Papyr* often found itself bound alone due to its length. And its controversy.

The ribbon harkened to a section of the scripture Dawkin hazily recalled from past homilies.

A sole god – a king with the sand and ashes beneath his feet as his subjects – remains. He wanders the world he rules, his reign empty, his kingdom composed of nothing. In the absence of a conclave and of subjects, madness swells within his being, one which knows no bounds.

So the earth answers, just as a dog mirrors his master. That which should not occur does, giving rise to anomalies small and significant, minute and vast.

Wood that does not burn.

Steel that does not rust.

Glass that cannot shatter.

Dawkin blinked. He had read the passage a hundred times in his youth, at moments of study, without giving the words a second thought. Yet something about them struck him as odd this time.

He skipped ahead.

Mar overturns all. With his word, the ground becomes sky while the blue above turns to soil. At his touch, everything turns aflame, even the words on ancient pages he once penned. His stare wilts every object in his sight, the expanse of his view a plague.

While the realm of men lies consumed by his grief and regret, Mar contemplates the unimaginable: The End of All Ends.

The unsettling feeling lingered. Still, Dawkin pressed on, thumbing through the pages as he ignored his intuition.

The thumping of determined footfalls disturbed Dawkin from his reading. He shot a look at the two Voiceless approaching.

"I thought I told –"

It rose — the commotion from beyond. Dawkin hurried to the nearest window to spot the mass of commoners gathering before the neighborhood's town crier, Master Reysen. Though lacking in stature, the short orator never acted as though without when it came to addressing a crowd. Until now.

"Come," Dawkin commanded his Voiceless, shoving his book toward one of them to carry.

Outside, the turmoil reached a boiling point. Shouts rose from the mob, as did fists and hands beckoning the crier to speak his piece. Inclined to seek out the magistrate,

Dawkin nearly pivoted before seeing the man of the law among the crowd. Shocked – and for a moment, forgetting his charade – he stormed up to the justice of the peace.

"Are you mad?" Dawkin demanded to know as he grabbed him by the collar.

"Bugger off!" the magistrate barked.

"Do your duty!"

"We have a war on our hands, you idiot!"

War? The thought hit Dawkin, but like that, so did the magistrate. A sloppy fist to the shoulder, mind you, though a strike nonetheless. Dawkin nearly lunged at the lawman before a Voiceless wrapped his arms around His Majesty to pull him back, while the other of his guards swooped in with the butt of his dirk to deliver the king's justice.

As the magistrate writhed on the ground, his hands to his head, the crowd nearest to him quieted a bit. The lull in chaos allowed Master Reysen the opportunity to garner their attention.

"Hear ye, hear ye!" he shouted. "I know rumors have swirled about His Majesty's wedding..."

Oh... no. Dawkin, having never been so intent in his life, listened. The crowd, though less invested emotionally, showed their own brand of concern.

"Let me assure you, the word is our King survived."

Thank Mar.

"To assure you he lives, I shall read his proclamation, copied from the letter written in his hand:

"'To my loyal subjects, I, King Jameson of Kin Saliswater, Monarch of the island of Marland, send dire news from the mainland. It is with a heavy heart I mourn the loss of our own. On the night of my wedding, the twenty-seventh day of Syr, the army accompanying the Court and I came under assault. Though the details are forthcoming, the damage was immediately apparent: three-hundred twenty-eight dead, with only three survivors, as the carnage proved so catastrophic."

The crier paused, the punctuation marking the time he took to catch his breath being an eon to the crowd, to none more so than Dawkin. In the act of duty, the Voiceless tugged at his arms, begging their King to retreat to safer quarters. Yet the King would have none of it. He needed to hear this.

"In the commotion of that fatal night, many of our own scattered. As a result, identifying the departed has been difficult, as we work on accounting for the missing so as not to send word prematurely to those who have lost loved ones.

"Of the few we've identified, word will soon be sent through our royal couriers to their kin. To them who receive such fateful news – the direst I could never hope to imagine – they have my deepest sympathies. Those brave men perished in service to God and the Throne, to Mar and Marland. Their sacrifice will forever echo in our hearts as they enter the Heroes Hall in the Castle of Mar. Though they will be missed, their efforts to ensure a better Marland for us all will not have been in vain.

"As details emerge over the next few weeks of the casualties – and our constant efforts to find the perpetrators – I will send swift word. Due to the foul nature of this massacre, I issue this royal decree: all reserve troops from every corner of Marland are hereby summoned to Arcporte to report to the Royal Proctor left in my stead, my grandfather,

Baron Artus of Kin Saliswater. Under his watch and with the guidance of the Conclave of Barons, the reservists will patrol and keep the peace in whatever manner they see fit until I issue my next command or I return after having secured vengeance for our brethren, whichever comes first.

"Rest assured, my dearest Marlish men and women, your security is always at the center of my mind and heart. It is my hope that you remain safe, away from foes near or from afar, and that you know that the Throne will issue Mar's justice to all who seek to harm us.

"Until my return, may Mar bless you and your kin. May Mar sanctify Marland, now and forever.

"His Majesty, King Jameson of Kin Saliswater, Monarch of the island of Marland."

Master Reysen lowered the letter to cast his sights on the crowd. The raucous atmosphere which had greeted him before stood replaced by stillness, the absence of rage supplanted by a sense of malaise. Tears meandered down the cheeks of some. Most just looked on, their souls robbed of any means to comprehend or express the remnants of what remained within.

Thump... Thump...

Dawkin turned, along with many. To his left, slightly behind him, a man in his fifties clenched his fist. He held it before his chest, extending it outward, before beating it over his heart. The thud left the man unaffected, his eyes unflinching, as he stretched his arm to repeat again and again.

A veteran. Dawkin could be sure of it, for he knew the look from every one of the battle-scarred soldiers from the Century War who made their way through Arcporte Castle, those who came to pay their respects to his father, the King under which they had served. Their unique sense of duty, even with the totality of what they had seen, never seemed to depart from their sensibilities, no matter their environment.

Thump...Thump...

A soldier's salute. To the fallen. The brave. An honor to those we could never reclaim.

Thump... Thump... Thump... Thump...

Others joined him. The youth. The elderly. Men. Women. Even Master Reysen, not accustomed to involving himself with a crowd he addressed, clapped his closed fist against the meat of his chest.

Several moments passed before Dawkin acknowledged the thud occurring over his own heart. He stared down at his right hand, which had instinctively united with the chorus. He glanced at the Voiceless beside him, whose own fists beat in accompaniment.

Thump... Thump...

Dawkin's mind swam. Aye, what a time it had been. That morning, he had retreated to the confines of Sir Nygell's to escape his duties and find solace. Instead, he found himself thrust into a world of chaos, one in which a lifetime of events and emotions had merged into the span of a single day. Love, or the prospect of it. Faith, and the consideration of its fullness, the extent of its opportunities and challenges. Now, war. Dawkin hoped against hope the label would turn out to be an embellishment, a hyperbole referring to a conflict or a battle that would fade to become some uneasy peace.

In his experience, that seemed unlikely.

Those on the fringes of the gathering began to disperse, taking with them the somber tribute. Seeing his window to withdraw, Dawkin kept his head bowed as he marched away, his footfalls in line with the echoing memorial.

Thump...

With his eyes downcast, Dawkin caught a glimpse of *The Adumbration* in the left hand of his Voiceless. The book, earlier granted as a gift, taunted him, its contents flooding Dawkin's thoughts. He knew of none of the details of what had transpired the night of his brother's wedding. His anxiety became the worse for it, with the absence of knowing compounding his fears. His imagination fermented scenarios both extreme and improbable, drawing upon the ancient text and its descriptions of Mar's – and the world's – possible demise. Floods of blood. Fires consuming oceans. Blades wielded by no soldiers nor knights, rising on their own to slaughter mercilessly.

Dawkin shook the ridiculous notions from his head. *No,* he reminded himself. *This isn't me.* He looked to his right, where the street stretched toward the harbor, allowing him the gap to see the waters beyond. *My brothers are safe. This is precisely why our father hid us, with only one before the public at a time. To protect us, to serve the Throne, to ensure the line of Kin Saliswater.*

His senses returned to him. Dawkin leaned into the knight at his left. "Go to my grandfather. No matter who he is with, I require an audience with him. At once."

The Voiceless nodded, the purpose of his duty waking him from his trance. He ran ahead as the other Voiceless matched his stride with Dawkin's, his sense of responsibility returning. The two passed Sir Nygell's. Dawkin, considering what he had to discuss with his grandfather, glanced longingly at the bookshop.

Not now, he reprimanded himself. *The Throne calls. Later.*

He winced at the lie he told himself. Later. Love. Life. One of his own.

It will never come.

For the greater good, Dawkin told himself, as he considered the realm of his sacrifices. *I do it all for the greater good.*

Chapter 7

"Calm down, brother."

Gerry stared at Ely, incredulous. "*You* are telling *me* to calm down?"

"Don't take that tone with me, you runt. I mean, look at you. Pacing like a penniless whore awaiting her next patron."

Gerry fumed. "I, why, you shouldn't –"

"Shush, shush, shush. You must control that temper of yours."

The irony of Ely's admonishments did not escape Gerry. "You never listen when we try to talk sense into you!"

"Because I, unlike you at this moment, always have sense. It never leaves me, so there is simply no reason for me to listen to you or our brothers. Sure, I tuck it away on some days, which allows my other – say, qualities – to produce themselves. But I am never, ever, without sense. Really, brother, it is ridiculous of you to suggest such a thing." Ely, having spoken his piece, reclined before their table as he sipped his wine.

Frustrated and at a loss of words, Gerry snapped away to resume his pacing. Twenty minutes had passed since the top of the hour, meaning their brother was twenty minutes late. Such tardiness could only mean one thing: a problem. Or, to be more specific, a *new* problem. For dilemmas abounded in the days since the Marlish encampment and

Castle Arinn endured assault. In response to the tragedy, barons from both courts plied the royals for audiences with the monarchs. Not that it did a lick of good. King Felix would meet with his subjects in his Throne Room, while Symon did the same in a tower provided by Kin Garsea. But with the two sovereigns committed to appeasing their countrymen, their decisions and promises often fell at odds with one another, which led to more questions from their supporters – along with a mounting communal sense of doubt. The incertitude compounded the already tense relations between the visiting Marlish and host Ibians, so much so that word of Symon extending troops to guard his people had reached Ely and Gerry's ears.

"I wonder if the reason for our brother's delay is his marital duty," Ely mused.

"Whatever do you mean?"

"Well, he has wed Prin – forgive me – Queen Taresa."

"He would never. Why he has a duty to us to attend to..."

"Oh, he has a duty he does. One that involves him between her legs."

Gerry lashed out at Ely. Fortunately for his brother, Gerry proved to be a horrible judge of distance. Unfortunately, his swing still connected – with Ely's bronze goblet of wine. The receptacle bounced off the floor as its contents splashed onto Ely's doublet.

"You vile fox!" Ely snapped, grabbing the fringe of his violet silk and crushed velvet garment. "This was my favorite doublet!"

"Serves you right!" Gerry shouted back, his nerve not wavering. He met Ely's incredulous stare with a steely look all his own. Such demeanor from his more petite, often meeker, sibling put Ely at odds with how to respond.

"Why, I should, you..." Ely drew his dirk. He glanced at Gerry, who responded by drawing his blade. Ely, suddenly robbed of his brash confidence, looked around. For an opening? An escape? Who could say? Not one, though any soul could attest that Ely wanted nothing to do with Gerry.

The heavy door to the chamber opened. A Voiceless marched in, halted, and stared from one brother to the next. He stood so stunned that Symon had to step around him to enter.

"What in the name..." he shot a glimpse at the knight before catching on to his line of sight. Seeing his siblings armed and facing each other prompted him to charge forward. "Disarm yourselves!"

Gerry obliged, as did Ely, though the latter waited for Gerry's dirk to clang before he dropped his own.

"Now, what is the meaning of this?!" Symon demanded.

Gerry the meek returned. "He said –"

"I did not!" Ely interrupted.

"He spoke ill of Taresa!"

"Symon, I merely suggested that you and her –"

"Quiet! The both of you." Symon rounded the table. With his jaw clenched, his stare narrowed, and his brow furrowed, the commander within emerged; the kind in no mood for antics nor games.

Symon stomped up to Gerry first. He loomed over his smaller brother, the latter having forgotten to wear his lifts. Gerry, his momentary rage toward Ely subsiding in the face of a more worthy threat, slunk into the chair at the table. Symon then directed his ire toward Ely, who met his brother's façade with rolled eyes and a huff but ultimately relented as he took his seat.

"I ought to flog the both of you," Symon seethed, "to find you fighting over a war of words while the fate of our kingdom hangs by a thread."

"Very poetic, brother," Ely quipped.

Symon, enraged, nodded to the Voiceless who had entered with him. In one full motion, the mute knight removed his buckled scabbard as he unsheathed the sword. Ely stumbled out of his chair as the Voiceless stepped toward him – to drop the sword on the table. The hilt clattered atop the wood as the blade, coated in dirt and ash, snapped into a handful of fragments. Gerry recoiled at the ringing sound of steel splintering.

"*That* is what happened while you two were fooling around." Symon pointed at the weapon. "My men recovered it from what little remained of our camp. The rest – bones, teeth, charred remains – fell to bits in their hands as they tried to pick it up. Not that the lot of you care."

Gerry's hand gravitated to the closest shard. But returning to his senses, he withdrew, out of respect for the poor soldier who no doubt fared worse than the broken blade before him. He nearly raised his voice to Symon to offer an apology until he noticed Ely heaving.

"How dare you!" Ely fumed.

Symon, like a deer caught by surprise, straightened at the unexpected affront. "What?"

"You think we didn't know what was going on? That we were unaware? As though we were hiding underground in Terran like we were children? I stood by and watched as you gallivanted around the ballroom while I discovered the vipers in our midst. I took to the streets to spy on our so-called allies in their den of foxes while you and your bride wetted the bed. I went through great lengths to secure as many secrets as I could while you rushed half-naked into a battle that was over before it had begun. And now, you stand here, accusing me of not caring? I tell you, *brother*, I care more now than you ever dare to know. Or does that come as a shock to you? It must. I bet you never even bothered to read the dozen notes I passed through our guards to provide intelligence I knew you could use. But did I ever receive a response? An acknowledgment? A thank you? No. Not once. So ask yourself, who amongst us cares, Symon? Who *really* cares?"

The chamber descended into silence. The Voiceless – perhaps thanking Mar for his muteness – remained at attention. Gerry looked to Symon, who stood stone-faced. Gerry had known that expression since youth. It came when Symon found himself challenged by two competing emotions: humiliation and rage. Today, the rage came from discovering his siblings quarreling, though the bulk no doubt was the product of the week's preceding events. And the humiliation... Well, Ely had done his part to provide that.

"Your findings," Symon began through gritted teeth, "while thorough, lacked truth. Or how would Dawkin say? 'They needed to be validated,' or, 'They're hearsay,' or some sort of rubbish. I know you took to great pains to retrieve the information. But what you found could easily be rumors or lies. There is simply no way to know."

Ely, never the one to be proven wrong – even when he clearly was – did not relent. "Tssk, tssk, my careful warrior.

Rumors abounded, yes, in the aftermath of the attack, as we can agree upon. Many falsities spread, the product of anxiety and fear. I am well aware of the inclinations of the beast of paranoia; believe me, I am, which is why I took great lengths to vet the entirety of what I heard. If you had read those notes I sent, you would have discovered that for yourself. Since you did not, let us here and now review what I learned, shall we?"

"I don't have the notes you sent on me –"

"I thought you wouldn't. Pity. The soldier runs into battle half-naked once again."

Ely reached behind his back to retrieve a small journal he had tucked under his belt. He flipped through the pages before arriving at his chosen sections, no doubt his latest set of observations.

"Now, let us see..." Ely scanned the journal's contents. "Gerry, be a good chap and bring the maps I brought. From the satchel in the corner."

Gerry, ignoring the condescension behind Ely's request, dutifully fetched the rolls of parchment from the sack. Picking them up, he regarded the antiquity of the maps, as well as their origins. *These aren't Marlish,* he noted. *These are Ibian. Local.* Indeed, Ely had certainly done his research, so much so he would have put even Dawkin to shame.

He laid the maps, six rolls in total, before Ely on the table. Ely offered a respectful nod to Gerry in thanks. *He actually believes in what he discovered.* The thought – of Ely maturing from an imp of foolishness to a royal of value – enticed Gerry to lean over the table. Even Symon cast aside his wounded pride to direct his focus to the drawings.

"I collected these, at a considerable expense of coin and

time, while sneaking around Arinn."

"I hope you didn't –" Symon started to warn.

"Relax. I didn't do anything to attract attention. I gathered these with care."

"Did anyone –"

"I used fading potion. And quite a bit. Nearly the lot of what we brought with us. So anyone, whether Ibian or Marlish, who encountered me was robbed of their memory almost immediately. I even put on my best disguises to accessorize my caution. Plus, I gifted the Voiceless at my side with my genius of disguise. Isn't that right, my mute friend?"

Ely shot a glance at the Voiceless, who had retreated to the corner. The guard, not one inclined to Ely's brand of humor, responded with a scowl.

"You were careful," Gerry said.

"Always, brother, always," Ely boasted. "And it paid dividends. I mean, look at this." Ely unfurled the largest of the maps, revealing a majestic drawing of Afari, the skill of which dated it to the Epoch of Artisans. Across the whole of it, though, lay markings in Ely's hand.

"Ely!" Gerry exclaimed. "This map was priceless."

"Oh, posh! I can find ten just like it if I had to. Besides, I improved upon its contents. See." Ely pointed first to the bottom center of the map, which displayed the peninsula of Belgarda and its principal city of Vloma. There, Ely had marked: *The Supreme Devout speaks of threats upon the continent in his yearly address to his Conclave of High Bishops.*

"I do remember that mention from the note you sent," Symon mused. "It arrived soon after I received word from

Felix's private horse messenger, who rode day and night to deliver news to him personally from the Court of Vloma. I simply assumed you had somehow intercepted the report from his parcel before transferring it to me."

"You assumed wrong. You see, certain details have a way of making their presence known far ahead of any royal messenger, even one as expeditious as that of King Felix."

"But how?"

"A mage never reveals his secrets."

"But what's so noteworthy about the Supreme Devout's address?" Gerry inquired.

"I'm glad you asked. You see the shorthand beside iconography of Vloma?"

Gerry made out a series of numbers and periods. *147. 6. 1302. 5.*

"The date of the royal wedding?" Gerry blurted, looking to Symon then Ely.

"Exactly. The Supreme Devout gave his yearly address three weeks earlier than he usually does, on the same day that Symon married Taresa." Ely turned to Symon. "You said His Grace apologized for Tongelus di Valia not being able to attend your nuptials."

"Yes, I sent word to you two on the matter via one of my letters from the castle, as I recall."

"A slight to both Kin Garsea and our own house, wouldn't you say?"

Symon rubbed his chin. "I suppose."

"And would your supposition evolve to certainty if I told you of the contents of his address?"

Symon straightened. "How could you possibly know

that? The contents of any Conclave's meeting, especially the covert gathering of High Bishops, are iron-clad, never to be discussed until announced in court, which Tongelus has yet to do."

"A mage –"

"Right, right, never mind." Symon waved his hand. "Now, out with it."

"The Supreme Devout made his disapproval of the royal union known. He said, and I quote from a slew of reliable sources, 'A threat has landed upon our shores, one intent on joining his evil with our goodness, who will taint our purity with his kin's legacy of sin.' The indication is as clear as snowmelt. He could have said 'their' or 'its.' Instead, he said 'his,' referring to he, or him. You. He spoke of you, Symon. On the very day you wed."

Symon's hand stayed planted on his chin. Though never one to attach much meaning to a war of words, the coincidence of the pairing was not lost on him. "What else?"

"I'm delighted you asked. The Supreme Devout droned on and on about the affairs of Afari. Or at least that's what my contacts confirmed. Much of what he said could be dismissed by the everyday audience as boring drivel. In reading through the notes on his address, I nearly fell asleep at several points myself. Until the pieces took on a pattern, and certain facts began to make themselves known." Ely, beaming, gestured to the top-right quadrant of the map.

Gerry leaned over, squinting, for the referenced section of the parchment appeared stained by some dark liquid. Nonetheless, he could spot the outline of the kingdom of Volkmar. Beside its borders lay Ely's scribble: *Ludwinn – sent delegation to Vloma.*

"That's all?" Gerry asked.

"All?! It is, in fact," Ely replied defensively.

"You'll need to fill in more of the gaps," Symon added.

"Oh, fine. Don't you think it's too much of a coincidence? With Ludwinn sending a delegation to Vloma? Before Tongelus gave his address?"

"Ludwinn is always dispatching his delegations. They're little more than bands of thugs who appear in courts throughout Afari, demanding bribes so their troops don't rape and pillage the surrounding countryside. That's why Father continued to ban them from his court after the Century War ended."

Tis true, Gerry recalled. Their father had often spoken ill of the Volkmar, almost in the same vein as he regarded the Foleppi or Mynhard. Though larger and more powerful than the previously noted enemies, with a lineage that stretched back before written record, in the eyes of Audemar they deserved no more respect than rats nor their lice. In fact, every Saliswater monarch had expressed a similar level of disdain for the northernmost kingdom of Afari, even in the days when relations between the Volkmar and Marlish stood as tepid.

Ely paused, perhaps considering their father's attitude for their enemy, before perking. "Oh, oh, I forgot to mark on *this* map what I found on *that* one." He reached for the map furthest from him, the smallest, and did quick work to lay it before them. As expected, the land it depicted was more modest in scope, with chevrons and curves dotting the whole of it to note mountains and hills throughout.

"Northern Afari," Symon stated. "Or a part of it."

"The soldier knows his geography. Who says troops

can't be smart." Ely shot a glance at the Voiceless in the corner. "You could learn a thing or two from my brother."

"Come now, Ely," Gerry urged.

"Right, yes. Well, you can see from the map a series of parallel lines cutting through the ranges and weaving through the hillocks. The more width or space between the pair of lines, the larger the road. The biggest is there." Ely pointed to what amounted to two thick lines that snaked from the left corner of the map to its right edge before turning south to end at the bottom of its center. "That is the road the delegation took once they sailed from their seat in Karr down the Delke River to the port of Frossberg. An overland route as broad as that could accommodate a small army, wouldn't you say?"

"Could," Symon replied. "Did it?"

"I have... sources... working to confirm those very details."

"Are you saying the Volkmar are trying to invade Vloma?" Gerry inquired.

"No," Symon interjected. "They wouldn't. Even in the hype of the wedding and the attack on the castle, we would have learned of a force *that* large. But a smaller, expeditionary detachment, one sizeable enough for a kingdom to convey a commitment to a powerful alliance... It would be a move of diplomacy."

"Two brutes flexing their respective muscles, huh?" Ely poked.

"Yes, brother, if you say so."

"Oh, but I do. Plus, there is more I discovered to support my theories, such as –"

"That'll do," Symon commanded, holding his hand out

to Ely.

"You need to hear this."

"Oh, I will. I'll listen to it all. As you will to me. Under the right conditions." Symon turned to the knight. "Gather the truth serum and memory tea. We're having back-to-back sessions," Symon nodded to Ely, then Gerry. "Ready yourselves."

Gerry breathed. He had consumed what amounted to a thick manuscript of narratives, with no detail omitted. As the effects of the memory tea began to wane, he glanced at Symon and Ely, who lay on cots opposite of each other, recovering from their truth sessions.

Surprisingly, his head didn't throb, as it often did after a long session. Since he endured two sessions of moderate length, which taken together constituted the most extensive hearing in his experience, he considered himself fortunate. He couldn't say the same for his brothers, who twisted and writhed. Though their eyes remained closed as they tried to sleep, their grimaces with those contorted lips spoke of residual pain from their extensive recollections.

Gerry sauntered over to the chamber pot, about to relieve himself, when a strong hand pushed him aside.

"Hey!" he blurted before realizing it was Symon.

"My apologies, brother," Symon offered, though he still stood before the pot to empty his bladder. "But all that truth serum makes one... full. Not to mention the memory tea I drank when Ely spoke his turn."

"You're full? What about me? I had to swallow a pot of that tea listening to the both of you."

"And what did you learn?"

So we're on to this? Gerry mused as Symon finished up

to step away to the nearby washbasin. Gerry eagerly took his place as Symon waited for his reply. "I gathered all you and Ely know. The massive fire. The explosion of the tower. Ely's espionage. His wild theories. The entirety of it."

"And?"

"And what?"

"Who do you think is behind it?

Gerry, done with the chamber pot, moved to the wash-basin. "I have no bloody idea," he said as he cleaned his hands.

"Then you have the right of it." Symon rubbed his chin, considering.

Gerry wanted to ask questions, to say something, but what could he? His brothers had released the full contents of their minds so that nothing remained. Nothing hidden. No secrets. Nary an unspoken thought or unexpressed emotion. Every suspicion in the recesses of their wits had been laid bare.

Therein was the problem. For all their collaborations with the court and each other, the three of them had no idea what to do next.

And now it's my turn to be King.

The anxiety of his ascension had been suppressed by the prospect of listening to his brothers. But with their pieces done and with no plan to follow, the weight of what waited for him – the possibility of everything – struck him hard.

His breath became shallow. His heartbeats quickened. His vision blurred.

Dear Mar...

Then a palm collided with his cheek.

The chamber spun, as did Gerry, before he fell against the wall. He fought to regain his footing, but before he could, Symon pounced before him. His steady hands gripped his shoulders to hold him in place and prevent him from escaping.

"Don't you ever do that again!"

"What?! *You* hit *me!*"

"I did. And I'd do it once more, or many times, if given a chance. But out there, when you're on the throne or standing before the court, I won't be able to save you. Those shakes of yours, the bits of anxiety, why – Gerry, we are not princes anymore. We are kings. Kings. You can't turn the coward or act the fool when the duties of the Throne overwhelm you. There are too many eyes on King Jameson at present, especially now that we the King have wed Taresa. You must... do all you can not to act... like you."

Symon had never been so bold before. Sure, he had pulled Gerry away to offer counsel or correct his form during a sparring session. Even when he had admonished him in front of others, be it their siblings or the Voiceless, never had the frankness of his words overtaken his compassion.

Until now.

Those eyes could pierce a steel helm, their intensity more shocking than a fleet of arrows. By Mar, he doesn't blink. He's more serious than I've ever seen him.

"I'm scared, Symon. I don't know what to do."

"I know. That doesn't matter. No one knows what to do. Not one. Sure, every baron of Marland will beg a private audience, to push their interests or opinions on you. The Ibian barons will do the same, though because you are not their king, they will yell and argue for your attention. Not to mention the bishops, the mages, the commanders – Gerry, for all their confessed skills and instincts, they are children looking to their father for guidance, knowing their father hasn't a clue on the evils ahead."

"And you want me to be the father? To a kingdom? To our peoples?"

"You must, Gerry. We were born for this. To lead when we are lost. Tis our fate."

Our fate? Or yours? Not that it made a difference, for Gerry knew the right of what Symon tried to say. Despite the apprehension in his gut, the end action would not change. He needed to take his Mar-given place at the Throne.

Gerry nodded. The gesture seemed to placate Symon, who eased his grip, allowing Gerry to shake free.

"I'll help you prepare," Symon offered.

"What of him?" Gerry asked, motioning to Ely.

"Let him be. Given his history with the bottle, he's more prepared than us to recover from the bad effects of some serum and tea."

The two withdrew to the barracks Felix had granted Jameson for his guards. The vaulted brick chamber offered little in the way of comforts, with only one hearth for long hall capable of holding a hundred men and few alcoves for their arms. Nonetheless, as they always did, the muted guards had made the space as hospitable as possible. Beside the hearth, the Voiceless had partitioned a section for the brothers to allow them a smidge of privacy. Gerry's cot and his belongings rested against the corner. While he dressed in his regal fineries, Symon offered snippets of encouragement and advice, undoubtedly to save face after admonishing his little brother earlier. Although earnest in his efforts, Gerry still harbored the sting of his honesty, causing him to regard little of what his brother said. Until...

"Gerry, did you hear me? About Taresa?"

Gerry, shaking himself from his bitterness, perked. "What about her?"

"I said when you retire on your first night, take care to be gentle."

"Gentle? Why?"

Symon sighed. He shifted in his seat on the cot. Gerry, not accustomed to seeing his soldier-of-a-brother unsettled, turned the whole of his body to face him.

"After the feast, we withdrew to the wedding chamber, like I said. Then I told you and Ely about rushing off to the fire, then the explosion at Castle Arinn."

"Right."

"What I failed to mention... The whole night was one of uncertainty. The bed, the act... prolonged... or put off... When I left our wedding chamber the night of the fire, I had not... done my duty."

Gerry's heart leapt. *Is he possibly saying what I think?* "Symon... Is Taresa still... unclaimed?"

Symon, never gracious in defeat, looked away.

By Mar. I will be her first, and she mine. "Thank you."

Symon rose, muttering something incomprehensible.

"Does she, you know, expect anything of Jameson?" Gerry asked as Symon opened the flap of the partition.

Symon paused, choosing his words carefully. "She needs a man."

In other words, not me. "I understand."

"A gentle man, as she lacks experience, but a man

nonetheless."

So I am to be a king, a hero, and a lover during this turn? Gerry reflected as Symon gestured to the opening. Gerry ducked under the parted flap before Symon followed after. He accompanied Gerry through the barracks then to the end of the hallway, where the main bailey and the rest of Castle Arinn waited.

"I told Sir Everitt to wait just outside come morning," Symon offered. "I said I needed to stand on my own, to offer a few words of encouragement to the men and counsel each of them through the long night, without my retinue being present. He obliged, knowing I'd be safe among my men. He or a guard he assigned should be on the other side, ready to escort you."

"Very well."

"Good fortune to you," Symon stated.

"I appreciate it, brother."

Symon turned to march back down the hall. Gerry reached for the door ring, bracing himself for the fate awaiting him on the other side.

"Oh, and Gerry."

Gerry glanced over his shoulder.

"Don't embarrass us. As I did."

Symon, solemn and doubtful, stared at his brother. Then, offering nothing else, he exited the hall.

Just another day in our kinghood, Gerry assured himself, as Symon had failed to do. Heart and mind racing, he opened the door to find his Right Captain standing at attention, just as Symon suspected he would.

"Are you well and ready, James?" Sir Everitt asked.

"Never better," Gerry lied. "Now, take me to my queen."

Chapter 8

Why is this damn seat so hard? I thought I asked the attendants to replace the cushions.

In truth, the pillows were far from the problem. As Artus shifted in his seat, the soft plumage of goose down encased in velvet cradled his rear, providing a buoyant layer between himself and the white oak panels of the throne chair. He could not have asked for a more comfortable piece of furniture.

But the posture, the duration he spent with his knees bent and his back straight, *that* was the source of his agony. From youth, his regal upbringing had instilled in him the discipline to sit properly, so he looked the part no matter the news delivered. Whether of war or windfall, a monarch had to appear stoic, unspoiled by the rumblings or emotions of court. 'Twas his duty.

That duty had worn on him, though, as the years supplanted his vigor with aches and fatigue. Not quite into his second hour of court and already Artus started to endure the restlessness of body and wandering of mind.

Bloody nobles, he muttered silently, his lips moving with no words spoken. The baron before him cared not of what his lordship nor the rest of the audience thought. He simply droned on and on, each phrase spilling forth, followed by another even duller than the one before. *Get on with it!*

A man, perhaps as fidgety and ill-tempered as Artus at that moment, shouted what the former monarch only thought. "Speed up, you bloody hound! The lot of us haven't got all day!"

A number from the crowd clapped and cheered. The nobleman, Baron Mortimer of Har-Kin Watteau, sneered as he swung around to reprimand the heckler. "How dare you!" he barked, his voice indeed sounding like a mutt, prompting some in the audience to chuckle.

"Me?" retorted the outspoken man, who remained obscured by those around him. "There are a hundred more awaiting an audience with his Liege Artus, and there you stand, wasting precious time with your drivel."

A hundred more? Artus rose. The subjects in his wake silenced, expecting the former sovereign to utter an admonishment or edict in response to the disturbance in the court.

He stood, his awkwardness dwelling within even as his regal exterior persisted intact.

What do I do?

Perhaps in anticipation of a tongue-lashing, the lord of Har-Kin Watteau bowed his head. "Baron Artus, forgive my ill-mannered ways. I allowed my pride to wrestle my wits, and in doing so, forgot my place in court. I apologize."

Artus nodded. Seeing an opportunity for respite, he addressed the crowd. "With our noble sovereign away, along with many of his ministers and confidantes, I know our patience is tried, especially after hearing about the massacre at Castle Arinn."

"We want justice!" shouted another hidden man in the crowd, this one with a hoarser voice.

Insolent subjects! If I were but younger and stronger, none would dare to raise their tone with me!

Ever the regal, Artus quieted the warrior within as he tilted his head upward. "And you shall have it! Marland will seek vengeance. Of that, I am certain. I know the King, sired from my line, holds the same intention. But justice with haste leads to hell, as many of those in the audience who survived the Century War can tell you." Artus paused, grateful for the older gentlemen in the crowd, who picked up on his cue and nodded in affirmation. "Until the day when we will have our reparations in full, Marland will carry on, as we always have. Now, considering the tone of this court, let us recess, so the more passionate among us may calm. I will return then, and not a moment sooner."

Artus descended the stairs from the throne. Though no longer a monarch, those before him bowed as his guards escorted him to the side door.

Now that's more like it.

Not until he entered the safety of the adjacent corridor, away from prying eyes, did he allow himself the privilege of sighing. The exhale resulted in his shoulders slumping forward, which came too easily to his aged frame.

"Are you well, my lord?"

The question startled Artus. He looked to the Voiceless around him before his eyes found the freckled face of Sir Higgins.

"Why, yes, my lad. Why do you ask?"

"Oh, it's only that you seemed... never my mind."

Yes, never mind you. Artus straightened and huffed but offered nothing more in response as he strode off. The young knight, oblivious to the slight he had just imparted, fell in line behind him and the three silent guards, his loose-fitted scabbard slapping his thigh. The claps of the boy's sheath reminded Artus of the oath he had made his Right Captain and Higgins' grandfather, Sir Segar of Har-Kin Birkenhead, to watch over the lad. In the moment of making a promise to a dying man, Artus had never considered that a man's last wish could be so burdensome. Or annoying.

Arriving at his chambers, Artus raised his hand, signaling his detail to halt. "A moment alone, good sirs."

"Shall we sweep the chamber? Not for grime, but for assassins?"

Artus clenched his teeth. "My boy, the guards regularly inspect the royal quarters when the King or I are at court, at least once an hour, time permitting."

"So, 'tis safe?"

"Why I just –" Artus bit his lip. He shifted to the Voiceless at his right side. "'Twas inspected?"

The knight nodded.

Artus turned to Higgins. "There you have it."

"I am pleased, my lord."

I'm not. "You've done your duty well, Sir. Go and rest. I need only twenty minutes to rest my eyes."

"Then I shall return in fifteen."

So I will be gone in ten. "As you wish."

The lad grinned. Artus pivoted, hoping to Mar his freckled guard would fall into the hole of a privy.

After a brief respite, a new man emerged from the royal chambers. Artus, feeling refreshed, strode from the entrance to be greeted by four familiar faces: three of the silent knights he had left and the other his grandson,

Dawkin.

"So, you bested the lad?" Artus quipped as he noted the set of impeccable freckles his kin sported, along with a convincing false red beard.

"Hardly," Dawkin answered. "Your escort had an incident in the privy, had to change his clothes."

Artus chuckled. "An everyday occurrence for that one, undoubtedly." Even the Voiceless in his band smirked at that.

"Grandfather."

"Oh, let me have my romp."

"The Court calls."

"Just like always. Very well. Let us resume."

The barons, having waited patiently – well, waited, at least – unfurled their requests one after another. From the baron of a western har-kin wanting to punish a farmer to the baron of a southern kin soliciting his men for service in the King's army, their unceasing tide of appeals knew no bounds. It struck Artus how *ridiculous* the kingdom was for having so many lords and ladies. *My goodness, how can an island hold so many nobles?* Not to mention that the Court served nobility first. The common folk – who thankfully kept their petitions brief – still had their turn the following day. *Ughhh.*

The last baron of the day entreated for a loan extension from his lender, for his sharecroppers' yields had been decimated in the Battle of the Ford. *So that is what they call the engagement now?* Artus thought as he waved his hand and nodded to grant the baron his request. Standing without waiting for the royal crier to adjourn the Court, Artus withdrew from the audience. The crowd had withered from the morning, with the remaining members offering obligatory bows and curtsies. They too seemed tired of the formalities.

Striding through the hall, the Voiceless kept their march in line with Artus' hasty pace. Then one broke from the pattern to approach at his side.

"You did well," Dawkin offered.

The lad comes to comfort me*? Mar, I'm not that feebleminded.* "I thank you."

"Will you supper with me? In the King's absence, no royal banquets have been scheduled, and neither the barons nor the bishops have begged for an audience with you tonight."

"Yes, yes, I would like it very much. Allow me a respite to change into some dining clothes. These regal costumes of Court could chafe a corpse."

Dawkin smirked, pausing outside the royal chambers. "I will see you at the private dining hall then."

Artus dipped his head as a Voiceless stepped in to open the door for him. He closed it as the former sovereign entered, emitting a long sigh as he found himself alone, at last.

The dining table in the private room stretched only six feet, serving as perhaps the shortest table in all the castle. Yet when Artus arrived to find his grandson standing at the far end, waiting, he could not help but feel a continent stood between them. *Why must everything in this bloody fortress be so grand?*

"Something the matter, Grandfather?" Dawkin inquired, undoubtedly in response to Artus' grimace.

"Nothing, my boy. I only hunger, tis all."

"Good. I had the cooks prepare all your favorites."

Indeed, he had. Duck basted in wild clover honey laid in the center of the table as the main dish, alongside wild rosemary potatoes, creamed parsnips, and golden dinner rolls accompanied with lavender butter. Other elegant touches dotted the table, including the silver cutlery set reserved for family celebrations and the gold-leaf goblets which had been heirlooms in the Saliswater kin for seven generations.

Though pleasing, the presentation struck a nerve with Artus, one which ran deep. His mood soured as he took his seat with a particular *thump*.

Not unaware of his grandfather's turn, Dawkin sat, dismissing the Voiceless present. At their departure, he reached up to his mouth to strip the false beard from his face. Artus, his hands on the table on either side of his dish, tarried.

"Would you do the honors?" Dawkin asked, extending the cutlery to him, motioning to the duck.

"Don't patronize me?!"

"I –" Dawkin's thought held in the air before he glanced away, another interrupting him.

"What?"

"Never mind."

"No, I insist. I stand in for King Jameson. You and your brothers. If I am to serve in this guise – or whatever it is this Throne has become – I need *you* to tell *me* if I made an utter fool of myself. I see the side glances they try to hide from me. The pause in their responses when I question them. Like I'm some old dog who will bite without notice.

Me! The Saliswater who served as monarch of the island longer than any of you, or your father –"

The last mention struck both of them especially hard. Artus, eyes widening with a flash of recollection, released the anger within, reclining in his chair with an air of self-defeat. Dawkin, his mood deflated, stayed on his feet. With utensils in hand, he took to his seat softly, laying the long knife and carving fork to his side.

The moment – eons in their mind's eye – lingered. Dawkin, first to break the silence, pointed to the carafe to his left. "Wine, then?"

Artus shrugged. Dawkin rose to pour his grandfather and himself a goblet each. He walked the length of the table to set the full glass before him.

"Thank you."

Dawkin returned to his chair to drink. He downed the first half of his glass, allowing the last half to linger as he swirled the contents within.

"This is the part," he began, "where you offer me some anecdote. You start lightheartedly enough, mayhaps with a joke or a quip. Then you turn nostalgic, regaling me with a tale from your past. I would venture to say a memory from the front lines of the Century War. No, wait, one involving my father. You spout some recollection about how he was like me, or he like you. We chuckle at the thought, then relinquish our bad tidings to enjoy this wonderful spread before us. Yes, that is how this part of our story should unfold. Or, at least that is how the scribes of old and new would say it should go, according to all the tales I've read and the manuscripts I've studied. And who are we to go against the tendencies of our greater narratives?"

For all his lofty words, of which Artus had little appreciation, the sentiment remained clear. Artus lay his elbows on the table, his hands meeting before his face. Then, just as Dawkin opened his mouth to speak again, he swept the spread before him from the table. The cutlery clattered while the dishes shattered, summoning the Voiceless into the room.

Dawkin raised his hands to stop them at the door before ushering outside again. The silent knights relented, though their concern persisted as they left. Alone again, Dawkin lifted his chair to carry it around the table to his grandfather's right side. He set it down gently as the old man lowered his head to his hand, where he cradled it in angst.

"This position," Dawkin said, "weighs on you."

"As it does you and your brothers."

"No. Tis different. Different from all the times you served as King, for which we are all grateful. And I mean that in the most sincere, un-patronizing way possible, Grandfather."

"I know."

"Today, with the barons, what troubled you?"

Dear Mar, do I even know? "I, I suppose... Oh, hell, who bloody knows? Everything. Everything is the matter. The Century War ended after my reign, with your father at the helm of this kingdom. The whole of our lives should have coasted into a stretch of peace. Your father serving out his days solidifying his legacy, his only annoyance being bickering barons. You and your brothers growing from your princehood into your kinghood with ease. Then the lot of you married – though even I admit, I see the folly of *that* being without consequence. Still, you having princelings of your own, your father and I watching them grow as we settle into the end of our years. That was how it was supposed to go.

"Now, the past year or so has unraveled my life's work. Along with your father's and yours, even with your reign has just begun. First, his death, at the hands of our own nobles, no less. Then this mess on the continent, on the King's wedding day of all things."

"We addressed the King's assassination with steel and gallows. Justice was had."

Oh, to be so young and trust in the certainty of such ideals. Artus grinned at the thought. *Never lose that, my son, not as I have.* Artus shifted in his seat to face Dawkin. "It was. Only to be lost. The memory of such amends has turned into a shadow overcome by the impinging darkness, my boy. Marland recalls not the efforts of your princehood, nor the discovery and dealing of a conspiracy, nor the triumph of your coronation. All they see is the assassination of one monarch followed by the near-miss of another. You are in a weakened state, Dawkin, not in truth but in rumor, which is so much worse. Our alliances become frayed. I can feel it, sense it with every fiber of my core. The nobles respect us less and less each day. Your petition to them in the Conclave saved the legacy of our kin. But for how long? I fear for you and your brothers. It's a dread which weighs on me, with every baron who speaks and each head I see bowed. I tire not from service, nor the boredom, nor the length of either. On the contrary, I wear down with the threat my efforts will prove futile, for the future of my remaining blood, which fatigues me more than any obstacle or battle I've experienced."

Artus stared into Dawkin's eyes, seeing a cadence between his spoken words and the process of his grandson's understanding. How many times had he tried to impart the same lessons of kinghood into Audemar? Then his grandsons? Too many. True, his past attempts had not been in circumstances so dire, so desperate. Those lessons benefited from being doled out in the lulls of their days, such as during the hikes of a hunt or by a hearth after supper. This, however, stood as different. The kingdom hung in the balance of every minute or every hour of the days to come.

Moreover, so did the lives of four kings serving as one.

Dawkin leaned forward. Intently, he narrowed his eyes. "What should we do?"

I have no idea.

The absence of a reply gave Dawkin his answer. He reclined in his chair, waiting for the sting of defeat to pass.

"We must do something," Dawkin mused.

Chapter 9

He seems so unlike himself. A different man from the one I married. How long has it been? A week? No more than two, for certain. Still, it all seems like a lifetime ago. Just as my husband before me appears. Then again, how well can I say I really know him?

The carriage hit a particularly large bump in the road, sending Taresa up in her seat. Not that carriage rides were ever comfortable. But notwithstanding their jarring nature, all felt it when they hit a divot or rise of considerable note. Nataliya would giggle, even in the presence of her elders, while Ermesinda would shift in her seat, acting unfazed though every jolt threatened to upend the contents of her stomach. Their mother would huff and sigh, often adding a comment about the tribulations of country travel. Taresa hadn't a clue how the road affected her father, for he always rode alone, save for the rare instances when he allowed a minister or duke of renown to join him. However, she did know his attendants always supplied a collection of snuff boxes, each with a different strain of crushed tobacco. On particularly rough trips, she would catch him handing an empty snuff box through the window curtain of his carriage, where a servant hanging from his side railing would take it. On some occasions, he would pass several outside. Why he could not bear to have an empty container in his presence stood among many oddities Taresa noted of her father.

Another dip bumped Taresa from her seat; only this time, she heard a crack. The noise resonated beyond the interior of her carriage as well, for within moments, Jameson parted the curtain with his sheathed sword to glance inside.

"Are you well?" he inquired, leaning over from his saddle.

Taresa smiled. "Never better."

Jameson frowned. He shouted to the coachman. "Hey, you there! You call this a King's Road? I've seen rock-strewn hillocks flatter than this path."

Taresa blushed, embarrassed. She could only assume the royal driver fumed at the slight. "Dear, I don't believe the coachman understands you. He doesn't speak Marlish."

"Oh, he knows. Marlish or not, he comprehends what I'm saying."

Taresa sat back in her seat. *So imprudent.* She considered offering another word to her husband. Before she could, he rode ahead, nary looking back.

She reclined in silence, spreading her hands on her lap to keep from fidgeting. Usually, she welcomed the opportunity to ride in a carriage by herself, away from the bickering and idle talk of her mother, sisters, or ladies of the court. Those rare occasions offered her the chance to settle her mind, to peek out the window and admire the countryside without commentary from another, save her wandering monologue.

The present excursion turned out to be an exception. Not that the road had anything to do with her sudden distaste for solitude. She didn't mind the bumps and bounces.

No, the discomfort came from riding apart from her husband. Not that she expected him to accompany her within, for few men in their prime, whether Marlish or Ibian, rode in carriages with women, be it their wives, daughters, or other kin. Still, ever since the night of their wedding – when all hell broke loose – she found herself without his companionship, as every baron, knight, captain, and even her father required his attention. Conferences in the War Hall, attending sessions of court, private meals with generals and barons to converse on security matters – those were but some of the events that occupied Jameson's long days. Taresa had no place in any of them, except when they permitted her to stand or sit in some far corner to watch.

She had accepted the constraints of court her entire life, biding her time through maidenhood, all the while waiting for the opportunity to broaden her behavior. She thought her betrothal to Prince Denisot would have allowed her more liberty, but with their brief espousal soon dissolved, she never experienced anything beyond scrutiny in the form of hushed whispers at court. Then came her next Promised, Prince Jameson, a regal she believed different from all the rest. Indeed, in Arcporte, he had demonstrated himself to be a man of skill and authority, evidenced by his deeds during her first visit to the island. Even in all the formalities of their union ceremony, she held out hope Jameson would be a king apart, a true soul to whom she could finally reveal her true self. But ever since their wedding night – with the attack on his men and the castle – he had become aloof. Distant, even. Every hour and day that followed, he sullied her faith in him through his many responsibilities and meetings. The rare instances when she found herself alone with her spouse hadn't helped, for he often turned in early, having exhausted himself beyond the point of offering more than a grunt or a nod to her until sleep overcame him. She realized the duties of the Throne weighed heavily on him, as did the sudden death of his father and now their present circumstances. She wasn't naïve of any of it. *Still...* she considered, fighting the urge to entertain her grievances. *He could try more at this marriage.*

Another bump in the road befell the carriage. The inclination to squirm proved almost too much to endure. Then she heard him. Again.

"I told you to watch the road –"

That's it!

Taresa stuck her head out the window. "Stop the coach."

The servant hanging from the carriage railing nearly fell off at Taresa's sudden appearance. "Beg your pardon, Your Majesty?"

"I *command* this coach to halt this instant!" she shouted, loud enough for the servant and the coachman to hear.

"Whoa, whoa," the coachman said to the draft horses before him as he leaned back on the reins. The carriage barely rolled to a stop before Taresa opened her door to descend. She waved the attendant off as he brought the step stool, choosing instead to hop down from her perch.

Landing on her feet, she stared up and down the road, acutely aware of the ruckus she had caused. The sudden stop drew the attention of all in their small caravan, from the squires to Jameson's Right Captain to the King himself. Good.

Jameson, all of the sudden less assured, trotted up to her on his horse. "Something the matter, my wife?"

"I need some air."

"Oh, well, we can stop for a spell –"

"No, let's not stop. I only want to breathe as I ride."

"The servants can tie back the curtains." Jameson tilted his head to study the gray sky. "Though it threatens to rain."

"I have a better idea."

Taresa marched to the front of the carriage, not bothering to lift the hem of her dress as it dragged over the dirt. She came to stand beside the coachman, who rose from his seat awkwardly to lean over and offer a near-bow.

"You have done well, Royal Coachman. Now, if you don't mind, I'll drive."

Agape, the driver stared at her, frozen in his hunched stance. As did the servant who had hung from the carriage railing. Then there was Jameson –

"Well?" she asked.

The driver looked to the King, who dismounted.

"Dear," Jameson said, concerned. "I think this may be improper. I mean, if it begins to rain, or the wind picks up –"

"Do you think me incapable, husband?"

"Why, no. Never!"

"Then I shall do it."

"Have you ever driven a coach before?"

"Once, when I was twelve. The Royal Coachman then allowed me to drive once, around the bailey almost three times until Mother came out to chastise me." Taresa climbed the footholds to the driver's seat as the Royal

Coachman hopped down from his perch. This particular carriage lacked the width of others in their collection, so only one person at a time could fit in the front seat.

The coachman scarcely had a moment to step away from the front wheel when Taresa braced herself on the footboard before snapping the reins. The four horses jolted ahead. Taresa lurched forward in response, prompting everyone in their caravan to reach out – albeit with none within arm's length – to catch her. She quickly composed herself, though, even managing a chuckle as she hurried down the King's Road.

The retinue in her wake scrambled to chase after, with Jameson being the first to catch up to Taresa. He trotted beside his wife, just across her left side, as she gave the reins another quick snap.

"A bold move," he commented.

"You think me foolhardy?"

"I didn't say that."

"You're thinking it. If not, the others are."

"Why the sudden, um, change in demeanor?"

The clattering of the carriage wheels, the vibrations of the seat irons, along with other sources of commotion, put Taresa in no mood to shout the particulars of her thoughts. "We'll speak about it when we arrive at the manor."

They needn't wait long, as the bend in the hedge-lined road revealed the gatehouse of Manor deila Krestta Deorro, a country estate that had been in her family for over seven generations. Originally a vineyard and winery whose operations dated back to ancient times, the previous proprietors had begun to outfit the grounds with defenses at the outbreak of the Century War when her kin took it over. Her ancestors had undoubtedly finished the job yet left much of the millennia-old enterprises intact, such that ramifications overlooked or stood beside vineyard rows, storehouses, and winepresses, making for a juxtaposing sight.

Anticipating their arrival, the drawbridge to the manor laid before them as the attendants and guards of the royal residence stood aside. Their shocked looks at spotting Her Majesty atop in place of the Royal Coachman brought a glimmer of amusement to Taresa's face, so by the time she pulled to a stop in front of the carriage house within, she beamed.

Not one to be outridden, the King dismounted right after Taresa descended from the coachman's step. He offered her a hand to escort her from the shadow of the carriage. In turn, she didn't so much refuse it but ignored it. She pressed on without so much as offering a glance to her side.

"Princess, I, pardon, my Queen –"

"Oh, so I am someone to you."

Jameson looked around, not accustomed to the curious looks of so many servants who respectfully kept their distance while remaining within earshot.

"A word?" he pleaded.

Very well. Taresa offered a curt nod to the reception hall bordering the bailey. He followed beside her until they reached the entrance, which he opened for them.

Modestly furnished with waiting chairs and sofas, the reception hall offered a respite from the watching eyes beyond. Taresa marched inside, waiting for Jameson to close the door behind him before turning with arms crossed.

"Forgive me," he started once they stood alone, "did I do something to offend you."

"I don't know, did you?"

"I –"

"Think upon the details of the past several days, James. In all that time, what happened between us?"

"Why, nothing..."

"Precisely! Nothing. Not a damned, bloody thing."

"Well, I, I had duties."

"Duties aplenty, I realize, as you always have. But now add to that one wife, whom you hardly have spoken to since..."

Her voice trailed off. She blushed. The near-union of their bodies on their wedding night flooded her memory. So tender had he been with her, so unlike what she had imagined. Then, *poof*, it had disappeared. An instant of love replaced with an eternity of formalities. Back to the life she had always lived. A statue, one of beauty, though of stone nonetheless. Just like her mother, or her grandmother, and every regal woman before. Robbed of a voice, of life, merely a pawn of court. Again. Forever.

Jameson withdrew a handkerchief from the inside pocket of his doublet, offering it to Taresa. She paused to question why before becoming aware of the tears cascading down her face. Reddening further, she took the silk square to wipe her cheeks dry.

"Thank you."

"Of course," he said. His mouth chastened into a grin. Suddenly, the King who had upset her converted into a figure more diminutive, almost... approachable. Hadn't he just been more regal? Stronger? Taller? The one she presently saw appeared as none of those things. Instead, he stood in the guise of an ordinary man – a kind soul.

Perhaps, a loveable one?

Taresa, not knowing what to do next, looked down. "What happens now?"

"I have a private meeting with His Grace, the keeper of this manor and your great uncle, I believe?"

"His Grace, the Grand Duke of Ryncon."

"Yes, him."

"Very well."

She offered the handkerchief back to Jameson.

"Please," he said, gesturing for her to keep it.

"Thank you."

Jameson twisted as if to turn when he caught himself. "What if, say, I didn't meet with the Grand Duke?"

Taresa perked for an instant before remembering her family's reputation. "That would be most unwise. My great uncle would never forgive such a slight. The men in my family are, how should I say, a proud line."

Jameson chuckled, allowing Taresa to catch a glimpse of his boyish demeanor. "Oh, if you only knew *my* family!"

"I hope to, soon."

"Yes, well, at least join us."

"In a session about the matters of the kingdom?"

"Why not?"

Shame washed over Taresa as she realized her behavior had shifted her husband's entire focus away from his duties. While she desired nothing more than for them to run off and enjoy each other's company for the first time in their marriage, she knew such childish wants were unwise.

"You go ahead," she insisted. "I'll be fine. Honestly, I could use a fresh bath and some rest after that horrific coach ride."

"Well, at least the last bit of it roused the both of us."

Another smile? Is he bantering with me?

Taresa offered a grin, accepting his playfulness. Satisfied the tension between them had diminished, Jameson finally did turn, finding his Right Captain and guards behind him, waiting.

Who is this husband of mine? Really?

Taresa's fingers lingered, intertwined with the stretched curls of her hair. Her comb lay suspended in her right hand as she waited, listening.

The echoes grew louder. *He's coming.*

Taresa stood from her nightstand. She glanced around the chamber.

"This is ridiculous," she told herself.

Taresa had done far too much to cater to his whims, and she knew it. Their room spanned the width of the tower, allowing space enough for a dining area, hearth, a canopied bed, and a small nook by the entrance where they could receive guests. In every parcel, she had laid out some token to satisfy him. On the dining table, she had his Marlish attendants arrange his favorite foods and spirits. In the receiving area rested volumes of manuscripts and books from her great uncle's library, with titles in Marlish and Ibian for his reading pleasure. She had his chest brought up so she and her handmaidens could refold and stack his clothing, even adding sprigs of evergreen or mint for a pinch of aroma. The shuttered windows lay open, as the clouds of earlier had dissipated to but a few, giving way to a warm breeze that she allowed to filter through their quarters. Finally, on the bed laid their nightclothes. His, a pair of trousers and a nightshirt, both of fine, downy wool. Hers, a nightgown, which by comparison appeared a thread to his wardrobe.

She nearly hastened to clear some of the embarrassment when Jameson arrived. He came halfway through the door and paused, his hand still on the handle as he looked around. Taresa, caught in the act of covering her tracks, stood with her hands by her sides.

"Welcome," she said.

"For me?" Jameson asked.

"Ummm, why, yes. I suppose." *Stupid, stupid girl. Why is this so hard?* "I wanted to make you feel at home."

"Oh," he replied.

The boy she had glimpsed earlier, small and unsure, returned. He admired the contents strewn about, but in essence, she understood his feigned attempt to avoid looking her in the eye. Because – if she had to be honest with herself – she pretended to do the same.

A boy. A girl. Wed. Yet still, they did not know each other.

We must change that.

"Come."

Taresa marched forward. She grabbed Jameson by the hand, noting how much softer it seemed than the last time she held it weeks before. She pulled him out of their royal chamber to find a Voiceless stationed outside in the hallway.

"No, no," she insisted, her hand gesturing him back. "You stay. We'll be right back."

The silent knight, who would have otherwise followed, stared at his King. Jameson offered a slight shrug as Taresa continued to keep him in tow. To her content, the guard stayed, as did her own guard – a Realeza – posted at the bottom of the stairwell.

"Where are we going?" Jameson asked as they passed through the kitchen.

Taresa had a faint idea, though she voiced it not in case her memory failed her. "You'll see." *As will I.*

Thankfully, her mind served her well, for the game trail she recalled from the days spent playing outside the castle in her youth remained. Its path clear from the light of the full moon, she traversed it, all the while tugging at her husband's hand to ensure he kept up with her. After a while, the touch of his palm in hers felt natural, less foreign. She suspected he felt the same, for the stiffness of his fingers lessened as his grip eased.

The game trail wound its way beneath the leafy canopy of ash and rowan. Her slippers met short grass as the trail thinned and the trees closed in, offering a less dappled glow from above. The prospect of enveloping darkness quickened her heartbeat, as did the thought of that to come.

Resistance shook her from her musings. "Should we... be out here?" Jameson had turned wary on her.

"Why not?"

"The attack on my camp and the castle."

She hesitated herself at the mention. No. She dismissed their vulnerability.

"It will be fine. Only the guards saw us leave. And the game trail is little known, except to some of the castle servants and the nearby shepherds."

"Well, if you want to –"

"Yes," she insisted. For they needed this.

The path twisted from under the moonshade toward a small plateau, which overlooked the gentle slope of a hillock. *Yes*, she told herself, *this is it.*

In childhood, the outlook had offered her and her sisters the perfect vista of the countryside below. Rolling fields of every crop imaginable spread before them in those days, as the waning reach of the Century War allowed farmers to return to their lands to grow once again. Her great uncle, Omarr Garsea, encouraged the peasants of his dukedom to plant variety rather than focus on one staple, so as to provide for the range of tastes the coming peacetime would cultivate. In response, alongside fields of wheat and barley rose vineyards and orchards. Even nonedibles and spice crops arose, such a lavender, tarragon, and mustard tress. The result became a cornucopia of hues at harvest time, though the season for such brilliance had yet to arrive.

No matter. For with the night came a welcome benefit: solitude.

Just out of reach of the shade, summer clover spread the width of the plateau. Taresa led Jameson there. She sat first, glad to discover the nightly dew had not settled yet.

Her husband, as though a sheep seeing pasture for the first time, looked to and fro as he knelt beside her.

"Your uncle, pardon, great uncle, sends his regards."

"I'm glad."

"He said while he was surprised by our excursion, he understands the need for us – the newly minted King and Queen – to escape Arinn for a spell. He felt there were too many eyes on us in the city. And that's why your uncle agreed with your father's suggestion that we step away from public life, given the tragedy in my camp and at the castle. He went on to say some time to ourselves will serve the Throne well, make our subjects forget the tragedy only to embrace our union upon our return. He even went so far as to suggest we put on a display of sorts when we go back to Arinn, perhaps a jousting match or a parade of some sort –"

"Would you mind if we didn't speak about royal affairs? Just for one night?"

"Oh," Jameson paused, realizing his folly. "Of course, my dear."

An awkward silence settled between them for a bit. Taresa smoothed out the folds of her dress. Jameson shifted to sit on his rear, bending his knees before resting his arms on them.

"This, this is nice," Jameson commented.

"Isn't it?"

He continued to scan their surroundings. Taresa did the same for a bit before considering what to do next.

"Taresa –"

"James –"

"Sorry. Go ahead."

With her hands in her lap, she fiddled with the folds of her dress. "The night... of our wedding."

"I remember."

"We didn't..."

"No."

"Nor since."

"I know."

He reached out to take her hand. *He trembles*. "I, I don't ... there was much that happened. Horrible things I saw at that burnt camp. And I don't remember as much as I should. So please, forgive me if I ask about events I *should* know."

"Like what?"

"In our chamber? Did we kiss?"

"We did."

"And then?"

"You undid the straps of my nightgown. You laid on top of me. We almost, say, sealed our union."

Jameson looked away. His head turned quickly, but in the flash of an instant, he appeared... *Jealous? Of what?*

"And for you?" she pried. "What was the night of our wedding like?"

Jameson, his gaze still away from her, paused to dwell on her query. "It was as though... I wasn't there. Like I was some guest at your wedding, so it felt as the night unfolded. I watched you come down the aisle from among the pews. I saw you say the vows before Mar and the High Bishop. At the ballroom, I gazed upon you as you danced." He turned. Moonlight coalesced in his eyes, encapsulated by tears yet to fall. "I have never seen a bride, nor anything, so lovely."

"And later?"

"The same. I was a man apart. Not fully present, not quite there. Then the fire beyond the walls raged. And I was gone, scared, for the dream of our wedding had passed."

Taresa wrapped her other hand over his. "Nothing has passed. All we've been since we were wed is ours: your pain and worries, my frustrations and sorrows, along with our dreams and hopes, and all that will come. We will face the realm of all futures, in this life and the next, together."

A tear streaked down his left cheek. "We will? Us. Just us?"

"Only you and me."

He leaned in with a force that threw her back. Awkwardly, she landed on her back. Instinctively, she opened her mouth to scream.

Her cry stifled, his lips encased hers, wanting. Desiring. Consuming.

Then, also without warning, he withdrew.

"I'm, I'm sorry." Jameson propped himself on his hands, concern awash on his face as he stared down at Taresa. For her part, she remained down. "Are you well?"

Stunned was more like it. However, she had also found the object of her search.

The boy and the man. Compassion with passion. Vulnerability paired with strength. How could one man be all that plus more? She knew not the answer to such a question. Or any questions. Nor did she want to know anything else save for the man before her.

She leaned on her elbow to wrap her hand behind his head. She pulled him close, her lips finding his again. Then again. For a third time, followed by a fourth.

She reclined on the ground, the spread of clover serving as a bed to her and her husband. As they kissed, she undid the buttons of his doublet and the strings of his shirt. He unlaced her corset and all the ties of her dress.

However slow or fast they went, eventually, her hands found his bare torso. Then his back.

Above, the remnants of the day's clouds dissipated, allowing the stars to join the moon. Taresa admired the canvas of the night, its brilliance unveiled. At last.

Chapter 10

"An abomination to Mar, is it not?" Low Bishop Jervis of Har-Kin Kensley sputtered before his coughing cut off his line. "Tis... something... we should pull down."

Dawkin sat atop his destrier, smirking as the bishop continued to hack. In actuality, he liked the runestones. To him, they spoke of a forgotten past, harboring secrets and mysteries he hoped to one day discover through scholarship. They also served as an annoyance to the more conservative factions of the kingdom, a perk that provided Dawkin a bit of joy.

"Your Grace," called a paviser who stood before the runestone. "Methinks you should see this."

The Low Bishop rolled his eyes though obliged nonetheless, withdrawing his head from the open window of his carriage so the attendant could open it for him. A large gentleman with hooves for feet, he still waited for two attendants to take his hands to escort him down the stepstool and onto the soft ground of the field road.

Dawkin, seeing an opportunity to stretch his legs – again – dismounted. He strode in the shadow of the clergyman, careful to keep his distance as His Grace hawked into his handkerchief. The attendant to his right offered him a fresh cloth while the unfortunate one to his left accepted the spent one. Dawkin, feeling sorry for both, shook his head.

Jervis rounded the runestone to where the paviser waited. He nodded to the base of the obelisk once the Low Bishop came to his side. "I almost missed it, til me waterskin slipped from my hands and fell. Then I saw it."

Dawkin peered between the Low Bishop and the servant to his right to glimpse the point of interest: carved into the stone, beneath the ancient text, were words of a more familiar language.

Tosilian.

A layer of plaster coated the inscription, filling its grooves almost to the point of hiding the engraving altogether. Dawkin had seen other such attempts to cover up the graffiti of Kin Foleppi, markings their spies and invaders had left in the waning decade of the Century War, a desperate effort to terrorize the countryside with signs of their presence. Notwithstanding the fact few Marlish could read the foreign script, the foxes of Afari always left an unmistakable cipher of their ever-constant threat: a broken sword. Not the outline of a fox, complete with tale and head, as most would expect. Such a symbol would have been too prominent for the cunning Foleppi. So instead, they chose a sign prophesying the peacefall to come.

In days past, the countryfolk always alerted their barons and bishops upon discovering a new inscription. Most gawked and pointed at first before taking measures to protect themselves, such as fashioning new arms or increasing night patrols. Despite considering the markings to contain evil spells, the neighboring townspeople were primarily credited with plastering over the engravings, even as rumors persisted of faeries coming in the night to carry out the task.

"Like I said," Jervis said, his coughing fit paused, "an abomination."

"I... have a confession..." the paviser started, turning his gaze downward in shame.

"Out with it, boy."

"I, I touched it."

"What?!" The Low Bishop released his handkerchief.

"Forgive me, Your Grace. I don't know what came over me."

"Why, you need to be cleansed. Immediately!" He pointed to the servant at his left. "Fetch me a vial of holy water from my carriage."

"Your Grace, I think you should know –"

"Yes?"

"Tis fresh."

"Fresh?"

"The clay, covering the words in stone. It hasn't dried."

The Low Bishop, whose mood had only worsened with each mile spent in his coach, darkened further. "Are you certain?"

"I am. Tis soft."

"Then dark magic stalks these woods. Spirits filled in those engravings, and why they waited so long to do so with this stone, no mortal can say. But as it's been years since the Century War has passed, that means the incantations you discovered befouled this land for years and years after their original writing."

"They did," the paviser turned pale. "What will become of me?"

"I can't say, my son. But you must be cleansed, through and through. My meager stash of holy water will not do you justice." The Low Bishop sighed, composing himself as a magistrate does when handing down a death sentence. "You are relieved of your service as my escort."

"No –"

"Follow my carriage at least twenty paces back. Touch nothing. Not your fellow countrymen. Not my carriage. Not *me*. When we reach the abbey, the brethren there will take you in to begin the prayers and blessings necessary for the salvation of your eternal soul."

The color drained from the paviser. He managed a nod. Dawkin thought the whole spiritual ruse to be a bit much. Still, he held his tongue out of respect.

Jervis turned, making haste back to his carriage. The paviser followed, albeit at a slower clip. Dawkin held back, staring at the inscription to consider the other, more sinister possibility.

The plaster wasn't fresh because faeries and sprites forgot to cover it over. It hadn't dried because the etching was *new*.

But how?

With each opportunity granted to Dawkin, he inquired. It proved not hard, as the runestone and its recent inscription had turned into the talk of the countryside. When they paused to water their horses, a gathering of mothers and maidens by the stream washing their clothes spoke to Dawkin of changelings who stalked the forest and had carved the inscription as a warning to children. At the highway tavern, where the bishop stopped to gorge himself on mutton and ale, the barkeep said remnants of Kin Foleppi's spies still roamed the nearby hills and even boasted of killing one only weeks before. The shepherd up the road herding his flock claimed the same as did two sawyers who journeyed on the road with them for a spell. Everyone Dawkin encountered spun a yarn about the runestone, which only obscured the truth rather than bring it to light.

By the time they reached the abbey later that afternoon, Dawkin never wanted to hear of the blasted stone ever again. He tired of the tall tales of the countryfolk, preferring the promise of a quaint room – quiet, unadorned – among the quarters of the silent brethren. Only when they arrived, the brethren presented themselves as anything but tranquil. The mass of monks scurried about the courtyard while the Low Bishop's carriage pulled to a stop, with not one pausing to attend to His Excellency.

"Uh-hmmm!" Jervis grunted as a brother nearly hurried past.

The monk, as if seeing the carriage for the first time, straightened and bowed. "Low Bishop Jervis! You're here!"

"A condition of which I am well aware," the Low Bishop snorted. "What I can't figure out is why you and your brethren have left me to rot in this wretched wagon."

"I beg your forgiveness a thousand times, Your Excellency! It's only that –"

"What could possibly be so important as to keep the man who oversees a diocese waiting?!"

"I, I –"

"Out with it, man!"

"We have a, a situation, Your Excellency. A fever has overtaken the nearby town. Or an illness. A rash of ailments, maybe."

"Well, which is it?"

"We don't know, Low Bishop Jervis. Several

townspeople have come to us with a range of conditions; we can't pinpoint their cause. A few claim to have fevers, though, in my opinion, they feel only a bit warmer than normal. A group complains of aches in their hands and knees, which they say came about suddenly. Still more talk of headaches which won't go away ever since they... touched that stone."

"Ughhh..." Dawkin muttered, loud enough to draw a glare from the Low Bishop. Dawkin tightened his lips upon receiving the look, remembering his ruse as Sir Evenon, an additional escort to His Excellency.

"Well," Jervis resumed, directing his attention to the monk once more, "I can see my services came not a moment too soon."

"They did, Your Excellency! I'll be glad to escort you to the chapel where –"

"Patience, my boy, patience. I need to receive counsel from the Mar Himself, as the ailments you speak of are no small matter."

"Of course, Your Excellency."

"First, help me down from this death trap on wheels. Then, show me to your finest room, where I shall require a hot bath and one of your monks to iron out my garb, which has been sitting wrinkled in my chests for far too long. After, I will send word to your cooks of my meal. The proper sustenance is necessary for me to delve into the teachings of Our Lord, given by His scripture and through His direct conversation with me, of course."

Low Bishop Jervis threw open his door, signaling to all his intention to move. The carriage's attendants descended upon him, with their many hands and a step stool ready.

The brother sped to the transport as he motioned his brethren nearby to come to his aid. A small force soon enveloped the Low Bishop, lending him the air of superiority he so desperately craved.

Dawkin, glad to be rid of the idiots, dismounted. As part of his ploy, his job on this expedition involved securing the perimeter of every inn and host residence where they stopped. He took it semi-seriously at first since the bishop's family of Har-Kin Kensley still held one of the largest fortunes on the island. The threat to His Excellency could not be dismissed on the highways and secluded roads that lay just outside the city. However, this far out in the country – where the most significant threat to His Excellency became the boredom of listening to superstitions– Dawkin's resolve to guard an overfed, pompous figurehead of the Church waned.

He walked his courser to the stables, proceeding to unsaddle the horse and ensure it had fresh grain and water. With the task complete, he left his mare in peace as he slung his saddlebag over his shoulder to wander through the grounds surrounding the abbey. From what he had gathered before their arrival, the abbey abutted a stream opposite the town of Meadowdale, which offered rich pastures dotted with trees of oak and walnut. There Dawkin hoped to find seclusion away from the hysteria.

His encounter with the stream dashed his hopes. For there - watering their flocks, scrubbing their laundry, or just chattering without a chore – seemed to have gathered every loose-tongued mouth in the diocese. Elders with one tooth and as much sense jabbered with the middle-aged and youth of the town, their wild theories on the runestone and its supposed curses overlapping each other. Fevers that sprung with a touch or rashes erupting at the first thought of worry stood out as some of the observations shared among the groupings. Such professions glanced off of Dawkin's ears, as he had no interest in the ravings of an uneducated populace. For as a prince, he had witnessed the many supposed "plagues" which had gripped the island over the years. Ordinary folk would come from near and far to lament in Court of how their children and elders suffered from curses or of how pestilence would spread to the whole island. His father, as King, would console his subjects with promises of serious consideration. He would dispatch messengers and mages to the far-flung edges of the kingdom to investigate the rumors of plague. Only one in ten tales had merit, with all the rest stemming from hysteria which cost the country too much in wasted time, funds, and other spent resources.

Perhaps sensing his disdain for their gossip, a few sturdy glares feel his way. Dawkin shrugged them off, chalking the looks up to the wayward traditions of country folk. He continued on his path past the bulk of the townsfolk, their conversations fading as he made his way to the south fork of the stream. His demeanor lightened as more of the meadowlands opened before him, with only scant signs of commoners going about their daily tasks. Patches of short grass beneath awnings of sturdy, leafy limbs offered the perfect reading spots. He settled on a particular location, one with a spread of dry rivergrass under the shade of an aged black oak. He laid his saddlebag on the trunk of the tree, where he knelt to withdraw its contents. Aside from a wool blanket, he pulled out two volumes: the first aptly titled *Conversational Ibian* by Sir Roger of Har-Kin Caunter, the second being his most recent gift, *The Adumbration*.

He leaned against the tree base, ready to settle into *Conversational Ibian* just as he intended. But as the volume sat unopened across his lap, he could not help his eyes from gravitating to the cover of *The Adumbration*. The title, its embossed scarlet letters having faded with age, called to him. He knew the appeal stemmed not from the contents within. Rather, the source of the gift churned his intrigue, causing him to toss his text on Ibian aside to grab the sacred book instead.

With each holy passage he read, the memory of the maiden at Sir Nygell's clouded his focus. *The Angel of Fate visits the houses of the living, her sword delivering the wicked to their graves.* Those green eyes, soft in hue, more pleasing in sight than any blade of grass. *The masses fall by the hundreds.* Curled locks of gold fall. The treasures they hold prove endless. *Once of soil, the ground becomes ash; the sky is a robber baron of the day as smoke chokes out the light. In the chaos, the justice of Mar reigns. Through death, his word is delivered.* Oh, and perfect skin. Without a blemish. Truly, just perfect.

Dawkin shook his head. *Idiot!* One encounter, though fateful, with a dashing maiden had turned his once steady mind into a bloody mess. He tossed the book aside before running his fingers through his hair. *This isn't me. I can't let myself go on like this. Daydreaming as if a virgin bridegroom on his wedding day. Pffff! What lunacy. My thoughts run amok. My judgment clouds. It even has me hallucinating as though that dear maiden was right before –*

“Am I seeing this?!” Dawkin could not help but ponder aloud. For coming up the path on the far side of the stream strolled a maiden, not unlike Lady Cora.

She carried a wicker basket leaning against her hip. Anyone would have mistaken her for a commoner doing her daily wash in a forest green dress and white apron. She certainly looked the part, with her golden hair wrapped in burgundy cloth and the faintest hints of dust and dirt upon her cheeks. Remarkably, the smudges upon her skin and her homely attire only accented her beauty rather than obscure it. Without any intent towards presentation, her radiance shone like sunlight peeking through the leaves of a wind-tossed branch.

She shifted her wicker basket from one hip to her other. Dawkin blinked. Her image, in an instant, changed. She shimmered. Her likeness vibrated as though the air before her had broiled, sending up fiery tendrils. The waves blurred her form, not unlike a ripple upsetting a reflection. Dawkin blinked again, and with that, the anomaly before her vanished.

Dear Mar, I’m going mad with obsession.

If the lady had noticed the momentary oddity before her, she did not show it. She pressed onward, traversing the path through the grass to scout the best place to wash. Since the shore directly across from Dawkin appeared to be of soft mud without solid support, the lady almost strode past him.

Emerging from the shade, Dawkin hopped to his feet into the sun. “Aye! Lady Cora!”

The maiden, startled, froze on the path. She shot a look at Dawkin the way a deer spots a wolf.

Dawkin, having not considered his next move, offered a slight wave.

"You?" the lady offered. "How, what, what brings you here?"

Immediately, Dawkin fumbled with how to respond. "I, uh, I'm here…" *Oh, hell, tell her the truth. A bit of it, at least.* "I'm here as an act of service, guarding the Low Bishop Jervis."

"Really?" she smiled. "Odd, I think I would have noticed a bishop in our presence."

"He's resting at the abbey. Since he's in good hands and we're off the road, I took a moment to gather myself."

"Good for you." Lady Cora made a move to continue on her way.

"And you? What brings you to this area?"

"Me? Why, I'm home."

"I never took you for a resident of Meadowdale."

"Why not?"

"I, I only assumed you lived in the city."

"Why?"

Why, indeed? Lady Cora stared back at Dawkin with those green eyes, as entrancing as any set of emeralds or precious stones he had ever seen. So intense, so full of curiosity and wonder. Had that question come from any other, especially a commoner, Dawkin would have felt slighted. Though not with her. There stood no formality in her queries because pretense had no place; she did want to know his motivations, his reason for being.

"It's that we don't get many girls from the country in the city — none whatsoever like you. You, you carried yourself so well in Sir Nygell's. You had a sense of comfort, of grace, as if you had known the bookstore – all of Arcporte, really – your whole life. Such a trait, such boldness, is not all so common with transplants to the city."

"You are too kind. Your boldness is of note too."

"Mine?"

"How you meandered past the washers up there," she nodded back toward the crowded stream banks. "Passing so close to the locals as they discuss their affairs is considered rude in these here parts. I'm surprised you didn't receive a tongue-lashing."

Dawkin tilted his head, smiling.

"Did I say something amusing?" Cora asked.

"So you *did* notice me? Earlier? The look of shock I saw before when I called to you on the path, 'twas a ruse, wasn't it?"

Like a girl caught swiping a hot cross bun before her elders had helped themselves, the Lady blushed. "Oh, fine, so you caught me. Yes, I saw you from afar. A fool with his head held high, a stranger strolling amongst us lowly commoners, unaware of our local customs. I suspected you to be the same man I met at Sir Nygell's, but from such a distance, I couldn't be certain."

"Well, now you are."

"'Tis true."

"I, I should help you with that." He bent his head toward her wicker basket of laundry.

"Oh, don't bother. It isn't heavy."

"Please, I insist."

"As you wish."

Dawkin balanced himself on three stones leading across the stream to end up on the other side.

"Oh," she uttered.

"What?"

"Your eyes... Up close, they're different than before."

All of a sudden self-conscious, Dawkin averted his gaze. *Of all the times!* He had remembered to apply the potion the day before but had failed to administer another dose since then.

"I don't mind it," Cora added, trying to make eye contact. "My father, his eyes look different too, according to the light. Light green in the morning and soft brown towards the evening. Tis how the light hits them is all it is."

Dawkin, his worry fading, looked back to her. "Aye. My eyes suffer the same affliction, I suppose."

Soon he carried Cora's basket as she strolled beside him, answering his casual questions on Meadowdale. Their quaint conversation took them further away from the village on a path that curved with the water until they came to a bend, which revealed a grove of a dozen dwarf elms along with a slight anomaly.

A runestone.

Dawkin paused. Cora took a few steps beyond him before stopping to pivot and face him. "What's the matter?"

"Nothing. Just I didn't expect to come across another marker such as this?"

"Another?"

"On the way into town, the Low Bishop's caravan I was guarding stopped to inspect a runestone by the road."

"Aye, I know of it. Been there a while. Like this one. So why are you so surprised?"

Her questions, those eyes... Mar save me. "The runestone had been covered over in one section with fresh plaster.

That meant the inscription must have been new. Or newly discovered. It gave all of us pause. Such exploits haven't happened since the last decades of the Century War, when Kin Foleppi roamed these parts, terrorizing the countryside."

"And that is your fear? The foxes have returned?"

"Aye."

"Well, that's ridiculous."

"Is it?!" he blurted.

Cora's eyes widened. Dawkin bowed his head. "Forgive me for the outburst, my Lady."

"You are concerned, truly? Aren't you?"

Mar, this woman pulls at me. "I am. People dismiss such worries, saying the threats we notice – or I, more specifically – are imagined, the products of an over-active mind. But look at all that has happened in the past year or two. We've been assaulted on our northern shores, betrayed by our nobles, and in the end, we lost a king. Our kin."

The last note hit Dawkin particularly hard. He tensed, careful not to let any sign of his regal history escape, via a twitch or a blink. However, something even slighter must have shown, for Lady Cora's demeanor evolved, becoming somber and dutiful.

"You and your family were close to the King, weren't you?"

"Yes."

"I'm so sorry, Sir Jameson."

Damn, she still remembers me for the wrong moniker. "Actually, it's... Never mind. Thank you."

Cora offered a grin as she took the wicker basket from Dawkin. Laying it down beside one of the elms, she withdrew a clothesline, which she proceeded to tie to two opposing trees. "Your family," she began. "I suspect they were thrilled by the news of the royal wedding."

Dawkin hurried to help Cora, taking the other end of the line to tie to the nearest tree. "Why, yes. The announcement of the royals finally joining brought joy to our manor."

"If you don't mind me asking, were any in your family invited?"

"My whole family received invitations. My brothers went while I stayed to attend to my kin's affairs."

"Isn't that always the case? The best of us manage to miss out while all the rest have their fun."

"Aye. There seems to be the trend."

"So, guarding the Low Bishop counts as your kin's affairs?"

Aye, she's a crafty one. "The King requested my assistance. Well, his Steward, Baron Artus. With so many barons and their sons across the sea for the royal wedding, good help is hard to find."

"You're right. Without your assistance, I would have to hang my wash all by myself."

"Was that a jab, my Lady?"

"Mayhaps."

Dawkin, finishing his tie, cocked his head toward the runestone. "Tis an unusual place to wash."

"It's quiet. Solitary. Nobody dares to pass here if they don't have to –"

"Except you."

"I know the stories."

"Yet you don't abide by them."

"I view the stones as... companions. They sit here to rest. It isn't their fault some idiots chose to carve in them."

"You're peculiar."

"Thank you."

"And it doesn't bother you in the least these same innocent stones carry incantations, spells from demons or faeries no one can decrypt?"

Lady Cora threw back her head to laugh. "Really? No one can understand them, yet they *swear* they're bad for us."

"You mock superstitions? A moment ago, you chastised me for disgracing such local customs, even though you laugh at other ones right now."

"I pointed out your lordly air, which led you to cast a shadow across us meager town folk. I merely look at the facts, consider, and judge for myself the dangers, or lack thereof."

"So... What have you noticed about this stone?" Dawkin edged closer to the runestone. Across its face, the inscriptions dated to antiquity. Remarkably, it had survived unscarred from Kin Foleppi.

"It's shorter than many of its brethren, perhaps because it lies near a stream and not by a road or town center."

"Then why here? By a game trail bordering a stream. I mean, it would make sense if it stood by a ford or shallow pass of a major tributary. But a random stream?"

"Tis why it's special. A couple could have erected it here to commemorate a first kiss or the place of their union."

"Weddings occur in churches, my Lady."

"I wasn't talking about *that* kind of union."

At that, Dawkin blushed.

"Anyway," Cora continued. "The fact the stone stands aside means it was meant for the eyes of a few, not many. Like a book tucked away in a tall shelf, one you seek out because you – and only you – know of the treasures within. Or a cavern under a castle, one which holds chambers and recesses where children can laugh and play without the watchful eyes of their parents. Or a field with the joys of spring, blossoming with wildflowers for the first time, one you are privileged to enjoy before any other."

The girl within the lady shone forth as she shared her childlike visions. From another, Dawkin would have found such proclamations immature. Yet from her, they only added to her soulful qualities, drawing Dawkin ever closer to her presence.

In the distance, a bell tolled. Dawkin, straightening, looked toward the abbey. "Why does it ring?"

"Calm yourself. Tis only the mid-supper bell. It lets the locals know not to disturb the abbey, for after the quick meal, prayers follow."

"Oh."

"Do you need to check on His Excellency?"

"I suppose," Dawkin grumbled. In truth, leaving the Low Bishop's side for so long would be considered an offense to the church, one for which he would receive a reprimand if Jervis were even sober enough to notice his absence.

"Well, then, I suppose this is goodbye."

"Goodbye?!"

"I leave for Seafall next morning."

"But, I thought your har-kin hailed from here?"

"Yes, the bulk of us Glennish hail from here and other

nearby hamlets of the Foothills. But my har-kin married into other families all over, if you recall from our first encounter. My cousin wed into a har-kin last year, one residing just outside Seafall. She's expected to give birth any week now, so I'm going to help her with the babe."

"Oh, I see," Dawkin said, his heart sinking.

"Come now, Sir Jameson. Once a few weeks have passed, and my cousin has bonded with the babe, I can stop by Sir Nygell's again on my way back. By chance, we may even run into each other again there."

I don't want to leave such an encounter to fate. Damn the chances of my life. "What if I were to accompany you?"

"You have your duties here, with the Low Bishop –"

"Forget that pompous drunkard."

Lady Cora raised a brow. Dawkin found himself – again – tilting his head in another apologetic bow.

"My concern for your safety outweighs my other responsibilities," he offered as a show of remorse.

"That is too kind of you, my lord. You needn't worry, though. My uncle's apprentice has agreed to accompany me through the countryside so that I won't be traveling alone."

"An apprentice? Is he skilled in the art of war? Does he know how to ride? Or quarrel? How to fight three bandits at once?"

"Do you?"

"Why... Yes."

"Quite the accomplished reader-and-swordsmen, aren't you?"

"I suppose."

Lady Cora considered. "As you wish. My uncle won't be

too pleased with me traveling with a stranger, so you'll need to meet him first to garner his approval. He has a smith shop on the edge of town. It has a chimney of limestone leaning slightly north, so you can't miss it. Be there at dawn."

Dawkin's heart fluttered. "It will be my honor."

"What will you say to the Bishop?"

"I will say I need to excuse myself to attend to a family friend, to honor a word given."

"A little bit of a fib, wouldn't you say?"

"Tis true. If we are to head to Seafall, we will need to stop for a spell first."

"Why Sir Jameson, you presume too much."

"Not for *that*. I owe a favor to a friend. More of a brother, truthfully."

"Very well, but if you try... All I'm saying is I'm well-armed at all times." Lady Cora patted her left thigh, holding her hand there long enough for the folds of her dress to bend to the outline of the sheath beneath. One long enough for a dirk.

"My Lady," Dawkin bowed.

"Go on, now. The Low Bishop is waiting. I'll see you at dawn." The bell tolled once more as if to serve as a reminder.

"And leave you with laundry still to do. What kind of gentleman would I be?"

"Like all the rest, I reckon."

"You deserve a man apart." Dawkin picked up a soiled shirt and proceeded to the stream. Lady Cora followed with a garment of her own. She placed a jar of soap powder, a mix of fat and ash, between them.

"Enjoy."

Dawkin smirked, digging his hand into the pasty substance. The viscous mixture stuck to his fingers. He slathered a wad onto the shirt collar, which stood out as the area of the garment most in need of cleansing.

What am I doing? he asked himself. He had washed clothes once as punishment for horseplay resulting in a bowl of spilt stew on a baron. Such a memory stemmed from an incident eons ago, and the lesson of what needed to be done hadn't stuck. Nonetheless, Dawkin went on with what he thought was the proper way to wash. Absent of Lady Cora's corrections, he continued, with the Lady concentrated on her clothing.

So this is what I've been reduced to? A monarch washing the clothes of a commoner? All while my brothers lay with a Queen and feast with the Court. Dawkin mused. Nearly twenty years of courtly upbringing – almost two decades of princehood – had prepared him for a life absent of such labors, the mediocrity of peasant life. He sometimes wondered if he could survive the repetitiveness of the common folk, most of whom would no doubt live and die without ever leaving their hometown, let alone the island. No castles for them. Nor company of barons. Nor courts. Absent of any legacy.

He submerged the soap-covered shirt into the stream. Rubbing it beneath the water, he watched the grime and soap disperse into the current.

Their lives seem so empty. Meanwhile, I have the chance at legacy. So why... Do I feel this longing? This void? This weight I cannot shake?

He glanced at Lady Cora. A woman unknown, beneath

him in rank yet unlike any other.

Could she... Could it be?

The possibility hung in the air before Dawkin, with nary a word to encapsulate his thoughts. Instead, it stood apart as an emotion — an overwhelming one.

He smiled.

“What?” Lady Cora asked, noting his expression.

“Nothing,” he answered, lying a bit. *And everything.*

Chapter 11

This must be what Mar feels like. Well, not always. But at least part of the time.

Ely, suspended by the wild blue around him, glided in a circle. Beyond the clear waters stretched a canvas of midnight blue, which served as a backdrop to everything else in between. Schools of tiny, silver fish glimmered and darkened as they swam in then out of shafts of light. Forests of kelp pulsed with every shift of the moving sea, be it due to a nearby current or the pull of the tide. Beyond their reach, the silhouettes of larger inhabitants lurked, whether hillocks of submerged rock or creatures Ely had no desire to encounter up close. None of those stood out as daunting as the ship's keel, which Ely likened to the long, wooden fin of a beast housing both the unthreatening and boring.

The burning within Ely's lungs stifled his musings. *Oh, well. I suppose I should emerge, lest a knight tries to jump in and save me.*

Ely popped through the surface, spitting a surge of water into the air.

"Why in the bloody hell did you do that?!"

Ely grinned. Only Sir Everitt would have the guts to address him in such a manner out in the open. Even Symon – for all his posturing as his big brother – would not dare break character as one of his guards. Not with so many witnesses.

Ely treaded in a semi-circle to face the ship. The galleon towered above, such that Ely had to crane his neck to view the main deck. There, leaning over the railing, fumed his Right Captain. His face had a beet-colored tinge to it, a hue that only furthered the curl of Ely's lips.

"Well?!" Everitt demanded. "What were you thinking?"

"I just wanted to take a dip, my good man," Ely cried, spitting out seawater in between words.

"A swim? Unannounced? While you're still clothed?"

"I live for the moment. Not for telling someone what I want to do, then undressing, then waiting through you or the First Mate trying to talk me out of it, then the moment."

"Aargh!" Everitt threw his hands into the air as he pushed himself off the railing. "You're impossible sometimes. You know that, James?"

"I agree," Ely said as he extended himself toward the dinghy making its way toward him. "Sometimes."

He tilted his head to the quarterdeck, where he spotted his two brothers. Gerry, stricken by a blend of shock and embarrassment, had turned as white as a bleached sheet. Symon, his skin color somewhere between Everitt's and Gerry's, managed to stay composed save for his brow. Lowered, it cast an ever so slightly longer shadow over his eyes. 'Twas enough to convey his mood, the one Ely knew he'd pay for later.

With Ely aboard the rowboat, the sailors made their way back to the ship. The attendants waiting above deck had all manner of towels and coats ready, along with a cup of tea, fresh boots, and an assortment of bread and cheeses. *Honestly, this lot acts as though I've never been wet before,* Ely thought, taking a towel. *How ridiculous? Such fools!*

Though the cheese does look good.

As Ely stole a bite of hard white cheese, his Right Captain waited with arms crossed.

"Glad to see your appetite is intact, as is His Majesty," Everitt said.

"Well, of course. Even a quick swim builds quite the hunger."

"Quite."

"Well?" Ely asked, looking before the wide-eyed audience. "You had your spot of fun. I gave you a show. Get on with it. The shore lies there. We mustn't keep our host waiting."

Befuddled but always at command, the audience of seafarers and servants dispersed, each going about their duties. The clank of the emergency anchor rose to Ely's ears, as did the commands of Captain Danyll of Har-Kin Masste and his First Mate Josson of Har-Kin Hawley, neither of which appeared amused by his latest antics.

As the Captain pulled Sir Everitt aside for a word, Symon and Gerry came to Ely. Despite their attempts at a sly approach, their false beards, prosthetic noses, and dyed hair did little to conceal their concern.

"You wretched little weasel –" Symon started.

"Nah-uh-uh," Ely chastised with a wag of his finger. "Someone might hear you admonishing your King."

"Not one of them will care of my words when they see me bashing your head into the planks."

"Brothers..." Gerry whispered, looking around. "Careful." Despite their caution, several servants still moved about them within range of hearing.

Symon, his senses somewhat returning to him, nodded

to the railing. He, Ely, and Gerry sauntered over to the side of the ship, allowing themselves a tad more privacy.

"Seriously," Symon resumed through clenched teeth. "What was that?"

"A swim," Ely replied.

"*Why?*"

"I –" Ely stopped himself, as though having never considered the question.

"Well?"

"I needed to get away from the lot of you."

"That's your excuse?"

"Do you need another?"

"Ely," Gerry stepped up, anxious. "Are you well? You aren't..."

"I'm not mad, well, not in that sense." Ely glared at Gerry. "Still, you're far from my good graces after the stunt *you* pulled."

"You shouldn't... That's an entirely separate matter."

"Is it?"

"Damn it, yes! You would have –"

"Gerry, Ely, we've said our piece." Symon glanced over his shoulder, making sure their conversation remained unheard. "We've all seemed to have erred these days, as we're all on edge."

"Quite right," Ely said, crossing his arms as he shot daggers at Gerry once more.

"If this were Terran, I'd have the two of you fight it out, so you could release all this tension between you."

"What good would that do? I'd win, then I'd feel guilty for beating the poor runt." *Or maybe I wouldn't,* Ely considered. The sting of Gerry having Taresa first proved unbearable enough. When Symon broke the news to Ely during Gerry's ascension, Ely had thrown a pitcher against the wall before upending a table and tearing through every ware in the room. Symon stood by through it all, allowing Ely his moment of rage. The mania spent, even Ely believed himself under control until Gerry returned, only to reveal he had sent Taresa off to her aunt's palace in upper Ibia, under the guise she needed a period of rest and comfort after the blast at Castle Arinn.

'Twas a ruse, Ely reaffirmed in his mind's eye. *The little man wants Taresa all for himself. He had her first and now desires to keep her from the rest of us. Even Symon fumed after Gerry told of how he shipped off Taresa.*

Ely had moved to strike Gerry upon finding out, but Symon and a few Voiceless intercepted him. Though the mania of the moment passed, Ely could not help but harbor the desire to retaliate against Gerry someway somehow. The opportunity to punish Gerry had yet to come, so in the meantime, the mania returned. And with it, the overwhelming urge to escape.

Hence, the unplanned dip in the ocean.

As Ely dried himself, he took note of the flurry of activity. A sailor in the crow's nest shouted in Ibian, quickening the pace of the sailors on the ratlines and deck.

"What's the matter?" Ely asked.

Symon did not answer. Instead, he climbed the stairs to the forecastle deck. Gerry followed, leaving Ely by himself.

He rolled his eyes, trailing after them. "You know, I am the King here."

Coming upon the next level, he discovered the source of all the fuss. Ahead, the dark silhouette of the coastline had come into view again, with its ridges and hills. At one point, a flash of sunlight blinked not once but twice, then in three short bursts.

"What the bloody hell is that?"

"Maritime code. Mirrors on clear days, small pyres during fog and at night, larger beacons with white smoke in a call to arms." Symon, befuddled, turned to Ely. "You should know this. Our tutors drilled this into us at Father's command."

"Oh, well, those matters proved to be so boring, with no relevance to the real world."

"Until now."

"Fair enough."

"Quiet," Gerry said, his lips mouthing words. "I'm reading it. It says... Oh."

"Well?"

Gerry pivoted, aghast. "His Grace is dead."

Ely expected the reputed Grand Duke of Seylonna to be a man of immeasurable wealth if any of the rumors possessed a shred of truth. What he saw didn't *disprove* the notion, for fortifications and great halls – no matter their extravagance or austerity – required a massive amount of capital.

Still, the chamber could have done with a touch of charm. Perhaps some tapestries. Another window wouldn't have hurt.

Ely's focus returned as the new duchess of the manor approached. "Your Majesty."

"Yes?" he said low, so as not to disturb the other court members who had come ashore with him. The lot of them bowed their heads in prayer or looked solemnly on the casket and the corpse within, paying their respects to the Grand Duke.

"He waits."

Ely nodded, then glanced at Sir Everitt. The Right Captain fell in beside him, careful not to let his footfalls echo too loudly.

The pair followed Her Grace, Grand Duchess Gloria of Kin Amadorr. Newly minted in her title, she took to her new duties as the lady of the manor in stride, offering a curt nod to those servants she passed, all of who preceded it with genuflection. Though her father-by-marriage had just died, Ely believed her cold manner to be a bit much –

Until she led them to the master bedchamber.

The door creaked open, alerting the whores within. One bare woman lay atop a pile of pillows strewn before the hearth. Another, also naked though on her back, stretched her bronze-toned body across the receiving couch. Two others, in loose skirts and nothing else, stirred on the bed.

Only the recent Grand Duke seemed undisturbed by their entrance, even as his wife strode through the room to the desk at which he sat.

"Your guests," Grand Duchess Gloria announced.

"I saw them at the door," Ienello replied. His voice, deep and robust, contradicted his slender frame capped by narrow shoulders. Nonetheless, his lack of commanding presence did not diminish the confidence within, as his cold eyes looked up to his wife. "You need not have bothered coming all this way to declare it."

Her Grace tightened her lips but offered nothing more. She turned, the soles of her heels sending up echoes louder than those of when she entered.

Ely, still a ways from the Grand Duke, glanced at Sir Everitt. The knight, as bewildered as ever, turned to His Grace as he cleared his throat.

"If you require a drink, there is sweet wine at the table," uttered Ienello as he wrote, his quill wavering. "Mayhaps some water left if the maidens haven't finished it."

"Maidens?" Ely questioned.

The quill stopped. The Grand Duke lifted his brow, though his head remained tilted downward. "Pardon, Your Majesty. I misspoke. These women are harlots, through and through." The quill resumed meandering. "You may help yourself to one or two if you'd like. Your Right Captain too, if he fancies the company."

"Thank you, no," Ely responded, moving toward Ienello as Everitt trailed behind, keeping a respectable distance to allow the two some space. Ely strode right up to the table, setting his hands down as he leaned over to inspect the strewn parchments. Ienello, if bothered, did not show it.

"Interesting..." Ely muttered.

"If you're looking to garner my attention, you needn't feign curiosity."

"Your Grace, your wife fetched me and brought me here, I assume at your request. You could have easily let me linger in the foyer, allowing me the privilege to mourn your father. Or you could have set out a modest meal for our welcome, or sent us out on a hunt, or offered us any variety of distractions befitting a royal and his attendants. Yet you didn't. Why?"

The quill stopped. After setting it down in the inkwell, Ienello laid his elbows on the table, joining his fingertips together as he looked up to the King.

"Hmmm," he began, "As smart as you are, it's a wonder why you earned the moniker 'King Fool.'"

"My enemies try their hands at a sense of humor, I suppose."

"How's your Ibian, Your Majesty?"

"Passable."

"It will have to do, then. I have something to show you." Ienello rose and stepped from around the table, glancing at the Right Captain. Ely, now able to see the Grand Duke in full, straightened. In standing, Ienello exposed himself as more diminutive than Ely or Everitt could have assumed. Sure, he compensated, using all the trappings Gerry had tried in his adolescent years. Lifts in his boots, for sure, along with padding on his shoulders and within the sleeves of his shirt. His pants had been stuffed too, to give the impression of thighs and calves of toned muscle. While the Grand Duke's garb – and the padding inside – stood out as well-tailored, such efforts to conceal his thin, short frame could only do so much. His face remained gaunt, the sockets of his eyes hollow, set between ears too large. All those features populated a head sitting atop a spear shaft for a neck. All that, along with a stature no more than five and a half feet tall, made for a man most unlikely to rule a dukedom.

"If I may be so bold," Ienello said, oblivious to Ely's silent judgment, "I must ask your guard to stay behind."

Upon hearing the request, Sir Everitt moved his hand to the pommel of his sheathed sword. Knowing Everitt intended the gesture as much for him as for the Grand Duke, Ely held out his hand.

"Pardon my Right Captain, Your Grace. He puts service

before manners."

"As well he should. I mean no distrust... It's only..."

"Yes?"

"You'll see."

Ely studied his face. So perfect had the man's indifference been before, displaying a blend of confidence and boldness. Indeed, much of that persisted, though now there showed a slight crack.

"Sir Everitt," Ely said, "Stay here. I command it."

Everitt's hands fell to his side as he frowned. "As you wish."

The Grand Duke gestured to the side door. Ely fell to his side as Ienello led the way.

The exit opened to a spiral stairwell. Again, Ienello encouraged Ely to go ahead. The darkness beyond the lit sconces prompted Ely to hesitate. Pushing through his doubt, he descended the stairs, with Ienello close behind.

The stairs took them to an underground lair, a chamber cut through damp rock, ending at a shut door at the far end. Ienello, seeing the apprehension in his guest, now went ahead to the locked oaken giant. He pulled a ring of keys from the pocket of his doublet, finding a long bronze one which he inserted. At the click of the lock within, a whimper on the other side stirred.

Ely – drawing his hidden dagger – came up behind Ienello. He dug the tip of the blade against the back of the man's doublet, right where a kidney lay within.

"Explain yourself," Ely demanded.

The Grand Duke turned around carefully. The color had drained from his face while his stern expression remained, revealing a truth Ely had missed earlier.

He fights through the fear.

Ely withdrew his dagger from Inenello, though he still held it out toward him.

"Go on. Open it."

His eyes never leaving Ely, Ienello unlocked the door. He wedged it open. The whimper from within echoed more prominently, accompanied by sniffling. The dim room hid the source of the faint sounds.

"Allow me to reach in. For a candle."

Ely nodded, allowing it. The Grand Duke groped his right hand along the wall bordering the door frame until he found a candle on a concealed perch. Taking it to a nearby sconce, he lit it, then made his way into the room, where Ely followed.

Ienello illuminated the sconces inside, allowing Ely a view of the prisoner in the corner.

The scene put Ely's fear at ease, if only because he had imagined a nightmare far worse. Rather than a dank, dark cell, Ely found a cellar resplendent with shelves of books and trinkets from the world over. And while there resided a captive, he appeared well-cared for, with only a single iron chain at his foot. Within his reach lay a cot, blanket, and pillow for his comfort. A half-eaten wedge of cheese stood amongst a few crumbs on a plate, while a carafe of wine remained for his thirst.

Ienello strode up to the captive, who withdrew in a timid manner. Ely wondered if indeed this had been the man's first experience with incarceration.

"Do you recognize this man?" Ienello asked, waving the candle in Ely's direction.

"No," replied the feeble soul in Ibian, who cowered.

Ienello frowned, then threw the prisoner his key ring. "Go."

The man fumbled with the ring before finding the key to unlock his shackle. He scurried away from the Grand Duke, wary of keeping his distance from the King as he ran from the cellar.

"I assume that stunt put your concerns to rest."

"Hardly. These are the borderlands you chanced upon here, King Jameson. Our neighbors are Belgardians and Tosilians to the east and what remains of the Colinnese loyalists to the north. Spies are as rampant here as rats to a galleon. You could have hired that man as an agent through any of the intermediaries operating in the area. Still, some men in this part of the country continue to do their own dirty work, so it remained worth my effort to ask the prisoner, poor in strength though he was."

"And why that man, in particular?"

"He spoke Marlish. Without an accent."

Ely's eyes widened. Yes, he had sought information from several commoners and even a few nobility while back in Arinn. Using his connections – royal, unscrupulous, and all in between – he had sent word across Ibia and even beyond for intelligence on the castle blast and other affairs which may concern him. But to his knowledge, none of those on the continent were Marlish. All had been foreign correspondents whose allegiance to coin outweighed their honor to country. How had a Marlish man made his way this far south? To be mistaken for a spy? And for what side? Ely could not answer any of the questions which raced through his mind with any degree of certainty.

"Don't be so shocked," Ienello said, noting the surprise

on Ely's face. "We see visitors to these parts from all over the world, even from farther north than your precious Marland. Our ports teem with citizens from the world over. The fact that he spoke Marlish did not single him out to my men."

"Then what did?"

"He asked too many questions."

Ienello attempted a grin. No sooner had his lips curled though when his hands began to tremble. The shaking moved through his arms to his shoulders and the remainder of him. So violently did he convulse he dropped to one knee. Ely dashed to his side to catch the Grand Duke before he fell.

"The... potion..." Ienello managed to point to a rack of vials on the shelf across from him.

Ely sprang to the rack, which contained five glass containers of equal size. All but one stood empty. The one to the far right had a deep violet liquid, which appeared viscous in consistency. Ely grabbed the vial and ran it to Ienello, who immediately uncorked it and drank its contents with vigor.

Moments later, the shuddering ceased. Ienello, his breath slowing to a regular cadence, moved to rise. Ely made an effort to assist, but the Grand Duke waved him off.

"I'm fine, really," Ienello insisted.

"You seemed prepared." Ely nodded to the rack of vials.

"'Tis a common affliction of Kin Amadorr," the Grand Duke confirmed, making his way to the nearest end table to pour himself some wine. "Many in my family have known convulsions — mostly distant cousins. My grandfather on my father's side shook, though it skipped my father and brothers. Thankfully for my kin's reputation – or really, my father's – I was last in line to inherit his dukedom, as three brothers came before me." Ienello motioned to the far wall, drawing Ely's attention to the portraits of three vibrant young men. "Despite my father's plans, Mar had destinies of tragedy in store."

"I'm sorry for your losses, especially the most recent."

The Grand Duke waved his hand again, dismissing the notion of grief. "Kin Amadorr is no stranger to difficulties. Being this far from the rest of Ibia hardens the soul, makes us impervious to what others perceive as pain. Or so I heard from my father growing up. When he spoke to me."

"His Grace reminds me of my father."

"An honorable man, I hear. Though whatever their similarities, you have no idea of how *His Grace* treated me. You never had to contend with brothers, let alone ones who bested you just by living."

Nobleman, you have no idea. "Aye, I suppose."

"My father spoke well of him, the late King Audemar; Mar rest his soul. Not an easy feat to earn my father's respect. Impossible, I would go so far as to say. Hell, many say my father went to Colinne more as a favor to the Marlish king than to our own. Imagine that? Though it makes sense. King Felix never did much like the borderlands, let alone the barons and dukes charged with keeping the peace out here. We staff the towers and beacons with men we feed and train. We collect the tariffs and duties which Castle Arinn levies, leaving us hated by our kind. And for what? All so that some foreign dignitaries can come here and act on behalf of His Majesty, doing the bloody tasks he so despises in the guise of a diplomatic mission. No offense."

Ely smirked. He had thought the trip a fool's errand, believing Gerry had chosen this destination to put as much distance a between Taresa and Ely during Ely's turn as king. *Well, even I can be wrong.*

"Your Grace," Ely started, his curiosity growing. "The spy in your... well, captivity. Is that all you wanted to show me? Hardly seems a sight worth the trouble."

"Ah, yes. Well, you have me there." Staring down at the glass in his hand, which remained half full, Ienello paused. Then in one gulp, he emptied it. "You see, in my father's last days, he was hardly the Grand Duke he had once been. For the past few years, I've been taking on more and more of his affairs. With word of your impending visit, I knew I would have you as an audience for much of your stay, minus a courtesy meal you were to have with him and any public displays for the commoners.

"In the days and hours leading up to this moment, I had a plan. Our rendezvous would start in a situation not unlike this, with me having offered you some wine," he said, pouring the rest of the carafe into his goblet. "You and I would then go on to drink, share our stories, reminiscence. I'd guide you through the labyrinth my father and his forefathers carved out under this castle, one which leads to all manner of passages and tunnels.

"My brothers played down there when we were young. They never invited me, though. They told me the ghosts of times long ago would come out and haunt me, as though some specter could be worse than the tortures they unleased. Lice and fleas in my bed. Ground peppercorns in my porridge. Vinegar in my water. The list goes on.

"I digress. The fact of the matter is, I'm the least of the Amadorr's who should be here, the last of my kin. You, on the other hand, grew up the sole heir to your land, the favorite of your father, a man who relished in pride and comfort his whole life. That is when it occurred to me, only days ago, that all my planning to connect with you, to bond, to strike an accord as minds sharing the same... Hell, I don't know. Perspective? Upbringing? Anything common to men who grow up to become acquaintances, then friends.

"Alas, my father died. So it occurred to me, 'Maybe we could bond over that.'"

Ienello eyed Ely. In turn, the King shifted his weight, remaining standing, albeit uncomfortably. He had never had the stomach for mourning in general circumstances, what with the weeping, the sniffling, and all the bloody prayers. This, however, stood out as something entirely different. A loss without the sadness, a man of title with no formality, no sense of tradition. Cold in his regard, as though he felt no connection to the one he had just lost.

Before Ely could break the silence, Ienello continued. "In that supposed fellowship, I would come to conclude I could trust you. Me, a noble ignored his whole life, having such an audience with a king, so much so he'd grow to respect me, and I him. What say you? Can I count you as my sole friend?"

Ely paused, his mouth agape, his eyes widening ever so slightly. He uttered no words in response. For he didn't need them. His façade answered on behalf of his lost voice.

Whatever image Ienello had attempted stood stripped of nobility, exposing the frightened, unremarkable child beneath. His lifts. His padding. His cold, stark remarks in the beginning. His feigned tone reeking of emotional distance. All of it fraudulent. An act. A poor one at that. Of a man who had spent his entire life trying to compensate for everything he knew himself not to be.

"Honesty." The Grand Duke took a deep breath, inhaling the entirety of Ely's pity. He then downed the rest of his wine. He released his glass, which fell to the floor and shattered. Ignoring the pieces, Ienello stepped over to the far left corner. He removed a series of books from the middle shelf to reveal a false panel, which he removed. Reaching into the hidden recess, he withdrew four scrolls and a worn journal. He plopped the materials before Ely before leaving.

"We shouldn't be leaving under these conditions, Your Majesty."

Ely glanced at Everitt. "Stating the obvious, are we?"

"Tis my duty." The Right Captain looked up at the castle of Kin Amadorr. Perched on the cliffside overlooking the sliver of the port, it hung awkwardly over them as though a giant teetering on the edge of a small pool. "We couldn't spare just one night ashore?"

"Not from what I discovered."

"Which is?"

"Believe me when I say we haven't time to spare."

Everitt, relenting to the King's urgency, saluted. He strode off, directing his attention to the staff as they moved to pack the ship they had just unloaded. He passed two unsuspecting figures – a guard and a lead attendant – who immediately fell to Ely's side once Everitt climbed the plank to the ship.

"Symon," Gerry pleaded as he and Symon approached.

"Remember your manners."

"Brother," Symon started, beside himself. "Explain."

"I don't know that I can."

"This is no time for sly talk."

"I speak the truth." Ely glanced around to verify every eye in their midst was preoccupied. "The chest by my right leg. I laid the first scroll unfurled on top, to address what I knew would be your curiosity."

Ely looked away, pretending to survey the progress of the packing. Symon and Gerry knelt before the chest, unclasping the lock to peek inside. They held the lid ajar, with each a hand to it, as they read.

Symon looked up to Ely first. "My Ibian... It's not what I would like."

"But you understood enough?"

"A map of Marland, of this detail, in a foreign land... Yes, I suppose I can relate to your concern."

"My concern?" Ely glanced at Gerry, who had paused in his reading to direct his attention to them. "And you? What say you?"

"I gathered a number of names as well as Marland. Plus, those of kin and various har-kins –"

"You bloody idiots. Didn't you read the numbers?"

"I did," Gerry confirmed.

"So did I," Symon added. "Though the Ibian words by them... They lost me."

"They're dates, are they not?" Ely asked.

"Yes," Gerry answered.

"And?"

Symon and Gerry stared at each other.

"Whoever made this map," Ely said, perturbed at

having to spell out his conclusion, "took care to note specific shipments to the island. Small loads, certainly not everything a ship could carry, only those deliveries of importance — some perhaps small enough to fit inside a crate or two. There are several. On the second month, twelfth day, vials of pollen and dried petals from various Afarian plants. No doubt the ingredients to make poisons. Then on the twentieth of the third month, nitrates and explosive powders. Fourth day, fourth month, clays, potions, and creams used to alter one's appearance, for any range of disguises..."

Ely paused as a pair of porters approached to lay a heavy chest on the dock before taking their leave. He waited until he felt confident they stood out of range of listening to them.

"I get it," Symon replied, noting the porters as well.

"Spies..." Gerry gathered.

"We can only hope to assume," Ely said.

"Hmmm..." Symon mused.

"Deep thoughts?"

"This map is manifest of sorts, of a ship or ships visiting ports in Marland. So why is it this far south, away from whatever vessel could have carried it? It doesn't make sense."

"Sense went the way of Colinne, brother. Though if I had to guess, I would say the receipt of that map and the other parchments His Grace provided had everything to do with the agent he detained, along with whatever network that spy is a part of.

"You know of father's stories from the Century War. Intelligence of enemy movements and plans seldom fit together. The best we can determine is from bits and fragments, from sources who would sooner lie and cheat their own mothers than reveal the truth of their purpose. Faith and instinct must be weighed whenever judging what is at hand. Analysis of rumors and half-truths is as far from an exact science as one can be. A fool has as much a chance of guessing the right of it all as any sage or prophet."

"So that spy, the one who we can *guess* had this map to begin with," Gerry began, "the Grand Duke let him go just like that?"

Ely sighed. "Yes."

"And you did nothing to stop him?"

"I hardly knew who the man was, let alone why he was being held captive until His Grace spelled it out for me. Well, the little he divulged, at least. Hell, I still haven't the notion of what Ienello – nor his late father – have done all these years to gather such intelligence. Pfff, it's all just one big bloody mess."

"On that, we can agree," Symon stated, rising. "If you have doubts about the source and truth of this intelligence, then why leave now? In a manner that attracts so much attention?"

"I... Well, you'll need to read the rest of the documents in detail to understand. Not to mention... It's..."

"Yes?"

Ely paced, looking down the dock and up to the ship beside them.

"Ely?" Gerry prodded, his paranoia mounting.

"That Grand Duke, there's something *off* about him," Ely said.

"He recently lost his father," Symon reaffirmed.

"It's not only that. He was different. In the head. Unlike any other I've met... except..." *Me*, Ely told himself. *'Twas too much like me.*

"Very well," Symon replied. "We'll discuss this further onboard. If what strikes you as off has any merit to it, there may be spies in our midst now, who no doubt have noted us three gathered far too long together."

"Right," Ely said, noting his Right Captain returning. "We'll reconvene after we've left port."

His brothers dispersed as Sir Everitt marched up to him. "Is everything well, Your Majesty? You look dour."

How kind of you to notice. "Tis nothing. I only grow anxious as we have yet to leave. See to it, my good man. I'll be in my cabin resting until after we've left."

A roar roused Ely from the comfort of his sleep. He blinked, his sight seemingly betraying him.

A bright green light flashed through openings left by the partially drawn curtains. Then red. Followed by blue and yellow.

"Is a bloody rainbow dying?" he asked no one, shaking his head at the ridiculous notion. Though as he awoke, coming to his senses, he considered he might actually be right. For the colors burst with increasing intensity, their brightness growing to the point of nearly blinding Ely. He shielded his eyes with one arm as he raised the other instinctively to his ear. It did no good, for the *cracks* accompanying each turn of brilliance permeated the cabin, ricocheting off the walls to assault his ears.

Somehow, through the explosions of hues and noise, he picked up on the steady thud of bone on wood.

Knocking.

Ely squinted as he swung around toward the door, both his hands now covering his ears. He stepped cautiously, suddenly aware the ship swayed more vigorously than when they set off from port.

As he approached the door, which he had locked from within, two familiar voices spilled forth from the other side.

“I told you to get him out of there!”

“He won’t answer! I’ve been knocking for minutes.”

“Stand aside.” The thick birch door reverberated under Symon’s pounding, which dwarfed their sibling's frantic yet hollow attempts.

“All right, you hounds! Quit it!” Ely yelled as he turned the key to unlock the door. “You’ll alert Sir Everitt and half the guards.”

Symon barged in, shoving Ely aside as he took to the cabin to inspect it. He barely took three steps before a short orange burst lit up the chamber, forcing him to a halt. Ely shied away from the radiance as well, along with Gerry, who remained in his shadow.

“What the bloody hell –” Ely started.

“Hell is right.” Symon blinked as his retinas adjusted to the dusk.

Ely, his sight also compromised, groped until he found a lantern. With a spark from his flint, a flame came to life, a mere ant of fire compared to the monster which had just raged beyond.

The subtle glow revealed his brothers still in disguise. Though now they appeared more disheveled, undoubtedly from the recent chaos.

“Shouldn’t my Right Captain be here by now?” Ely asked, perturbed.

"He commanded me and two other Voiceless to stand watch while he convened with Captain Danyll and First Mate Josson."

"What? Does he think he can issue directives in a time such as this? Without my consent? That entitled bastard." Ely tore open the door to find two Voiceless waiting beyond the eave of the short hall. He broke into a trot. "Make way for your King –"

The air erupted again. Instantly, the cooling sensation of the sea air transformed into a thick, insufferable wall of heat. Ely – caught in mid-breath – gagged. The Voiceless, though shocked themselves, rushed to his aid. As they held him by the arms, his brothers fell beside him.

Ely, keeled over, struggled to straighten. He pushed away from the helping hands as the brightness dissipated and the air chilled once more. Shuffling onto the main deck, he scanned the sea and sky. Above, wisps of cirrus clouds held visual remnants of the blasts, the residual pigments fading into the stretched gray threads with each passing moment. The faint light cast from their heights shone on churned waters as white-capped swells rocked the galleon.

The steady motion accompanied by the gentle glow would have been considered a romantic sight in any other circumstance.

Unfortunately, the mood – as reflected by the faces of all on board – betrayed the beauty.

Terror had supplanted every emotion and thought they had harbored before the eruptions as their collective faces reflected parted lips and widened eyes. Like children confronting death for the first time, their hope drained from them. However scared they remained, the lot of them stared east toward the beast which had riled their souls.

With the shore about half a mile off their starboard side, Ely could make out the ridgeline of Seylonna. Much of it stood as it did earlier that day, save for the billowing nebula and the two flaming streaks beneath it. The orange and white lines rippled, intimidating even from Ely's vantage point. At once, he knew the raging fire at the water's edge to be the port. Though too far away to identify any of the particulars, he surmised the blaze had consumed the vast wooden planks of the wharf, along with its many buildings and perhaps even the anchored ships. But the second line, which stood parallel to the lower one, what could that...

"Oh, Mar..." he uttered.

The castle. The behemoth of stone. *Of stone!* Somehow it had flattened and burned, seemingly as quickly as pine needles to a cookfire.

Again, a blast erupted. The passengers and crew cowered, this time before a violet spark that sent debris up and outward. Boulders – some having once supported the castle's foundation – rose to far heights as though feathers caught in a draft.

As Ely blinked in the wake of the latest flash, Everitt appeared. "Your Majesty! You shouldn't be on deck. I gave specific orders –"

"Everitt," Ely cut him off, "what happened?"

"We heard it first. A rumbling coming from the cliffs, from whence we set sail. No sooner did I turn when I saw the first blast of color. Blue. Dark blue coming from the castle, with a wave of heat. The whole western wall of it collapsed, sending boulders tumbling to the port below. Then the port itself blew, burnt orange that time. On and on it went, one explosion then another, like they were trying to compete with each other, every one that followed bigger and brighter and hotter than the last."

"Very well, I see," Ely said, his hands extended in an effort to calm his Right Captain. Sir Everitt, sweat having beaded from his recollection, panted. Ely shared a look with Symon then Gerry, who expressed their silent concerns. Never before had their personal guard ever displayed such panic, however subdued it may have appeared to others.

"James," Everitt resumed, slowing his breath. "What say you of this?"

Ely perked, not accustomed to his Right Captain prompting him while under his guard. He became acutely aware of the eyes upon him, including those of his brothers.

Damn it, he thought. *If only I were in the sea* now.

Very well. They want the King. Give them the King.

"Our ally, the Grand Duke of Seylonna, is dead. He follows his father, also recently deceased, to Mar's Castle. As do the souls of those who perished in the fire, the names and likes of which we will never know.

"We do neither their Graces nor the subjects of their dukedom nor Mar Himself no honor by whimpering before a threat like beaten dogs. When the time comes, we will mourn their kind separately in a church like good Marlish folk.

"That time is later. Now, we ready ourselves for the fight ahead. Oh, and believe me, there will be a fight. For like the fire that claimed our brethren in Arinn, this too will not go unanswered. Inquiries will be made. Our suspects will be questioned and tortured. Those responsible will fall to the blade or the noose. Rest assured, we will see justice. We will have the final word. Our answer to fire and treachery will be steel and brutality. Vengeance will come!"

His final words hung on echoes of quietude, so alarming as to render Ely self-conscious his speech had failed in its intent. Then Everitt, ever dutifully, thumped his right fist over his heart. The sentiment spread as sailor and servant alike mirrored the Right Captain's lead until others felt so emboldened as to offer a cheer. One, then three, followed by many more exponentially. Soon the whole galleon clamored with applause and cheers.

Another blast ruptured the northwest wall corner of the castle, sending that section down the cliff into the smoldering remnants of the port. Those on the galleon paused to view the chaos once more. Ely stepped up to the railing to meet the wave of heat in its wake.

"Sir Everitt," Ely called, still emboldened by the reception to his speech.

"Sire."

"As I said, this threat needs to be answered. Sail north away from here as I mull our next course of action. And make haste. Whether up close or afar, we need to show this *enemy* their activities will not spoil our hopes."

"At once, My King." Sir Everitt glanced over his shoulder. The Captain and First Mate had come within earshot of Ely as he spoke, so they heard everything. With raised fingers and eyes focused, the men barked orders. The deck scurried in response to the flurry of directives from the ship's officers. Sir Everitt took his place between the two, so when they had finished, he conferred with them the details of their route.

Ely, satisfied with the alacrity of those on board, leaned over the railing to survey the coastline. The thin lines of fires still raged but seemed less intimating, even as the head of smoke above them had grown, as had the bright streaks of lights stretching even higher.

"A rousing speech," Symon commended, though the smirk on his disguised face said otherwise.

"Too much?" Ely asked.

"I liked it," Gerry squeaked, coming alongside Ely opposite of Symon. In the scramble which had become of the deck, no one bothered to query the costumed brothers on their duties.

"Thank you, Geremias," Ely replied.

"A little dark towards the end," Symon offered. "Even Father would have raised a brow at your choice of words."

"Didn't he always? Besides, the words matter not. The fact I said them sober, without slurring, would have been more than enough to make him proud."

"I suppose. Either way, it did the trick."

"I appreciate your enthusiasm for my methods of ruling, brother. Your petty focus on my prose aside, I meant what I said. This needs to be answered."

"Agreed."

"Was *that*..." Gerry started, nodding to the burning ruins of Castle Seylonna. "Was it meant for us?"

Ely and Symon fought the urge to glance at each other, though both failed.

"What say you?" Gerry prodded.

Ely considered. "Well, we can assume one of two things I gather: either the perpetrator planned for us to be there tonight and set in motion a trap to destroy us and the Grand Duke."

"Or?" Gerry asked, wary of the possible answer.

"The enemy watched us leave and then went about with the destruction. So we could see it. And hear the message: We're being watched. Stalked. Hunted. Two attacks that nearly missed us is no mere coincidence."

"It's a pattern," Symon concluded.

"So how do we answer it, as you would say?" Gerry replied.

"Tonight," Ely replied. "After Everitt has done his shift and set the night guards outside my cabin, we need to convene a truth session, then discuss next steps in our..." *What? Set of orders? The battle to come? Or worse? War?*

"Our what?" Gerry inquired.

"Our duty," Ely finished. For what more could he say?

"We also need to send word to Dawkin," Symon added.

"Yes, and expeditiously," Ely replied, nodding to the coastline. "Before he hears from other sources."

Following Ely's gaze, his brothers watched as a light came to life further up shore, solitary and controlled. A beacon. Its blaze burned orange, absent of any other hue or tone, casting up a column of white smoke. In response, another beacon ignited. A third, one to the far left, later replied. Like ghosts, wisps from their flames rose, foreshadowing to come.

"No mirrors, huh?" Ely quipped.

"What does –" Gerry began.

"Not now," Symon urged Gerry. "Let us disperse." He fought the urge to look at Ely. "You should walk the deck for a bit. Encourage the men. Look regal."

"Aye," Ely said. *For 'tis my role.*

With his brothers slipping away to resume the responsibilities of their personas, Ely strode the length of the ship. He slid his hands behind him as he consulted Sir Everitt before moving in for a word with Captain Danyll, then First Mate Josson. With each, he posed a few questions, suppressing his usual personality in favor of listening to counsel, just as he had been taught. He nodded when appropriate, then moved on, marching with his head held high. Attendants bowed as he passed. He looked on, tilting his head every so often.

Having made his rounds, Ely finally arrived at the quarter deck. By then, the ship had moved further offshore, though the coastline remained in sight. The blasts still consumed what little remained of the castle and port of Seylonna, though their subsequent eruptions turned smaller, their waves of heat and noise barely drawing the crew's attention. As a result, the streaked tones of the cirrus clouds held less of their colors. The bright reds, blues, and other hues of earlier now gave way to pastels, not unlike those of a sunset. At once majestic and depressing, Ely studied the whole of everything before him.

From within, the surge rose. His familiar companion, the depression he had come to expect in such moments. Having already suffered his mania from earlier, this imposing episode proved not a surprise.

Though what happened next was.

Without any thought or will, the feeling dissipated.

Ely, shocked, looked around. The ship went on as it had. Along with her crew. And the sea. Nothing in his environment had changed.

Only him.

So unfamiliar, Ely considered. Not entirely happy nor disappointed either, he knew not how to interpret the disappearance of the beast he expected. *I should be overcome with worry. Anxiety. I ought to be consumed with myself. But I'm not. Why?*

The image of His Grace, Ienello of Kin Amadorr, overwhelmed his mind. His stooped shoulders. His diminutive stature. His slight frame. His physical presence, however unimpressive, was a beauty compared to the monstrosity within him. A soul wracked by depression. Always longing, in need of constant validation, seeking the pleasure of drink and flesh to mask the pain.

Disgusting. Unwanted.

And a far cry from the man I want to be.

Such determination had quashed the onset this once, Ely knew. Would it always? Perhaps not, though this one time, Ely would relish in the victory. Not of conquering some enemy beyond his borders, who he had yet to meet. Nor of winning over the hearts and minds of his subjects, which he knew would not last. This stood apart as a conquest of one he had fought his whole life.

Himself.

He breathed in the salt air, which carried hints of smoke from the shore. Beneath, the sea churned in the wake of the rudder.

You damn fool, he thought. *Of all the times you should jump, you choose now to find yourself.*

"Bloody hell," Ely said, turning his back to the sea as he leaned against the railing. "Mar sure does have a wicked sense of humor."

Chapter 12

Clank, clank, clank, clank.

So on and on the racket went. Dawkin glanced at the column of young men, some younger than he, as they trudged in the opposite direction. His gaze fell upon their feet. Bare, caked in sweat and dirt, they bore shackles linked to the same shared chain which bound them all.

Who would choose such torment?

Atonement for sins was one thing. But this? Such agony, self-inflicted, for guilt? Dawkin shook his head at the notion. He could not compute the idea of a persistent feeling, much less a damning one, capable of leading to one's demise, however traumatic the inciting event may have been.

His mind turned to Ely. *That poor chap. 'Tis must be how he feels at times. Captive to his mania.*

"Judgment is expected."

Dawkin looked to his left. Lady Cora rode at a pace matching his own, one which had slowed as they had come within sight of the Lost Souls. Though neither had reason to fear the restrained, unarmed, and repentant mass, she avoided eye contact nonetheless. With her head lowered, her cowl nearly obscured the whole of her head, save for the skin of her right cheekbone and a single golden curl peeking out from the wool border. Enchanting.

"Judgment?" Dawkin queried, many moments after she had spoken.

"By onlookers who forget their manners." She twisted her head toward him, flashing a wry grin.

"I, I had no intention of staring."

"They want the attention, though in their humility, they would never admit it. Rumor has it they added the chains because their travels no longer garnered the admonishing looks their predecessors received. People had simply grown accustomed to seeing pious men in dingy robes. So they started to ignore them. Such apathy to outward repentance could not stand, so they added the chains for... shall we say..." Cora paused, the word she grasped for suddenly out of her mind's reach.

"Theatrics?" Dawkin ventured.

"Not the phrase I would have chosen, but it'll do."

"So, I do them a service by staring."

"Hardly my point."

"'Tis mine."

"You're imprudent."

Dawkin smirked. *Damn, this is fun.* His mood lifted. He sat taller in his saddle as the entourage – and their song of shame – passed.

For the past two days, their journey to Seafall had been uneventful. On the morning of their departure, Dawkin had obligatorily met with Cora's uncle to convince him of his intentions. Namely, that he would protect his niece and abstain from behaving as anything less than a gentleman. To Dawkin's surprise, the man seemed indifferent to him. He offered no protest to the proposed escort, nor did he question Dawkin about his family history or profession. The lack of interest disappointed Dawkin somewhat, for he had spent the previous night concocting an elaborate backstory tied to his alter ego.

In truth, Lady Cora had not expressed concern over his intentions either. She seemed far too lax over the past few days, hardly the demeanor expectant of a woman – or man – riding the highways. At taverns, she did not press him for her own room, though he always made arrangements for such. Around the cookfire, she did not flinch when he used his hatchet to split wood or draw his knife to cut meat. She acted as if she had known Dawkin his whole life, a sense of familiarity he found both puzzling and refreshing.

"Odd," Cora mused. "How such men can travel the countryside and not be caught up in its wonder."

"You certainly appreciate it."

"Ever since I was a child." Cora brushed one of her golden curls behind her ear. "There is a peace to these woods, a sensibility lost by being in the city or even in a village. Many people forget their connection to the natural world. The only place where the spirit can be free. Except maybe when reading a good book."

"Is that why you visit Sir Nygell's?"

"In part. Reading strengthens my mind while also putting it at ease. Sometimes my passion for nature and the written word converge, which is when I grow most excited to lose myself in that bookstore."

"Oh, pray tell. Any volumes of interest you can recommend?"

"Hmmm, for a fellow traveler and bookworm such as yourself? A delightful question. I'll need time to consider it."

Dawkin smirked, waiting for Cora to offer him a title he had yet to read.

“Have you ever considered being one?” Cora asked instead.

“What?”

“A Lost Soul.”

“Me? Why ever would you ask?”

“No reason, other than we just passed a lot of those fellows.”

“Still, I mean, your question seems so –”

“You think yourself above them?’

“I didn’t say that.”

“So you’ve never looked at the whole of your sins and thought, ‘I need to atone for this one.’”

“I didn’t say that, either. As for the Lost Souls, I admire their level of faith. Such dedication is admirable. It’s only that...”

“Go on.”

Mar, this woman knows no boundaries. “It’s a waste.”

“Of?”

“Everything. I find the whole notion of atonement a bloody, bloody mess. Consider the average faithful Marlish citizen, who spends his life trying to do what is right. Or hell, consider the whole of humanity for that matter. We strive for good works and strong faith our entire lives, only to be damned by actions and faults which make up a smidge of our time here on earth? Our one percent of errors wipe out the ninety-nine percent of things we do well? As if the blemish defines the enormity of ourselves. Tis a waste, I believe.”

Lady Cora burst into laughter, throwing her head back so that her hood fell back to her shoulders.

“Foolish, I know.”

"On the contrary. Brilliant. I've heard abbots and bishops go on and on about the meaning of Mar's will, including his perspective on sin. They bore me to no end with their references to *The Papyr*, quoting scripture as though they have some understanding of life, which they don't. You, on the other hand, give a refreshing take on an ancient dilemma."

"Which is?"

"How to talk of religion and not put your audience to sleep."

Dawkin smirked. He glanced at Lady Cora, who turned to him simultaneously, so their eyes met. No sooner did he look at her when a golden curl parted from behind her ear to bounce against her left cheek.

Suddenly mindful of his stare, Dawkin turned his head.

Fool, fool, fool. Am I red?

"Are you blushing?" Cora asked.

Damn it to hell. "The long ride has me working up a sweat. Tis all."

"Mm-hmm."

The last utterance made Dawkin even more self-conscious. He clipped his heels into his steed to trot ahead. In response to the gap between them, Cora started to whistle a tune as she gave the reins of her mare a hearty snap to catch up to him.

She needn't ride far, for at the bend of the road, Dawkin paused.

"What? What is it?"

A towering Marlish ash tree split the path before them. Dawkin recognized the fork in the road. But from where?

Right.

He turned to Cora. "Would you mind a detour?"

She replied with a raised brow, though not at all unbecoming to her.

"I have an errand... No, a debt. To an old friend. It won't take long. Plus, we can stretch and rest for a while. In a manner befitting my lady."

"Why, Sir Jameson, you wouldn't be seeking to dishonor me." A smile, as wry as they come, crept onto Cora's lips.

"The thought has never crossed my mind, not even with your present mention," Dawkin replied, proud his face had not reddened as before.

"So it seems. As you wish." Lady Cora looked to the fork before them. "Which way?"

"So, this is what you had in mind with 'a manner befitting...'" Lady Cora coughed, the heavy stench of must overwhelming her.

Not exactly. Dawkin eyed the black mold inhabiting the crack in the stone wall beside him. To say it was a solitary blemish would have been a barefaced lie. Moss crowded those gaps and splits by the windows even though most had been shuttered. Cobwebs claimed every corner they passed as a dour-faced servant decades past her prime, Lady Agnes, led them through the hallway. The flame of her candle served as their guide, moving past the streaks of dappled light peeking in from the poorly thatched roof.

Cora burst into another hacking fit. Agnes halted.

"Are you going to continue on with that racket?" she uttered through her three remaining teeth.

Delightful. Since his youth, she had served Har-Kin Furde. Even back then, she had struck him as a salty thing with all the manners of a backcountry wench. "Are the baron's quarters nearly this astringent?"

"A-what?"

"Oh, for the love of… Just lead us to His Liege."

"That's a where I was taking you, before all the commotion." She twisted to continue on her way, with nary a consideration towards whether they followed her or not.

"This friend of yours, I hope he's worth this drudgery," Cora said.

"He is. And more," Dawkin replied.

"Well, now I have to meet him." The Lady straightened, fighting the urge to hack once more.

Their haggard guide eventually paused atop a stairwell, where a large hall lay with a fireplace at the far end. There, embers smoldered, their center pierced by an iron poker held by the lord of the har-kin. The soft light from the hearth fell all about him and the chair in which he sat, revealing only the silhouetted left side of his profile.

"Me lord, you have guests. This one says he knows you, by way of your son –"

His servant paused as the baron lifted his finger. Though several dozen feet away, Dawkin noted it shook.

The servant motioned to her liege with her candle holder, turning her back on them without awaiting further orders from her master. Dawkin edged closer to the fire as Lady Cora trailed, allowing him the space she felt he needed.

"Baron?" Dawkin ventured. "Baron Ralf. Tis me."

"My boy?"

Dawkin stopped. Baron Ralf turned to lean over the arm of his chair. He searched the whole length of Dawkin, from top to bottom, eagerly seeking to recognize him.

Dear Mar. The hollowness of his soul struck Dawkin, an unholy union bequeathed by age. The innocence of a doe-eyed child coupled with the creased shell of the once-mighty man he knew. Those bear-claws of hands he had believed capable of crushing stone tremored, their motion reverberating up their host to the base of his thick neck. His head had shed the remnants of its mane save for a few strands of gray, wisps like those of the dying coals before him.

"My Lord... Do you know me?"

"My boy?" Ralf repeated. "My son?"

Tarnation, he thinks I'm Everitt –

"Adequin, come closer. Let me have a look at you."

Dawkin froze. He glanced over his shoulder at Cora. Reading him and his concern, she pulled the collar of her cowl closer around her neck, as unsure as Dawkin of how to proceed.

"Adequin, come."

Dawkin obliged. He inched before the hearth, so close the faint heat bathed him. In its warmth, he knelt before the baron. Ralf gently caressed his cheek.

"My son..." A tear cascaded down his cheek. "Tis been so long. An ocean of time. Why?"

"I, I... I have been away, serving my kingdom. In your name, our har-kin's name, Father."

"Right, this war. By Mar, will it ever end? So many good men lost. Like Baron Marvynn. Or even lords like Oweyn, who never seemed the same since he returned. All the rest, though not lost, scatter the continent fighting for the sake of Marland."

"Aye."

"Mayhaps Artus' son can make some headway in Afari, put to rest this longstanding conflict for good. Remind me, have you met the King? Admere?"

"Audemar."

"Yes, you've got the right of it. You know him?"

"Yes. Very well."

"Good, good. His father is a bit stale for my taste though I remember in my younger days... What, what is it?" Baron Ralf paused upon seeing a contained smile twist on Dawkin's lips.

"Nothing, it's nothing," Dawkin said, as the off remark about his grandfather put him at ease.

"Oh, well, as I was saying, I saw King Artus lead many a battle against the odds. So if the young monarch has the capability of his father and the gift of youth, well, I dare say we stand a chance to see the end of this war."

"King Audemar will do well to end it."

"Then lads like you can return to their manors to settle down. Marry. Sire a grandson or two." The old lord winked, satisfied with himself.

Dawkin glanced over his shoulder, not sure if Cora would take the chance to introduce herself. Baron Ralf, noticing his stare, leaned over the arm of his chair to peek into the shadows.

"Oh," he said, picking up on the outline of the lady. "I seem to have spoken a tad late." Ralf turned his attention back to Dawkin. "Is she... you know..."

"I am Lady Cora, my lord," she replied with a curtsy. "It is an honor to meet your acquaintance."

"No, my lady. The honor is mine." Baron Ralf stood from his chair. Dawkin sprang to his feet to help him. Ralf waved him off as he stepped forward to take Cora's hand and offer a gracious peck. "My manor is yours."

"I thank you for your hospitality," Lady Cora replied.

"My boy, where are your manners? Having a beauty like this stand in the dark while we banter? Offer her a chair."

"Yes, sire." Dawkin scanned the room to settle on a stool, which he pulled to place beside the lord's chair. He motioned to the squat seat as Cora took to it. Even in low light, the mischievous grin on her lips did not escape him.

"My Mar, you're as bad as your younger brother," Ralf went on as he settled back into his seat. "Where is Everitt anyway? Probably attacking the chickens again with some makeshift sword."

"I will check on him later," Dawkin assured him.

"So, Lady Cora, please forgive this old man for his memory. 'Tis not what it used to be."

"Pardon?"

"I swear we've met, though, for the life of me, I can't put a finger on when or where. Tell me about your family. What kin claims you?"

"Oh, I'm of Har-Kin –"

"– Mallory," Dawkin interjected. "A distant second cousin of Baron Gale."

"Ah, that old lord is still swimming. Well, then, Marland stands a chance at this war. Gale the Narwhale we used to call him. A true sailor, that one. He could swim all day and emerge from Mar's sea to take a sword and fight."

"With a reputation like that, tis no wonder how Uncle Gale earned his moniker," Cora added.

"Aye, is true. So my lady. Is this visit a prelude to a...

union?"

Lady Cora twisted away, blushing. In truth, Dawkin fought the urge himself.

"Is that a 'yes'?" Ralf inquired.

"No. I fear we are not there, quite yet," Dawkin replied.

"Pity. Some grandsons would do this manor some good."

"Tell me, sire. How long has your har-kin inhabited these lands?" Cora asked.

"Oh, well, it seems my son hasn't told you much. Shame on him. This castle once served as the outpost to the western edge of our lands. It started out merely as a tower before more defenses were raised during the beginning of the Century War. Though how quickly it has come to disrepair baffles me." Baron Ralf scanned the ceiling before his gaze searched out the rest of the hall.

"Well, it is a fine manor, indeed." Lady Cora looked around before her eyes settled on Ralf and Dawkin. "I hardly knew such luxury. My distant relation to the Mallorys – along with the stubbornness of my father – meant we roamed the countryside as he looked for work."

"Oh? What did he do?"

"A tad of everything, though his particular specialty was as a sawyer."

"Ah! Good man. The kin of Baron Gale has always produced fine woodmen, including sawyers. An honorable profession."

"One could say that."

"Adequin," Ralf leaned in towards Dawkin. "Do you remember when we hosted those builders at Manor Furde?"

"Oh, well, I don't seem to recall –"

“Yes, yes, you do. King Artus issued a decree asking the kins and har-kins to build the latest round of ships. A squall had claimed much of the fleet moored across the sea, so he needed replacements in haste. A manor to the north… Oh, what’s their name? Anyway, they sent a host of carpenters along with their apprentices down the road to answer the call. Trouble was the lot brought their families with them. How one har-kin could claim so many builders still baffles me. Still, they came from that nobleland to aid the King, so when they crossed into our estate, I took them in. They stayed all but a night and a day. ‘Twas long enough for this one though…”

Ralf winked at Dawkin, a twinkle settling in his eyes. Dawkin waited.

“You remember,” Ralf insisted.

“What?”

“The girl.”

“Girl?”

“One with light hair, though not as golden as that of our present company.”

“I –”

“Oh, you shouldn’t play coy, my son. It happened so long ago this one hardly has reason to be jealous.”

“I agree. Whatever transpired occurred ages ago.”

“Still, you should remember. The love-struck looks you two shared across the banquet hall. The whispers she shared with her sisters. Then how the riding master caught you two in the stables.”

“I think, I mean…”

“You *have* to remember your first woman. Honestly, how could you forget, Adequin…”

Baron Ralf paused. He stared at Dawkin, his eyes suddenly empty, as though the soul behind them had been robbed and replaced by stone.

Dawkin froze. He knew what the look meant.

Realization.

He had seen it before, in his grandfather. Mostly in his right mind, Artus nonetheless suffered rare bouts of memory lapse, which transported him back to the reality of a time long since passed. In his case, such episodes lasted but minutes. Yet upon their end, Artus would find himself returned to the present, with the shock of the occurrence causing a mixture of panic and embarrassment. In one instance, Dawkin stood present to witness the brief transition between forgetfulness and consciousness.

A pitiful sight it had been. Now, he counted himself fortunate it had not turned his grandfather into someone like the broken soul before him.

"You... You aren't..." Tears swelled from Ralf's eyes.

"I am not he," Dawkin confessed.

"I... Get out."

"My Lord, I am sorry."

"Begone."

"Forgive me. But I bear news from your other son, Everitt."

"Leave, you devil!"

"Certainly, you must –"

"You are no king of mine, Prince Jameson! You let your father die. Murdered. In your own castle. What kind of royal allows that?! I'll tell you — a worthless man. No, a shell of a man. A louse!" Baron Ralf rose to his feet, nearly falling over. Dawkin moved in to brace him only to be met by his hard hands, which shoved him away. "Out! Out!"

Lady Agnes returned with a candle in hand, along with a young lad and a portly woman at her side. The three, stirred by the raucous cries, stood by as Dawkin collected Cora from her seat. For all the frailty he showed before, Baron Ralf had now shed his slight demeanor. He tossed his chair across the hall, where it crashed against an end table, sending it toppling. He flailed about, throwing everything in his path until his eyes settled on the hot coals within the hearth. With his sense lost, he reached down into the smoldering mass, picking up coals by the handful to launch them at Dawkin and Cora.

His servants rushed to his side. They encircled him, their arms outstretched as they attempted to reason with him. However bold or vain, their efforts at least distracted him, allowing Cora and Dawkin the chance to escape.

"'Tis not your fault."

Dawkin nodded. He tightened the strap of Cora's saddle before moving on to his mount. From the stables, they heard nothing of Ralf's madness. Nonetheless, Dawkin made haste to ready their horses.

Stupid, stupid, fool, Dawkin chastised himself. *I should have known better than to humor an old man in such a state.*

"You couldn't have known," Cora added, as if in response to his self-admonishment.

"Let's go," was his only reply.

Dawkin set his foot in his stirrup, about to mount, when the *clip-clop* of another drew his attention. He pivoted to find a Voiceless - dressed in an unsuspecting doublet and trousers, save for the robins sewn onto his breast – galloping toward him.

"Wonderful," Dawkin muttered.

The knight pulled his steed to a stop. He dismounted. Scowling at Cora, he shielded his right hand from her. "What are you doing with *her*?" he asked with his fingers.

Dawkin pulled him around so that the knight's horse blocked them from Cora's view. "What is the meaning of this?" he inquired through the language of the hands. "You know better than to come to me as, well, you, unless it's an emergency."

"My news is important. But first, what is *she* doing here?"

"Why does she concern you so? She's merely a lady, a woman I met in Arcporte."

"You brought her from Arcporte?"

"No, I met her again when traveling with the Bishop. She needed an escort to Seafall, so –"

"Do not trust her!" the knight clenched his teeth, nearly hissing.

"Are you –"

"She's one of them." The knight peeked over the saddle of his horse to ensure Cora could not see their hands. "A sibyl."

Dawkin arced his head back to chuckle. He stifled himself though, as the knight's look of concern deepened into a glare.

"She?" Dawkin asked. "A witch?"

"Don't you see it? Her kind has a certain... look about them. She seems peculiar, does she not? As if you've never seen the likes of her before?"

"I admit, she is stunning." Dawkin leaned back, glancing at the lady from around the horse. He caught her calming her mount with the palm of her hand. Her milky skin once more stood out as flawless, as did the curls framing her face. And those eyes… "She, she is unlike any woman I've seen."

"There's a reason for that. Blond hair and eyes like those come from the Boreal Isles, further north than even Lewmarians care to sail. Legend has it the sibyls of old settled the ridges of our island in the harshest times of winter, in storms so bleak none would venture out to oppose them, as any reasonable man would expect the ice to claim them. 'Tis never been so, for the sibyls continued to live on, held up in their mountainous enclaves and wooded refuges by way of their magic."

"Legend is rumor without reason," Dawkin quipped. "She's harmless."

The knight sighed. "Fine. The stories may strike you as foolish. But is it worth disregarding a warning – and putting the Throne at risk – over a maiden?"

Dawkin balked. "I would never put the Throne in peril."

"So you'll stop seeing her at once?"

"We'll see."

The knight's hands nearly flurried in another protest before Dawkin interrupted. "How did you even find me anyway?"

"You should know we track your and your brothers' every move when in transit. Even when you manage to dodge our guard – which annoys us to no end – we always pick up your trail. Eventually."

"So what tipped you off this round?"

The knight tilted his head toward Cora. "That one. Like I said, there aren't many around like her."

"Fair enough. And this dire news you bring?"

"It's complicated."

When is it not? "Care to elaborate?"

"I'll show you." The knight mounted his steed. Casting a final glare in Cora's direction, he offered one last condition to Dawkin. "But she stays back."

For all the cover from the canopy above, the road before them remained clear, the dappled light from the wind-stroked branches offering enough radiance to guide them. Indeed, with the rustling of leaves, the caress of the breeze, and the babbling of the adjacent creek, Dawkin almost found himself entranced on the ride. The only detriment to his calm rode up a ways, as the Voiceless knight pressed on through the Marlish idylls.

Dawkin resisted the urge to swivel in his saddle. The pacing of hooves behind him vouched for Lady Cora's continued presence. Such confirmation – along with the idea of her stewing for being asked to trail behind – prompted him to keep his stare on the road ahead.

The halting of his horse lobbed him forward. The Voiceless, having stopped his horse before him, pointed. "Behind the bend," he signed.

Ahead, over the sound of the running creek, came shouts and splashing. The knight pulled his reins to the left, turning his horse to cross the ford. Dawkin, having no time to pose questions, followed. As he did, he motioned to Lady Cora. "Stay, please. We'll be right back."

He sloshed through the water after the Voiceless. Coming onto the other side, they traversed a game trail through the adjacent woods to a small ridge overlooking the creek's bend. There, Dawkin saw it.

Peasants. Dozens of them. Servants. Along with a baron and baroness. Even a handful of monks. Plus, wait... Was that Low Bishop Jervis?

They plodded through the current, their heads down, searching. Most ran into each other, which led to a shove or a shout before they returned to the quest at hand. A few dug their hands into the water, leading those nearby to rush in and do the same. Desperation ensued for whatever unseen spurred their envy.

And in witness to it all, across the creek from Dawkin and the Voiceless, knelt a dozen Lost Souls.

"In the name of all that is holy," Dawkin started. "What the hell is this?"

"'Tis the mania gripping the whole of the country. 'Fool's Fever' it's called. Come. You need a closer look."

They crisscrossed down the ridge to the water's edge, where they dismounted. While the Voiceless secured the horses, Dawkin waded ankle-deep into the creek. He kept a respectable distance from the subjects, who continued to slosh around, unaware of his presence.

Dawkin bent his head, curious as to what could inspire such madness. At his feet, the water rushed over his boots. Though they remained dry, the cold from the creek seeped into him, sending a chill up his legs through his spine and beyond. He ventured to guess how those before him - soaked through and through by the looks of them – would soon suffer from a long-lasting numbness, one which would claim a foot or leg from at least a few.

Aside from the smooth stones beneath the surface, not a thing caught his eye. He waded further as his guard beckoned to him, clapping.

"Your Majesty," the Voiceless signed once he had Dawkin's attention. "Not so deep."

"I'm fine," Dawkin insisted, though the rush of the current slowed his pace. With the water now just beneath his knees, he paused. Those in the tributary still made a mess of the water, as though salmon spawning for the first time.

Then, turning back to the creekbed before him, he saw it — a glint from the water. As quickly as it came, it vanished. Dawkin bent his knees slightly, narrowing his eyes when he saw it again. This time he held the sight in his view as he leaned in for a better look.

Gold.

His eyes widened. He plunged his hand into the water, his fingers slow to approach the treasure lest they lose it in the current. No more significant than a thimble, Dawkin plucked the nugget from the creek. It shone for him once more as he raised it before his face.

"There! He's got one!"

The scream shattered his concentration. No sooner did he lower his gaze when the baron in the creek tackled him, sending both of them into the frigid shallows.

Though not deep, the charge still sent Dawkin below water. He flailed, overwhelmed by frigidity, robbed of breath. He beat his fists against the lord who held him under for an eternity before the baron lifted him out to scream.

"It's mine, I tell you! Mine –"

Blood spurted from the baron's mouth, a gloved fist having connected with his jaw. His unconscious body collapsed into the creek as his wife rushed to his side.

"Ahhh! How could you?!"

The Voiceless ignored her shrieks as he reached for the King. Dawkin – gasping for air and his senses – readily took his hand. As he rose, his legs wobbly, the baroness heaved her husband from under the current.

"You bastard!" she yelled, swiping at the Voiceless with one hand, which glanced off his thigh. The knight forgave the slight, grinning as the baron slumped from the woman's one-handed grip to reclaim the water.

Others gathered around the baron and baroness, less to help and more to search for whatever nugget had led to his incursion. As the mass moved in to slosh through their small section of the creek, Dawkin emerged, shouldered by the Voiceless.

Lady Cora, drawn by the commotion, descended from her vantage point on the ridge.

"By Mar! Look at you!" she exclaimed.

"I've fared worse," Dawkin proclaimed, even if he couldn't remember when.

"Come," she insisted, ducking under Dawkin's other arm to support him.

They guided him away from the creekbed to a stand of birch trees, where the Voiceless had tied the horses. Dawkin mounted his steed while the Voiceless helped Lady Cora atop his. The knight led them back up the ridge, glancing toward the hysteria still unfolding in the creek.

For his part, Dawkin resisted the urge to glance at the chaos – until he mounted the ridge. As the Voiceless and Cora rode ahead of him, he offered a fleeting look at the creek.

The baron and baroness floundered toward the nearest shoreline. The rest of the folk meandered through the current, their momentary frenzy having receded, replaced by the more steady delirium of resuming their watery pursuit.

And looking on – unmoved by the baron's madness, or anyone else's – knelt the Lost Souls. They remained on their knees, their hands clasped before them, in dense, grim-stained robes. Their position continued unchanged, with no difference in appearance, save one.

Now, they didn't look toward the creek. Instead, they directed their eyes to Dawkin.

Chapter 13

The hump crested. Then it sank below the surface. Symon needn't ask his men if they saw it. Their faint whispers and pause among them provided confirmation.

He smirked, knowing he shouldn't relish in their fear. But he couldn't help it. Judging by its size, the leviathan could not be much older than a hatchling. Yet even he had to admit that in the dark such a sight was unsettling, as the sleek, black body bobbed in and out of the water, slowly encircling their skiff, waiting.

Clack!

The wait ended. A lightning bolt struck the surface a stone's throw from their stern.

The men scrambled from the rear of the skiff. The leviathan slapped its tail above as it dove under their boat. All while Symon chuckled.

"It's not funny," Everitt insisted, hand on the pommel of his sword.

"It's a baby," Symon insisted. "Perhaps, what, three, four feet in length. Now the mother, phew, she probably grew to be a good thirty or forty feet. Not as large as a giant sperm whale or colossal squid, mind you, but a good size, I would imagine. I wonder if she is near here..."

"Must we speak of all the creatures in these waters that can kill us?"

Symon quieted, holding out his palm to signal him

relenting, even as his smirk remained. The idea of his Right Captain cowering should have alarmed him. However, it put him at ease. Since youth Everitt had hated lightning, believing in the superstitions surrounding the phenomenon that his nana had ingrained in him through lore and sayings. As a man, Everitt showed no hint of the boy who believed such nonsense, proving himself time and time again in battle or duty. That is until now when the combined threat – however imaginary – of lightning and open water shook the knees of his most trusted guard.

Symon, ever smitten, took a seat on the bench of the skiff. As in answer to his moment of rest, the first drops of a shower started.

"Lovely," Everitt said, withdrawing his hand from his pommel to raise his hood.

"You should be relieved," Symon insisted.

"Relieved? It's raining!"

"Hardly. On our island, this is a sprinkle. Nay, a drizzle."

"Well, then, the lightning..."

Symon raised a brow. "You forget your lessons?"

"Of?"

"Of Ibian weather. The mage gave us a briefing in case we encountered the temperamental nature of our hosts. Lightning and rain never mix in this part of the world, for whatever reason Mar cooked up. Storms pause – perhaps so the angels can ready their bolts – sparks ensue. Then the rain – usually a mild one – follows."

"And that's it?"

"No. The pattern repeats itself. Rainfall, lightning, rainfall, til the storm passes."

Everitt scowled. "Mar, I hate this country. Such idiocy, madness, even with their weather. I can't wait to be rid of this place."

Symon cocked his head, agreeing – and grinning.

Suddenly, the scared boy Symon had mocked vanished.

"Your Majesty," Everitt growled, the soldier within rising. "Duck down. Lower your head. Just in case."

Symon obliged, glancing over his shoulder as he did so. Onshore, not more than a few hundred feet from their position, waited a line of longbowmen. While none had drawn bowstrings, their quivers lay empty. The fletching of upright arrows – their heads buried in the sand before the archers – caught the brilliance from the nearby braziers. Ominous, none of the longbowmen moved, even as their shadows flurried from the breeze-fanned flames of the beach fires.

"Your command?" Everitt asked Symon.

"We land at the beach, as intended. But to be safe, offer the cross of your sword."

Everitt frowned yet did as directed. He stepped to the bow of the vessel. Undoing his belt, he raised his sheathed sword before him, its tip pointed down.

If the archers took notice, they certainly made no motion to confirm.

"Row faster," Symon commanded.

"James, you serious?"

"I am."

Everitt extended a hand to the railing of the boat as the rowers quickened their pace.

"Quicker."

The sailors hastened. By then, the waves approaching

the beach began to crest, pushing the skiff ever forward.

The first line of waves crashed into their stern with a mighty thud, sending the bow down.

"Row hard. We have to stay ahead of the next break."

"James, our men know how to land on a beachhead."

"This one's different."

As the next wave rose behind them, abruptly, they stopped.

"Row, row, row!" Symon yelled.

The sailors obliged, instilling their fury into their oars. The wave, uncaring of their fear, arched its long head above.

"Hang on!"

Whatever had held them in place relented, allowing their boat to float just ahead of the crashing whitewater. The foam splashed the men who, while relieved, did nothing to slow their pace. A few minor wave breaks later, the skiff slid onto the sand.

Symon jettisoned onto the beach as Everitt hastened to his side. He marched toward the line, which remained in position.

"Very well," Symon called, "Which one of you bastards issued the command?"

Silence met his question. A moment later, the last figure of the line – just out of the light of the braziers – stepped back and answered him.

"Pray tell, what command?"

Symon perked, snapping his head in the direction of the shadowed speaker.

"The command not to warn us of the dangers landing on this beach."

"But you knew the dangers."

"Barely. From the tales my father told, which I recalled at the last minute."

"Then the fault is yours."

"You're our host. You have a responsibility to see after our safety."

"We care for guests, not for adversaries. I haven't decided which one you are."

The speaker, having circled behind the bowmen, flicked his fingers. As if able to see his gesture, the archers swooped down, nocking their arrows and drawing their bows.

Symon grit his teeth. "I would expect better from even you, Xain."

"Xain? Why, he's not here."

"Then which Garsea are you?"

Symon kept in stride with the small man, whose gait turned out to be remarkably quick for one with such short legs. Then again, everything about the Badger of Arinn seemed out of sorts.

His less-than-gracious host had presented him with two options on the beach: Return to his galleon or come with him. As Symon had no intention of rowing back with a line of archers to their rear, he elected the latter option, albeit with a sharp glare from Everitt in protest.

The Badger skipped ahead a beat as they came upon a crossroads. He peered around the corner, observant as any vanguard even though his men had already scouted the passage.

"I thought you owned these streets?" Symon prodded, recalling the various tales of the Duke's maliciousness.

“Oh, I do,” Duke Vicentius replied, “in the same way a butcher owns a mutt. Sure, a few scraps of meat buy the beast’s favor, perhaps its loyalty. Yet never assume you control the dog, which will bite you lest it forgets the hand which feeds it. And believe, Your Majesty, animals do forget.”

The Duke eyed a beggar, asleep at a stoop close by, as he finished. He tilted his head toward the man. One of his henchmen – who led a ring of guards as they strode – approached the man, his blade at the ready. Symon paused.

“A tad unnecessary, don’t you think?”

“It will serve as a warning to those who dare to follow us.”

“I must insist.” Symon moved his hand to the pommel of his sword. The Badger’s men – be they Realeza in disguise or hired hands, Symon could not tell – unsheathed their swords. Everitt and the Marlish under his command, following behind Symon, did likewise.

Vicentius rolled his eyes, less out of threat than annoyance. “Fine, Your Illustriousness. Far be it from me to try to keep a royal meeting a secret.” He flicked a finger towards his man, who nodded and halted his approach to the beggar, though he kept his blade out.

The pair moved on up the path, which wound through the lesser parts of Arinn bordering its harbor. In the distance, voices from taverns and brothels echoed while a dead quiet met them in their immediate vicinity. The shuttered windows, the unlit buildings, the streets absent of even feral creatures – Symon knew the void of the living to be the work of His Grace.

“Are the streets always so peaceful?” Symon asked

hesitantly, dreading the answer. *I must ask something if only to size up this one.*

"The King issued a curfew. He urged his subjects to practice restraint in their nightly endeavors. I, for one, agree with his mandate. I would go so far as to say it's long overdue."

"Oh? Has Arinn suffered from crime as of late?"

"If it's lawlessness of which you speak, then, no. In all honesty, Arinn is one of the safest cities on the Continent. Sure, we have a few misdemeanors here and there. Even the occasional stabbing or murder. Yet when one considers the expanse of our city and all the inhabitants within, the perpetrators of such violations account for nothing more than a fraction of our peoples."

Symon nodded, the thick accent from the Duke ringing in his ears like a song that had just ended. Though in this case, Symon had never wished for his ears to be chopped from his head.

"So why, you may muse, have I longed for a curfew?" the Duke went on, oblivious – or not caring – of Symon's disinterest. "I could give you a thousand and one reasons. All with merit, I assure you. However, tonight I offer one. The Church of Mar."

Symon paused. "The Church?"

"So, you were listening."

"What does our religion have to do with the safety of Arinn? With the threats against the King?"

The Badger – with his crooked nose, small chin, and greasy skin – bared his teeth. Never had Symon seen a set so white, so immaculate, without a stain. His mouth settled into a smile, accompanied by a stare so unnerving Symon struggled not to look away.

"My dear king," Vicentius began, "our faith has everything to do with, well, everything. It propels our people to toil through their miserable lives, to be dutiful to a Throne that barely acknowledges their existence, all in the belief their humble, meaningless efforts will lead to eternal salvation. It unites our many barons who, without a deeper cause, would continuously battle one another.

"More importantly... It gives us a chance to exalt ourselves. For if we have faith and our enemies do not, who is always in the right?"

Symon breathed. He had half a mind to stab the Duke – or even himself – just to stop the talk from assaulting his ears.

"No words, Your Majesty?" the Badger asked.

"What does any of what you said have to do with the curfew?"

"A man who requires a more direct line of logic, I see. I like that. My uncle was once such a man, though that was such a long time ago, when he was in swaddling clothes... Oh, look at me going on and on without providing you with closure. Forgive me, Your Majesty. It has been far too long since I've spoken to a foreign dignitary, much less a sovereign as illustrious as yourself. Yes, the curfew. Well, setting boundaries instills a sense of discipline on a kingdom's subjects, as my uncle has so often concluded. And what better measure of discipline – or really, of allegiance, loyalty, and the like – than a curfew? Those who obey respect the rule of Kin Garsea. The others found roaming the street, drunk or otherwise, in clear violation of a most basic mandate, do not. Such an easy way to distinguish your foes from your allies when it comes to analyzing a kingdom's subjects, wouldn't you say?"

Before Symon had a chance to consider any part of the Duke's rants, the Badger perked. "Look at that; we're here. Pardon, Your Majesty. I insist on checking with that guard up ahead, the one disguised as a sawyer, to ensure we are clear to proceed. One moment."

As Vicentius slipped away to speak with the man, Everitt sauntered up to Symon's right. His eyes never left the Ibians around them, who remained in a ring around Symon and his Marlish detail.

"I swear, James," Everitt whispered, "if this continues, I'll defy my duty and kill the man if only to shut him up."

"You'd start a war with my wife's kin for a moment's peace?"

"Dear Mar, yes."

"Good man," Symon smirked. "Still, if you could find it within yourself to hold off, I'd be obliged."

"You nearly ask too much."

"Aye. But the worst of this mission is far from over. Something tells me we'll be tried further before the night is done."

"I hate this place, James." Everitt scanned the outlines of the buildings that stood sentry to their wait, seemingly hollow figures casting real and imagined shadows. "So much..."

"I know."

The Duke whistled, jolting the two from their conversation. He waved them forward. Symon and Everitt strode up the cobblestone path leading up to the Badger.

"He's waiting." Vicentius nodded to the building

looming over them.

"A sawmill?" Everitt sniffed.

"I suppose you were expecting a grand hall for our secret meeting?"

The Badger chuckled, as did some of his men. He moved from Symon and his Right Captain, not waiting for the Marlishmen to enter.

"Like I said –"

"Your duty, Sir Everitt."

Everitt set his jaw, fighting to say more, then nodded.

Inside, the mill teemed with life. Workers carried planks and rounds of freshly-cut wood from roller conveyors. Alongside them, woodworkers labored at benches and tables with crosscut log saws and panel saws in hand, sawdust rising from their every pull and push of their blades. Most worked in pairs save for one in the back, who took to his piece of lumber with the ease of a master.

"Uncle!" Duke Vicentius shouted over the clamor of the mill, being the one closest to him.

King Felix looked up from his bench, revealing the beads of perspiration on his brow. He waved the lot of them toward his workspace as he removed his leather apron, revealing the sweat-stained shirt underneath.

"Nephew," Felix acknowledged as he cast his apron on the bench. "King Jameson," he added, looking toward Symon.

"Your Majesty." Symon bowed his head.

King Felix waved for him to lift his head. Symon glanced up, finding the King had swiped a block of wood from his bench. Taking a carving knife from his pocket, he began to whittle. "I learned the details of your visit to our close friend and ally, the Grand Duke of Seylonna."

"Yes. 'Tis tragic what occurred."

"Nonsense. I'm glad to be rid of him."

"Your Majesty?"

"The old man who held that dukedom had been descending into madness for some time. He kept sending his men on wild outings, claiming that foreigners were raiding his lands and harassing his people. Our agents – some of which were his own spies who bent to the Ibian throne – revealed the truth: the reported provocations came from his men-at-arms, not from anyone else."

"I suspect that's why his son took the reins. Unfortunately, he too perished."

"Bah!" He flicked a wood shaving from his carving. "Replacing a senile old man with a runt proved little better. I saw His Grace, Ienello of Seylonna, only once in my court. A sad little man, and not a pinch more. With such a bloodline, it's no wonder that kin fell into ruin. I'm only surprised it didn't happen sooner."

Vicentius snickered. The Realeza within earshot smirked.

"So the attack," Symon added. "It doesn't worry you?"

"I've already sent emissaries to those kingdoms bordering the Seylonna... Lower Volkmar, Tosily, Belgarda..."

The mention of each name sent a shudder through Symon. His breath deepened. His eyes narrowed. He fought the urge to close his fists. All such gestures unfolded with subtlety as he made a dedicated effort to maintain his composure. Yet failing, Felix noticed, his stare firmly planted on Symon.

"You disapprove?"

"You know my kin has never trusted the Family of the Fox, not to mention their cozy neighbors."

"I never said I trusted them either."

"And still, you dismiss the notion they had anything to do with the attack on Castle Seylonna."

"As your people say, 'Aye.'"

"Then, with no fear of those who border you, why all the secrecy? The longbowmen on the beach? The..." Symon glanced at Duke Vicentius. The Badger smiled, flashing his ivories. "... other precautions?"

Felix dug the point of his knife into his carving. Perhaps to create an eye? A mouth? "I know it seems strange. The current plight we're facing. An attack on the border. Then before that, the fire to your camp, followed by the collapse of one of my towers. In the face of everything, you would expect differently of a man such as me, wouldn't you?"

The King paused, waiting for Symon to answer.

"Any man would," Symon offered.

"I'm not asking about any man. I'm asking you. From one monarch to another, what would you do?"

"What my people would expect. Secure the capital. Call up the reserves. Station my troops at all major fortifications and send scouts to gather intelligence from all corners of the kingdom. That is what I would do."

"A soldier at heart. Like your father."

"And *you* disapprove?"

"I... disagree with such a predictable approach."

"Why?"

Felix paused. "Leave us."

The Duke of Tehonne, who had allowed himself to recline on a stack of wood pillars, perked. "Uncle?"

"Go on."

Vicentius rose to his feet, shrinking after the Realeza and the Marlishmen who returned from whence they came. Everitt retreated just as warily, lingering long enough for him to spot a raised hand from Symon, a command as strong as any. With their departure, Felix put his carving before his lips, blowing away the shavings. The fluttered in the air, like so much sawdust, lingering.

"Your father, he was an honest man?"

"Aye."

"Same as you?"

"Better."

Felix grunted. "What did he think of me?"

"Your Majesty, he spoke highly –"

"Lies!"

Felix reddened. The knife in his hand stuck end-first into his carving.

"What... did... he think... of *me*?"

"He believed you to be a runt."

Felix stared ahead at Symon, unflinching. "And?"

"Inept at battle. Strategy, commanding, all well and good. But amid the chaos of fighting, on the front lines, he thought you lacked the capacity to lead."

"He said that?"

"In those very words... no. In bits and pieces, he would recollect on the Century War. He would never comment on any commander or king in whole. His opinions, he shared them in small doses."

"Allowing you to read between the lines, gather his sense on all regal matters."

"My father was a man of few words."

"Wise. Not a bad way to rule." Felix laid his carving knife on his workbench. "You question my actions, King Jameson?"

"Pardon?"

"No need to deny it. Not here, with us alone."

"I... wonder a great deal about many things I've seen in the land. Including your rule, yes."

"Things you discuss with your court."

"Yes."

Felix sighed. "The attack on the tower, the night of your wedding. I confess: it wasn't entirely unexpected. Nor was the assault on Grand Duke Ienello and Castle Seylonna. Tensions have been brewing at home and abroad, which affect all of Ibia. Do you remember what I told you the night of your coronation?"

Damn it to hell! Symon did recall Dawkin, who served as Jameson that fateful night, speaking of his exchange with King Felix. But even with dose after dose of memory tea, Symon could not retain the entirety of what had happened – it was too bloody much!

"No matter," King Felix continued, noting Symon's pause. "'Twas a long day for you, I'm sure. The mention I refer to was when I spoke of your promise to my daughter. Unofficial at that time though it was, I nonetheless saw the event on the horizon, and with you finally crowned, I made sure to pull you aside to address the matter – king to king."

"It's starting to come back to me," Symon offered, feigning familiarity with Felix's memory.

"Within the company of our confidants, I approached you. I extended my congratulations and well wishes for your reign as any monarch would do, whether ally or foe.

Then, with the members of our court losing interest in our pleasantries, side conversations broke off, allowing us to make idle talk until we finally shifted away from the ears of our courts onto the balcony."

Symon strained into the recesses of his consciousness, the faintest hints of the moment coming together as Dawkin's recollection of the coronation melded with Felix's words.

"In our solitary discussion, I gave you one piece of advice. One bit of counsel to remember, should you ever find yourself with enemies aplenty, especially after uniting with my kin by marriage. Sorry to say, my attempt at guidance turned out to be a fleeting effort, lost on a freshly-minted sovereign." Felix darkened, the creases of his eyes deepening as his eyes narrowed, transforming his façade from a mask of disappointment to one of indignation. The slight of having forgotten his advisement would not easily be forgotten – nor forgiven.

Damn it, you fool! Symon chastised himself. *What did he say? Remember, you brute. Remember!*

Then, it dawned on him. A moment too late. For as he opened his mouth to utter, Felix continued.

"Never be predictable."

"As, yes. I recall –"

"Liar! You forgot. Not surprisingly. I knew your father to be the same way when he first took the throne. Edict after edict he issued, one decree after another, all easy to foretell, as though he had them written out for him years beforehand. Word of his rule reached my court by couriers, and in my youth, I relished in how I could guess at your father's directives before I received them. Even on the front, he remained as such, proving steadfast in his resolve as all the world danced around him.

"Perhaps his course saved his reign in those critical first years. I knew monarchs who grew *too* reactive upon transitioning from their princehood, so that their foolishness stained their rule, preventing any duke or baron from ever considering them seriously. Whatever his mindset, your father wised up, as they say. Still, it proved too little, as you witnessed with not one but two attempts on his life –"

Symon winced. The last part struck a nerve. And Felix knew it.

"See. Predictable." He pointed at Symon.

Symon swallowed. "So, this is why we're here? In a sawmill instead of your Throne Room? To err on the side of caution, throw off our enemy's assumptions?"

"Precisely. Though I've grown too accustomed to using this location as a front for my clandestine meetings. You see my favorite workbench there? Along with my apron and carving knife?" He picked up the blade from the bench. With a flick of his wrist, he flung it over a stack of lumber. It rattled on the floor beyond Symon's line of sight. "My preference for this site has become a liability. After our meeting, I'll instruct my nephew to burn the whole of it to the ground. I'll miss this place." Felix turned his back to Symon to gaze upon the rafters and breathe in the sawdust.

"Your Majesty..."

Felix looked to Symon.

"What would you have me do? Become unpredictable? Brazen? Is that it?"

"You haven't been picking up on my nuances, have you?"

"Regretfully, no."

"You needn't act irrationally nor without reason. You shouldn't act without counsel nor reflection. I just want you – for the sake of your kin, as well as my daughter – to avoid, shall we say, patterns."

"Patterns?"

"Patterns. Schedules. Agendas. Models of behavior and certain orders of thought, one any idiot can guess at without having met you, much like how you've behaved with my daughter following your marriage. Your retreat to Manor deila Krestta Deorro following the wedding – and attack on the castle – was unexpected, perhaps inconsiderate to the kin of the soldiers and barons lost in the fire. But it showed you to be capable of change so early in your reign, unlike your father and many others. And then you sent her off, ahead of you, to upper Ibia. Mayhaps a stroke of genius, an unforeseen decision, for any other newlywed would be keeping his wife close in times such as these."

"So... you approve."

"Of how you've moved to protect my daughter, yes. Unorthodox though your actions may be, even questionable. But upon review, understandable."

"And my other decisions? As monarch?"

Felix took a step forward. His gesture did little to close the gap between them, for several paces still separated them. It nonetheless established an increase in their proximity, such that Symon could not look away. The intensity of Felix's gaze... Symon wanted to turn, for the moment felt akin to being pierced by a red-hot iron poker.

Resisting the urge to move, Symon planted his feet.

"Need improvement, I'd say," Felix continued. "From

the time of day you hold court with your barons and ministers to when you supper. All those activities would be fine in *normal* circumstances. These days following your union with my daughter have been anything but. For certain, your court, along with your Right Captain and your guards, will insist on set times for all your duties, arguing they need to know your schedule so they can know when and where to find you. And you should concede to many of their demands. Just not all of them. Change at will. Without warning. Your reign depends on it."

Beyond, a dog barked. Distant and unthreatening. Felix tilted his head toward the sound, his intensity broken.

"Alas, I haven't heeded my own advice. I've droned on too long, as any man would expect of me." Felix whistled. From the hidden corners of every woodpile, the Badger and his Realeza emerged. Everitt and the Marlish guard followed, a clip behind their movements. Though not off their guard, they seemed rushed; the slight distinction in timing between his men and Felix's was not lost on Symon.

Nor Felix.

He offered no wink or grin at the moment of realization, one that bonded them to a mutual understanding of their conversation. Instead, he turned as his retinue closed in, marching toward the rear of the building.

"You have a minute before a fire engulfs the whole of this place. Leave now. Don't look back," Felix said, his back to Symon.

Symon turned to his men, waving them toward the front.

"Your Majesty."

Symon looked over his shoulder. Felix had ducked out

of sight, as had his Realeza. Only the Badger had fallen back.

"Compliments of my uncle."

The Badger tossed an item to Symon. He threw it too high. Symon managed to snatch it from the air, to prevent it from sailing overhead.

In his palm lay the King's carving. A squat rendering of a soldier, complete with helm, sword, and shield. Dug deep into the face of the shield lay the sigil of Marland, of his manor: the four-pointed compass.

"Careful you don't let it burn," the Badger muttered of the carving as he dashed through the pilings after his uncle.

Symon closed his fist around the soldier. "I won't."

Chapter 14

All this is happening too quickly.

"Your Majesty."

The voice, a meek one, hit her ears like the piercing call of a siren. Then came a gentle knock at the door.

"Can't I have a moment's peace?" Taresa asked herself.

"Pardon?" the female attendant asked from the other side.

"Nothing. I'll be right out."

Taresa rose from the latrine. Straightening the folds of her dress, she glanced at herself in the mirror, ensuring she looked proper. She flattened the creases over her abdomen, laying her hands to rest there.

Somewhat satisfied, she took a deep breath, her hands falling to her sides. She threw the door open.

"Your Majesty." A handmaiden not quite sixteen curtsied before her, her head bowed. "I was told he waits."

"How kind to allow a lady above his station a brief respite."

"Yes, my lady."

Taresa frowned. "Forgive my manners. My frustrations are not your doing."

The girl glanced up at Taresa. "Is there anything I can do?"

Gag the bastard. Wait, don't. He'd probably enjoy it. "No. Nothing. Come with me."

The servant followed Taresa as she proceeded out of the royal chamber. The crisp sea air greeted them, as did the clanging from the yard below.

Taresa glanced over the railing to spy several more companies of soldiers at practice than she had seen earlier in the day, the torchlight throwing their shadows onto the ground and the surrounding stones. Though no battle awaited them, a great many bore the surcoats she loathed.

So it begins.

One after another, heads bowed before her. A flurry, really, in answer to her quickened gait. The servant girl in her wake broke into a trot more than a few times to keep up with the queen, nary offering a protest or any other type of peep. By the time they reached the doors of the grand hall, the girl's breathing had hastened.

"Are you well?" Taresa asked.

The girl held her breath to answer. "Forgive me, Your Majesty. I am from the inland, where the air is much drier. This seaside air bothers me, it seems."

"No apology is necessary, my dear. So inland, you say?"

"Yes, Your Majesty. Zamerra."

"And my mother informed me you are to replace my previous handmaiden?"

"Yes, if Your Majesty will allow me."

I'm about to leave for a new land, so I must allow it. The time for her to vet a candidate herself had passed. Her last handmaiden – removed from her presence before she could inquire – was rumored to have become pregnant with the child of a rising squire. The irony of losing her attendant to such a situation when she would soon need her most was not lost on Taresa. Still, it hardly proved a reason to be so curt with her new handmaiden.

Taresa paused. "What's your name?"

"Celia."

"Lovely. Celia, please forgive my tone. Like you, I have struggled to adapt to my new surroundings." Taresa glanced around. The two of them stood at the curve of a hall, one absent of any windows, with light ahead to guide their way. The cold walls rose high about them, like sentinels of stone, serving to remind them that they did not belong.

"Your Majesty, I could never forgive you."

"Pardon?"

"I mean, not that, only... You could never do anything wrong. To me. Or anyone. Thus, you never require a pardon all your own."

Celia curtsied as she shied away, expecting an admonishment.

Taresa smirked. "You and I will get along splendidly, Celia." She continued onward, waving Celia along. "Come."

Their path ended before a set of doors carved from gray ashwood, which nearly blended in with the walls. Ibian guards, bearing the crest of an Ibian cedar flanked by red eagles, stood at attention. Taresa minded the sigil with caution, knowing the men within her sight – and those inside – answered to another.

"Take a seat on one of these benches while I attend to the guests," Taresa said to Celia.

"My Queen, shall I come with you?"

"You needn't bother. But thank you."

Celia obligingly sat on the nearest bench, carved into the stone wall abutting the hall. Taresa smoothed the lines of her dress once more before turning to face the doors. Nodding to the guards on either side of her, they opened the massive cedar beasts, revealing the artifice within.

In the few hours since she had visited the hall, the chamber had transformed into a receptacle of vanity. Nobles of every rank – from high knights to viscounts to lower dukes – reclined on any seat available. Some had even brought their own chairs and couches, the gaudiness of their bright, unmatched colors and elaborate decoration an assault to the eyes. Their "guards" looked no better, with their halberds loosely clasped and their armor unpolished. Groups engaged in card games while their masters lounged about, the latter either too drunk or too cowardly to address their imprudence.

At the head of this monstrosity sat her prized guest: the Grand Duke of Almata.

She strode through the unkept entourage to the fringes of his circle of Realeza, who thankfully still bore manners enough to tilt their heads at her approach. Taresa paused to curtsy before His Grace.

Xain, lounging across two voluptuous young women seated on a wide couch, set aside his chalice before rising. "Cousin," he started, his speech only slightly slurred. "You need not bow before a commoner such as myself. It is I who is honored by *your* presence." He dipped his head before her, so low he lost his balance. He touched the floor with his fingers before righting himself back up, laughing as he straightened. His entourage also chuckled with him, discarding any pretense of etiquette in the presence of the royalty. Only Taresa retained her dignity, unamused by her cousin's antics.

“You look... stiff.” Xain meandered to the side table at his right, where flagons aplenty awaited.

“You made quick work,” Taresa eyed the depravity around her, “of our aunt’s manor. Even for you, I’m amazed.”

“Why, thank you,” Xain replied, failing to catch on to her undertone. He grabbed a stein more fit for ale from the edge of the table and filled it to the top with a fine vintage of amber red wine.

“She won’t be too pleased.”

“Oh, Aunt Eldonza doesn’t care. She loves it when I visit. I’m her favorite.” Xain glanced over his shoulder. “Well, her favorite nephew, anyway.”

“What are you doing here?”

“Well, can’t I –”

“Xain!”

The last utterance exploded and echoed to cut through every parallel conversation. The hall quieted, with every tongue held still as all eyes turned to the Queen.

Xain, as though not surprised, peered over his shoulder to give Taresa a blank stare. He swung around to splash the stone tiles before her. With her feet planted, unmoving, she glared at her cousin as he tilted his stein back to gulp the contents within. All the while, the whole of the hall watched soundlessly.

After finishing, he wiped his lips on his sleeve. Then, setting his stein on the table, he clapped two short bursts. “Very well. You heard Her Majesty. Her directive was indirect, but nonetheless, expressed. Leave us at once.”

Moans and sighs spouted as the audience turned away. They obliged, if only because the promise of further theatrics had faded for the moment. The mob filed out into the foyer. The remnants of the guards – the last to exit – closed the doors behind them. All the while, Taresa remained firm in her stance as Xain carelessly rounded the chamber, picking through the remnants leftover on platters and dishes.

“Should you *really* eat considering what you consumed already?” Taresa glanced at the wine-stained tile before her feet.

“Concerned, cousin?” Xain popped a pitted olive into his mouth.

“For the cleanliness of our poor aunt’s manor, yes.”

“There was a time when you didn’t care so much for such droll states. Not long ago, a little girl with no concern for being ‘clean’ or ‘polite’ ran through this very hall in a soiled dress and muddy boots.”

“‘Twas ages ago.” Or so it seemed. “I’ve matured since then. It appears I’m the only one.”

“Ouch,” Xain replied as he feigned a wound to his gut.

Taresa continued to stare at him, awaiting substance to their conversation.

“You tire of banter, I see.” Xain set himself upright, seeming to sober immediately. “As you wish. Now is as good a time as any to speak candidly. What is it you wish to know?”

“Your intentions,” she reiterated. “Your reason for being here.”

“Have you visited our poor aunt?”

“I have.”

“Then your encounter no doubt answered at least part of that question.” Xain’s eyes went to the southwest corner of the hall, where dusty, faded portraitures hung. The curtain before them remained closed, concealing their finer details in dimness and shadow. "Our poor aunt. I do say I always felt sorry for the precious creature. Which is why I'm relieved she'll soon be put out of her earthly misery and join our dearly-departed cousin, if you believe in such a thing as the afterlife."

Blasphemy. Delightful. Though as Taresa considered the object of Xain's attention, she could not help but partially agree with him. The likeness of their cousin Matteus rested in the center of smaller, inconsequential pictures, taking prominence amongst them. Even in the low light, she noted the soft lines and gentle tones of his youthful face, coupled with eyes so innocent she wondered how such a child could ever have existed in this cruel world.

"What say you?"

Taresa, her mind having wandered, turned to Xain. "Pardon?"

"Do you think I'm right? About Aunt Eldonza only having days – perhaps hours – until she passes and we finally inherit what is due to us?"

Taresa reddened. She marched up to Xain, so close she could smell the bile on his breath. "You are a wicked one, you know that, don't you?"

"Of course."

"Why have you come here, *really*? You are in no danger of losing any part of Aunt Eldonza's estate by being away. When she passes, royal messengers will be dispatched to all of us who will inherit her endowment. A chancellor will read her will, which my father's counsel has already reviewed." She narrowed her eyes. "Her assets will be distributed evenly amongst us, her last remaining kin. That is the law. You being here will not change that."

Xain stared back at her. To anyone else, his façade would have come across as one of stone. But she knew better. The creases of his face held the promise of a grin, an expression suppressed when one knew a secret all the world should have guessed.

"Your Majesty," he began. "You are correct. No surprise, seeing as how you are never wrong. True, my portion of the inheritance will be equal in size, my allotment no different than yours or my uncle's. The chancellor will confirm so during his reading of the will."

"However..."

"The proximity of my piece... is where the true treasure lies. About six months ago, while you and your minions were residing in Arinn, preparing for the royal farce that was your wedding, I was here with Aunt Eldonza. Her state of mind proved well enough where she was able to approve of an addendum to her will."

"But the law –"

"Yes, yes. I know I can't receive *more.* I can inherit a piece of my choosing, with our aunt's blessing, of course."

"Piece. What piece?"

"The bulk of Aunt Eldonza's estate, the source of her wealth, is cedar. The largest forest in the north resides under her name. The woods are dense, though, with the only roads into them those adjacent to this very castle. Beyond them, only game trails and small footpaths lead into her vast tracts of land, and none of those are wide enough for woodsmen to cart out timber. Hence why so much of her acreage remains untouched.

"The exception is what nature intended, a product of Mar Himself." Xain nodded toward a landscape painting adjacent to the collection of portraitures, one of a fishing village on the banks of a river. "The Taguas River. Small, not very wide. Hardly an expansive waterway. Yet a calm one, with no rapids nor falls, save for those in its eastern tributaries. Free of crags or torrents, it's perfect for skiffs and vessels, including barges.

"On such a watercraft, I took a short trip on the Taguas with a few surveyors. Mapping the terrain around it, I figured the land around its banks to be a size appropriate to my part of the inheritance. Not more substantial than my share, mind you, just a bit more valuable than the rest.

"While on my excursion, I also confirmed the existence of twelve villages and towns on the river. I managed to spend some time amongst their peoples, being an unofficial ambassador of Kin Garsea. I learned a bit about our beloved Uncle Quento, who had a soft spot for the river villages that populate the Taguas, seeing as he descended from a kin of fishermen. Aunt Eldonza held onto such a sentiment when he passed, allowing them to dwell as they have for centuries without being taxed or burdened by sharing the costs of running a dukedom."

"And you plan to change that? To line your own pockets?"

"Tax the poor? That will hardly make me rich, now will it?" Finally, the curl on his lips, which he had withheld all this time, emerged. "Their labor, well, that is another story.

"When my time comes, they will have a choice: pay tribute to their new landlord or work off their debt to the dukedom. All will be persuaded toward the latter. Docks will be expanded, quays built. And most importantly, the virgin forests along their shores will finally be harvested, with the logs felled and the cut lumber from newly-minted sawmills available to float down the Taguas. As was always intended."

Taresa, catching the folly of Xain's grand plan, replied to his scheme with a grin all her own. "My dear cousin. While Ibian cedar is prized, it is also readily available, especially in the south, where most dry docks and carpenters reside. They have stockpiles aplenty, even when you consider the increase in demand due to our new treaty with Marland.

"Even with the coerced labor you dare to mention, you would need a sizeable fortune to start such a venture. And you'd need a spike in demand to eventually pay for it. Why, if history is any indicator of the economy, there hasn't been such a market for Ibian cedar since –"

The life drained from her. Her grin faded while his remained.

Dear Mar.

"Exactly," Xain confirmed.

"Do you... conspire..." She scarcely uttered the last word, managing only to push it out as a whisper.

"No, no, cousin. Even I don't have so much influence. Besides, long, drawn-out wars are hardly my thing. Sure, I enjoy a good contest as much as the next man, but the blood and gore... No, I have no hand in the war to come.

"I'm simply an opportunist, one who sees on the horizon what others fail to acknowledge... though we all know it's coming."

"You assume too much," Taresa squeaked, growing

exasperated by how timid she sounded. "The recent events have been unsettling, yes, I'll grant you. But they are the mark of a madman, or a rogue group, looking to disrupt the Throne and sow chaos. No kingdom would dare to go to war with Ibia, especially now that we are united with Marland."

"My dearest Taresa." Xain extended his hand to caress her cheek. He nearly succeeded. Taresa pulled away just before his fingers brushed against her. "You perplex me. In a single breath, you speak like a sovereign and sage molded into one. Then, in your next uttering, you reveal your persistent naiveté, that ragged and carefree princess whose mind never matured." Xain stepped up to her. Taresa, standing her ground, nonetheless could not help but lean back. "It's clear your marriage to King Jameson hasn't served to better you. If only you had accepted my proposal. I could have been your Promised, then your husband, and by marriage, the King of Ibia. Your own personal monarch. The counterweight to all your flaws – your innocence, your great hope, all of your blind trust. We could have balanced each other. Ruled as a royal couple like no other."

"You and I, we were never meant to be."

"You thought otherwise once. On the night of your Promise to Prince Denisot. When I found you in the stables, crying... I comforted you..." Xain leaned forward.

Taresa slapped him across the face –

She leapt away. Shuddering, she kept her hand up, half-expecting him to attack.

Xain, though shocked, smiled. He extended the tip of his tongue to dab the top left corner of his lip, which bled.

"I knew it," he beamed. "You still care."

"I do not!"

"If that were true, you'd be shouting for your guards as we speak."

Taresa fumed. "I want you gone. Out! I don't care what Aunt Eldonza said. You are to leave the estate this instant!"

Xain stood back and straightened. He dipped low to bow, his gaze never leaving Taresa. "As you wish, Your Majesty."

With more composure she'd expect of a drunkard, he strode through the chamber. He slipped out to leave Taresa alone.

The final click of the closing door released Taresa from her stance. She exhaled. Her legs wobbly, her hands shaking, she hastened to the nearest table still harboring a touch of wine. Finding no steins nor goblets, she uncorked a half-empty vintage and drank straight from the bottle. She managed to gulp almost all of it before pausing to catch her breath.

That bloody louse. She wanted to curse his name. Curse his imprudence. Curse his every suggestion. His every word...

But she couldn't. For she knew – and hated to admit – that he was right.

Chapter 15

Symon rubbed the sinuous fibers of the rope between his fingertips. The habit gave him a short reprieve from the grinding of his teeth.

"All clear."

"Finally," Symon uttered under his breath. He took to the ratlines on the side of the galleon two tiers at a time, brushing off the extended hands from the nearby sailors offering to help him.

He hurdled over the railing onto the deck, ready to address any threat presented. Only his anticipation went unmet, except by the company of the ship's captain and Sir Everitt, whom he caught in mid-sentence.

"Your Majesty," they both said, their heads bowed.

"The report."

"Nothing taken," Everitt replied. "At least, not at first inventory. They did manage to make a mess of everything, however, so I've set my men to do a second sweep of the ship to be certain."

That bloody bastard turned out to be right. Symon nodded to his Right Captain. "And how about our men?"

Captain Danyll cleared his throat. "I saw to them personally, My King. Fifty-two sailors, guards, and attendants disembarked from the ship aboard all seven of our remaining skiffs. Forty-seven came back on our six, as expected. The seventh skiff escaped, having made its way towards the flyboat we spotted on the horizon before the fog rolled in. With any luck, those sailors on board the flyboat are truly ours and accepted our five men and their cargo with haste."

"And did the Ibians suspect anything amiss?"

"The Realeza didn't bother to stick around to count those who returned, having left once they concluded their search. I made certain to cause a ruckus during their raid, to sell them on the outrage of my protest."

Symon raised his brow. "You stayed aboard?"

"I did, Your Majesty. 'Tis my ship, after all."

"You had my permission to disembark with the others."

"I recall."

"In case the Realeza proved to be... more aggressive than necessary."

"'Tis true, Your Majesty. But this ship is my child and those men who boarded... I wasn't about to leave them alone with her. Not with your permission or even by Mar's command." On that last note, the Captain bit his lip, expecting an admonishment or word of further caution from His Majesty.

This one could be a Saliswater, through and through. "I would expect no less from a Marlish sailor, let alone one we've entrusted with a royal vessel. You have my thanks, Captain."

Danyll clipped his heels and beat his closed fist over his heart. He bowed as he excused himself from their company, withdrawing to the other railing where his First Mate waited patiently for a word.

"That one has more saltwater in his veins than a Saliswater," Symon admitted.

"Yes, a loyal one he is."

"Maybe even more so than Har-Kin Furde," Symon offered with a smirk.

"Now, now, James."

"Fine, fine. Seriously, what say you?"

"The ruse worked. The men relinquished the ship for the raid. The Realeza searched every last one of them before they disembarked. Thankfully, they made no effort to check the skiffs, though."

Lucky bastard, indeed. "And my quarters?"

"A bloody mess, like the captain said." Everitt shook his head. "They tore your room apart. No respect that lot has for anything, the wicked heathens. The Badger probably ordered them to do it."

"Good thing you let him live then."

His Right Captain grimaced. "What can I say? I had my orders."

Everitt escorted Symon back to his room, where two Voiceless stood at attention outside. Within, two more waited in full armor. Having directed their attention to the disarray, they pivoted at their entrance, saluting.

"You," Everitt said to the Voiceless at his left, "who was the fifth Right Captain to King Aethelrik?"

"Everitt, really? You already conducted a sweep with these men."

"Aye, I swept the room. Now, I question the men, in case the Realeza planted agents capable of overtaking our guards, Mar forbid." Everitt turned back to the Voiceless. "Answer. And raise your visor before you do."

The Voiceless paused, looking to Symon. Symon nodded. The Voiceless raised his visor, revealing the bulbous nose and sharp brow of the knight within.

"Right Captain Sander, of Har-Kin Herbert," the guard signed.

"And you," Everitt said to the Voiceless at his right. "Who was the sixth Right Captain of his predecessor, King Andreu?"

The Voiceless remained still, perhaps in consideration.

"Well?" Everitt asked, his patience tried.

"I have no idea..." the knight answered in the language of the hands before raising his visor.

Symon held his breath. Everitt's hand fell to the pommel of his sword.

"... because King Andreu had only three Right Captains during his reign, not six." The Voiceless held his hand at the ready, prepared to reply again if prompted. The light blue eyes of an earnest guard met Everitt's inquisitive stare.

"Very well." Everitt turned to Symon. "I recognize these men. Newer guards they are, having joined our ranks shortly after your coronation. Their eyes – and responses – ring true."

"I'm sure of it myself."

"Good night, James."

"Don't stay up too long yourself. We sail at dawn."

"I'll oversee the final sweep, then retire." Everitt tilted his head toward Symon before marching out of the room.

As soon as the door closed, the Voiceless to his right removed his helm. "What stick up his rear does Everitt have this time?" Ely asked.

"He's on edge, 'tis all."

"For the past thirty-some-odd years."

"Was it that bad ashore?" Gerry asked as he took off his

helm. As he did, the interior glanced upon his nose, putting it askew. The result smudged the prosthetic against his left cheek, giving an appearance both grotesque and comical.

"Aye, what he said," Ely added, chuckling.

"Aye," Symon confirmed.

Ely perked. "So I was right, wasn't I? Say it, brother. Say it!"

"You were... partially correct."

"Meaning?"

"Your guess about the Realeza proved true, I'll admit." With their arrival at the Harbor of Arinn, Ely had sent their flyboats ahead to gather intelligence from the capital. The resulting surveillance provided tales of a city – and kingdom – on guard, with the news of Castle Seylonna having reached them only the day after its fall. In the wake of such details, Ely suggested a bold move to protect their recently acquired maps from Ibian eyes. Symon, then Gerry, resisted his proposal, believing paranoia had overtaken their brother. But the raid proved their more irrational sibling to be correct, much to their chagrin.

"Then what was I wrong about?"

"The Grand Duke, unfortunately. He wasn't by His Majesty's side, as expected. He moved north, supposedly to rally the support of other kin necessary to respond to the recent threats."

"Taresa –" Gerry uttered.

"Will be fine," Symon insisted. "We intended to pick her up with haste anyway, having sent word ahead by flyboat to the royal estate where she stays."

"Right, the flyboat..."

"So His Majesty orchestrated the raid on our galleon,"

Ely said. "I'll say, a bold move by our father-by-marriage."

"I didn't say that."

"Oh, come now. You're going to stand there and tell me –"

"I'm not going to tell you anything!" Symon growled. He shot a disapproving glance to Ely. Gerry placed his hand on Symon's shoulder only to receive the same glare. Symon shrugged off his little brother's gesture to retreat to the corner. There a flagon of wine waited along with three glasses. Symon ignored the glasses as he uncorked the bottle from the table. He took a long draught as his brothers watched in silence.

The drink dripped down his chin. He wiped his mouth on his sleeve before glancing at the words etched onto the flagon. "Rosi... rosaa?" He slammed the bottle back onto the table with a thud. "Damn Ibian language! And their accents!"

"Brother..." Gerry whispered.

"It's all wrong since we came here. The feasts. The galas. The show of force, only to miss the enemy by so little, before they, they... taunted us. Uhhh!" Symon threw his hands in the air. "So much useless, idle talk. And for what? Nothing!"

Symon rubbed his temple while Gerry shrunk back. Ely, grinning, stepped between them. "May I speak now?"

"What?"

"You needn't fret, brother. We have the advantage."

"Advantage? You're mad. Bloody mad."

"Am I? Consider our situation. We are allied with Ibia at long last, which was a union decades in the making in our dearly departed father's eyes. We have maps from the

Grand Duke of Seylonna, Mar bless his soul, which no one seems to know anything about. They have dates of voyages, details of manifests, in short, more details a ring of spies could ever hope to discover. Once Dawkin sets his eyes upon them, I'm sure he'll sort out their meaning. And finally, we – or at least him," Ely snapped, jerking a thumb toward Gerry, "has Taresa."

"What's she have to do with all this?" Gerry asked.

"She's our, um, how would those maritime merchants put it? What with their contracts, trade routes, handshake deals. She's our collateral. Nay, our insurance."

"She's neither contract nor coin."

"Aye, she's better. For whether we're taunted by Xain, or the unknown menace whose been attacking these castles, or King Felix himself, none would dare to strike our queen."

"You're damn sure?"

"I am. Damned and sure. We all are. She's bloody protecting us, she is. If ever a fool were to harm her, the Ibians – King and all – would rise in arms."

"They're doing that already," Symon quipped.

"True. The Ibians want justice, as do our lot. But in this conflict, brothers, we do not stand at the front lines. Those *talks* you abhor, Symon, are our salvation. They buy us time. Resources. Even allies. Albeit not the most savory ones, but allies nonetheless. Don't you think Father tried a hundred-thousand times to do the same during the Century War? But do you ever recall him saying his attempts ever became fruitful? Never. But, here and now, we have the opportunity to do what he could not. Not as one. Rather, four. We can be the diplomat he never achieved. This shared conflict – or nuisance or threat or whatever you want to call it – can bind us to the continent's superpower. If only we show this chance the restraint, the respect, the cunning it deserves."

Ely looked to his brothers. Blank stares met his eagerness.

"Really? Nothing?"

"I, I don't know, Ely," Gerry confessed.

"Your passion is, say, notable," Symon added.

"But you're a tad... How would Dawkin say? Naïve."

"Agreed. The Ibians aren't pawns. We can't count on gaining any momentum by trifling with –"

"Shut up. Both of you." Something outside the rear cabin window had captured Ely's attention. He strode across the room as his brothers followed. They leaned over the bench bordering the window, straining their eyes for a closer look.

Adrift, a skiff floated. Unmanned. A swell rocked the boat. As it did, the lantern placed upon its center bench came to life.

"Is... Wait. Are those oreflares inside the lantern? How are they..." Ely's voice trailed off, puzzled.

"I know how," Gerry said, beaming. "Remember? You take a handful of large oreflares and jostle them around. They brighten due to the motion. They never stay lit for long."

"Smart lads," Ely mused. "I didn't even ask them to do that. I merely suggested they include a sign of some sort, one to signal their departure from Ibia yet one not so obvious as a shining lantern, lest the steady brightness tip off the King's agents in these waters. Hmm, not bad."

Symon looked upon the empty boat. Never before had he ever been so glad to see a vessel unmoored and unmanned.

The maps are safe, at least. Our sailors managed to escape. Dawkin will be warned – as will Grandfather and the rest of Marland – ahead of our homecoming.

"You did well, Ely," he said in earnest, knowing the fight ahead would be far from fair. "We need more of that wit from you. And from our men. From all of us."

"Your accolades unnerve me, brother."

"As they should."

For even with our advantage of intelligence, with our secrets and all, the enemy still assails us. Here, during our royal union. Abroad, during a mission of diplomacy. Perhaps even at home? Is Dawkin safe from the threats we've faced? Are any of our countrymen?

Symon set his jaw. Whatever their circumstances – with all the world of possibilities, however improbable, swirling in his mind – he knew one thing to be true: They would act. For they had to, as waiting in the shadows and biding their time benefited not them but their enemies. Yes, they would put a series of events in motion. With haste, in the face of immediacy. With prudence, when favor allowed. With force, to show those at home and afar that Kin Saliswater should never be opposed.

"We will use your spies, Ely," Symon announced as he looked out the window, as much to himself as to his siblings. "Gerry, we will use your modesty, to deceive our enemies. And Dawkin, his mind, as annoying as he is with his book knowledge and such. And I... will use shield and sword. We will stop this threat, using every trick and edict at hand, no matter how questionable. We must stand against this... tide... This surge rising from the continent, which seems to assault everything we touch. We must plan. Move. And strike."

Chapter 16

"... and here is the manifest." Artus laid the leather-bound book before Dawkin. "The Head Magistrate delivered it this morning. I have yet to review the log for the contents reported as missing, though he did mention a few of the stolen items. Hardwood from the Eastern Woodlands. A bundle of feathers. Crystal orbs."

"Crystal?"

"Aye."

"Half the shipment had been arranged for our mages, who use them for storing certain potions or fashion them for their devices, telescopes, and the sort. The Cutters Guild bought the other half, its contents earmarked for the lapidaries of Arcporte. Their orders will be delayed due to the loss of their wares."

"Of course," Dawkin replied. *Fewer crystal goblets and vases for our precious nobility.* "Is that all of it?"

"There is one other small... matter."

Dawkin tapped his fingers on the table with one hand as he pinched the bridge of his nose with his other. He had wondered how soon it would take his grandfather to arrive at the dreaded topic.

"Go on."

"The Voiceless, having monitored your quest through the countryside – and thank you for adherence to your royal duties, by the way – well, they brought to my attention the company you kept during a portion of your trip."

"Grandfather, I am not a member of the court." Dawkin dropped his feet from the edge of the table. He shifted in his seat, planting his feet on the floor and his palms before him. "Speak your truth."

"Very well, Dawkin." Artus leaned forward; the lightness of his demeanor had vanished. What replaced it appeared akin to a wolf staring down its prey. "Your association with a sibyl is a threat to the Throne."

"She is a descendent from the Boreal Islanders. Her association with witchcraft ends there."

"How can you be so sure? You hardly know the girl."

"I came to know her... Well enough."

"Dawkin?!"

"Not in *that* way. Merely as a fellow traveler. We rode together, conversed, shared meals, even a skin of wine."

"Oh, why that changes *everything*."

"Poke fun all you like."

"If someone of repute saw you together –"

"So what if they did? I acted in disguise. She doesn't even know who I am. The real me." Dawkin slumped in his chair. "No one does."

Artus leaned back from the table, though he kept his back straight. "Just be mindful."

"I always am."

Artus rose. He opened the door to the Fourpointe Chamber, finding the two Voiceless outside where he had left them. He nodded, prompting the knights to move down the hall out of Dawkin's view.

"Will you be joining us?" Artus asked.

Dawkin fought a sigh. "Aye." He grabbed the helm from the table, fitting it atop his head. He donned the full plate and armor of a Voiceless from crown to toe, serving as a proxy to Artus' Right Captain.

They ascended from Terran in silence, accompanied by the pair of Voiceless. Rising to the floor level, a subdued version of castle life awaited them. Servants strode with a blend of haste and worry, treading carefully to ensure their soles made nary a din. The yard – usually ringing with the clack of metal and the grunts of soldiers – lay bare and quiet. Even the stables they passed offered little in the way of liveliness as the steeds looked on at their passersby.

Only the hall leading to the Throne Room offered anything recognizable. Even if Dawkin hated it.

Clap, clap.

Dawkin shuddered. He had only heard the ominous echo of the vaulted hallway a handful of times in his life, when he and the children of court – and on rare occasions, his disguised brothers – had played. Such instances of frolic proved scarce, for many nobility and clergy often crowded the space, even at odd hours. Still, at times early in the morning or after supper, the hall cleared, allowing youth to run amok as they pleased.

His playmates, who were always too busy giggling or chasing each other, never expressed discomfort upon hearing the vibrations around them. Only Dawkin seemed to pause – albeit briefly – when the stone columns and panels of the gallery began to sing. Or wail.

Clap, clap, clap.

Each acoustic wave ran long and deep, spilling into every crevice of the hall, including the ears of the few present. In the absence of other sounds to provide distractions, their pitch stood out as unavoidable, omnipresent.

As Artus and Dawkin approached, the guards at the main entrance pulled open the doors to the Throne Room.

Beyond the arch awaited their guests: the senior clergy of the Church.

The audience stood seven in all, including the highest-ranking member of the Church of Marland, High Bishop Perceval. Resplendent in the forest green robes and golden trim of the Church's northern branch, the whole of them turned to their host, eyes wide in anticipation. Each held an ornamental staff crowned with a silver-inlaid adornment of a hand holding a downward trident. The symbol, meant to indicate peace and fellowship, never struck Dawkin as righteous; for him, it implied an inevitable doom.

The clapping continued as they entered the Throne Room, with the low and high bishops bowing their heads to Artus. The former sovereign dipped his head in response as his guards – Dawkin in disguise as one of them – strode on behind him. Artus took to the throne just as the sentinels at the door closed them. Then, silence.

"Your Majesty." High Bishop Perceval bent into a low bow.

"You're too kind, Your Eminence," Artus replied, remaining seated. "Sire will do."

"As you request." Perceval glanced at his colleagues to check their attention. The six, standing tall behind him, stared forward, their concentration on the Throne. Perceval shifted his eyes back toward Artus. "We thank you for the invitation to this private court. Your time – more than any other Marlish noble – is of the utmost value –"

Artus raised a finger. Perceval paused.

"I beg your forgiveness, Your Eminence. But with the matters we're considering, I suspect we can skip the pleasantries." Dawkin, standing on guard at Artus' right, caught a futile look in his direction. "Speak your truth."

"Very well. Your men apprehended five of our pupils, just outside Evanshire, the day before last. Two days before that, I learned of three others who were stopped and questioned in the Upper East Waterlands, while other novices expressed similar concerns of experiencing scrutiny from Marlish soldiers."

"Eight inconvenienced? That hardly seems worthy of calling a meeting."

"There are more reports. Many more. I only abstain from mentioning specifics in this present moment to save the Court... any further scandal."

"Careful, Perceval. I like your har-kin enough, and I respect your position, but I won't tolerate any implication of wrongdoing, whether in private or public."

The High Bishop tightened his hand around his staff, never breaking his gaze with Artus. "You asked me to speak my mind."

"Yet you hold to some pretense, suggesting rather than stating boldly."

Perceval smirked. "My apologies, Sire. I should have remembered the tales from my father, who always spoke of the Gauntlet with reverence, even when you vexed him."

Dawkin winced, for once grateful of the helm and visor which stifled him. He knew his grandfather held the moniker with ambivalence in his calmer moments and with hatred in his worst. Not because the former king had any love for Kin Foleppi. Far from it. He hated the Tosilians perhaps more than any Marlishman. Rather, he loathed any mention – even an epithet intended as praise – which reminded him of the adversaries who had killed three of his children.

"Aye," Artus replied stone-faced. "Baron Dederic. A stubborn though wise man. He served Marland well."

"As have all of Har-Kin Hamage, which is why I break from protocol to offer these words now: the Lost Souls are not to be harassed."

Artus raised a brow. "Honest. Like your father."

"He lost many a debate with you."

"His will, though strong, often held at its base assumptions and bias, which is why I steered clear of his advice. Much like I deny taking yours at present."

"Though unlike your discussions with him, I feel you may be more inclined to listen. Especially given the words I speak are not mine. They come directly from Vloma." Perceval held out his free hand. One of the bishops behind him produced a scroll from his sleeve, which he placed in Perceval's palm. The High Bishop handed it to the Voiceless nearest him, who in turn passed it to Artus.

"It is an official decree from the Supreme Devout himself," Perceval noted as the former sovereign unfurled the parchment to read it. "He declares the current state of Afari and its outlying isles – including Marland – are in disarray, lost in sin, enslaved by lawlessness, debauchery, and disobedience. Due to such widespread, wanton heinousness, he has declared this present time to be an Epoch of Lost Souls. I suspect you know what that means?"

Dawkin expected an "Aye" from his grandfather. Yet none came. The Saliswater kept on with his reading, with only his eyes moving to and fro to indicate he remained cognizant.

Finally, his eyes ceased shifting. They turned upward away from the scroll toward Perceval.

"The Supreme Devout has some nerve. I'll grant you that."

Perceval reddened. "Blasphemy!"

"'Tis true. Your lord's action seems out of sorts."

"I was referring to you, my liege."

"Oh, I know. But remarkably, you fail to acknowledge your leader's faults while pointing out mine. An Epoch of Lost Souls? Truly? An edict like that is reserved for the otherworldly, such as when Mar traded his trident for the shield and sword or after he wandered Afari after slaying his brother. Even in the Century War, only one Supreme Devout dared to declare an Epoch – His Eminence, Antoni di Luggano."

"I know my church history, Sire."

"Then you recall his edict was rebuffed. Every kingdom dismissed his decree and sent their armies to the borders of the Devout State as a show of force. Fortunately, Luggano never made good on the promise within the decree, in which he threatened to declare war on those who assaulted or harassed the brethren or bishops of the Church. So with his warning ignored, do you know what happened next?" Artus shifted to the edge of his seat, his elbows on his knees. "The kingdoms continued with their duty, vetting those corrupt church officials who conspired against them: the brethren of the cloth, men sworn to serve man and Mar, only to betray both in the name of the fox. Monarchs not in bed with Kin Foleppi sought out such vile traitors –"

"Sire, I must object –"

"You are in the King's Court! The court of my grandson, in whose absence I represent. So long as a Saliswater sits on this throne and speaks, none shall interrupt."

The clap of echoes thundered in the expanse of the Throne Room. A force capable of weighing down everything it touched, the furor burdened all, such that even drawing breath became laborious. Artus' bellow continued to rumble, the stone walls reverberating his words back and forth until they faded into an awkward silence.

The quiet seeped into Dawkin's bones, as did the unsettling concern something so much worse would transpire from this encounter.

Say something, Grandfather. Dawkin nearly screamed his thoughts. *Speak any word. Save this moment.*

Artus rose from his chair. He descended the short steps from the throne to approach the High Bishop. Though he remained in place, Perceval swallowed a breath as the former sovereign came up to him, having to tilt his head down to stare into his eyes.

"You broke from the unspoken code of this Court to offer a truth you knew I did not want to hear. Now let me return the favor by doing the same: Kin Saliswater has the final say over all matters in Marland. Like many, we've bled, we've lost, we've suffered for our land. However, like few, we rule. Our burden is known by a select minority, our curse..." Artus scanned the Throne Room. His gaze found Dawkin, though in his caution it thankfully did not settle.

"... Well, our curse is unique. Ours alone. This reign only works under the condition of absolute rule. We hold court not to bend to this will or that, but to consider the totality of circumstances and opinions before issuing our decrees.

"I am only a steward to my grandson. He is his own man, with a perspective all his own. Nonetheless, never doubt we are one mind when it comes to how we demand the utmost obedience. Every subject who inhabits this sacred Marlish soil must follow our commands. No one – by which I mean no mortal, no soul – shall defy us. Nor are any in a position to tell *us* what to do. Understood?"

Perceval held his stare. The High Bishop bent his head as though to nod, then continued to dip into a bow. He took a few steps back before turning. The other bishops followed in his wake as he left.

Dawkin descended from the throne platform as the doors creaked with their exit. In the presence of his grandfather and the Voiceless once more, Dawkin removed his helm.

. "Grandfather, was that truly the wisest course of action?"

"No."

"Then why?"

"I took over for my father after more than six decades of war. There were times – nay, years – when I made one bad decision after another. Not due to stubbornness, nor pride, nor ignorance. Because there were no good options to make." Artus pivoted to Dawkin. Whatever furor he had held when speaking to Perceval had drained from him. The iron monarch of only minutes before had faded, having been replaced by a frail old man. "Commands, good or bad, must persist. And good or bad, your reign, however short or long it will be, shall endure under a solitary condition: your will. Decide, and never doubt yourself thereafter. By that condition, you and your brothers will survive."

The breeze nipped at Dawkin. He pulled his scarf close, even if the effort failed to stop the coldness from seeping through the wool to reach his neck.

"Bloody wind," Dawkin mumbled.

He hastened his pace to warm himself. The wharf proved too crowded for him to move much faster, however. He managed to strike ahead a few quick steps before the path narrowed, with the flock clogging the avenue further.

Dawkin cursed under his breath; he resumed shuffling with the rest of the pack. In such tight quarters, the stank of Marland came upon him. From the unwashed freshly departing the ships, or the crooked green teeth of the poor begging for alms, as well as the patrons of pubs, the lot of whom had no sense of personal space.

For all their odors, their talk assailed Dawkin more than anything.

"Move on, you bloody wanker!"

"Piss off, you scoundrel!"

"Make me! I dare you!"

"Spare a bit of coin, will you, mister? You look like you can. Come on now."

"Watch where you're going!"

"Hey, hey, look at that one! That blonde wench right there."

The last comment crystallized Dawkin's attention. He snapped his head, both to find the speaker and the subject of which he spoke.

"Who in the bloody hell would wade into the sea in this weather?" said the same, unknown voice.

"A whore with a burning in her nether-regions, that's who," chuckled another.

Dawkin elbowed his way to the seawall, which ran along the harborside of the wharf. Although also teeming with the masses, it offered pockets of space, which provided a brief respite from the horde. He wedged his way toward one, where he finally paused. He searched the length of the stone barrier, peeking his head over the short crenels until he spotted the woman mentioned.

She waded knee-deep into a shallow harbor section, just beyond where the last grouping of docks ended. There, amongst the tidal pools, she scavenged for mussels and clams. Hardly a surprising activity, Dawkin mused, had the weather been more agreeable. In the current conditions, however, she gathered alone.

With her back to Dawkin, several hundred feet away, he held out hope she was the one he sought. She had the slender build and height of Lady Cora, along with her hair. Such similarity provoked Dawkin to stare with an unknown intensity so that his vision began to blur as the very air around the maiden quivered.

Again? he thought.

He blinked, shaking his head. Refocusing on her, she turned, revealing herself to be another lady, fair in skin but far removed otherwise from the woman of his desires. Disappointed, he leaned away from the wall, rubbing his eyes. Everything cleared, with not a speck or blur before him. Satisfied his vision had corrected itself, he moved onward.

Sir Nygell's lay absent of any patrons when Dawkin entered. The aroma of fresh cardamom and cinnamon greeted him, as did the smile of the shopkeeper.

"Greetings, Sir Evenon!" Master Franque chirped.

"Good afternoon," Dawkin replied, moving toward his usual spot.

"You won't be wanting to go there, not without your next read."

"Oh, actually, I wanted to peruse a bit, perhaps find something –"

"New? She thought you might say that."

Dawkin perked. "Oh?"

"Uh-huh." Franque's grin widened. "I must say, whoever your companion is, she has been good for business. Such a well-to-do lass, always seeking out rare manuscripts and purchasing them too. Not like most who come in only to purchase a spot of tea and read without buying the damn book they touched." Master Franque caught himself. "Present company excluded, of course."

Ignoring the unintended slight, Dawkin strode to the head counter. "My companion? The one you mentioned, the blond-haired woman?"

"Why, yes. She purchased another present for you. She asked that I hand it over on your next visit."

From the lower shelf, the shopkeeper furnished a leather-bound manuscript. Dawkin's eyes widened upon seeing the violet-colored hue of its cover, noting such craftsmanship proved rare due to the time and expense of coloring leather in such rich tones. Further to its exquisiteness, the border and lettering of the title were inlaid with silver leaf, which glinted before Dawkin's eyes as he took the book in his hands to inspect it.

He ran his fingers over the silver inlay of its title: *The Weald Tales.*

From the top peeked a rectangular piece of paper. Dawkin pulled it out, discovering it to be a small letter:

In this manuscript of woodland creatures and spirits, my love of the natural and of words collides. May you find your meaning within these pages as you read them. Touch them. Feel them.

C.G.

"Lovely, isn't it? And worth a bit of coin too." Master Franque winked.

Dawkin's silence gave him all the answers he needed. The shopkeeper receded to the teapot he had placed at the far end of the counter to pour two cups of steeping brew. He put one cup to Dawkin's right – just out of reach, to prevent it from being accidentally tipped – as he sipped from his.

"One wouldn't think her kind to afford such a luxury."

"Her kind?"

"Oh, I don't judge. The fair-skinned blondes from the northern isles have assimilated well with our kind, faring much better than those barbarians from Lewmar ever could. Still, not many have the coin to spare on luxuries such as this beauty, what with the bulk of their people tending to the fields, or focusing on the healing arts."

"She's more than a farmer or curer." Dawkin ran his fingertips over the inset lettering. "Much more."

"Whatever she is to the rest of us, you surely made an impression on her." Master Franque set down his cup. He reached beneath the counter again, this time withdrawing some scones. He offered Dawkin one, who politely declined. "It is curious, though, what with her being so lavish in her gifts to you when she can't even recall your name."

Dawkin chuckled. "The fault for that is mine. In my... eagerness to speak with her, I blurted out the king's name when she asked me about mine. I haven't had the heart to correct her yet, you see."

"Oh, really? Odd, still. She didn't refer to you as His Majesty's either."

"Huh? You sure?"

Master Franque popped the last morsel of his scone into his mouth, nodding.

"Well, what name did she –"

An orange flare burst out front. The windows exploded, sending shards inward, while the door blew open. A suffocating heat poured in, sending Dawkin to his knees, gasping.

His eyes watered. His ears rung from the explosion. His mind, clouded, throbbed from a pain that shook him to the core. Somehow, he managed to catch wind of the shouts from the street.

"After them!"

"Watch out!"

"The flames! Fire! Over yonder!"

Dawkin staggered to his feet. The curtains straddling the windows had been set ablaze, along with those stacks of books closest to the entrance. He drooped over the counter, spotting the shopkeeper face down on the floor.

"Master Franque!" Dawkin yelled. He coughed, the shout having allowed the scorching air to assail his lungs.

The man lay unresponsive to Dawkin's call. Dawkin

hobbled around the counter, his forearm to his mouth in a vain attempt to filter the smoke. He wheezed while he turned Master Franque over on his back. The man responded with a flutter of his eyes yet remained on the ground.

"Up with you," Dawkin urged.

Dawkin lifted and propped him against the counter shelf. He then wedged himself under his left arm, prompting Franque to struggle to his feet.

"What? My, my shop..." Franque uttered.

"Bugger it! I'll buy you a new one."

With the shopkeeper leaning heavily on his shoulder, Dawkin stumbled out the front door into the chaos.

From the epicenter of blackened cobblestones, tendrils of fire raged, consuming all. Splintered wood. Torn clothing. Flesh.

Dawkin could hardly tear his gaze away. Dozens of townspeople reeled on the ground as many and more crowded around them to help. Most of those just beyond the fatal reach of the explosion had been knocked down in shock, left to cradle their wounds, unseen yet devastating.

Within the radius of blast and fire, a more sinister scene lay — eight lifeless bodies. Charred flakes of black replaced the sight of smooth hands and faces. Clothing had burned away, as had hair and even the stiff leather of the victims' boots and shoes. Yet the worst of the scene was not what the blast had engulfed.

Rather, it was what it had torn.

Bearing witness to limbs strewn and scattered, Dawkin could not decide whether the carnage looked more related to the work of a butcher or a pack of wolves. One arm had severed cleanly from its victim, whose sinew and flesh had been instantly cauterized by the fieriness. Nearby, a leg had been ripped to shreds. The spectrum of gore littered the cobblestones, turning the once-road into a crematorium.

Beyond the bloodshed, a group of monks hurried up the street, trailed by a mob of townsfolk. One of the brothers paused, pivoting to face the horde. The throng halted, with many backpedaling from his presence.

At once, it became clear why. The man-of-the-cloth – in a stained, off-white robe – produced a wine bottle from his robe. A handkerchief protruded from its neck, which the monk set ignited with the flick of his flint. The top aflame, he hurled the projectile into the crowd.

The mass scattered. The bottle shattered on the cobblestones, spewing tendrils of golden light. Even from afar, Dawkin had to shield his face from the surge of heat. Seconds passed before he dared to lower his arm, finding the flash had claimed a bystander, who sunk to the ground enflamed.

Enraged by the horror, the mob resumed their chase, closing in on the seven brothers. They caught up first with the one who had lobbed the last bottle. They pinned him to the ground in a hail of fists while the rest chased after the others. In spurts and waves, they soon claimed the remaining monks, who defied their captors with slurs and threats.

"You cannot stop us!" one brother yelled before a solid punch broke his jaw.

"Death to Marland! Death to her people!" cried another.

"Damn the King! Damn him, I say! Damn the King!"

The furor of the mob drowned out the rest. Their cries

and shouts blended, morphing into a collection of curses from hundreds sharing the same mentality. Dawkin strained to make sense of the disorder, able to pick up a spare word here and there. Then a peasant chanced by him, the loudest of the bunch.

"The Cathedral! They seek sanctuary. Stop them!"

Dawkin withdrew from the tumult to lay Master Franque under the awning of a cheese shop. A firm hand gripped his forearm, swinging him around. Dawkin launched his fist, only to stop it an inch away from the nose of a Voiceless.

"Your Majesty," the knight signed. "We must go."

"What in the bloody hell is happening?" Dawkin caught sight of one mob moving toward an oak tree, where the length of a hastily-made noose dangled from its thickest branch.

"We'll provide a full report to you back at Terran –"

"Soldier!" Dawkin roared. The Voiceless released his forearm.

"Best we know right now," the Voiceless began, "is that some explosives were discovered on a ship by a surprise inspection. The vessel was crewed by their kind." The knight gestured to the monk at the oak tree, whose neck had been fitted with the noose. "Now come."

Dawkin turned to Master Franque. The shopkeeper stirred, his eyes parting as he extended his arms to support himself. Though dazed, he at least proved alert.

The knight pleaded with His Majesty once more. "Please! Now!"

Dawkin conceded, allowing his detail to lead him through the streets. They steered clear of the remaining sections of the mob, which swelled their ranks by the minute from those commoners looking to see justice had.

As they escaped, one question burned through Dawkin's mind. "Where's their ship?" he asked the Voiceless. "Where is the monks' ship?" The Voiceless shrugged as he continued to march. Dawkin thought of pressing him once more. His chance escaped him, for as they turned the corner to come upon the wharf, he found his answer.

A riot engulfed a large galley. Several commoners had taken to the deck, tossing its cargo into the water or tearing at its sails. Many more gathered on the dock, taking aim at the ship with any item within their reach. They largely ignored the tongue of flame, which climbed up the right side of the mainsail, flanking the crest:

An Ibian cedar.

Chapter 17

The ale was sour. The corner dark. The banter around him unamusing.

All just like his mood.

"The gale continues. That wind be something of a blessing: strong, straight, and true," said one sailor.

"Just like our king with his new queen!" shouted another.

An uproar rose from the gallery. Even the cooks in the kitchen heard the crude joke, adding their chuckles. Only Gerry remained apart, raising his stein to his lips for a long, long draught.

"Best mind your tongue," advised one sailor, whose lack of slurred speech conveyed the right of his thoughts.

Finally, Gerry thought. *Some sense.*

"Bah," replied the jokester. "The officers don't care what we say down here."

"But up on deck –"

"Her moaning will drown out the lot of us!"

The laughter exploded. As did Gerry. He slammed his stein onto the table and shot from his seat. He made a line toward the drunk buffoon – intent on shutting his mouth for good – when a set of strong hands grabbed ahold of him, ushering him to the stairs.

Gerry shook his shoulders to try to break free before realizing the quarters swayed back and forth. The jolt to his feet had been too sudden considering the ale he had consumed. His stability compromised, he leaned into the Voiceless guiding him, who had picked up on Gerry's need for support.

The two emerged onto the main deck, where the brisk sea air invigorated Gerry. He inhaled, the sweet wind cleansing him. And without further provocation, he retched.

"Aaargh!" the Voiceless exclaimed, the guttural sound rising.

"I'll take him from here," Symon offered, nodding to the knight's now-soiled boots. "Go, clean up."

The Voiceless obliged as Symon guided Gerry to the railing. There, Gerry proceeded to spew the contents of his day.

"Impressive," Symon began as Gerry vomited his last. "You made a mute man speak. Not much different from their grunts during training, but still."

"More jokes," Gerry sputtered, wiping his mouth with his sleeve. He slumped down to the floor. "Don't you start."

"You all right, little brother?"

"How, how could he? How could *she*?"

"'Tis our duty, remember?"

"You didn't –"

"We were attacked that night."

"But before, during your truth session, you said you couldn't –"

"*That* was different. Had I... not been interrupted, I would have done my duty. Understood?"

Gerry nodded, though he didn't believe him. Then again, he could hardly comprehend anything. "I need a drink." He propped himself on his hands, about ready to rise.

"No, no. You've had enough."

"You're not the king of me!" Gerry, somehow, stumbled to his feet.

"I am," Symon insisted as he wrapped his arms around him.

"More ale."

"No."

"Then wine."

"No."

"Well, give me something."

"I will."

A moment later, the cold rush enveloped him. Gerry opened his mouth to scream, only to have his cries drowned. His breath burst into bubbles around his face. He wrestled against the firm grip of his brother's hands on his head and shoulders. Finally, Symon relented, allowing Gerry to fall away from the water barrel.

"What the hell was that?!" Gerry demanded from the ground, soaked from the shoulders up.

"A lesson."

"In what?"

"Public display." Symon extended his hand. Gerry took it begrudgingly, only to be propped back onto his feet in an instant with Symon's strong pull. "Never get drunk while in disguise. Never."

"But Ely does that all the –"

"Ely knows how to control himself, even when drunk. Him acting on his control, well, that's a different matter entirely, as Dawkin would say." Symon jabbed Gerry with his finger. "You, on the other hand, can't control your spirits."

"I can. A little."

"You can't."

"I'm just, I..." Gerry gestured toward the King's cabin. His shoulders slumped, defeated.

"Understood." Symon patted Gerry on the shoulder. "Your disguise washed off. Come, before anyone sees you."

Minutes later, in the privacy of their alcove within the Voiceless' quarters, Gerry slipped a dry shirt over his head. As he tied the tassels, Symon offered him a warm mug of tea.

"Drink."

Gerry raised it to his lips, then paused.

"Did you..."

"No fading potion. Nothing in it but honey and the brew of leaves. Honest."

"Maybe there should be." Gerry took a sip. "I should all but forget tonight ever happened."

Symon pulled up a stool and sat across from him. He leaned in, placing his elbows on his knees. "Gerry, I know it's hard –"

"Do you love her?"

"What?"

"Taresa."

"I know who you're referring to, I just, I..."

"She was my first. I know you and Ely and even Dawkin have had other women before, both as the Prince and in your excursions from Terran, but I haven't."

"Really? Come now. You spoke of visiting brothels and taverns when going out on your own, in disguise."

"Lies. All of them. Sure, I went out hidden in one of Ely's

ridiculous fronts and came back to tell of some misadventure. But 'twas a ruse. I never lay with another. I only drank and sulked in the corner of those establishments, reporting of what others did, never of myself."

"Gerry, we all think we love the first one we lay with. But those feelings pass."

"Do they? Always? She isn't some whore from a tavern. I'll see her for the rest of my life. What I feel... it won't fade. Just the opposite. It'll grow stronger. I know it."

"Then, Taresa, she means something to you?"

"Aye."

"I see."

"No, you don't. Perhaps you care for her. And Dawkin. Maybe even one day Ely, that rotten bastard. Still, you don't know what it's like. To carry the burden of –"

"Don't you dare."

"I didn't finish."

"Nor will you." Symon rose to pace. "Gerry, *we* share the same burden. Us four. No one else will ever know the responsibility we share. People look at us and think we have only the good life. They never consider the stress we feel as baron after baron laments at our court. Or how we must make decisions that affect not only our kin but our kingdom. Then in battle or conflict, they never have to see those we command, then lose... the dead we see..."

Symon paused, leaning against the wall across from him. Though the light was low, a host to dimness and shadows, Gerry knew it alone could not account for the mood he saw. The blood drained from his façade. The drooping mouth. The sunken eyes.

"You know what day it is?"

Gerry shook his head.

"It's been a year."

The shock thundered through his consciousness, such that his worry over Taresa abandoned him.

How could I have forgotten? Idiot! I, of all my brothers, should have remembered. Mar, I discovered his body. I was there... I was there...

The deluge of that fateful night sank in, overwhelming him. The bloodied sheets. The gasps of the knights and the cries of the attendants who crowded at the doorway. The mangled flesh... of his... of his...

Tears cascaded down his cheeks as his nose ran and his mouth quivered.

Symon bent his head down, knowing he had touched a nerve, a wound that had never healed. He dipped his hand into his breast pocket to retrieve a handkerchief, which he extended to Gerry.

"Like I said," Symon whispered as Gerry took his cloth. "I see."

"Dear Mar," Gerry said, dabbing his cheeks and nose. "Father. I recall him, in that tragic moment, as if it was happening right before us. And yet, so much has passed since then. It seems like ages ago."

"Much has passed."

A king's year is a peasant's lifetime. "Aye. Now look at us." Suddenly, through the remnant of his tears, Gerry chuckled.

"What?"

"Such fools we are! We lost our father, became kings, married into a family who hates us, and traveled to a country where death has stalked us at every corner, and we *still* can't bother to get along. Honestly, how did Father put up with us all those years?"

Symon grinned. "True. If he had stuck with us, to see what we've done, what we have become, how we sulk about our trials – He would have flogged the lot of us. With Ely alone, his arm would have tired from inflicting his discipline. Seems we haven't matured much since our younger days."

"We're as green as ever."

"Still, I wish Father was around to see us."

"Aye. In spite of my sniveling, I'm sure he'd manage a grin. For all our faults, our mistakes, we somehow secured the coronation of King Jameson. And a queen, on top of it. Within the year, if it can be believed. For all we've endured becoming whatever – or whomever – we are now, Father would be proud."

Clang! Clang!

Both Symon and Gerry perked. The main deck bell outside rang. Footfalls beyond their cabin pounded and shuffled. Amidst the commotion, a familiar voice rose.

"Lower the dinghy!"

"Ely?" Gerry stammered.

Symon threw a hooded cloak to Gerry, not bothering to wait for him to put it on. With haste, he made for the door.

"What in the bloody hell?" Symon uttered.

On deck, they found a ringlet encircling Ely, who rang the brass bell at its center. Sailors and servants alike stared at their sovereign, then each other, unsure of how to act or what to say. It took Captain Danyll wedging his way to the head of the crowd before Ely finally relented.

"Oh, there you are," Ely said.

"Your Majesty," Danyll began, appearing equal parts annoyed and befuddled. "What is the matter?"

"My good sir, this ship is the matter."

"Forgive me, My King. Do you care to elaborate?"

"It is much too far from our fellow galleons. A king needs to be able to access all of his fleet at a moment's notice. I mean, this mist which obscures might as well be a wall of fog, seeing as I can't see the next ship."

Now strictly agitated, the Captain approached Ely. "Your Majesty, our ships are at your command, as are we, your faithful crew. While out of your immediate view, I assure you, the fleet is but a signal away."

"Pray tell, good captain, if *my* fleet is so close, how long would it take for me to reach them?"

"In the event Your Majesty would need to disembark, reaching the next ship would take only a matter of a minute or two, with the support of a small rowing crew, of course."

"Very well. See to it."

"My King." Danyll cleared his throat. "May I ask *why* you need to leave *now*?"

"If you must," Ely sighed. "Ask."

"Why must you disembark now, Your Majesty?"

"Good sir, a king cannot wait until court is in session to rule – what with the frivolities of a crown on his head, a scepter in hand, and all that sort. The moment to serve, to reign, can happen at any moment, at any time, whether it be during court, at supper, even in the middle of the night. Do you follow?"

"Aye, Your Majesty."

"On that accord, a king operates much the same way in

all aspects of his life. His sleep patterns vary from that of the ordinary man. His eating habits can change. As his moods. And desires."

Captain Danyll raised a brow though he continued to listen. Others among the crew did likewise, while Gerry shared a look of bewilderment with Symon. *Where the bloody hell is he going with this?* Gerry thought.

"It so happens this is the case with me, your beloved leader," Ely continued, oblivious to the stunned crowd around him. "Such a fancy struck me just now whilst you dined or rested. My mind, it began to run. A longing, a passion, to be among all my people, thundered within. You have had the privilege of being in my presence since we left Arinn to pick up my queen before heading home. But what of the others? Those who crew the other galleons and support vessels? The barons and members of the court who came to represent Greater Marland? Even the multitude of servants, from the refined attendants to the lowly maidens. They need to feel my presence."

Oh, for the love of Mar. Gerry dropped his head, the cowl obscuring his face as he shook his head. He pinched the bridge of his nose with his fingers to further hide his embarrassment. He glanced at his left to find Symon – his jaw clenched, his skin red – seething at their brother.

"Remember what you told me," Gerry whispered. "Public display."

"I'll display him all right," Symon replied softly. "How dare he!"

"He's only..." *Seriously, what is he thinking?* "He's Ely. He can't help it sometimes."

"He has a wife in his bed, and still he can't stop whoring

around for one night. And as King Jameson!"

"Shhh!"

"He is acting as the Throne. As all of *us*." Symon glared at Ely. "He should be with Taresa. Not about to leave her."

At the mention of her name – and in consideration of Ely's departure – Gerry smiled.

The winches rotated to life. Ely and the four oarsmen braced themselves as their dinghy descended. The vessel splashed lightly before the small team pushed off the side of the flagship. At the dinghy's bow, Ely swept his arm out as though commanding a warship in battle.

"Man the oars, gentlemen! See we arrive at the next ship in haste, for she awaits us! What is her name again?"

"*The Blessed Virgin*," answered one of the sailors.

"Oh," Ely replied, pausing. "Well, not for long. Am I right? Am I right?"

The four oarsmen laughed, albeit awkwardly. From above, Captain Danyll stood at the railing with the remainder of the crew and passengers, watching as their sovereign rowed away.

"Our glorious sovereign," Danyll said, though not so loudly that those in the rowboat below could hear him. "He's gone mad tonight, I fear."

"King Fool," muttered a sailor, hidden amongst the crowd.

"No sedition on my ship," Danyll chastised, at the same time realizing his folly. He leaned back from the railing to glance over his shoulder, finding First Mate Josson to his right. "Get the men below deck. Gawking at His Majesty will not be permitted."

"You heard the Captain," Josson bellowed. "Back to your

business. Any man found wasting his time up here will earn half rations and double shifts for the rest of the voyage. Go on, now!"

The masses scattered, with Symon heading back to the knights' quarters. Gerry trailed behind him for a bit – but with Symon stewing, not look back – he fell away. He considered his options, his gaze gravitating toward the stairs leading to the sterncastle.

Moments later, he knocked on her door.

"Go away!"

Gerry cleared his throat. "My Queen," he uttered, attempting to sound as much as his regal self as possible.

A patter of muffled footfalls followed before the door opened. Taresa's handmaiden, Celia, stood aside to allow him to enter. Even the suppressed look of a servant at that moment was enough to put Ely to shame.

"You may leave," Taresa said to Celia.

Ely entered, stepping aside to allow the handmaiden to pass. Celia curtsied. She slinked past Ely.

"Lady Celia."

Celia paused under the frame, looking back to Taresa.

"Thank you."

"Your Majesty." Celia curtsied once more to Taresa. She turned to Ely. "King Jameson." She closed the door behind her.

Ely peered out from under the rim of his cowl. Taresa, shocked and angry, met him. The left strap of her nightgown had been ripped, though the rest of her clothing appeared unruffled. With eyes wide and bloodshot, she glared at Gerry.

"Remove your hood. I want a good look at you," she

insisted.

Gerry lifted his head. He pulled back the edge of his cowl.

No sooner had it fell to his shoulders when her hand slapped his cheek.

“Do you have anything to say for yourself?” she asked, standing in the doorway, unwilling to let him inside.

“No.”

“I thought not.” She slammed the door in his face.

“Damn it, Ely,” Gerry cursed beneath his breath.

“What was that?” Taresa said from the other side of the door.

“I said I’m sorry,” he lied.

“You can be a real bastard sometimes. You know that?”

“Aye. You have the right of it.”

“How could you?”

“I’m sorry.” Gerry tilted his head back, his mind racing. *How the hell am I going to pull this off?* Whatever had transpired between Taresa and his brother remained unknown to him. He did not have the advantage of Ely’s truth session, so he could not pretend to recall any conversation or experience they had shared. What’s more, he dare not walk away from her now, lest he anger her further.

“Is that all you have to say for yourself?”

“Yes?”

The door swung open. Taresa glared at him, her surprise at his return having faded, replaced in full by fury. “Seriously?! You have nothing else to say?”

At once, he truly felt sorry. Not for what Ely had done. No, it was for the loss he felt, the mourning of the connection he had shared with Taresa their first night together.

Staring into her eyes, he knew it no longer persisted. Whether due to Ely's folly, or his general absence from her, their bond had faded from existence.

"Forgive me." He met her glare, never wanting to turn aside. "I failed you."

Unprepared for his earnestness, Taresa relented. She stepped back, allowing him to enter.

Gerry's eyes fell to the bed. The top comforter and sheets had been pulled away, exposed the lining beneath. Beside the bed, shards of a shattered goblet littered the floor, while on the nightstand a carafe of wine lay upturned, its contents dripping onto the puddle beneath. Whatever Ely had tried with her, he had done so in his classic style of haste.

"I thought you left," Taresa said, crossing her arms.

"For good?"

"You threatened to leave the ship, saying you needed some time to think. You went on and on about someone taking your place, what was meant to be yours, whatever that bloody well meant."

"I did. I... I needed time to return to my senses, 'tis all."

"Well, how kind of you to choose the *most opportune moment* to take your leave."

Damn it, Ely. Gerry rubbed his right temple. "My dear... I apologize, I mean, in all the excitement of our night, did we, um..." He motioned to the bed.

"Honestly, how drunk were you?"

"It wasn't the drink. Just my general mood. My disposition."

"No, you damn idiot. We didn't lay together!"

Thank Mar. "I see."

"James, what is with you tonight? You couldn't control yourself with me. We nearly... started... until I told you..."

Taresa cradled her head in her hands as she wept. Gerry, in witness to her pain, approached her. Still wary, he held out his hands, ready to comfort her. If she would allow it.

"Taresa, the whole memory of these past several minutes is a blur. The whole night, in fact."

"Do you really expect me to –"

"He died. A year ago to this day. My father."

Gerry's hands fell to his sides. Taresa straightened, a sense of shame, albeit slight, welling within her.

"James, I'm sorry. I had forgotten."

"Aye, so had I. The whole day nearly passed without me thinking of him. Til tonight."

Taresa took his hands in hers. "I can't imagine what you must be going through."

"Honestly, I'm not sure of it myself."

"Understandable. I'm sorry."

"You needn't apologize. I have a habit of reacting poorly at the worst possible times. As you'll come to learn."

"Well, still, in light of what today means, I should have chosen another day to tell you..."

"Tell me now."

"What? Again?"

"We'll reset the clock. Pretend this never happened. Please. Let us have a chance to do this right."

"This seems ridiculous."

"I'll act as if I never heard your news before." *For I haven't.* "Anything and all which is on your mind, I want you to tell me."

Gerry strode to the bed to sit on its edge. He patted the space next to him, inviting Taresa. She smirked, taking her place by his side.

"Tell me. Everything."

"As you wish. You recall our visit to my great uncle's manor?"

"I remember. How could I forget?"

"Well, we went there together... And we left with another."

Gerry cocked his head. "Another?"

"I am with child."

Chapter 18

"He's being careful."

"Too much?" Gerry asked.

Symon squinted. "We'll see." *What are you up to, brother?*

Three flyboats spread about in the water ahead, forming a V before their flagship. A guardship approached them from the opposite direction, bearing a square sail with the sigil of Kin Saliswater. Only vessels directly under the King's command – or at the directive of his steward – could carry the trademark. With such a seal, the flyboat had the authority to allow them to pass or turn them away altogether. The fact the ship took such a precaution against the royal fleet – which both Dawkin and Artus knew well – spoke volumes about their trepidation.

Symon turned his attention from the grouping to the stone monolith watching over them: Arcporte Castle. Still far off at the opposite end of the harbor, it nonetheless commanded a presence over the city. It reminded Symon of the folktales he knew as a lad, especially those about the giants who had supposedly roamed the island.

"Spyglass." Symon held out his hand to Gerry.

"Where's yours?" Gerry replied.

Symon glanced down at his garb, partly to answer him. He wore the suit of a maritime soldier, composed of light, breathable leather armor and oversized clasps for quick dismantling should he fall into the water. Not quite the clothing which allowed pockets for storing personal articles.

"Oh, right," Gerry admitted. He handed Symon his spyglass.

Symon lengthened the scope as he turned back to the porthole. He raised it to his eye to scan the coast.

The lone pillar jutting from the strip of land moments before suddenly dominated Symon's view. Every detail magnified, from the straight edges of its crenellations to the polished helms of the soldiers marching its parapets, the number of whom had increased threefold since their departure. With the landmark as his reference point, he panned the tip of his spyglass down and to his right, setting his sights on the cliffs stretching underneath the stone colossus.

Unfortunately, the Sirens' Cavern eluded him. Due to the flagship's current position, simply too many spires and arches stood between them and the cliffside of Terran.

Symon handed the spyglass back to Gerry. "I can't find him. Doesn't mean he can't see us."

"You worried?" Gerry asked.

"Bout, bout what?"

The slurred question came from behind them. Gerry turned, though Symon did not.

"Nothing that concerns you," Symon stated flatly.

"You don't know that," Ely sputtered with a bottle in hand. Though the water had calmed, Ely managed to crash into the wall to his left. He fought to maintain balance as Gerry rushed to his side.

"No!" Ely pointed his finger at Gerry. "No. Not you.

You're the reason I'm like this." He raised the bottle to his lips and somehow still managed to spill on his shirt.

"Me?" Gerry stood back, astonished.

Symon sighed. *This again.*

'You, you took her. You put a baby inside her. So, I put a drink inside of me."

"Twas my right!"

"Gerry," Symon warned. "Your voice. You're King this time around, remember?"

"Right. I'm needed on deck. Maybe if the guardship sees the king himself, we can hurry home."

"Why?" Ely hiccupped. "What waits for us there?"

What indeed? Symon mused.

"Say as little as possible. When in doubt, nod and listen. Tell all who ask of your command you must take time to consider the wisest choice. Do not let them press you for an answer, no matter how loud they bark or roar. Hold your ground, brother. Stay the course."

Gerry gulped. Ely glanced at him, then Symon. For once, his trademark snicker did not come into play. He withheld his eye-rolling and smirking too, for the scene before them proved too serious – even for the likes of him – to incite an airy reaction.

Companies of soldiers patrolled the wharf. Symon counted three in his view, each four wide and six deep. The crowd before them parted. Such reverence for men-at-arms typically occurred closer to the castle grounds. Here, on the pier, a grouping of soldiers nearly always had to muscle their way through the rough folk who worked and braved the docks. Though not today. The commoners allowed the troops to pass out of respect – or fear – their eyes lingering on them in their wake.

The same collective sense of caution met them at their dock of arrival. The royal detail had doubled in size from the one which saw them depart. Moreover, an armored carriage awaited His Majety and the new queen, a vessel more befitting for a sovereign in a war zone than royals in peacetime.

"Your Majesty," Sir Everitt said as he came to Gerry's right side while Symon and Ely – in their disguises – fell back. "I did not approve of this."

"My grandfather, then?" Gerry queried.

"Aye, I suppose. Though I insist on questioning the royal driver and the carriage attendants before we depart."

Symon eyed the crossbowmen at the railing, with Captain Danyll and First Mate Josson among them, ready for their next order. Every one of them stood on the starboard side, their sights facing the very men supposedly assigned to accompany the royals. The strength of their focus, of their apprehension, spoke volumes of the fear awaiting them onshore.

As the plank wedged into position, Sir Everitt moved to conduct his inspection. All eyes fell on him as he approached the royal driver. A handful of Voiceless knights and castle officers joined those two, swelling the gathering around the armored carriage.

"Symon," Gerry began. "I have a feeling about this... A bad one..."

"Do as Symon told you," Ely urged. "He knows what he's saying."

Gerry offered a glance in Ely's direction. He turned back to Everitt, who withdrew from the carriage to march back up the plank.

"See you in Terran," Symon stated as he and Ely fell away.

They watched as the Right Captain returned to Gerry to whisper into his ear. Too low to hear from their positions, the uttering was brief. Gerry nodded and pointed to the royal chambers in the aftercastle. Together, the two marched into the quarters, returning with Queen Taresa a short time later.

"What say you, brother?" Symon asked Ely as he watched the Captain and First Mate exchange a few words with the king and queen. "What new trouble is all of this?"

"This isn't just from the news of the continent," Ely whispered. "Even if all we endured made its way home and somehow became embellished, the people would never be so unnerved. Something happened here. And not unrelated to the affairs in Afari, to be sure."

"Aye." *The one time King Fool had to be right,* Symon thought, *is the one time I wish to Mar you were* wrong.

Symon and Ely departed last from the flagship, following in the wake of the security detail. The entourage of guards and soldiers crowded the width of the dock so much so Symon wondered if the wood would hold their weight. Hold it did, though a few creaks unsettled his faith in the pilings and their boards.

The trip from the wharf to the castle grounds turned out to be quicker than expected. Whatever efforts the castle guards had taken to clear the path of onlookers had worked, for crowds lay only at the fringes of the road, with none dallying before the procession. Symon suspected the multitude of heavy cavalry archers among the column had everything to do with the clearing, for such mounted units rode the length of the parade, their eyes keen to the movements of the crowd. More than a few times, they paused, raising their bows and nocking their arrows as they scanned their surroundings in search of threats, both real and imagined.

Only when the entourage came upon the barbican's drawbridge did the column slow, with the guardhouse captain and his men ready to meet His Majesty. Sir Everitt, atop his steed, departed from the side of the armored carriage to have a word with the captain.

"We'll never make it through with Gerry and Taresa," Symon noted. All in the procession had stopped save the carriage, which crawled forward to the head of the line. "The guards will let them pass ahead – as expected – while the lot of us will be searched."

"Very well," Ely said, scanning the crenellations above and the guards who watched from their perches. "To Terran."

They marched to their underground lair with nary a word to each other. An occasional murmur from the passing common folk assailed their ears until they moved on past the city walls, where the sounds of distant wave breaks and chirping birds became their only aural companions. Only when they squeezed into one of the narrow openings of Terran did the familiar clang of armor meet them.

"My good man," Ely perked, though Symon sensed the melancholy of his tone. "How good to see you."

The Voiceless stared Ely up and down as a second, then a third knight, emerged from the shadows.

“Good Mar,” Ely gasped, hand to his heart. “A little warning would be nice.”

Ignore him, Symon signed. *As always.*

The Voiceless, considering Ely’s expression and Symon’s reaction, glanced over his shoulder and signed. *It’s them*, he motioned.

They strode the passageways into Terran, Symon noting the fresh troops at guard postings interspersed more closely than when they had left. With their visors raised, some bore the façade of squires, a mark of the untested which nary sat well with Symon. Both he and Ely forewent stopping in their rooms to proceed to the underground bailey, where a cacophony of grunts and clashes awaited them.

There, encircled by a ringlet of five Voiceless in padded sparring armor, stood Dawkin.

He breathed deeply, his hands on his thighs as he shook the sweat from his brow. He glanced up at his companions, the entrance of his brothers gone unnoticed, as he urged them to attack. “Again!” he commanded.

The five rushed in at once, thrusting their weapons forward. Though the tips and edges lay wrapped in padding, Symon still shouted. “Don’t!”

The directive came too late as the points drove inward to their mark — five at once. An impossible volley of strikes to escape.

Which Dawkin managed to avoid nonetheless.

He ducked out of range of three points, his padded sword blocking the other two. Sweeping to his far-right, he moved from the center of the circle to its outer edge to take on one knight instead of five. He disarmed the one

Voiceless quickly enough with a two-step incursion, then moved on to the next knight, who exchanged three parries with Dawkin before the king found a weak spot below the pit of his right arm. Emboldened, Dawkin rushed to engage the other three. A bold – and stupid – move, which ended with Dawkin on one knee, his sword swept from his hand.

"Brother," Ely said as he broke through the training scene, ignorant of Dawkin's combat folly. "That was impressive."

"Then why am I unarmed?" Dawkin pressed.

"You may have lost, but it was in grand fashion."

"A loss is a loss in battle." Dawkin took Ely's extended hand as his brother helped him to his feet. "Welcome home."

"Hardly a warm welcome," Ely said, noting the Voiceless around them. "What in the hell happened?"

"Yes. What?" Symon interrupted, holding the padded sword Dawkin had just lost. He untied the leather wrappings around its blade. "These aren't sparring weapons. These... These are from the war armory."

"The war armory?" Ely repeated, puzzled. "We have one?"

"These arms haven't seen the light of day since Father's time, when the Century War ended. You dare use them now?"

Dawkin waved Symon off, withdrawing from the fighting circle to a bench where a few waterskins lay. Symon, not relenting in the conversation, met Dawkin at his seat.

"Dawkin. Answer me," Symon insisted.

"No sense in confirming the truth you hold in your

hand."

"Why?"

Dawkin gave Symon a wry look before glancing toward Ely.

"Don't look at me. He's a bit sour, I admit. But honestly, I'm a tad curious myself. Best to answer."

"You sure you want the whole truth *now*? You've only just returned. Don't you want to rest, regain yourselves?"

Symon studied Dawkin. Something about his brother struck him as off.

With the side of the sword, he tapped Dawkin on his right shoulder. Dawkin winced.

"I knew it," Symon replied. "You're fighting injured." Symon tossed the sword to the nearest Voiceless, who barely caught the weapon by its hilt. "Now, tell us what happened."

Three solid hours passed uninterrupted. In that time, under the influence of truth serum, Dawkin revealed all that had transpired since his three brothers set sail. His mind spilled forth into the waiting ears of his two brothers, who sat on nearby stools. By the end of Dawkin's monologue, Symon found his concentration spent, his mental strength drained. Even three strong cups of memory tea could not prevent the headache he endured by the end of Dawkin's deluge.

Dawkin proved worse still, arising from the reclining sofa in the Fourpointe Chamber as though bruised and battered all over.

"Maybe… you should… rest," Ely suggested as he battled his own throbbing.

"I'm fine," Dawkin insisted, though his hoarse voice told

otherwise. “I have to return to the bailey. To train.”

Symon perked in his chair. “Dawkin! You’re hardly fit to speak, let alone resume sparring.”

“I just laid down for a few hours.”

“For a truth session! That wasn’t rest.”

“Bugger off.” Dawkin waved his hand toward them as he shuffled toward the door.

Symon, as mad as he was dumbfounded, turned to Ely. “We have to stop him.”

“I need a drink. Tis not right to feel this migraine without the benefit of spirits.”

“He could hurt himself.”

“He already hurt himself. Never mind his stubbornness. He’ll try his hand a few more times, then tire out and go to bed.” Ely shuffled over to the end table to pour himself a drink.

Symon sprang from his chair. He made for the door, making it only a few steps before the total weight of the truth session weighed on him. He paused – though his head didn’t – to lean against the wall.

“See!” Ely boasted with a goblet in hand. “Dawkin will fare little better.”

Ignoring his slight, Symon braced himself as he trudged forward.

“You say I’m mad!” Ely cried after him. “Better mad than stubborn. You two are a pair of arses. You know that?!”

Good Mar! Symon thought through his headache. *Turn him into a Voiceless, I beg of you.*

Ely’s jests faded as Symon made his way back to the underground bailey. With each step, his wooziness faded as his equilibrium returned. By the time he entered the expanse, he almost felt normal.

He couldn't say the same of his brother, who had taken to practicing spear thrusts with a figure of straw and burlap. The Voiceless there had dispersed, leaving Dawkin to grunt and struggle alone.

Symon slowed his approach to study his brother, who paid no attention to his menacing presence. So, Symon rounded him. He came to the bench where the waterskins lay to grab one.

Then, with his right side to Dawkin, he waited.

Dawkins shouted a war cry. His blade ripped through the burlap skin of the mannequin, splicing straw before striking the wooden skeleton within. Dawkin grunted as he pulled back his shaft, drawing the spearhead from his target. He cocked his arm, ready to repeat the attack –

Before the cold leather of a waterskin slapped against his face.

He slashed his spear in Symon's direction. "What the hell?!"

Symon, far out of range, offered a blank stare in return. "Me?"

"Yes, you, you rotten bastard." Dawkin raised the butt of his spear and hurried toward him, ready to club him –

When another waterskin collided with his nose.

Dawkin's free hand went to his face as Symon rushed in. Before his brother could react, Symon had disarmed him of his spear. Enraged, Dawkin grabbed the waterskin and lodged it at him. Symon, his façade as blank as ever, deflected the leather flacon with a swing of his new spear.

Dawkin clenched his fists. But before he could charge,

the tip of his spear met him, inches from his chest.

"You need rest," Symon insisted. "You have passion; I give you that. However, your stabs lack precision, your form is sloppy, and above all, you're predictable."

"Well..." Dawkin began, reddened. "What do you expect? I've been at it for hours."

"Which is why you need to stop. Or at least meet me halfway and slow a bit."

"Weren't you listening?! The whole of Marland has gone mad. Fanatics roam the streets, terrorizing both nobles and the common folk with their random attacks, while gold fever hypnotizes the rest of the country. I've never seen anything like it. And then the news from Afari, which seeps in from every sailor stepping onto our docks, only adds to the mania."

Symon lowered the tip of his spear. Dawkin, panting, turned away as he ran his fingers through his hair. The whole of him had become a far cry from the man they had left on the wharf of Arcporte weeks earlier. That version had been a scholar, a king of reason and thought, capable of sifting through a world of chaos while all others sunk with fear.

Now, though... A soul unsettled stood before him. A mania had overcome Dawkin, removing all sense of the practical. Symon believed it stemmed from the events of the past few weeks. Or perhaps, it was due to something more sinister?

Darkness without cause.

Symon forced the possibility from his mind. He set his sights on Dawkin, even as his brother looked to and fro.

"Dawkin."

His brother stared back at him.

"Show me what you found."

He nodded. Then he led Symon to the castle dungeon.

The pair strode in silence. Dawkin focused on the ground before them, as if careful to watch the loose stones and not trip. But Symon knew something else resided in his mind. He considered speaking first, though decided waiting until they reached their destination would be better.

Two Voiceless waited outside the cell deep within the underground prison. With a glance from Dawkin, the knights proceeded to unlock the door with a giant key. The pins within awoke and groaned, their metallic sigh echoing down the length of the tunnel. With all their weight, the two knights pushed open the iron-banded giant.

Upon entering, Dawkin motioned to a single small barrel the size of a babe. It lay in the center of a chamber large enough to house a full-fledged leviathan, with portholes cut into the vaulted ceiling to allow in shafts of light. Symon peered into the shadows, half-expecting to find more barrels stacked against the walls. He spotted none.

"This is all that's left?" he motioned to the barrel.

"I told you we sunk the rest of it," Dawkin snickered.

Symon frowned. The truth session still fresh in his mind's eye, he recalled Dawkin's snippet about the cache of barrels the magistrates and their patrols had discovered, part of a smuggling operation orchestrated by the Lost Souls. Dawkin had overseen the disposal of the illegal cargo, which involved a small fleet of flyboats sailing to deep waters. There, Dawkin and a handful of Voiceless had loaded the barrels into nets weighed by stones they then tossed overboard. Dawkin had reported saving a sample of the cache, one he believed captured the might of the cargo: A single, puny barrel.

"Were all the barrels this size?" Symon asked.

"Aye."

"And tell me again, how many?"

"A total of two dozen intact. We figured another eight was part of the cache, which the Lost Souls used in their attack once we uncovered their plot. That includes the two they set off on the dock, the ones I told you killed the magistrates and their patrol..." Dawkin's voice trailed off as he knelt before the barrel.

Three magistrates, five soldiers dead, another magistrate and six soldiers wounded. The planks and piling of an entire dockside blown into the harbor, while the stone length of a quay lay reduced to gravel. As Dawkin's words reverberated through his mind, Symon struggled to wrap his mind around the power of the blast. Dywar's Tears and oreflares in such small batches had the potential at best to dislodge rock and crack stone, unless aged for long periods to allow their properties to settle and mature. At least, that was how Symon remembered the mages explaining it to him.

"You ever seen a torn body?"

"What?" Symon asked.

"A corpse, his personage mutilated." Dawkin had drawn a small knife from the cuff of his sleeve, positioning its tip into the edge of the barrel's lid, ready to pry it open. He paused to look up at Symon. "You've seen your men bloodied and bludgeoned when you led the Battle of the Chesa. We were there for the Battle of the Riverford. We've seen the casualties from the punctures of spears and swords. Or the cleavings from axeheads and halberds. The shafts of arrows in our troops, both those who survived and the ones who fell. All horrible atrocities to witness, without question. Yet none as frightening, so ghastly, as seeing innards strewn, tissues butchered and flayed. Parts fully removed. A leg here, an arm there. Then there are those faces, with eyes looking back at you, ingraining their trama into your soul."

Symon knelt before Dawkin. "Brother."

Dawkin stared at him, blankly.

"What is it you fear?" Symon asked.

"The end."

Dawkin wedged his blade into the lid of the barrel to open it. He dipped the tip of his knife into the pitch-black liquid inside.

"Dawkin," Symon continued, hoping the moment to connect with his brother had not passed. "Whatever you saw on the streets, no matter the threat you faced, we, your brothers, are here now. We can help. We can battle this evil together."

Dawkin glanced at him. "That worries me the most."

With a flick of his wrist, Dawkin flung a drop of the dark substance at the dungeon wall. The solid mass erupted in a flash of orange light, spewing rocks and dirt back into their faces. Symon shielded his eyes with his forearm as he leapt back to stand straight. Dawkin merely glanced away from the blowout while he remained kneeling. A plume of smoke rose above them, from one shaft of light to another, as the Voiceless guarding the door entered in a panic.

Dawkin extended his hand. "'Tis fine. A small demonstration for my brother here. As you were."

Puzzled and perhaps a bit perturbed, the Voiceless

nodded before withdrawing from the chamber. Symon, even more astounded, turned to Dawkin.

"I should have warned you, I know. I only wanted to show the full might of what we're dealing with, so I felt it best a moment of surprise was in order."

"That... Is what happened on the streets?"

"At times, yes. Grandfather allowed Mage Wystan and his apprentice to have one vial, so they may conduct their experiments while I did some tests of my own. We came to similar results. Best as I can figure, the color of the blast depends on what the substance comes in contact with, whether diluted in some other liquid or the object it encounters when dispensed. Or both."

The blasts from his wedding night, from the encampment consumed by fire to the destruction of the castle tower, overwhelmed Symon's memory. As did the collapse of Castle Seylonna.

"No potion known to us can account for this devastation. And yet somehow, in our ignorance of alchemy, a ship carrying enough to level Arcporte made its way into our harbor." Dawkin leaned in to whisper as if there were others around to listen. "We captured a few Lost Souls, who believed foolishly in the power of sanctuary. We plucked them from the Cathedral, and those not brave enough to fight or too cowardly to slit their throats, we locked away in cells for an inquisition. With Grandfather's reluctant approval, I wrote notes in his hand, inviting the most dangerous Century War veterans to pay our guests a visit.

"Using their methods of persuasion, the Lost Souls confessed: The contents of the barrels were meant for Highmoorr Castle."

Symon's eyes widened. Not so much at the ploy. But upon hearing it for the first time.

"You withheld this from your truth session?" Symon asked, astonished.

"I did."

"How? Why?"

"To answer the first, with a bit of practice, truth serum can be overcome. In smaller doses, some of the time.

"As for the why... The incident on the Curved Wharf inspired people to talk. Bits of gossip about the Lost Souls wafted up to the barons who remained in Marland during your wedding. They pieced together a conspiracy aimed at the next Conclave of Barons, though the details of what would occur vary from manor to manor or tavern to tavern. Now that the whole Court has returned with your fleet, the rumors will only fester. No baron will dare meet at Highmoorr Castle once they know of the plot, whether real, imagined, or otherwise.

"Consider if they knew the truth, of the potency of the liquid the Lost Souls tried to smuggle, of how the potion could level any castle or even whole neighborhoods of Arcporte itself. The presence of the Lost Souls already unsettles our subjects. And then there's this business of Fool's Fever, with gold suddenly appearing in the countryside. Just one more mess – like this added threat – would turn the barons mad."

Symon glanced down at the small barrel. "Who else knows?"

"Other than you and me, only Grandfather. I made sure those who helped me interrogate the Lost Souls had their share of fading potion. I couldn't risk them going off like

Ely to some tavern to spill their guts about the confessions we pulled."

"Dawkin, you should have told us this during your truth session. Including Ely. Such an omission goes against our oaths, the very laws of Terran –"

"Forget our oaths! The laws don't apply to us anymore. Father made them up to keep us in line, part of some fairy tale about how we were special and had to be protected as babes and all that nonsense.

"Listen to me, brother. We are Terran. The Law. Arcporte. Hell, the whole of Marland. We represent the four corners of our island – a kingdom that stands threatened on every side. I've seen the mania in the countryside, in the streets, on the docks. Barons and peasants brawl for a single nugget of gold. Mobs flog heretics sent from Mar knows where. Neighbors spy on neighbors, wondering when the other will lose their sense and go mad.

"And yes, all that has affected me. Me, the smart one, from this ragged family forced to hide in the shadows decades after assassins nearly wiped out our kin. So I have acted, training by day while in disguise by night, torturing and questioning our prisoners in between. Because without that action, my expressed determination... I fear... we'll lose more of ourselves... much more than we already have."

Dawkin fitted the lid back onto the barrel. The stout container wiggled under the weight of Dawkin's hands. Symon instinctively knelt to help, but Dawkin waved him off as he finished, before slowly rising. "So you can see why a bit of fatigue and some bruises are of little consequence to me."

Symon stood in kind, his sights never leaving the barrel

until he came level with Dawkin. In the dimness of the cell, the low light enhanced the languor sown into his face. The heavy eyelids. The parched lips. Those sunken eyes.

"None of this is you, Dawkin. Your brilliance has left you. The, what is the word? Reason. You are without reason."

"Logic is for the realm of libraries. Through hard lessons, I've learned the difference between the lessons of books and those of the field. You, of all people, should know that. How many have you seen fall in your battles? Dozens? Perhaps by now hundreds?"

"They died with honor. But torture –"

"Is it not torture to burn by this fire in the streets? Or to suffer poison? Stabbing? And then attend the funeral of it all?!"

Dawkin's reference to their father was not lost on him. Hell, at that moment – with his brother's fatigue suddenly vanished – he even looked like him. The set jaw. The narrowed eyes. Along with something more –

The desire for reprisal. The hunger born out of wrath. The vengeance.

"We need a resolution to these events," Dawkin continued, "which I know all tie together. With you three back home, I can finally stop acting through Grandfather and emerge from Terran as the king this country needs."

"I'll call an emergency session of the Fourpointe Chamber. The three of us will vote for you to stay bound to Terran until you return to your senses. If the Voiceless can't restrain you, then the rest of us will."

Dawkin turned deadpan. "You'll do nothing of the sort."

Symon opened his mouth to protest further. A

quivering suddenly overtook him. First in his lips. Then his hands. Followed by the shaking of his knees.

"Can't talk? A fish on your tongue?" Dawkin sighed. "I didn't want to do it. However, I knew you would speak the loudest against me once you learned all the trouble I went through in the absence of you three. I considered withholding the revelation of Marlish events from you altogether. I knew such secrecy would be far from right, though. We've had too much of that in our lives, wouldn't you say?"

"You... When?" Symon spat out.

"Just a dab of fading potion on the rim of your cups, the kind Mage Wystan mixes with herbs to induce deep sleep. I knew the memory tea would mask any hint of taste."

Symon sank to his knees, holding onto the ground as the cell around him spun.

"The ill effects will subside soon enough. You'll close your eyes soon, as will Ely. The two of you will even wake refreshed, a full day after Gerry returns and I ascend."

"How... could... you? You?!"

"Ely did it a half dozen times to us as adolescents. Don't you remember? You even tried your hand at it once, though I spat out the brew because your ingredients were off. And how many doses have we given Gerry over the years to calm his nerves after every time Father chastised him?" Dawkin patted Symon on the back. "Yes, it's unlike me, I'll admit. It's a good thing, I assure you. It signals I am ready to do what is needed. You'll see."

Darkness overtook Symon as he fought the weight of his eyelids. They won as a curtain fell over his hearing, the fading echo of Dawkin's footfalls like an audience applauding the end of a play.

Chapter 19

Dawkin rubbed his temple in earnest, attempting with all his will to show interest in the nobles who spoke.

He failed, the events of the morning slipping into his consciousness, planting seeds of guilt.

What have I done? he asked himself, partly in reflection but also in admonishment.

He sat. He listened. He considered the arguments, both those petty and those deep.

"He was gone too long!" one noble said as he glared at Dawkin.

"To secure an ally!" Everitt pounded his fist on the table before them, a long stretch of birch where every conceivable map of Marland rested.

"Little good that did us," the same lord barked. "Consider the hundreds we lost the night of his wedding." Baron Belin of Har-Kin Cely plopped back in his chair, as spent as he was reddened. Many of the other nobles in the audience around the table showed similar displays, with only the younger barons still planted on their feet. Everitt, standing in for his father, was one of them.

The Right Captain rounded the map table, locking eyes with as many men as had the strength to look upon him. "We lost a great deal many. Aye. No act of contrition by you or me or even King Jameson himself will ever serve to honor their memory rightfully." Everitt paused, glancing toward Dawkin. Whether he expected a nod or scowl, Dawkin could not tell, as his Right Captain went on, turning back to the gathered nobles. “We owe it to the departed to decide once and for all how to answer this threat. They did their duty. Now is the time for ours.”

“Are we even certain of who we’re fighting?” Baron Gennon asked. Like his older brother, Mage Wystan, the lord of Har-Kin Danverrs, had piercing eyes of glacial blue. Even when he spoke casually, his gaze bestowed a sense of formality Dawkin envied.

“Certain? No,” Everitt answered. “We have... suspicions, though.” Upon those words, he stopped. He looked upon Dawkin, knowing his place.

Dawkin shifted in his seat as he narrowed his eyes as if taking the time to draft a response. In truth, he fought the mental fatigue which had set in to cloud his judgment. *I tire before a handful of barons,* Dawkin thought. *How can I expect to face the Conclave?* For once, he wished for the constrictions of Terran. In his youth, their walls had many a time served as a prison in his mind. Now, they offered sanctuary.

“My King?” Everitt started, searching for an answer.

Artus, sitting beside Dawkin at the head of the table, cleared his throat. “We know those in Afari who move against us. They may have conspired to attack our diplomats the night of Jameson’s wedding or Seylonna just before the King’s timely departure. Or they may have simply known of it. Or had no idea of either event at all, save after it happened. No matter. Those who threaten us *now* are complicit.”

“Here, here!” shouted a few nobles.

“Good Marlishmen, this gathering here at the War Hall is not to assign guilt or answer danger. We must simply decide on a venue for the next Conclave.” Artus shifted his focus to the three men on his right, members of the Reigning Council. The three held the responsibility of voting not only for themselves but also acted as proxies for others.

“Lord Artus has the right of it,” Baron Karles of Kin Tenholm added. “Whatever you venture to say this day about our supposed enemies and allies matters not. We will decide the venue for the Conclave and nothing more.”

Dawkin noted his salt-and-pepper mane had grayed considerably since the last time he had seen him, no doubt due to rumors his son – who had taken his place of honor at the royal wedding in Arinn – had perished in the tower attack. The official list of the departed was slated for review that evening by the royal scribes and mages for accuracy. An attendant to King Jameson had informed Dawkin the news would not be in Karles’ favor.

“Where we will then arrive at an answer to such matters,” Artus concluded. The added comment did little to quell the barons in attendance, who did not protest per se but grumbled.

Good luck at that, Grandfather, Dawkin thought. His fingertips gravitated toward the transcriptions his attendants had recorded of the prisoners’ confessions, which lay under the edges of the large maps draping the table. Though coerced, the consistency of the Lost Souls’ remarks on their plot could not be denied. Their alarming familiarity with the architecture of Highmoorr Castle – the full extent only Dawkin had surmised – suggested a ring of accomplices vast and connected. And if in their activities they had learned of one of the most secure fortresses in Marland, how many others were under threat?

Dawkin rose suddenly. He fought the urge to stretch, though his body ached. He resisted his want to rub his eyes, though sleep beckoned him. Instead, he forced himself to straighten. To act... kingly.

"My lords," he began. "Let us recess for a spell. Your counsel, wise and thoughtful, is appreciated. We can afford a respite to muse on all we've shared." Dawkin rounded the table as the nobles likewise stood, bowing their heads as he passed.

The air in the corridor blasted him, jolting him to his senses, if only for a moment. Undeterred by the cold, he pressed on past the Voiceless, who clopped behind him at a steady pace. He prayed they mistook his haste for determination rather than the anxiety which had settled within.

As he headed up the staircase to the King's Chambers, the pair followed. Another silent knight, stationed at the top of the steps, saluted as he went, trailing after him once his brothers-in-arms had ascended. Then there stood the one at his door, who opened it, pivoting to enter and stand guard in the receiving area.

Dawkin paused in the entryway, his hand extended. "Please," he insisted. "I require privacy."

Having just come from the War Hall, no Voiceless signed to question him. They simply bowed, retreating to the length of stone comprising the hallway, taking their places.

Dawkin closed the door.

Thank Mar. He leaned against the door, looking upward. Instinctively, he sniffed.

Cloves. Mildew. Musk.

The scents of his father.

They had faded from the quarters in the past year, though in Dawkin's mind, they persisted as strong as ever. Even during his father's long campaigns, as a lad, Dawkin would often enter the room to find the familiar smells. Servants would bring in cloves harvested from the red and yellow spice trees of the Sovereign Gardens to crush and mix with boiling water. The aroma – according to Audemar – masked the mildew which always found its way back into the tapestries, blankets, and garb housed in the castle. And then there was the musk – the key ingredient to the King's cologne – which could not be expunged from the chamber, no matter how many times the attendants cleaned. In his days, Audemar's fragrance sometimes overwhelmed his sessions at court. Now, more than a year after his passing, Dawkin considered the day when he'd walk in and discover the absence of such scents altogether.

Dawkin, attempting to shake the sorrow of nostalgia, turned to the far left corner of the bedchamber. He marched to the wardrobe, a hulking beast of carved cherry wood and bronze hinges. He opened the left door, reaching up to slide his fingers along the inside of the top lip.

Click.

Snapping the tiny hidden lever, Dawkin glanced down at the hooves of the dresser. As expected, its wheels had dropped into place. With ease, he slid the wardrobe away from the wall, revealing a small door.

The masons had protested in fits of sighs and groans when ordered to cut into the ancient rock. No matter, since after each shift they were given a helping of fading potion.

Their daily dose was just enough to cloud their memory but not so much they couldn't continue their labor the following morning. The secret project had not taken them long. When finished, it provided a direct corridor to the study of Prince Jameson.

Dawkin opened the small door to peer into the darkness. *Had this been constructed in my father's day, would he have had a chance to escape his fatal destiny?* He must have mused on the possibility every time he came here. Like all thoughts concerning his father, he buried it. He stepped inside.

He emerged from the hidden corridor into the study. The stained glass of the arched windows glowed, indicating the sun outside had burned through the morning haze. The brightness illuminated everything within, including the large table where Dawkin's collection of manuscripts and scrolls lay. He sighed, glad none of his brethren had rifled through his work since their return.

Most of the contents atop remained in disarray, with an open book here or a loose scroll there, save one: *The Weald Tales.* The gift from Lady Cora appeared untouched, for it essentially was. Dawkin had yet to bring himself to do more than glance at its pages. With every thought to do more than peruse it, some more pressing matter always seemed to arise, whether it involved his grandfather beckoning him or the Voiceless delivering news of court life. Such interruptions weighed on him, especially these days, so that even the simple pleasure of reading – without his mind lost to wander – sat out of reach.

Approaching the table and its contents, Dawkin paused as he heard a set of footfalls mirroring his own. He turned to the foyer connecting the princely bedchamber to the study.

"I had a suspicion you'd come here," Artus said.

"You had the right of it," Dawkin admitted. He sighed, disappointed his promise of solitude had been stolen.

"No doubt you wanted to be alone."

"Yet you're here."

"You and I. We were hardly on the best of terms with your brothers away."

Dawkin nodded.

Artus strode further into the study. His sights gravitated toward the small door from whence Dawkin came. He chuckled.

"Another hidden passage. Mar, how many does that make in this castle?"

"Thirty-eight by my count, if by castle you mean the ones above. If you include Terran, two dozen more."

"That was a rhetorical question, my boy."

"How so?"

"Because who among us can be sure of all the secret passageways and the hidden halls this castle has to offer? I remember when your father and I had this study built as a gateway to Terran. The scheming and planning involved, the supplies we had to ship in under cover of night, the doses of fading potion we administered to the workers. 'Twas a monumental effort in and of itself. Thank Mar Terran did not have to be carved from scratch, with it being a secret repository during the Century War."

Dawkin listened patiently, having heard it all before. His attention drifted back to the table.

"You're just like your father, you know?"

Dawkin perked. He stared right into Artus' eyes, which had followed his gaze to the documents he longed to study.

"Me?"

"Aye, you. You thought I'd compare my son to anyone else? Symon, perhaps?"

"Well, yes."

"Hmm. True, my son became the dutiful general in his later years. He always had an inclination, a natural talent, for fighting, especially swordsmanship. Much like your brother.

"However, when he started as king, Audemar... He struggled. Like you. He so wanted to figure everything out. He loathed the sessions at court. The dinners with barons. The false chuckles. The bald-faced lies. To him, they were ambiguous, complete wastes of time that led to empty promises and half-hearted commitments.

"Then, on the front, he encountered the real trials of rule. The slain. The enemies we took prisoner. The calls for their hanging. The threat of revolt and desertion from his men. All those troubles coupled with the rumors he was showing signs of... being unable to sire an heir."

"He held counsel meetings well into the next morning. He read his manuscripts and maps, straining to find any tidbit of wisdom or knowledge which would give him an edge."

"Did he?" Dawkin asked.

Artus shook his head. "Nay."

"So he gave up? Turned away from his studies to focus his prowess on the battlefield."

"No. He found another way to improve, to deal with the crushing weight of kinghood."

"What was it? His secret?"

"He matured."

Dawkin didn't know whether to throw his arms up, roll his eyes, or snicker. He considered doing all three.

"Not the answer you expected?"

"It leaves me wanting."

"Which is exactly how he felt. Those years of his early reign were some of the toughest of the Century War. Certainly the most challenging either of us had seen. He experienced... hardships, the kind not seen by myself or other Marlish kings in recent memory. In hindsight, my attempts to counsel him were poor."

"How so?"

"I acted like a stone-cold bastard."

Dawkin raised his brow. Artus replied with a nod. "It's the truth. In his trials and obstacles, I simply told him to strengthen his resolve and never show weakness. He struggled to take my words to heart, and in his anguish, sought other methods to deal with his problems." Artus paused. His gaze drifted from Dawkin to the shelves around them before glancing upward to the windows and the carved marble reliefs of the dome. Dawkin followed his cue, unsure why the forest scenes beckoned to his grandfather at that moment.

When Artus relented, tilting his head downward, Dawkin saw tears in his eyes. "His maturity came with a heavy price, son," his grandfather continued, "after many mistakes he could have avoided, had those he loved been there for him. I know you consider my counsel an act of meddling. I accept that. But heed my words: Exert caution in your dealings, for there are still foxes in every corner of this kingdom. Practice restraint when you want nothing more than to shout and fight. Show compassion when vengeance calls. When your thoughts feel as if they will explode, quiet your mind. Guard your soul. By Mar, do whatever it takes to keep the crushing weight of your kinghood off your shoulders."

Artus reached out to Dawkin, his lips quivering, his face turned pale. His hands trembled. Dawkin grabbed them, expecting him to collapse.

"Grandfather!"

"There is… so much more I need to tell you… About your birth… The secrets you carry…"

Dawkin held him by the hands. Eons had passed since the last time he had embraced his grandfather, a reality not lost on him. Though the flesh, the muscle underneath, felt familiar to some degree, in that touch, so much revealed itself to be missing. The strength for one. In his youth, Dawkin thought his grandfather powerful enough to crush stone between his fingertips. Now those same digits shook, vigor and control lost to the decades. Along with the determination, focus, and iron will Dawkin believed – nay, knew – his grandfather had possessed. Nearly all of what he had known of the man – his kin – stood as an imprint from the past, a dream of what once existed, replaced by nothing.

Dawkin squeezed his hands.

"King Artus."

His grandfather ceased shaking. His eyes, wide in terror and sorrow only moments before, narrowed to focus on Dawkin.

"Sire. My Liege. Your Majesty."

"Why, it's been years since I bore the title, been

addressed that way. I relinquished my crown."

"Nay. No man can ever stop being what he was meant to be," Dawkin said, not knowing if he believed the words from his mouth. *What am I saying? How can I lie to him? Or do I speak the truth?*

Artus, suddenly wary of the way he had been acting, straightened. He released himself from Dawkin's grip. His vulnerability dissipated. He brushed his tunic as if readying himself for court.

The shift in his appearance, nay, his entire self, alarmed Dawkin. Akin to one of Ely's fits, Dawkin knew not if the weakness he saw only moments earlier had disappeared entirely. Or did it lay hidden, concealed, ready to rear its head?

Dawkin studied the man, the goliath he had always worshipped, even more than his so-called god.

You're there. I know it. Show me.

Then, he caught sight of him. Artus, his proper self returning, stared back at his grandson, the twinkle of a kind yet wise soul.

There he is. The monarch of my childhood. The king I know.

Dawkin fought off a smile, not wanting to make his grandfather more self-conscious.

Out of the corner of his eye, he glimpsed a length of coat in the shadows. They were not alone.

"Yes?" Dawkin called.

From the edge of the study, Everitt emerged. He looked to Dawkin, then Artus, as if having offended both. "Forgive me, Your Majesty. With your absence, then your grandfather's, I made inquiries. The Voiceless advised Lord Artus had headed this way, so I took a chance."

Dawkin glanced in the direction of his secret corridor. *So much for my covert efforts.* He returned his attention to Everitt. "Is something the matter?"

"No, nothing pressing," his Right Captain replied in a muted tone, one which hardly inspired confidence. "Once you two left," he continued, "two more nobles entered the War Hall, having just arrived at the bailey. Barons Hudde of Har-Kin Clarre and Cason of Har-Kin Birkenhood."

Artus' face reddened at the utterance. "For the peace of Mar!" he exclaimed. His thumb wrapped over his fingers as his hands turned to fists. "Of all the lords to join our council, those two windbags had to show up. I say flog the bastards!"

"Grandfather. Your manners."

Artus snickered, looking away. Everitt raised his brow slightly, unaccustomed to seeing the former monarch unarmed of his manners.

"Pardon my opinion, Your Majesty, but your kin may have the right of it. No sooner did those two nobles enter when they were embraced. They suggested – not overtly, one could argue – the kingdom was teetering. 'On the brink,' Baron Cason said. Said such times required 'real men.'"

"You allowed them to say such lies?!" Artus exploded.

"No!" Everitt shouted in defense. He pursed his lips, controlling himself. "I lost my temper. I threw a flagon of wine against the wall. Some shoving between the barons ensued. I ordered the War Hall cleared until the time of the King's return. The Voiceless and the rest of the guards have the lords in the Throne Room, allowing them more space to cool. And sulk. They await your return."

Lovely. "Very well. I'll go back –"

"Son," Artus said, holding out his hand. "Do not honor their impertinence. Let them wait further. Then allow them to stew. They'll figure out your continued absence is a result of their malfeasance."

"How can you be so sure?"

"Because I'll tell them." Artus looked to Dawkin, then Everitt, offering the hint of a smile. "Stay. Collect yourself. Have a meal or a ride in the country if you prefer. I'll have those worthless souls shamed and respectful upon your entry." With an assured, steely look, Artus took his leave. Dawkin watched him go, noting the prowess had returned to his gait.

Both waited until the echo of the door closing reached them. Dawkin turned to his study table, where his maps and parchment, ever forgiving, waited.

"Have you noticed something amiss about him lately?" Dawkin asked.

"The old Gauntlet has his off moments, even days," his Right Captain admitted. "He still can outflank my father on his worst day if it's any consolation."

"It is."

"And you?"

"What?"

"How are you holding up, James?"

Dawkin looked to the details of the drawings before them as if they held the answer. "I honestly don't know."

"This business with the barons. Them learning of the plot on Highmoorr Castle and all." Everitt circled the table, glancing at its contents, feigning interest. "'Tis not right."

"Nothing seems right nowadays."

"Funny thing about what seems correct. It doesn't have to be true. Take my father, for instance. While we were away, two strangers paid him a visit."

Dawkin leaned on the table. "Oh?"

"He mistook the man for Ade... my late brother, and the lady as his companion. He said the pair asked him some questions. Nothing sensitive, I'm told. Hell, when he spoke of the incident, I nearly thought he imagined the whole ordeal. Until..."

Everitt leaned over the table. He dipped his head. At first, his palms braced him before he bent his arms to shift his weight to his knuckles.

Damn it to hell, does he know?

"She stole from us, James."

Wait, what? "Stealing... Who?"

Everitt lifted his head. "Agnes. The lady who has served my har-kin since before I could remember."

"Everitt, I'm sorry. I promise she will meet the King's justice."

"Never mind. I dealt with it already. I banished the thief and her family from the grounds. Let us leave it at that."

"Exactly how did you come to find out?"

Everitt chuckled. "Fool's luck, I suppose. Once I concluded my inspection of Arcporte Castle and you gave me leave, I rode back to Randell Forest. I didn't arrive until well after nightfall. I intended to go straight to my father's room when I caught sight of candlelight from the servant's quarters. Even for them, the hour was late, so I went in to check on the lot. I found Lady Agnes and her dastardly offspring emptying the manor of every piece of steel, silver, and any other good they could carry.

"Turns out, the visit – from whomever – made them suspicious. The *lady* and her kin believed the guests to be spies sent on my behalf. Thinking the agents noticed something amiss with the manor or my father and worried about their return, Agnes and them prepared to escape into the night when, by sheer chance, I discovered their plot.

"I merely had to roar and brandish my sword a few times to get them to confess. They left the same night all right, but with little more than the clothes on their backs and the ass dragging their cart."

"And your father? What of him?"

"Safe, thank Mar. I managed to take him to the nearest abbey, leaving strict instructions no one speaks to him until my return."

"Good. Good."

"Whoever those two were who spooked Agnes and her family – be they imposters, thieves, or beggars – they served a purpose."

"What are you suggesting?"

"How many times have you... Nay! How many times have *we* lied to our men, James? Boosted their morale when they tired of training in the yard? Hell, in the battle against the Lewmarians, when we stood outnumbered and outflanked?

"This is no different. I know you curse these meetings under your breath. Hell, I do too. But..."

"Don't hold your peace with me, Everitt. Out with it."

"Your dealings with the Ibians, I know, I saw they got to you. With every word they spoke, they left a trail of lies. And at the end of it all, you stood changed. Affected.

Turned. Why I saw so many different versions of you, I couldn't keep track."

Dawkin winced. *So much for maintaining continuity, my brothers.* "Even now, you notice me acting this way?"

"You remain quiet upon your throne, feigning an appearance of listening."

"I heard everything the barons said."

Everitt shook his head. "Your mind sat elsewhere."

"Easy to judge from your vantage point."

"Really, James?"

Dawkin ground his teeth. "I am still *your* king, Sir Everitt. Don't you forget that!"

"Yes, yes. There's the son of the Foxcatcher, the offspring of the Gauntlet."

"You dare provoke me further?"

"If I have to, I will. James, I've sworn to stand at your right side through every battle and encounter. Not only the brawls and battles. But also the sessions at court. The meetings. The conclaves, whether with one or a hundred barons. There, the King is needed most. Along with the sum of regal skills. A forked tongue instead of a sword. A quick wit in place of a shield. Your presence – alert and vigorous, absent of any fatigue – as your greaves, your breastplate, your helm."

"And the lies?"

Everitt sighed. "Remember the Battle of the Chesa?"

"No one will let me forget."

"Your lies: the trees. Your fibs: the leaves. Any falsity or perjury you say: the bushes, the stalks, and the logs we hide behind for our ambush. We deceive on the battlefield to win, James. Courts are no different."

"I'll turn into King Fool."

"No. Just King."

Everitt cracked a smile. Dawkin fought the urge to shake his head. *The bloody bastard's right.*

"I'll take my leave, grant you some peace." Everitt strode back toward the hall.

"How'd you become so righteous?" Dawkin asked.

"I lied."

"Pray tell."

Everitt turned away. "When I sent Lady Agnes off with her kin, I said she left with an ass pulling her cart, didn't I?"

Dawkin nodded.

"I left out the part about her second one." His Right Captain paused. "I flogged the beast, James. Right in front of them. Then I butchered its head off, told them they'd get worse if I ever found them again."

Everitt reddened. Whether the memory stirred his blood or welled up the shame of the incident, Dawkin could not tell. Before he had the chance to inquire, his Right Captain marched off, his footfalls heavy, his breathing silent.

Alone at last, Dawkin returned his attention to the table strewn with parchments and manuscripts aplenty.

The knowledge. The wisdom. The facts. All a waste.

Misinformation. Deceit. Favor. Promises. Lies. The currency of kinghood.

Dawkin shuddered at the truth. His mind drifted to the events of the morning, imagining Symon immobile in Terran while he stood in his place, apart from his brothers, as King Jameson. The thought of betraying his brother for the greater good suddenly seemed easier for him to consider, as insignificant as bumping a stranger in a crowd or tipping over a stein in a tavern.

Mar help me, Dawkin reluctantly prayed, *if this is what it means to lead.*

Chapter 20

"Your Majesty, her fever hasn't returned. She remains committed."

As I knew she would. "Many thanks to you, Mage."

Wystan bowed his head. "I live to serve, My King."

The Royal Mage withdrew. Gerry watched him stroll away. *My King.* The title never stimulated his sensibilities when used in public, such as in Court or when announced in a procession. In private, the moniker carried a heavier weight, stirring Gerry's consideration. Even more than a year after the coronation, Gerry had to fight the urge to pivot and search for his father.

King Jameson. King Geremias.

Gerry shook off the notion. He nodded to the Voiceless flanking the doorway as he entered.

Lady Celia retreated from Taresa's bedpost upon seeing His Majesty. Gerry waited for the handmaiden to close the door as she exited before he took a seat beside her. As he did, Taresa twisted onto her back, her eyes shut.

"James," she uttered.

"I'm sorry. Did my voice carry from the door?"

"Your smell. I can pick you out from afar, my dear."

"A pleasant one I have. I hope."

"Most of the time."

Gerry cracked a smile. Taresa's eyelids fluttered open.

"What time is it?"

"You needn't worry about that. We'll leave when you are able. Unless you prefer to stay –"

"Don't you dare. I already spent too much time away from you, with my father sending you off on that ridiculous diplomatic mission."

She raised herself on her elbows even as Gerry shushed her to stay in bed.

"Don't excite yourself," he chided. "You need to rest. You have to stay calm."

"I'm always calm," Taresa replied curtly, perhaps in response to Gerry, mayhaps because of something else.

"Very well."

"I only want *us*," her hand gravitated to her abdomen, "to be close to you."

Gerry sighed. At the last Court's last session, some of the bishops and barons had raised issue with the Queen traveling to the countryside in her condition. "A fortress is no place for a lady expecting."

That comment provoked a scowl. "King Jameson, we Ibian women are not the feeble maidens of your island. We are iron-willed strongholds, especially when with child. If you believe a minor carriage ride and a dirt road will deter me from spending time with my husband, then you don't know me at all."

Well, I tried. "As you wish, My Queen."

Only half an hour passed before Taresa's ladies-in-waiting had the Queen ready. In that time, Gerry busied himself by inspecting the guards and sentries on the castle ramparts before directing his efforts to the soldiers who lined the road leading out of the grounds. He had only minutes to examine the latter before Sir Everitt rode to his side.

“My King. Her Majesty is waiting.”

“And the royal carriage?”

“I just came from the coach house. I personally went through every axle, wheel, and strap. Thrice. There is no finer conveyance in the country for Queen Taresa.”

“Good.”

“A bit heavy-handed with this trip, aren’t we?” Everitt looked to the men-at-arms standing at attention on either side of the road.

His Right Captain was hardly wrong. After Dawkin had announced the Conclave venue half a fortnight earlier, the barons in attendance responded with protests and suggestions aplenty. Once again, Sir Everitt had to clear the War Hall. What is more, Dawkin had been so bold as to demand a personal audience with each lord to instill the full weight of his mandate and the consequences for anyone – be it commoner or baron – who dared to question his authority. The move worked, with the lords in attendance conceding to King Jameson’s choice for the location and date of the next Conclave. But in the process, the stakes had been raised. In every day following Dawkin’s command, he and his brothers made sure they displayed their authority.

Today proved no exception. Gerry glanced around him. The polished helms of his men held spheres of reflected sunlight. Their crisp blue capes flapped in the subtle breeze, never losing the lines of their ironed cloth, each one a wave in the sea of soldiers. Their freshly-oiled boots and scabbards exuded the pungent odor of leather as though they stood in a tannery.

“The details matter,” Gerry quipped. “Nothing is gained by relenting our perfectionism now.”

"Aye," Everitt conceded, smirking.

"What?"

"I see you took what I said in your library to heart. Well done, James."

"See to my queen, Sir Everitt."

"Yes, Sire."

Satisfied with his king – and seemingly himself – his Right Captain clicked his heels into his steed and rode back to the bailey.

Gerry trailed back at his leisure, stopping every few paces to search the soldiers for flaws in their appearance. He found none. He arrived at the royal carriage satisfied, just as Taresa stepped into the open air of the yard with her flock of attendants.

"Husband, you almost kept me waiting," Taresa chided.

"Never, my lady." Gerry dismounted, handing his reins to a nearby servant. He took his wife by the hand as Everitt dismissed the coachman to hold the carriage door open for them.

"A last-minute fourth inspection?" Gerry asked.

"Of course," Everitt said.

"It met with your satisfaction?" Taresa inquired.

"Yes, Your Majesty." Everitt looked at Gerry. "At your word, we leave."

Gerry took his seat next to Taresa. Through the open door of the carriage, he scanned the grounds one last time. He glimpsed blue capes, watchful attendants, and the caravan of wagons and carts to accompany their majesties on their journey. All sights of castle life he had known his entire life. Not a banner, cart, nor personage stood out of place, though the laughter in the yard did pique his interest.

“Ah, the toys,” Taresa said, her sights following Gerry’s. Across the royal carriage, two giggling children bearing paddles sidestepped as they hit a rubber ball between them.

“Just how many did your retinue give away? And to whom?” Gerry asked.

“Oh, my attendants passed out gifts to all the servants’ children.”

“Oh, how thoughtful.”

“Then they took all the rest into the city, where they distributed them to every boy and girl in view.”

“Taresa, I should say, that is…”

“What?”

“Well…” Gerry grasped at a spare thought. *What would Dawkin say?* “Some parents may object, as idle play may distract the children from their labors. I assume some of those citizens will find their way to my court. And then there are the guilds, those who make toys for sale within Arcporte and beyond. I imagine they wield considerable influence.”

Taresa furrowed her brow. Gerry raised his, anticipating a backlash. Suddenly, his wife burst out laughing.

“That’s the most ridiculous thing I’ve ever heard,” she said, her high-pitched words punctuated by chuckles.

“Is it?”

“I brought those toys for the specific purpose of securing favor. And you admonish me?”

“I didn’t mean –”

“You sound just like my father.”

“I daresay –”

"It's a compliment, James. He's a reasonable man, much like you. The truth is, the giving of gifts when two royals marry is an Ibian tradition. It signals the coming of a grand gift – that of an heir – for the subjects to welcome."

"Oh."

Taresa took Gerry's hand in hers. She placed his on her abdomen.

"In our case, a present well on its way."

Gerry smiled. He peaked out the window again to watch as the two children chased their ball from the yard into the corridor halls.

Castle life. Everything in its place. Perfect.

Too perfect.

Gerry, fighting the darkness within, leaned to the opposite window. "We depart," he commanded.

Sir Everitt bowed. He needed only to step from the carriage window for his men to note his cue. They hurried down the caravan, taking their places on carriage perches or in saddles, readying to depart.

Taresa offered a wave to her attendants, oblivious to the missing detail her husband sought. An extra Voiceless amongst the guards. A servant sauntering through the stables. Or an apprentice meandering the yard in search of the master he didn't have. The mark of a familiar gait. A man of a certain height. In disguise. Hidden. Yet familiar.

No sign of his brothers. Anywhere.

Terran had been tense in the days leading to his current ascension. Once Symon managed to shake off the potion Dawkin had slipped him, he roared with rage, threatening to cut the limbs from the brother who betrayed him. With Dawkin already above at the time, it fell to Ely and Gerry –

along with every Voiceless in range of their shouting – to subdue their strongest sibling. Having no choice, the two brothers confined Symon to his room.

Dawkin, hearing of Symon's fit, descended early, bringing news not only of the upcoming Conclave but of Taresa's fever as well. The totality of events created a conundrum. Dawkin, having just served his rotation – in deceit, no less – and Symon in no manner to control his temper left only Ely and Gerry fit to ascend next. While Ely stood next in line to serve, the details of Taresa's illness turned his stomach, leaving Gerry to rise sooner than anticipated.

The placement, in actuality, did nothing to disturb Gerry. In any other circumstance of his princehood, the thought of ascending out of rotation would have stirred his bowels and caused headaches without end. Instead, a calm overtook him, a sensibility which only persisted when he saw her first upon his ascension. He visited her straightaway to discover her forehead beaded with sweat and her body consumed by fever. While the Royal Mage had already directed the attendants to her needs, Gerry still barked orders to have her linens changed and her limbs massaged. He stayed by her side through the night until the time came to attend the morning's court session.

The totality of the experience invigorated Gerry. Never before had such a sense of purpose been instilled in him. Knowing it had come from within, of his own accord – not because his brothers decided, his grandfather urged, or the barons insisted – stoked his energy all the more.

Still... With the absence of his brethren, he remained incomplete.

"Dear," Taresa said. Gerry shifted his sights from the

grounds to his wife. With her eyes pressed shut, she squeezed his hand. “Tell me a story.”

“A story?”

“When we last spoke, the night before last, your attendant had some maps and scrolls with him. You told me you sought a place with meaning for the Conclave, and in your search, you found some places with stories all their own. Tell me one. About where we’re going.”

Gerry studied her face. The sunlight from the window painted a diagonal streak of cream across the lower half of her face, while the top half held a slightly darker, though no less stunning, version of her beauty. Eyes closed, draped in shadow, she rested in the comfort of his hand’s embrace, her fingers delving further into his.

“Please,” she uttered.

“As you wish.” Gerry cleared his throat. “My father often spoke of the Sayonn Days, when kin and har-kin roamed the island, moving with the seasons to gather and fish. The peoples fashioned their lives on simple principles, with the blessings of Mar himself so abundant they never stood in want.

“That is not to say their lives were perfect. When tempers flared between barons or kings, the threat of war loomed then as now. Even as nomads, they knew to build safe havens for those times. Metallurgy and masonry had not yet developed, so what did our Marlish ancestors do? Using their tools of wood and stone, they constructed earthen fortresses, predecessors to our castles.

“Most were but hillocks or mounds fashioned with burrows for foodstuffs and supplies to serve an army during a siege or battle. A chosen few rose to prominence, becoming the inspiration for legends in which faeries found homes in the rafters of some while behemoths squatted in the larger ones left abandoned between conflicts.

"In any case, while the myths and stories arising from such garrisons survived, sadly, most of the structures did not. The rains of centuries ate away at their heights, the wind leveling their rises. Some went on to serve as the foundations for today's castles, stacked by rock and mortar. Only a handful survive in earnest, including the persistent structure of Glic Anglisk Castle, a mighty fortress of packed dirt and petrified wood built by the founders of our capital... Dear?"

The rise of her snoring answered his query. He chuckled, left to wonder where in his blathering he had lost her to slumber.

A gentle tap on the door diverted his amusement. Gerry drew the curtain over the window to spot Everitt riding atop his destrier outside.

"Thought you should know." His Right Captain pointed ahead.

Gerry yanked the curtain back. He peered forward. A line of blue-draped soldiers separated the row of carriages from the common folk. Unalarmed by the show of force, the citizenry cheered, their palms waving and fists rising. At first glance of the uproarious crowd, Gerry nearly sought to question his Right Captain.

Then he saw it.

The crook of a staff. Not an unusual sight in and of itself. Its difference stood as one of sheen and tone, with the gleam of the white, polished wood catching Gerry's eye. A ceremonial mitre accompanied the crook, its gold and scarlet trim an oddity amongst the surrounding swell of pulsating hands.

"Slow," Gerry commanded.

"Are you certain?" Everitt asked.

"Aye."

Everitt clipped his heels to ride up to the royal coachman. The driver shrugged before tightening his grip on the reins. The horses before him neighed as they curbed their gait.

With the reduced speed, every stone and divot in the road bounced the carriage – and those it carried – a little higher. Gerry doubted the image of him hopping within his transport would impress the bishop. Still, he issued no order to adjust its speed. The carriage clambered ahead.

Ahead, a red ball no larger than a fist bounced into the road. A boy darted after the toy, between a small opening amongst the soldiers.

The sandy-haired lad reached his ball right in front of the first line of royal draft horses. The steeds flailed and neighed, coming to an abrupt stop as a soldier rushed to scoop up the boy from the road.

The momentum lurched Taresa forward. Gerry caught her in his arms as she awoke, startled.

"There, there," he said, setting her back into place.

"James."

Taresa looked past him, her complexion drained. Gerry shifted in his seat, following her lead.

The carriage rested before the High Bishop. As though on cue, the commoners before Perceval parted. He stood immaculate in his crisp white robe, overlaid with a sash of gold and scarlet to match his mitre. For all the beauty of his garb, the austerity of his posture appeared – well, off. Gerry could not place it until he spotted a nearby peasant glance down at the High Bishop's feet, then his own.

The bottom trim of his robe flowed with a breeze, revealing feet blistered and caked with grime.

Gerry lifted his eyes. Yes, it became clearer now. Perceval held his staff more firmly than one ought, leaning on the pole for support. He shifted his feet with subtle grace, though with each turn, he held back a grimace.

His eyes told of it all. The pain. The humility accompanying his formality. The depth of faith prompting him to such lengths. Along with the rage. The rage of having been betrayed by the Throne.

Perceval pursed his lips. Then they parted.

"Sanctuary."

A solitary word. It carried a chill that reverberated down the whole of Gerry. For it bespoke of a power no other utterance could have held.

Dawkin, Gerry said to himself. *Do you have any idea what you have done?*

Gerry had heard the recitation of events during a personal truth session with Dawkin. The magistrates had stumbled upon the cache of explosives the Lost Souls tried to smuggle into Arcporte. A fight ensued, resulting in a few explosions from an incendiary substance. A handful of Lost Souls managed to escape, to find their way into Mar-by-the-Sea Cathedral. There, they fell to their knees to plead to the High Bishop for sanctuary, which he was honor-bound to grant per the doctrines of the Church. A decree noting the act of sanctuary was then nailed to the door of the Cathedral, in accordance with custom.

Dawkin, acting through their grandfather, would have none of it. He ordered the Cathedral stormed in the middle of the night, where the soldiers rounded up the Lost Souls under its roof and placed them under arrest.

After hearing of the scandal Dawkin ignited, Gerry went on to endure many more earfuls from Court, from merchants enraged at the Lost Souls to apologetic barons whose sons had joined the controversial movement.

Absent from the litany of accounts were those from the Church of Mar.

No bishops, high or low, came to Court. Nor did any clergy attend the daily masses scheduled in the King's chapel. No scrolls or letters arrived bearing the seal of the Church. All correspondence vanished, thereby crystallizing the Church's unspoken message:

The sacred covenant of sanctuary had been violated.

While Dawkin had expressed his disapproval of religion over the years – with his frequent jabs and criticisms – Gerry had never believed he would act on it.

You fool! The Throne is now an enemy of the Church.

The butt of Perceval's staff clapped the ground. As if commanding the air itself, the surrounding noise dissipated. For any who had missed the High Bishop's first announcement, there was no mistaking his last.

"Sanctuary."

His staff struck the cobblestone again. Perceval said nothing. Yet with the thump, a man of the cloth emerged from the mass, to take position by His Eminence.

"Sanctuary," said the lowly cleric.

Clack!

Another, this time a monk, came upon Perceval's left

flank.

"Sanctuary."

The staff beat the stone without haste. One by one, more men of the Church emerged. They spoke the same word with the same inflection, same tone, never tinged with anger nor hate nor any emotion. Their phrase always came out the same. Clear. Cold. Unmistakable.

Through the gathering, Perceval never broke sight with the King. His dark brown eyes held true, piercing the expanse between them, burrowing themselves into Gerry's permanent memory.

On the periphery of Gerry's vision, the kingdom waited. Peasants and merchants stared, partly in disbelief, while also afraid of what would come next. Having rounded the carriage on his mount, Everitt lingered for Gerry's directive, his men in view also expecting.

Then a hand, both soft and comforting, rested on his shoulder—Taresa's.

Gerry breathed. He lifted his hand out the window, never breaking his stare with the High Bishop. He pointed forward to flick his index finger.

Everitt lifted his head high. "Move out!"

The coachman snapped his reins. The wheels clapped over the cobblestone once more.

Gerry shot a look back at the High Bishop. The crook of his staff rose, then fell. Although Gerry could hear nothing beyond the carriage wheels, he knew the sound would beckon forth another. A man of faith. One with soiled feet. An unshakeable force.

"Thank you," he said.

He stared at Perceval for as long as he stayed in view.

And even beyond that. Taresa's hand fell from his shoulder as she settled back into her seat. Within moments, her snoring resumed.

The clatter of hooves trotting joined Gerry's carriage. Everitt appeared alongside his window.

"That was ill-timed."

"You have a way with words. You know that?"

"May I suggest a detour?"

"We have a schedule to keep, don't we?"

"Your Majesty will want to see this."

The keystone held in place. A remarkable feat, Gerry considered. He strolled beneath it. The engraving stretched under and throughout, paying homage to all kins and harkins, families he had long known or heard of in his lifetime.

"I never believed they would finish it so soon."

"I only learned of it myself the morning before," Everitt admitted. "Our masons manage quick hands, I suppose."

"To say the least," Gerry added, remaining in marvel at the craftsmanship.

A vision from heaven, the curve of stone bore a ribbon of seals. Gerry had known them all his life, and yet, seeing them chiseled into the massive block imparted a sense of honor, a mark of pride somehow strange to him. Perhaps it was all due to the fact he had commissioned it – The Marlish Academy of Alchemy.

"'Tis coming along nicely, James."

Gerry failed to answer. Instead, he took in the expanse of the unfinished grounds. Inlaid in the earth stretched the broad trenches waiting to be filled with rubble and mortar for the foundations of the adjacent buildings. That of the Atheneum of Alchemy – intended to house the library and offices of the mages – had been complete, with the most massive pillars put into place. Of those, two supported the arch designed to hold the entryway. There, the keystone sat in the balance, the crowning achievement of months of preparation and labor.

"You should be proud," Everitt added, coming alongside him.

"So should you."

"Pardon?"

Gerry pointed upward.

The seal of Kin Saliswater – a fourpointe compass – rested at the center of the keystone. To the right of the crest lay that of another family, one with three robins in the foreground.

"I don't understand," Everitt admitted.

"I had the master sculptor add the design for your family."

"That's very kind of you, James. But, um, well..."

"Yes?" Gerry couldn't help himself from grinning.

"The details are a little off. There is no diagonal stripe on my family crest. And traditionally, those seals around or bordering those of the King are not of har-kins."

Gerry's mouth widened into a smile. He waited. Finally, after a moment longer, Everitt's jaw dropped.

"Ha!" Gerry exclaimed.

"You mean, my family – a har-kin – has been elevated?"

"The Furdes have been the strongest allies of the Saliswaters for years, long before you became my Right Captain. With your valor at the Battle of the Riverford, I knew the time had come to honor your family, who has done everything possible to protect mine. Believe me, Everitt, this was long overdue."

"Your Majesty..." Everitt bowed his head, ever the formal knight.

Gerry, still beaming with delight, returned his gesture with a wave of his hand. "'Tis nothing."

"The barons of greater manors, they won't appreciate a har-kin jumping ahead of their positions, especially in such public monuments which clearly display my favor. The Conclave must still approve of my family's appointment to a higher rank."

"The barons! Let them huff and protest all they want! They cannot doubt the many sacrifices of you and your ancestors. Some may cast votes against the promotion out of spite or envy. Let those bastards rot! Enough will support your ascension to make it official. You'll see."

"Hmm. Kin Furde. Kin Furde," Everitt said aloud to himself. "It rings true."

"That's the spirit."

Everitt glanced away, contemplative. "I'll need to pick the proper moment to tell my father. He'll need to be of right mind to appreciate this honor." Everitt considered. "It's possible the Conclave will bring up his condition."

"Aye, they might."

"He has yet to concede his status as baron, even when he is not of right mind."

Gerry turned to his friend. "The Conclave – and I – have the authority to do something about that too."

Everitt sighed. "'Tis not right."

"Everitt, you were always in line to inherit your manor

with all its privileges, including rank."

"No, not always. Adequin... Never mind."

Gerry winced. The mention of the eldest Furde sibling, Mar rest his soul, stirred memories of grief, reopening wounds never fully healed. With the exception of Symon, neither he nor his brothers knew how to traverse the sensitive subject with any measure of success.

Still, I must try. "A Furde rising to the rank of baron of a newly-forged kin. Why, there is no circumstance in which your family should not celebrate, including your father, no matter his mental state. You can even bring him here, after you've become a lord, for the inauguration ceremony. He'll come, see the crest, and know the pride of his family's accomplishment. You'll see."

"James, listen to yourself," Everitt chuckled. "You sound like a young lad dreaming of knighthood."

"Too much?"

"No, no. 'Tis lighthearted is all. And, honestly, you're right. It will be a great honor, regardless of my father's state. I am in your debt, James. Thank you."

They stared up at the keystone together.

"You two seem awfully smitten, having left a queen to wake alone in a carriage." With a shawl pulled across her shoulders, Taresa sauntered up between them.

"Your Majesty, the fault is mine. I suggested His Majesty veer from the royal procession to inspect the progress of the Academy grounds, the construction of which is well ahead of schedule –"

"Everitt," Taresa interrupted. "I was only joshing you."

Everitt blushed. "'Twas a fine joke, Your Majesty."

"Everitt, what have I told you?"

“Taresa. You got me good, Taresa.”

“Better.” Taresa turned. “Are you boys done? One of the servants from the procession retreated to us, said quite the crowd has swelled to greet us in the township just below.”

“James?” Everitt glanced at Gerry.

“Right. On with it, I suppose.”

Everitt fell in beside Taresa to offer his arm and escort her back to the carriage. He deftly pointed to every tiny crag or recess before them, eliciting a smile from His Queen.

Gerry held back, allowing himself a moment to take in the grounds by himself. He glanced upward, his gaze settling on the top crest of his kin on the keystone.

The crowd below did not disappoint. As Taresa had said, it had grown more significant than those which had greeted them upon departure. The commoners lining the road spilled before their path, despite the efforts of the soldiers to keep them at bay. As a result, the royal coachman drove the carriage at a snail’s pace, the lack of momentum inspiring some of his more coarse phrases.

From within, Gerry and Taresa watched the jubilant onlookers, offering a wave here and there.

“James,” Taresa ventured. “Is this common?”

“Why, no, it isn’t. The people are merely excited to catch a glimpse of their new queen, ‘tis all.”

“No, I mean... How do I say this? Your Throne seems to have a tradition of being very accommodating.”

“How so?”

“That wasn’t the right word. But it does strike me as odd at how often you must answer your Conclave.”

“Oh, hmmm,” Gerry recalled a recitation Dawkin had

uttered during one of their truth sessions. "I'm aware your Conclave is less... diverse."

"Pardon?" Taresa replied a touch defensively.

"Kin Saliswater has not held the kingdom nearly as long as Kin Garsea has held theirs. Your family has had the product of time to forge alliances, marry into other powerful kins and hard-kins, establish trade agreements, and so forth. Us Saliswaters have not possessed such an advantage. Why, half our dynasty has been marred by the Century War, which we barely survived..."

Gerry trailed off even as Taresa looked on, expecting more. *After all our victories, the deals, the decades holding court, are we still so vulnerable? Have we any real power at all? Or is it one long ruse to be shattered as quickly as a crystal goblet falling from a table?*

"My dear?" Taresa prodded.

"Kin Saliswater has endured many challenges. Every monarch we've placed on the Throne has held their head high, even as their crown weighed heavily on them." Fatigue settled on Gerry, suddenly and without the promise of an end. "So yes, we answer to many, hoping against hope for the masses of both peasants and nobles to bless us with a few more years to reign."

Gerry peeked out the window, offering a hand to the audience. They responded with jubilee, unmatched by his mood.

Taresa slid his hand in his. "You are King Jameson of Kin Saliswater. If one man can hold this island together, it is you. Besides, you don't have to do this alone." She squeezed his hand.

Aye, he mused. *I don't. If you only knew how true your*

words rang.

Delivering himself from his thoughts, Gerry watched the crowd as they inched past. Their shouts intermingled; he sought out their calls at random.

"Blessed is the King!"

"Your Majesty! Your Majesty!"

"Long live Kin Saliswater!"

"The book! The book I gave you! Dawkin, you must read it!"

The last utterance stirred Gerry. He released Taresa's hand to lean on the window, scouring the flock of onlookers.

"James, what is it?" Taresa asked.

"Dawkin! Dawkin!" The words glanced upon Gerry's ears again. He searched to his left, from where he could swear the voice came. In a flash, he caught sight of a head of golden locks, along with a waving hand. But the crowd, dense and without end, swallowed her as the carriage pressed onward. Or perhaps she never was there at all? Gerry searched the audience again, finding neither her nor even the place she stood. The moment, whether true or not, vanished.

"James, did you see something?"

Did I? I know I heard the name Dawkin. Didn't I? Certain of nothing, Gerry shook his head. "'Tis nothing, I suppose." Gerry leaned back in his seat, his mind awash in uncertainty.

"Remember." Taresa took his hand once more. "You are King Jameson of Kin Saliswater. You can do anything."

Gerry smirked. He gripped her hand, though no words left his mouth in answer. Turning back to the crowd beyond his window, he waved.

Chapter 21

"Here they come," Ely said, just before he tipped a glass of sherry into his gullet. "The suckling pigs."

"Where is he?" Symon inquired. He peered out the window of the bartizan, eying the first carriages of the caravan. Guards lined the bridge stretching over the brackish water of the moat. The forward barbican had fallen into ruins many years before, its moss-covered stones a testament to the mighty blocks which once composed its heights. Likewise, the drawbridge had disappeared, replaced by the recent addition of sturdy planks to accommodate the carriages and horses of the day's Conclave gathering. Neither banded by iron nor secured to chains and windlass, the makeshift bridge could not be withdrawn, leaving only the wide doors of the gatehouse – with possessed no portcullis – as the only barrier to the threats outside.

Ely smirked. *The defenses must be driving Symon mad.*

"He's in the carriage house, inspecting the chests and such," Gerry answered. "Said he might have forgotten something."

"Good," Symon uttered. "Let him search 'til the end of the Conclave. Will be better for him."

"For us," Ely added, pouring himself another glass. "We haven't time for your antics."

"No, we haven't. With a castle as poor as this, we

haven't the luxury of anything, especially security. Damn it, Dawkin! What on earth was he thinking, choosing this place?"

Ely shared a look with Gerry. Never did he imagine the two of them would ever have to take on the anger of their bigger brother to protect their smartest one. Having done it once already in Terran, when Symon first awoke from being drugged, resulted in a monumental effort Ely did not ever want to attempt again.

"I believe," Gerry started, albeit squeaking like a mouse, "there is working more toward our advantage than against it."

"You mean the valley? The gap we all had to pass through? Pfft," Symon scoffed. "The surrounding rangelands aren't so high as to stop the most determined. I venture there are dozens of paths crossing these ridges for shepherds and their flocks."

"True," Ely admitted, emptying his glass. "Yet that can be said of any mountain hideaway or highland fortress." Ely strolled up to Symon, calm as a babe approaching a wet nurse. "Brother, whatever your feelings toward Dawkin, his efforts in our absence unveiled the treachery of the Lost Souls. His truth session told all about their plot. With their plans to blow up Highmoorr Castle, we had no choice other than to find an appropriate alternative."

"Appropriate?" Symon jabbed his finger through the window. "We have no barbican! We have no drawbridge!"

"We also have no dungeon. No vault. No underground tunnels or lairs to speak of. So we run no risk of the Lost Souls having stocked their explosives in alternative locations, as Dawkin learned during his... questioning of them."

Ely shuddered at the idea of his brother torturing prisoners. In truth, for all his nights drinking and carousing, not once had Ely lost so much sense as to consider tormenting another. The entirety of the concept – the screams, the sweating, the blood – upended his stomach.

"Are you well?" Gerry asked of Ely, noting his suddenly pale façade.

"Quite so," Ely insisted. "Just need more drink, 'tis all."

"Explosives can be hidden," Symon persisted. "Holes dug and covered. This fortress is of earth and timber. It wouldn't be hard."

"True," Ely relented. "This castle, like any other, could burst. Combust. Yet you forget Dawkin consulted the mage before proclaiming his decision. That old chap Wystan conferred with our brother, advising such incendiary devices would, um, how did he say?"

Ely shot a cursory glance at Gerry, who pivoted to his brother. "'Blow *up*,' the mage said," Gerry added. "The liquid the Lost Souls brought expands rapidly. It climbs for air like a hungry fire, which is why placing it underground bears so much of a threat. The underground passages of this ancient fortress filled with mud and debris centuries ago, becoming like mortar, as Mage Wystan concluded."

"Precisely, little brother." Ely clapped Gerry on the back, nearly knocking him forward. "So you see, Symon, even if the Lost Souls found some miraculous way to hide their explosives in some nook, when set off, the main force of the blast would shoot into the air. Like an arrow having lost its way."

"Towers can still fall. And walls." Symon crossed his arms, clearly not buying into the rationale.

“Yes, but the foundations would hold; the integrity of the fortress would not be compromised. In the case of an explosion, only those within the immediate vicinity of the blast would be harmed, the rest of us spared.”

“Mage Wystan compared such a scenario to a mine collapsing within versus a rockslide on the side of a mountain,” Gerry stated.

“Precisely!” Ely exclaimed.

“I still don’t like it,” Symon insisted. “The Conclave being held here and all. ‘Tis not right.”

“Good Mar! There’s no pleasing you.” Ely downed another glass of sherry before motioning to Gerry. “You deal with the sour louse. I’m going downstairs to find –”

“Grandfather!” Gerry exclaimed.

“– I was going to say another bottle.”

“No, you fool.” Gerry looked to the road below. “Grandfather, he came after all.”

“He’s right. ‘Tis his bannerman at the front,” Symon added.

Ely furrowed his brow. “Dawkin advised him to stay at Arcporte Castle, on account of his...” Ely struggled for the phrase so often applied to himself. *Mania? Incident? Episode?* His voice failed him. His mind, suddenly anxious, hung in the balance.

Symon glanced at Ely. Gerry, too intent on meeting their grandfather, hurriedly passed the helms to his brothers.

“Come!” Gerry said. “Let’s see him greeted properly.” Without waiting for either of them, he made for the stairwell.

“I’m sure Grandfather’s fine,” Symon noted.

"How can you be certain?" Ely asked.

"A Saliswater knows." Symon patted his shoulder before following Gerry.

Then perhaps I am no Saliswater, Ely mused as he trailed after his brothers.

The central yard bustled with activity. Though as large as any, the stables and carriage house – recent additions to the ancient structure – could only accommodate a handful of carts and a dozen mounts. Such confines meant the arrivals, who couldn't be bothered with walking, had to be dropped off within the yard before their carriages were led to the grounds outside to park. Such a circular parade made for a ringlet of frustration amid chaos, one Gerry navigated with enthusiasm as he strode to the rear of the line, where Artus waited.

Everitt, speaking with his men, fell in beside Gerry.

"James," he called. Gerry slowed, allowing Ely to catch up and linger behind them.

"Everitt. How goes the inspection of the grounds."

"There is much here to be desired, Your Majesty."

"Oh?"

"The ramparts are low, barely a story and a half in some parts. The quarters are dank and dark in most places, with only the hall without leaks, as of now anyhow. Not to mention..."

"Everitt, is it secure?"

"Yes. All in all, it's safe, James."

"But?"

"I still don't like it." Gerry glanced back at Symon, who, like Ely, wore a full visor and helm. Ely – not needing to care who saw him –

turned in full to his brother.

"What?" Symon asked of Ely in a whisper.

"You've poisoned our Right Captain's thoughts against the lot of us," Ely snickered, also low.

"The man has a right to his opinion."

"Sure, yours."

Symon and Ely fell silent as Gerry took Everitt away by the shoulder.

"I know you're concerned," Gerry said to him. "And I appreciate your candor."

"Don't patronize me, James."

"Truly, I'm not." Gerry paused. "What more would calm you?"

Everitt considered. "The woods near the south have been cleared from the fortress' edge, for the most part, yet remain thick in many areas. I would prefer more scouts assigned to patrol them. And more sentries on this joke of a parapet overlooking them."

"Can you spare the men?"

"Aye. The yard is too cramped for the castle patrol anyway. I can use them."

"See to it."

Everitt nodded to Gerry before marching back to whence they came. Symon and Ely parted to allow him to pass. Gerry, grinning, went on ahead to the rear of the line, where their grandfather's carriage lay in sight.

"He's getting good at this," Symon stated, beaming.

"This?"

"His kinghood."

Well, best it not go to his head, Ely thought, a tad envious.

Ahead, their brother broke into a trot. "You arrived!" Gerry shouted.

Artus swung open the door to his carriage. A servant swooped in with a stepstool, one which the patriarch quickly waved away. Stepping straight into the mud, Artus extended his hand to Gerry even as his grandson leaned in for an embrace.

"How did you fare on the ride?" Gerry asked. He looked to Symon coming up on his right, who now sported his helm, its visor closed. Ely, who also approached in the guise of a knight, escaped Gerry's gaze. Unlike Symon, he held back a tad while remaining within earshot.

"I would have been better off riding," Artus replied. "Good Mar, how does anyone stand a coach? I felt every stone, dip, and twig in the road, I did."

"'Tis easier on your bones than atop a horse," Symon uttered through his visor.

"You only say that because you think I'd fall."

"I'd never think that, Grandfather," Gerry pledged. "Honest."

"Your word is never anything but true." Artus clapped Gerry on the back. He scanned the yard. A smirk took form on his face. "What a bloody mess."

"At Court, the barons insisted on being let off in the yard, just as they would have in Highmoorr Castle."

"Highmoorr has a lane for such deliveries. Along with two gatehouses, to ensure such congestion doesn't occur."

"Aye, Grandfather. We made this known to our lords. Still, they insisted."

Artus squinted. Darkness overtook him. Ely inched closer.

“The barons,” Artus seethed through clenched teeth. “They expect too much.”

“Yes, Sire,” Gerry said, his shoulders foretelling his move to step away.

“Such entitlement will need to be addressed. Not today, I suppose.” Artus removed a scroll from the pocket inside his long coat. Though rolled, the seal had been broken. “This came to the castle after you left, just as I was readying to leave. Pardon my curiosity. I thought it better to open and read it, should the news prove worthy to wait.” He extended the scroll to Gerry, but before releasing it, nodded to the gatehouse. “Perhaps some privacy?”

Gerry nodded. He, Artus, and Symon retreated to the alcove of the gatehouse, which sat unoccupied save for the flickering light from a sconce. Ely went after them. He paused just within the entrance of the passageway, where the three stood in his sights. He turned away slightly, acting as a sentry on guard, though he perked his ears more than any soldier would.

Symon, in the safety of shadows, removed his helm. Gerry unfurled the parchment as Artus glanced at Symon. Then Ely.

“What’s it say?” Symon asked. “Spare the details. Give us the basics.”

“Word from across the channel, from Vloma, by way of Port San-Mont. By the hand of High Bishop Jaquot of Har-Kin Senddula...”

Gerry paused. Symon crept closer. Like Gerry, he peered over his shoulder to ensure none other than their brother stood in the corridor. Ely moved in too yet maintained a respectable distance, keeping up his ruse as a guard.

"It reads, in parts: *Word of our violation of the sacred covenant of sanctuary has reached the Continent... The Conclave of High Bishops, along with Kin di Valia, have heard of these crimes against the Church... they are displeased by these reported sins... A tribunal will be initiated to investigate... We demand the clergy have a seat at your next Conclave of Barons to discuss...*"

Gerry's words trailed off even as he kept reading. He lowered the scroll to look at his brothers and grandfather.

"You know what this means?" Artus asked ominously.

"What?" Symon asked. "A few strong words from a High Bishop across the Channel? Hardly a –"

"Brother," Gerry started, "have you forgotten your history?"

"No," Symon answered, even as his tone spoke to his uncertainty.

"Port San-Mont is the unofficial seat of Belgarda's military power in northern Afari, the ancestral home of Kin di Valia. During the Century War, a scroll issued from their mist-shrouded isle meant only one thing: a declaration of war."

"Bah!" Symon glanced away, then faced off with Gerry. "An old legend, 'tis all. That isle has sat quietly for over two decades. Why I've never even heard of a threat or an opposition coming out of this so-called island fortress. Could be abandoned for all we know."

"The stronghold you dismiss so easily is as mighty as ever," Artus insisted. "Do not disrespect that which you do not know."

Taken aback by his grandfather's admonishment,

Symon stuttered. “Grandfather, I meant no contempt. I merely... I value the sacrifices you and your generation made to thwart our enemies... The Century War produced many a worthy adversary...”

Artus raised his hand to stop his grandson. “Put your tongue and mind at ease. Your attitude is not unlike that of the barons in my day. Myself included. We, too, thought less of the northern stronghold of Kin di Valia. Those who did not live through those days can easily breeze over the absence of the Devout State of Belgarda from our history texts. And who can blame you? Officially, Belgarda never aligned with any power in all the years of the Century War. Even in the years of their False King, the Devout State managed its neutrality. To the deception of us all.

“Yet make no error, the rare times when Port San-Mont issued a decree...” Artus touched the top edge of the parchment. “... something would happen. The tides would retreat from the channel standing between the isle and the mainland. The monks would traverse the momentary peninsula. Days or weeks later, carnage would ensue, with one sides’ army obliterated. By whom exactly, ‘twas never announced. Still, always afterward, the monastic force would be spotted returning to their stronghold, nearly in full force, to lay dormant once more until another edict by their High Bishop was issued.”

Artus paused, his face bearing the weight of a heavy truth, both grave and unrelenting. Symon, looking to the parchment in Gerry’s hands, tugged it from his brother. He held it to the flame of the sconce until it caught, the threat it held consumed by fire.

“What do we do?” Gerry asked.

"What we must," Artus replied. "His Reverance, Perceval, is due at the Conclave, is he not?"

Gerry looked hesitantly to Symon, who shared his sentiment. "His brother, Baron Dederic, did insist on his brother joining him at the Conclave. So out of respect for his Har-Kin, we did extend an invitation. That was before... Dawkin broke sanctuary."

Artus threw his arms into the air. "That boy! He took too much liberty with my name. Never in my wildest dreams would I have thought to keep a watchful eye on that one." Instinctively, his eyes glanced in Ely's direction, who at once knew the implication.

Yes, Grandfather. I am the one they call King Fool. You never believed one of your other beloved grandsons could earn the moniker, could you? For once, Ely was thankful for the visor across his eyes, lest his grandfather or his brothers read the scorn his face no doubt carried.

"He is nonetheless expected to attend," Gerry continued, albeit without haste. "Our men spotted the High Bishop and his clerical retinue on the Amberglen Highway. On foot, no less, to make amends to Mar for the sins *we* in Marland have committed."

"Hmm, that would explain why I didn't pass him on my way here." Artus scratched the stubble of his chin. "And his journey here speaks volumes about his willingness – mayhaps that of the Devout State – to come to an agreement."

"And put this whole business with the Church behind us," Symon added.

"What say you..." Artus pondered, "to us sending a royal escort to His Reverence? Say your carriage? And wagons for his retinue? That would speed his progress here and reflect his prestige, his coming as a guest of honor."

Ah, hell. Enough of my ruse! Ely abandoned his pretend post at the mouth of the corridor. "The barons will be outraged!" Ely exclaimed, removing his helm. "You give favor to any one of those elitists in attendance, and the whole of them will protest. And to a clergyman no less. Plus, the son of a har-kin?! The higher ranking kins will erupt with outcries."

Gerry stepped up to him. "Is that such a bad thing?" He turned to his grandfather. "The barons will be displeased, yes. But given the news from Afari – which will eventually reach their ears – they will come to understand our offering. Plus, Perceval will be flattered by our show of respect, which will make waves across the continent back to Vloma, and the ears of his leader, the Supreme Devout."

"No member of the clergy can resist such puffery," Artus mused.

"Nonsense! The lot of them will see through the move." *By Mar, am I the only one not gone mad?*

"I can't believe I'm saying this, but Ely *may* be right," Symon admitted. "Then again, so may you two."

"We can't not make a royal offering to Perceval," Gerry said. "Any statement or move by us might be misconstrued. I know the risk. Yet the longer we wait to make amends, the worse the consequences be against us."

The four considered Gerry's words in earnest. Ely snarled. *Damn the little bugger. He's right.*

"Well, then," Artus nodded to Gerry, "have your carriage readied for the jaunt to Amberglen. The High Bishop will be saved the humility of arriving on mudfoot, somewhat to his chagrin. Though I wager our kin he will accept our mode of transport with some hidden sense of relief."

Gerry, beaming from his grandfather's encouragement, smiled. "I'll give the order, Grandfather. I will." With haste, he marched from the gatehouse.

"Best I keep an eye on that one." Symon strapped on his helm. "He's become too emboldened as of late."

Well, he took Taresa to bed. What were we to expect? "Me too, I suppose." Ely made a move to put on his helm.

"Ely, before you do, a word," Artus insisted.

Ely paused. Symon, giving him a look, shrugged before lowering his visor and following after Gerry.

"What troubles you so, Grandfather, that you need a solitary audience?" Ely inquired.

"You, you were put in a rather peculiar position back at the castle, were you not?"

Ely cocked his brow. He suspected he knew what his grandfather was referring to but would not venture to guess. "Meaning?"

"Gerry left without you three. A rare move, given how you and your brothers have staged your ascensions – and subsequent guardianships – since the first day of your kinghood. Do not bother to deny it. In princehood, your father insisted on only one of you – whether in disguise or not – being ascended while the rest were confined to Terran. He and I managed to keep you four committed to such a regimen in your younger days.

"Alas, as you matured, you desired to escape in not-so-secret ways. To explore Arcporte and beyond. He and I permitted such slights.

"Now, as men, the laws of what we outlined in Terran bear you no consequences. As monarchs, you must bend or discard restrictions at will, either for your wellness or the greater good. Such moves have seen your rule consistent, the eternal bond between you forged. Until recent days…"

Artus looked away. First, to the noises from the yard, which echoed through the stones of the gatehouse. Then to the flickering light of the sconce, which captured his attention too long. Lastly, he peered into the shadows, the darkness of no particular interest.

"You left with Symon, while Dawkin came much later afterward. But not before you made inquiries while the Voiceless held Symon in his confines." Artus finally turned to Ely. "You must have spoken to every single Voiceless about what transpired while you were away. Did you not? A hard endeavor, considering the years you have mocked our mute guards."

Ely held his tongue, wanting to answer with a humorous quip. "Aye," he said instead. "I made inquiries."

"You asked not only about Dawkin… You asked about me."

"Aye," he replied again.

"Why?" Artus asked. His eyes narrowed in admittance to the fact he already knew the answer.

"Dawkin, during his truth session, he, he recalled moments of concern." Ely wavered. Eyes, light brown with flecks of gold, burrowed into his soul, searching for answers. *The Gauntlet lives. Making this all the more difficult.*

"Moments?" Artus prodded.

"You, at times, seemed to lose your wits."

"And?"

"Your nerve faltered."

"Go on."

"Grandfather –"

"Ely!"

"Fear," Ely blurted. "Dawkin, he kept referring to your fainthearted behavior. Your frail demeanor. He saw you afraid. A... fool."

Artus lowered his brow as his nose crinkled. Ely expected a tongue-lashing. Instead, he faced the backside of a silver mane as his grandfather snapped away. The old man stretched out his hand to the stone wall, in as much to steady his body as well as his anger. "Does the kingdom see me this way?" he finally inquired. "The peoples. Our subjects."

"I honestly don't know."

"My entire reign was marred by war. When peace finally came during Audemar's time, I thought my legacy – our legacy – was secure. A father having endured the brunt of the fight, one who passed a kingdom on to his son, who then quelled the remnants of our chaos." Artus glanced back to Ely. "I hope you never know what I have. A father, losing a son."

No waterfall of tears followed his sentiment. Not one droplet. The veil of the Gauntlet held firm.

"How do you do it?" Ely asked, at a loss. "Lead? Represent the Throne? Knowing that every moment of weakness – no matter how strong you try to be – becomes an arsenal against you, one our enemies and our very own barons keep in their pockets, to use at their leisure? Honestly, when I falter and then return to my senses, I see the looks of those who witnessed my mania, my outbursts... their smug faces, and I, I..."

I turn into the Fool. Again. My anger seethes. I want to

beat those dastardly subjects, with their treasonous thoughts behind polite smiles. Lock them in chains. Throttle them by the noose!

Ely had glanced aside of Artus' stare. Recovering his wits, he lifted his eyes to catch sight of Artus watching him, the pendulum of concern having shifted from grandson to grandfather.

"Ely."

"Yes?"

Artus hesitated, his mouth agape. Both a moment and an eternity passed before an interruption bellowed through the corridor.

"Grandfather?!" Symon shouted from beyond. "Brother?!"

"We're here," Artus answered.

"Perceval has arrived by coach."

"So soon? Gerry only issued the order –"

"Not ours. Another baron picked him up along the way, besting our efforts. The yard is astir. We should begin. Shortly."

"Aye. We come." Artus went on after his Symon's voice, but not before lingering by Ely. "You've spent a lifetime trying to rein in King Fool, keeping that part of yourself confidential, along with the other workings you and your brothers have experienced." Artus leaned in as if others stood closely within earshot. "Our secrets have done much to save us. Now, they do us harm."

"How?"

"One day – soon – I will need to tell you four. Altogether. Of a hidden chapter of the Century War. One I had put out of memory, buried deep, only to see it rise again."

Dear Mar, has he truly gone mad? "When?"

"Soon."

With that, the old man – perhaps giving way to the Gauntlet within once more – hastened away, his legs somehow gaining the speed and strength of a fresh squire. Ely scarcely had a chance to raise a hand and a word to stop him before his grandfather turned the corner to leave him in the shadows.

Secrets? More? Ely plodded to the mouth of the corridor. He peered from the dimness as he fastened the strap of his helm under his chin.

In the yard, High Bishop Perceval stepped from a carriage bearing the crest of five spades of Kin Hamistale. His feet planted themselves on the mat an attendant had laid before him, a vain effort to protect his mud-caked bare feet from further grime. Another servant wrapped a red sable cape over Perceval's shoulders while a third presented him with a platter bearing him a cup of steaming hot tea along with an assortment of dried fruits and nuts. Outside the circlet of doting attendants, nobles of every har-kin and kin waited for their chance to greet His Eminence.

Perceval, basking in the attention, tilted his head toward the sun as he spat out a prayer of thanks.

"What a whore," Ely whispered to himself. He lowered the visor to his helm. *May Mar strike me down if ever I desire so much flattery,* he thought, before remembering so many similar actions of his. *Wait, don't.*

Circumventing the crowd gravitating toward the carriage, Ely tromped to the Great Hall of Glic Anglisk where – eventually – the lot of barons and bishops would find their way for the Conclave.

Chapter 22

"Our mage says it looks like rain." The gap-toothed attendant squinted as he stared into the haze. "Can't say I see it myself. Mayhaps a fog."

Dawkin grunted as he set the trunk against the wall. He pivoted on his heels, ready to retrieve another.

"Whatcha doing?" the attendant screeched.

Dawkin ground his teeth. "My work."

"Not like that, you won't. Don't you see those stains on the wall? If it rains like the mage says it will, the water will run down the wall –"

Dawkin held out his hand, noting the darkened trail past rains had left. "I'll move it. I'll move it."

The attendant opened his mouth wide, revealing his gums, as his hands shot into the air. "Bloody knights." He stomped away. "Not a tad of sense with that lot, there is. Can't even move a trunk without ruining it."

Dawkin breathed deep as he bent down to drag the trunk from the wall.

Five more trunks later – which he moved and moved again – he came across the one he had set out to find. Braided with bronze studs over ribbons of embossed tin, the leather-covered trunk required a bit more heft on Dawkin's part. He carried it to the main storage quarters along with the others, waiting for the carriage attendant to depart for the privy before moving it to the barracks assigned to the Voiceless.

There, he threw open the trunk. He drew a few volumes from within, including the one he had sought. Laying them on one of the bunks, he admired their calligraphy for a moment before retreating to the washbasin in the corner.

Removing his prosthetic nose, chin, and cheekbones, Dawkin scrubbed the makeup from his face. A knock from outside the locked door caught him with a towel over his face.

"Occupied," he shouted, hoping the knight on the other side would recognize his voice.

"'Tis me," Artus replied.

Dawkin sighed. He unlocked the door for his grandfather, retreating to the trunk he had brought as he entered.

"They're about to begin the Conclave," Artus announced.

"Good," Dawkin said, his back to Artus. He knelt to throw open the lid to his trunk. "The sooner they start, the quicker we end this. This place is so, so damp and cold."

"You picked it."

"A choice I now regret. I thought earthen forts were supposed to be packed tight to avoid all these drafts."

"Like other castles, they have ventilation shafts. I suppose some may have broadened or swelled over time."

"Perhaps." Dawkin tossed aside a few wares from the trunk, whose contents had shifted considerably on the carriage ride over.

"May I lend a hand?" Artus asked.

"Thank you, no."

From behind Dawkin, Artus sighed.

"What?!" Dawkin asked.

He pivoted on the balls of his feet, ready to meet his grandfather's disapproving stare, perhaps even a scowl.

Whack!

He met the back of his fist instead.

Dawkin tumbled onto his back. Stunned and shocked, he looked up at his grandfather. The old man, with fists closed, towered over him.

"What in the blazes was that?"

"A lesson."

"Lesson?!"

"You're not a spoiled, sniveling prince anymore. You are a king. Act like one."

Dawkin sat up, caressing his jaw. It did not hurt per se. Rather, the mark stung his pride more than anything.

"Are you angry?" Artus prodded.

"A tad."

"You should be. Your behavior as of late has been deplorable."

"What?" Dawkin shuffled up to his feet. "What are you talking about, Grandfather? Have you lost your wits?"

"No. Have you?"

"Me?" Dawkin, dumbfounded, knew not whether to seethe with anger or retreat in guilt. "You, I, I – What is the meaning of this?"

"You truly don't know?"

Dawkin knew. His eyes narrowed at the name flashing through his mind.

"Say it," Artus insisted as if reading his mind.

"Symon."

"Aye."

"But he, he questioned me."

"As is his right. Like your other brothers."

"He's different. That damn warrior. He disappears for months at a time – with Ely and Gerry and nearly the whole Court – and then returns to scrutinize my every move, as I knew he would. Him and his pious, self-righteous attitude."

"Listen to yourself." Artus approached Dawkin, unclenching one hand while the other remained balled. "You know your brother. You anticipated his behavior, his reaction, to what you did in his absence and that of your brothers. And *still*, you act blindsided, offended by his criticisms. What's more, you turned craven. You decided to sedate him rather than stand by your actions and defend yourself in the Fourpointe Chamber."

"The lot of them would have confined me to Terran."

"So be it. 'Tis their right."

"They have no claim to judge me. They weren't here. They didn't see what we – what I – saw. In the countryside. On the streets. The madness. Hysteria. The loss of control. One that would have surged from the gutters and sluices of every slum we have."

"Dawkin –"

"You don't know what it's like."

"I do!" Artus – straightening further, now with both hands balled – stood squarely up to him. "The Century War did this to many. Far too many. I watched as men with wit and courage such as yours would march off to the battlefield with ideals and dreams of glory aplenty. They would pass a town or village close to the front, maybe one pillaged, and witness the horror of war on the common. The fear. The desperation. From an enemy real or imagined, there one moment and gone the next. It was never the actual combat that claimed them. It was always what they saw before or after which came to haunt them. And not just the foot soldiers. Knights. Barons. Kings..."

The last utterance hung in the balance, crippling Artus' resolve to speak sense to his kin. His concentration wavered. He leaned away from Dawkin.

"Grandfather?" Dawkin began.

"Audemar. My son..." Artus turned away. Whether he spoke his name out of nostalgia or had lost his senses – believing now the one before him was the late king – Dawkin dared not say.

"At the castle, when you met me in the library, you said you had something of importance to discuss. With me. Along with my brothers. About our father. And us."

"Oh, that. Yes."

"Grandfather, what happened?"

"You... you were... born..."

The door creaked open.

Dawkin exploded with rage. "Who dares to disturb the King –"

The soft white face of Taresa peeked in, her eyes set on the two.

"You."

Artus spun around to meet her stare as well. He and Dawkin – as if ghosts caught in the act of a haunting – remained agape as Taresa entered. Doe-eyed, she approached, with the slightest of smiles repressed from her lips.

"What are you doing here?" Dawkin blurted.

Taresa bristled a tad. Her hint of amiability dissipated, replaced at once with regal formality. "I am a queen of

Marland now, am I not?" she pressed.

"Why, yes."

"In Ibia, a queen has the right to enter every chamber of a royal residence, be it a temporary shelter or permanent dwelling. My tutors of etiquette informed me this is also the case here on this island. Were they wrong?"

"No."

Taresa nodded, accepting the confirmation. She glanced at Artus. "The lords collect in the Hall. You are expected. Before the king."

Taresa laid her hands over her waist, waiting for a response. Artus and Dawkin shared a look. Artus finally relented. "I take my leave." He looked to Dawkin. "I will see you before the Conclave, King Jameson." Then to Taresa. "Your Majesty."

Taresa waited until the door closed, leaving her alone with Dawkin.

"I suppose I must prepare," Dawkin said.

The Queen glared at him.

"The barons will be waiting," he continued.

Her silence assaulted his confidence.

"Is there something on your mind?"

"Why do you do this, James?"

"Pardon?"

"Your behavior. How you treat me. One minute, you are the kindest, gentlest man I've ever met. The next, you turn me aside like some used harlot."

"Taresa. I –"

"I'm not finished!" Taresa breathed, composing herself, as Dawkin pursed his lips. "Just when I think I know you, you show me... another side... of yourself. One righteous.

One awful. All those in between. I meet a different man every time."

Taresa paused. In that respite, Dawkin considered the possibility of discovery. *How much has she seen? Does she suspect? Worse, does she know?*

Before Dawkin could compose himself to answer – rather than sputter – Taresa pivoted. She searched the room, circling the bunks and racks of the barracks.

"You quarter your mute knights here?"

"Aye."

"They truly cannot speak?" She wafted up to a rack of halberds. She extended her hand to a curved blade, her fingers tracing the air just beyond its edge.

"Words aloud, no. They lack the ability. They communicate by way of their hands."

"Have you ever known them to have outbursts? To blurt out a phrase they later had to apologize for, earnestly?" At the last word, she ventured a gander at Dawkin.

"No. I haven't."

"You would do well to learn from them." Taresa pulled her hand away from the halberd. She retreated from the rack, taking position only feet from Dawkin.

"I suppose you're right," Dawkin relented.

Taresa looked away for a moment, thoughtful. Dawkin considered saying something before her stare returned to his eyes, arresting the whole of him. "I never thought I'd want a man to mince his words with me. I always believed I wanted something – anything – different."

"Different, how?"

"I've only known my father and mother as composed. As a solitary figure, people see King Felix as a stoic, careful man. I've witnessed only a few bouts of emotion from him, such as a raised voice here or a reddened face there. Yet never has he allowed himself to show a bit of his true form, whatever that might be, to the Queen. He addresses her like he would a duke or baron of the Court.

"And my mother, she just accepts it. She talks and talks as if she's in the presence of one of her chambermaids. She giggles. She screams. She even curses. All he does in response is wait, his tone never an octave higher when he's finally granted a moment to speak. That's who he is in the presence of his beloved, the woman who bore his daughters. A statue."

She relented, searching for a wisp of empathy, any sign that the man across from her could relate.

As a matter of fact, Dawkin could.

How many times have I been groomed, trained, instructed to act not only as a royal – but the *royal people last saw? How often has Ely returned from a manic episode or Symon from a sparring match, with me expected to pick up where they left Jameson? Even now... Who am I to this woman? My wife. The queen.*

The mother of Gerry's child.

"Taresa," Dawkin started, then stopped himself. Not met with interruption, he continued. "I fully expect you will see sides of me both royal and intimate. While I have been groomed for the Throne my entire life, I can not, will not, portray any part of my personage fraudulently to you.

"That will undoubtedly... present some problems at times. Perhaps even today, if these barons manage to crawl under my skin. Rest assured, when I lose my senses, I intend to return to them, and you, if you'll have me."

Taresa grinned. She extended her hands to Dawkin's, her fingers interlacing with his.

"I shall like that," she replied.

Dawkin held her stare. Far shorter than a husband should. And yet longer than appropriate for any man with the wife of another, even that of a brother.

"I have something to show you," he exclaimed, cutting short the occasion.

"What is it?"

"I, uh, um, these books here." He pointed to the volumes he had laid on the bunk. "My grandfather came to check on me, on these, to make sure they arrived in fair condition. The lot of them have been passed down from generation to generation."

"All of them? Some look so new."

"Well, a few are. Like this one. And that." He pointed to *The Weald Tales*. "I've carried on the family hobby of collecting rare books. It's a Saliswater tradition. One I hope we can carry on someday with our son."

"Or daughter."

"Yes. Either would be brilliant. Like their mother."

Taresa blushed, turning away from Dawkin to kneel before the bunk. She placed her hand atop each open volume as she glanced from one to another.

"You may take a few volumes back to your, I mean our, royal quarters if you like," Dawkin said as Taresa admired the manuscripts. "Even in this drafty fortress, I heard from the attendants that the hearths warm the rooms well. I'll have them start a fire, so you may enjoy a cup of tea while –"

"Oh, how interesting."

"Yes, the volumes offer such a wide breadth of prose and poetry."

"No, that isn't it." Taresa placed her hand atop one of the pages of *The Weald Tales*. She stretched her fingers as she pressed her palm to the parchment. Then, she withdrew it. "Look."

The calligraphy, having been of solid black ink, flashed alive in tones of copper and auburn. The lettering shone brightly before returning to its original hue, save for a few letters which stood apart, telling their own story.

Dawkin bent beside Taresa, mesmerized by the phenomena. "What did you do?"

"I only touched it."

"Is it..." *Enchanted? Magical? No, it cannot be. There must be some logical explanation.*

It dawned on him. "Put your hand to it again. Then pull away quickly."

Taresa did as instructed. Upon drawing her hand away, only a few letters came alight.

"Now rub your hands together vigorously. Create some heat and press both hands to the page."

She followed his directive. After ten seconds, Dawkin reached for her forearms, which he raised from the book.

Beneath, the lettering flickered, lush and bright.

"Brilliant," Taresa murmured.

"Heat," Dawkin whispered. "It responds to heat." He straightened up before pivoting to scan the barracks.

Atop a bench laid the standard-issued supplies all Voiceless carried on assignment. Dawkin rummaged through the nearest, finding the objects of his need: a flint and candle.

He lit the candle, his hand cupping its flame. Taresa scooted aside as Dawkin approached the manuscript.

He held the leaf of fire a finger-length above the page. It flickered to no particular breeze, the wax it melted threatening to fall.

"Careful," Taresa whispered.

"I have it." Dawkin held his free hand under the coalescing beads. A droplet fell to his index finger. It stung. Yet Dawkin did not wince. For before him, the parchment transfigured.

A spectrum of tones – some metallic, others with deep hues – sparkled as the black ink faded. As bright as reflected sunlight, it shone. Dawkin and Taresa fought the urge to look away.

As quickly as it flashed, the scene subsided, though this time, the letters left in its wake persisted for seconds. Long enough for the two of them to read.

"I can speak Marlish," Taresa began. "But my reading of your language is lacking. I only managed to pick up every other word or so."

"Then your comprehension is fine." Dawkin blew out the candle before tossing it aside. He slammed the book shut. "It's Old Marlish." He rose, taking Taresa by the hand.

"James, what is the meaning –"

"We need to get you to safety. Quickly. Before it's too late."

Chapter 23

"They grow restless. Are they almost through?"

Symon turned from Gerry to sign to the Voiceless at the entrance. Half a head taller than most, the knight - Sir Gylbarde of the Fourth Silent Order – peered into the shadowy corridor leading into the hall. He glanced back to Symon, using his hands to confirm the number left: five.

Five more lords. Entitled barons. And two guards apiece made for ten more on top of that. Fifteen men waiting to take their place. To sit among nearly a hundred others who came before. Lords and knights. Bishops and their brethren. All searched for weaponry, having endured the humiliation of their word meaning nothing, their honor impugned.

All manner of spirits waited for the barons at their tables. The lords drank heartily, consuming the darkest – and most potent – of ales and wines first. While intended to appease the nobility, the drinks managed to have the opposite effect. Murmurs unbecoming spilled forth, bouncing from table to table. A few barons shoved at one another, their near-fights stopped by guards, who stood in the dim light of perched torches and sconces.

Gerry watched the scene in stride, goblet in hand, as he paced before the tall chair set up for him. Symon stood at attention to the right of his seat, beside the side table where various pitchers and carafes sat, while Ely kept guard at his left. Beyond the platform supporting the three, their silent knights had fanned out, patrolling the Great Hall of Glic Anglisk.

Through the slit of his visor, Symon caught sight of Gerry again, just in time to find his little brother mid-gulp. He circled to the front of his chair, his back half-turned to the audience.

"Slow down, Gerry. That's your third goblet. You'll need your wits for this crowd."

Gerry tipped the goblet before his mouth, more to hide his lips than to drink. "I know, brother. I had my attendant fill my wares with unfermented drink."

He is *learning. Smart lad.*

From behind his visor, Ely scoffed. "Pity. You'll consume a week's worth of pitchers tonight, only to rob yourself of drunken joy while having to fight the urge to piss yourself."

"Ely!" Symon shushed.

"This lot can't hear us," Ely said a tad louder, though still in a somewhat hushed tone. "Our voices are nearly drowned, I tell you."

He had the right of it. Though wide and deep, the hall hardly stood tall by any standard, be it contemporary or ancient. At only a story and a half high, the vaulted ceiling and walls reverberated rather than absorbed the lamentations. Peculiar, considering the walls consisted of packed earth overgrown with moss, while above soft timber secured by petrified vines made for the roof. Even the ground beneath their boots cushioned their footfalls, suggesting another surface that should have tempered the discord.

Gerry swirled the remnants of his wine in his goblet,

turning his back to the audience as he did so. "Where is he?" he asked Symon.

"You sent him to the perimeter," Symon answered.

"With the intention that he returns." Gerry downed the last of his drink. "You don't think –"

"Nonsense. The Voiceless gave a security report before we opened the doors. The grounds are secure, the soldiers at their posts, with all accounted for except those of patrol."

"Including Everitt."

"Aye."

"Perhaps he had the good sense to disguise himself as a mute," Ely uttered low, tilting his head toward the closest of their silent brethren.

"Nay. He would have told us that much. Where is he? Maybe I should –"

"Don't you dare, brother," Ely admonished, almost loud enough to be heard beyond their reach. Though he did not turn and kept in character like Symon, the edge of his tone manifested itself with every word he spoke. "You dismiss this lot without just cause," he continued, "at a meeting to discuss avenging the very fathers and sons these men *know* they've lost, why, they'll never heed another edict we ever declare. Our messengers will be stopped at their barbicans and gates only to be dismissed. Taxes and customs will go missing. Our sessions of court will be empty. All that before the Conclave calls their next meeting, to vote on our ousting."

"Well, what would you have me do?" Gerry begged. He glanced at Ely, and all those around them, before settling on Symon.

Symon sighed. "You know what Father would have

said."

"When the doors to War Halls close or the flaps to War Tents seal, the King must decide on his commands, no later the foxes laying siege to his men. Otherwise," Gerry hung his head as if searching his memory, "Otherwise..."

"... their blood would have been spilt in vain," Symon finished.

"Very well. Right Captain or not, we will proceed."

"I remember that morbid bedtime story," Ely quipped.

Ignoring his brother, Symon eyed the final baron making his way into the hall. Baron Dederic. Brother to the High Bishop. As a Voiceless patted the baron for arms, Dederic's eyes found Perceval across the chamber, their stares locking in place, sealing an understanding only kin could share.

We're in for a war of words. "Gerry," he whispered. "Listen carefully."

Gerry shot him a glance in acknowledgment, though he continued to scan the room. "Go on."

"Whatever happens, do not let the barons speak out of turn. Do not let them join forces in conversation, even if they happen to support you. Everyone here is to speak one at a time, no exceptions."

"This is a Conclave, brother," Ely reminded him. "Need I remind you of the Reigning Council?"

The three glanced in the direction of the table to their right, which sat on its own platform equal in height to the King's. The Council's six barons rested silently, goblets in hand, no doubt mulling over the raucous scene before them.

"This isn't like our last meeting when the fate of Kin

Saliswater was on trial. Our position has since been secured. Yes, the Conclave holds authority in their gatherings. But this isn't Highmoorr Castle. This session stands apart. Here, on grounds the King of Marland has a duty to protect, the Conclave will allow us – I mean, Gerry – to impart the rules of debate. Hence, why so many Voiceless were permitted."

"Sure," Ely nodded back to the head Voiceless at the entrance. "Much good they will do. They're unarmed."

"Along with every man here," Gerry quipped. "We're on equal footing. All of us."

"Yes, some barons feel vulnerable," Symon admitted. "Others, perhaps not. Whatever their mood, no matter your level of comfort or anxiety, remember: one voice at a time." Symon, through his visor, set his eyes on Gerry. At this range, his brother could stare back through the slit. Nonetheless, he avoided such contact, choosing instead to focus on the bottom of his goblet, which he quickly drained.

"A daring proposition," Ely added, "to impart our rule, whether our right or not. No matter our gifts of tongue or sword, the *best* of us would have trouble convincing this lot to maintain their manners."

"I know what you're implying," Gerry said. He slammed his goblet on the armrest of his seat, breaking its crystal stem. The small shatter echoed as a sigh in the sea of noise. Still, it caught the attention of the closest barons, who pointed and shared low voices as Gerry marched from his seat to the head table of the Reigning Council.

"He knows he shouldn't do that," Ely said. He paused as one attendant came to sweep up the broken glass as another brought a fresh goblet filled to the brim with wine. Once they departed, he continued. “It’s unseemly for a king to leave his seat to address nobility. That’s why we have servants.”

Symon noted the attendants at their platform base, who had no choice but to stand and watch agape as the one they served did their duty. Before the head table of the Reigning Council, Gerry leaned in, his lips moving passionately though his soft words remained unheard. The nobles in the broader audience paused to take notice, including the silver-maned patriarch sitting in the far corner to their left: Artus.

“No one will think much of it,” Symon said, hoping against hope.

“And if they do?”

“Mar help us.”

Gerry returned to his throne, plopping himself into his seat. As Baron Dedric came to the last open space among the lords, the eldest of the Reigning Council – Baron Malerius of Kin Enfield – rose first. Using the butt of his staff, he pounded the floor three times. His colleagues, along with Gerry, quieted. A hush fell over parts of the hall as all stood until, at last, the conversations subsided.

“My Lords,” Malerius began, “today is an ominous day, one which has us here, away from our stronghold for the first time since the end of the Century War.”

Murmurs erupted. Malerius waved his hand to his guard, who beat the butt of his halberd on the platform. On the eighth, peace finally fell back into place, for the moment.

“The decision to relocate to Glic Anglisk Castle did not

occur with haste. We did not embrace the matter lightly..."

Malerius droned on and on. Another of the Reigning Council chimed in, along with perhaps a third. No matter. For Symon's concentration on the feeble words of old barons waned, gravitating instead to the one on his left.

Gerry.

The journey to Ibia had done much to mature him. The nights with Taresa mayhaps did their part. Not to mention the news of a child, foreshadowing his upcoming fatherhood.

Gerry raised his new goblet to his lips. With narrowed eyes and clenched jaw, he sipped. He set down his glass, turning his hands inward as he pressed his fingertips together and listened.

Subtle yet powerful. Patient and strong. A move Father would have made had he been here, entertaining the dull pleas of barons.

Good Mar, he looks like a king.

But is he?

Symon prayed the words he spoke earlier would be heeded. Not only the ones from moments before. All of them. From their training sessions to their council in the Fourpointe Chamber, Symon had done his due diligence to prepare their younger brother for this very moment. They all had in their own way. Even Ely – despite his joshing – did not want to see Gerry fail.

Yes, the gatherings at Court served as a precursor to this very meeting. Along with the sessions with mages. And high bishops. All that preparation. No monarch-in-training could ask for more.

Still...

His doubt lingered. His hopes diminished. Yet all Symon could do was stand there. Stay silent. And wait.

Symon blinked, realizing quietude had fallen over the hall. Malerius sat, as did the chorus of barons both at the table of the Reigning Council and the rest of the room. Gerry – his elbow on the arm of his throne, his right finger at his temple – waited. For what?

At last, their grandfather stood.

"Good men of the Reigning Council. Barons. Bishops." He nodded to a few. He glanced away from others as if they were part acquaintances, part strangers. "Lord Malerius did well to lay out the reasons for our being here today. I shall not repeat his sentiment, for with it lurks the threat which brought us together.

"We can but guess at the motives of our enemies. Yet one thing is for certain: we must act."

Grumblings erupted, as expected. Symon caught Gerry stroking the tiny whiskers at his chin, which foreshadowed a beard. He remained silent. Perhaps contemplative. Or hesitant.

Artus parted his lips as if to speak but caught himself when a lord at a nearby table rose:

Baron Rayvenn.

His stare, a winter unto itself, held the eyes of Artus. Even as he slurped his ale, his look never trembled. Along with the other nobles, Artus bowed his head as he placed his fist over his heart.

"My condolences to you and your kin," Artus said.

"Save you words," Rayvenn replied. Looking down into his brass goblet, he sneered. Then, he poured the rest of its contents onto the table. Those nobles closest to him slid away in their seats.

"What is the meaning of this?" Malerius asked, though with a tad less solidity than expected.

"This is waste," Rayvenn muttered. "Like what happens when poor leaders do nothing about a massacre."

The last drops of ale splattered on the table. Rayvenn cast his goblet aside, which clattered on the ground.

Artus turned to Gerry. Gerry, remaining silent, eyed his grandfather – along with the Voiceless who had inched closer to Rayvenn. He raised his fingers, motioning them away from the baron.

That's it, Symon thought. *They believe you. They see you, King.*

"My lord," Gerry began. "My grandfather has the right of it. We mourn your son. Baron Hewe was an honorable man."

"Honorable? I remember you once referred to him as the Swineherd King."

Symon ground his teeth, glancing sideways toward Ely, who stood unmoving in his Voiceless armor. *Damn you,* he silently seethed at his brother. *Your mouth will be the ruin of this family.*

Gerry, too, took a gander at his brother. He feigned clearing his throat before turning back to Baron Rayvenn. "I won't deny a slight against your kin. The error was mine. I correct myself now for that comment and any others against your son. He was honorable."

Many in the audience nodded in approval. Two even clapped, albeit briefly. Symon grinned.

You have them, brother. Keep it going.

The lord of Har-Kin Warci, however, remained

unswayed.

"So noble of you, isn't it? To admit the truth. So tell me, my good king: What is to be done about this threat to our kingdom?"

Gerry shifted in his seat. "As my grandfather started to say, we must take action. I've conferred with my advisers, whose recommendations we will discuss in detail, such as increasing the patrols on the Curved Wharf and Smallquarter, which saw damage and losses during the most recent attacks. Or raising the militia to attend to the rivers and streams where this gold fever has been reported. And doubling the magistrates who inspect –"

"All hogwash!" Rayvenn bellowed.

Barons gasped. Well, some chuckled. Gerry, as shocked as any, paused.

"Well..." he stuttered. "That is but a preview of the possibilities –"

"Your possibilities will not avenge my son!" The baron reddened. The few guffaws of the crowd quieted. The whole of the hall iced as what little camaraderie evaporated.

Gerry breathed deeply. He reached for his goblet on the arm of his chair, only to brush it from its perch. Its crystal – base, stem, and all – shattered at Symon's feet. Shards clanked against his boot. Symon closed his eyes. He opened them to look down, finding not broken glass but the shaking hand of his sibling.

"Look! He knows it's true." Baron Rayvenn separated from his table, pointing at Gerry as he did. "Bah! What a fine king. Marching. Inspections. A bloody waste of time."

A wave of nobles nodded, this time clapping in unison.

Artus stood, motioning them to calm. He even tried to speak yet found his voice drowned by the clamor.

"I'll tell you how we right the wrong of Ibia," Rayvenn bellowed. "We send the might of Marland to their doorstep."

"But they're our allies," Malerius urged. He leaned over the table, the vein of his forehead pulsing. Two other lords of the Council – Baron Howward of Kin Fawcett and Baron Karles of Kin Tenholm – came to his side to calm him. Indeed, the elder appeared weathered by the commotion as he fell back to his chair. Rayvenn – and many more barons – noted the opportunity. They bolted to their feet. They shoved. They hollered.

All as Gerry looked on, shaking.

"Gerry," Symon whispered as he remained tall.

From all corners of the hall, the Voiceless gravitated toward the throne. Sir Gylbarde looked to Symon. Symon signed to him, "Protect your King."

The head knight nodded at the directive. He clapped his vambraces together. The steel *clanged,* throwing those nearest to him down onto their benches. The outer reaches of the hall barely noticed, their share of the audience still up on their feet in protest. Even so, the burst rallied the Voiceless from all points. The silent knights swarmed in. Within moments, they became a barrier between the King and the barons, a circlet of leather and steel.

Unarmed.

Symon scanned the Voiceless, relieved at their position while he cursed under his breath. The guards of the Reigning Council had inspected the Voiceless for arms in exchange for granting the guards the right to search the invited barons. The concession proved necessary to secure the trust of those in attendance. Yet, in hindsight, it left them – especially Gerry – too vulnerable.

Gerry heaved, the presence of his mute guardians having done little to quell his anxiety. As with the swell of his emotions, the nobles continued to take notice.

"See!" shouted a baron, cloaked by the standing mob. "King Fool returns!"

"King Fool!" cried another.

"Give us justice, Jameson! Justice!" shouted a third.

Surveying the mess, Symon clenched his fists. The scene having turned, the hall no longer harbored the lords, the manors, he had known from birth. It held... something else. Worse than all the conflicts and skirmishes he had known. For in those arenas, the threat stood clear, his enemies a separate force from his own. Here, the danger lay within, arising from the ones he should have counted among his allies, friends of the Throne.

So uncivil...

A chant from one baron, then several, swelled.

"King Fool! King Fool! King Fool!"

... This betrayal...

"King Fool! King Fool! King Fool!"

His grandfather faltered against the crowd, some of which turned to him for answers he could not provide. Artus braced himself against the edge of his table; his face reddened as he traded barbs with the nobles around him. He pointed at the platform before directing his finger back across the table.

The gestures. The shouts. The maddening.

Gerry took it all.

Pained. Beaten. Defeated.

He retched. The nobles, amidst their chanting, took notice. And laughed.

End this!

Symon knelt to Gerry's side as his sibling sat hunched over, wiping his mouth. Ely hovered behind Symon, aghast.

"Brother, pull it together," Ely urged.

"Enough!" Symon pulled Ely's ear close. "Gather three Voiceless and fall back to the doors. Gerry will give the order to clear the hall and restore order."

"But, he can't –"

"He'll give the order! It must come from the King!"

Symon stared into his eyes, his stare cutting through the slit of his visor to bore a hole in Ely's helm.

Ely, accepting the reality they knew to be true – what Gerry, as King, had to do to salvage his power – nodded. He fell away, taking the platform's steps two at a time as he stopped before the circlet of knights. He grabbed Sir Gylbarde by the shoulder, his hands fluttering, delivering his commands before the knight's face. Gylbarde, understanding the gravity of the situation, pulled two of his men away in turn. The four then delved into the crowd, all of which had risen, their collective mood focused on one:

Gerry.

"Gerry!" Symon yelled, forgetting to sign. "You need to stand. Give the command to clear the hall."

"I can't," Gerry squeaked.

"You must! Only a King can clear the royal hall."

"Me?"

"Yes, you! The King!"

Thump! Thump!

Symon snapped his neck. The echo, which would have blasted through every beam and crevice of the low hall if empty, barely reached his ears as a muffle.

Thump!

He caught the source of the sound that time — the doors.

Craning his neck, he caught sight of the back foyer, which had cleared with the barons clamoring toward the front of the hall. There, before the doors, Ely and his entourage of three Voiceless gathered.

Thump!

From beyond, a force pushed on the doors, nudging the horizontal beam keeping them closed. Ely leaned back from the thrust, wary and uncertain.

"Ely!" Symon yelled, realizing his folly as soon as he had said it. He dug his hands under Gerry's arm as he lifted him upward. "Come now!"

"Symon."

Ely, fixated on the hall doors, stepped toward them. His hand extended.

Don't you open them!

"Gerry! Restore order! Someone is trying to breach the hall!"

"My head..."

"No time for this! Yell! Command! Be a King, damn it!"

Gerry collapsed into his arms, the whole of himself gone limp. The lame weight of his body fell upon Symon, who struggled to prop him up, his own head suddenly throbbing.

Symon blinked. His focus waned.

At the doors, Ely held his hand out to the beam. Yet there it rested, unmoved, as Ely dropped to one knee.

Thump!

The doors shifted once again. This time, Ely looked upon them not as the barrier to a menace but as the obstacle to their salvation.

All around him, the atmosphere evolved. The mob – once an agitated, unruly mess – subdued, their raucous voices falling silent. Many of them gripped their torsos or their benches, as many more sat. Some retched. Those of the Reigning Council proved no better. Malerius fell to the ground, convulsing, while the others had only the strength to look on.

A certain few – barons, clergy, and their protectors – unaffected, inched away from the suddenly ill. They collected themselves at the far reaches of the hall, where the beams and pillars of the ceiling met with the earthen walls. They paused as one among them – High Bishop Perceval – snaked through the felled crowd.

"Your Majesty," he bellowed. Then, catching himself, he turned to the closed doors. "Or should I say, 'Your Majesties'?" He set his sights on Ely before looking up to the throne, where Symon stood with Gerry against him.

"Perceval?" Symon gasped, breaking with his clandestine protocol to speak aloud. "You did this?"

"Aye," he admitted before turning coy. "But I am not His Eminence –"

The High Bishop paused. A trembling hand – from Baron Rayvenn – grabbed ahold of him.

"You," Rayvenn uttered, "damn you."

"Nay, damn you." Perceval pointed at Gerry. "And

damn the King!"

He opened his palm, and as though by command, the hilt of a short sword met it. He dug the tip of his newfound blade into the nook of Rayvenn's neck. Instantly, the old noble gushed, his blood spilling forth onto the pristine garb of His Eminence.

"Give my regards to your son," Perceval snickered.

Rayvenn drooped to his feet. Perceval shook his sword at the lord, splattering blood upon his fresh corpse.

And all around him, those invited who remained composed did likewise. Brandishing all manner of weapons – swords, axes, maces – they took to those in their reach. They hacked. Stabbed. Bludgeoned. Nobles and clergy. Guards and soldiers.

But how? How?!

Though his peripheral vision blurred, Symon found his answer. Those traitors at the earthen walls snuffed out the torches and sconces as others groped the moss-and-vine strewn lengths, their hands disappearing into hidden gaps and holes. They pulled their arms from the concealed pits, dispursing the weaponry to their comrades, who made quick work of the victims.

Some of the less affected men fought back against the quislings, shoving or pushing them away. They fell like the others, their efforts delaying the inevitable by mere moments of resistance.

A line of armed men fell to either side of Perceval. The High Bishop, at the ready, approached the barrier of Voiceless. The silent knights appeared as crenels of their former selves, some having sunk to their knees while others remained standing, barely.

"If you concede and give yourselves up, I'll be merciful toward your mute knights," Perceval offered, slapping the width of his blade onto his free palm.

Thump! Thump! Crack!

Symon looked up as Perceval and his men pivoted. At the doors, Ely braced his shoulder against the beam, which now leaned upright. The doors burst open –

A Voiceless spilled in, along with a handful of his comrades.

Dawkin, Symon thought. Though clad head to toe in the armor of a silent knight, Symon knew. The posture. That gait. The way he moved. *By Mar, it's him.*

Bloody hell, it's him. Here. *With us.*

Perceval grinned, turning back to the Throne...

Only to discover Gerry, weakened yet determined, with Malerius' staff in hand. He held it out, the head pointed at Perceval like the point of a spear, as he heaved.

"As you wish, Your Majesty."

Perceval dipped his head as if to bow, only to wield his sword downward. The tip found its way into the narrow gap between the gorget and helm of Sir Gylbarde. The head knight struggled ferociously as he spewed blood.

Dawkin let loose a war cry. Gerry, in his own way, did so as well. Symon, through his pulsating mind, believed he did the same. Perhaps Ely too. Before the world descended into a blur.

Chapter 24

So much chaos. So suddenly. The thunder of conflict awash in a rain of blood.

Remember your training. You were born to be a royal.

Her father's parting words echoing in her mind, Taresa shook herself from the arrow slit and the scene unfolding below, even as the outcries and explosions clamored for her undivided attention.

Out of the corner of her eye, she caught sight of Celia. The handmaiden, covered in a shamrock-green cloak, braced herself against the innards of the bartizan, fighting the urge to sink.

Taresa hurried to her, taking her by the shoulders. As she knelt, she guided Celia to the floor, where she left her.

"Soldier!" Taresa called as she stepped to the tower entryway. Under the arch, a lone warrior – more of a squire than a knight – lowered his crossbow.

"Your Highness!" the young man called. He managed a salute, even while dividing his attention between her and the conflict.

"Take me to your commander," she insisted, ignoring the slight.

"He, he's..." The green recruit pointed at the next flanking tower. Only then did Taresa notice his trembling. His quiver empty, three bolts lay strewn about him, no doubt the product of his unsteady hand.

Down the rampart where he gestured, a man – the only one there still moving – struggled to brace himself against a crenel.

Taresa gandered at the line at her feet. The one where sunlight met shadow. She stepped from the darkness –

"My Queen!" Celia cried.

Taresa swung her head around while Celia's fingers clawed into her. As Taresa fell back, the soldier darted before her, blocking her path.

"What are you –" Taresa started.

He pivoted to face her, his eyes wide with anticipation. Behind him, the sky flashed. His back, to the light, curved toward her, unnaturally and suddenly. Taresa gasped as the full weight of the soldier toppled her.

All went black. The chorus of the battle quelled. Everything to the touch vanished.

Taresa blinked.

A weight rolled off of her. She gasped for air.

"Your Majesty! Your Majesty!" Celia exclaimed. She swept her arm under her head.

"I'm, I'm –" *What was she?*

"You're still here!" Celia cried, embracing her queen.

Taresa, also forgetting all pretense, held her. Another explosion beyond the walls shook them from their moment. Taresa scrambled to her feet along with Celia. She stared down at the fallen soldier. His back bent at a right angle, leaving the man in a grotesque, unnatural position. The blast had also tarnished his plate black and singed his exposed skin.

"My Mar..." Celia wept, closing her eyes and placing her hands to her forehead in respect.

Taresa did likewise, though her eyes remained open. Her stare settled on the man's arming sword. And crossbow.

"Did you send your riders?" Taresa yelled.

"What?" asked the commander, his hearing – and consciousness – fading.

"Your distress riders. Did you send them?"

"Nay." He patted the corpse beside him. "He had the message. To carry." Indeed, a small roll of parchment stuck out from the top of the departed's fist.

The commander's tapping slowed. His eyelids flickered.

"Commander? Commander?!"

He stared back at her, forever losing the ability to answer.

"My Lady," Celia urged. "This path isn't safe. We must go."

Taresa slid away from the crenel, grabbing the message from the corpse.

Below, the enemy had secured the gatehouse. Upright beams stood under the portcullis to prevent it from dropping while the broken chains of the drawbridge dangled. The Marlish forces had arranged the carriages in the bailey in an arch, to form a second barrier to entry. Every able-bodied Marlish soldier bore a bow or crossbow or sling, sending all manner of fire toward their opponents. The blockade served its purpose at the moment, even as the assailants lobbed their projectiles into the boundary.

Leading Celia by the hand, Taresa hurried down the stairway, which ended behind the makeshift boundary. Her head low, she prayed nary a soul would notice them.

Alas, one did.

A knight parted from the defenses to sweep in at the base of the stairs. Taresa raised her crossbow, then paused as Celia took her newfound sword to step between her and the knight.

"Lady Celia!"

"You friend or foe?!" Celia demanded.

The knight raised his visor. Taresa lowered her crossbow.

"Everitt."

"Your Majesty. With me." The Right Captain waved over those men closest to him. "Come. Defend your Queen!"

Five comrades who heard him instantly fell in line with Everitt. He led the duo to the nearest covered parapet. Under the ceiling of shelter, he removed his helm.

"Where were you?" Everitt asked, exasperated. "My men have been searching the whole of this fortress. When we found your other attendants slain, we, we thought –"

"Slain?"

"Yes, Your Majesty. Your Ibian retinue... They killed them. Our soldiers found the departed in your quarters shortly after the attack started."

"What happened?"

"I was doing one last patrol of the perimeter, where the forest is thickest, when..." Everitt flung his helm across the parapet. "I fell right into a trap." Everitt paced a length. "A cowardly bunch. They felled a tree before the vanguard and ambushed my men from behind. My commander took a bolt to the neck before we could sound the warhorn. 'Twas too late, anyhow.

"We fought our way out — me and two other men who made it. We came back to Glic Anglisk... Found the moat teeming with peasants and townspeople. The whole stream was suddenly awash with nuggets. The gold wasn't there this morning. Suddenly, the water offered a bounty.

"The soldiers on the battlements demanded they leave. And fired warning shots. Then the commander sent soldiers down to clear the grounds of the commoners. Me and my two surviving men joined the efforts. But the Fools Fever proved too strong. They refused to leave. That's when they attacked."

"Who?" Taresa asked.

"The Lost Souls. From the woods. From amongst the peasantry. In their hoods. Their disguises. They emerged. With their blades and weapons. And projectiles."

"And the King?"

Everitt sighed. "Two sets of doors lay between us and James. The first set leading from the bailey to the hall is barred from the inside. I dare not cut them down, lest James and the barons have barricaded themselves within."

"And if they haven't? If the enemy has found a way inside?"

"Then Mar help us all."

Taresa's hands fell to her abdomen. Celia rushed to her side. "My Lady."

Regaining herself partially, Taresa braced her hands on Celia's forearms. "Your distress riders? Have you sent them?"

"We managed one. His mount took a bolt to the hindquarters, but the horsemen kept riding. Not sure how much further he made it."

"Any more coursers?"

"Another. I'll need to track down a man with skill and

form enough to ride her. Perhaps from Har-Kin –"

"My Lady," Celia interrupted, looking to Taresa. "I can ride."

"You?" Taresa and Everitt asked at once.

"Yes."

"This will not be a leisurely trot," Everitt cautioned. "We need a horseman, eh, rider, who can –"

"Who knows how to give aids to a horse with her voice, hands, and legs? Who can change a broken bridle mid-ride? Who has mended a thousand bleeding fetlocks?"

"Why, yes."

"Then send me."

Everitt looked to Taresa. The Queen nodded.

"Very well," Everitt obliged.

He led them to the open-air stables located in the right corner of the bailey. As they hurried, Everitt gave Celia her needed directives. "Riding through the gatehouse is out of the question. Your only option is to go through the eye of the needle at the north wall."

"Eye of the needle?"

He pointed to a low door between the rounded curves of two nearby flanking towers. "The towers will provide you cover, so long as the men in it haven't perished. The frame is too short for you to ride your horse through, so you'll need to lead him by the reins until you're out, then mount quickly and gallop before any enemy projectiles can find you." Everitt paused, motioning to the ridge. "A hillock lies just beyond the north wall. If you can make it there, you might be safe. Unless –"

Taresa grabbed Everitt by the forearm. "Unless, what?"

"If there are any of the enemy beyond the ridge, lying

in wait, she'll ride right into them."

Taresa shuddered. Turning back to her handmaiden, she searched her face for any slight of fear or hesitation. A sign she would waver if she encountered such adversity.

Taresa found none.

"Let me go, Your Majesty." Her eyes set with determination, her tone resolute, she nodded to a stall in the middle. "That's your best remaining courser, is it not?"

"It is." Everitt unlocked the gate to its stall.

"Then let's ready him –"

"Sir Everitt! Sir Everitt!"

The three swung around to find a soldier racing toward them. He motioned to the gatehouse from whence he came. "The gate! The weapon! They're about to fire!"

Taresa squinted. From their vantage point, so much stood between them and the gatehouse – the barrier of carriages, discarded trunks, and then, the bodies –

Through it all, emerging from the arched tunnel, crept the curve of a large bow, set upon two wheels. Set on its riser protruded the head of... not an arrow... but a glowing orb, one of yellow crystal.

"Everitt..." Taresa began.

"My Queen!"

A brightness, blinding and brilliant, erupted. Taresa only glimpsed it as Everitt pulled her back into an empty stall. He fell atop her, becoming a shield to the wave of heat that washed over them.

Particles of debris showered her face. She shut her eyes tight until they stopped, then blinked them open to find the sky above scattered by ash. She scarcely had a moment to draw breath before Sir Everitt took her by the hand to pull her to her feet.

"Are you well?" he asked.

She nodded before noticing the streaks burnt across the top sections of his armor, stretching from his back. She glanced at his rear to spot the whole of his backplate blackened. "Are you?!"

"'Tis a scratch," Everitt insisted through a grimace. "Never mind it. We need to get you to safety."

He turned back to the gatehouse. Taresa did likewise, expecting to find the makeshift barrier in smoldering ruins.

Indeed, the skeletons of carriages lay, along with the defenders of Glic Anglisk. And yet, their attackers did not swarm over the carcasses as expected. Through the shimmering heat and haze of the rubble, Taresa spotted the assailants claimed by their blast, as though the explosion had blown back and charred them.

"Good Mar!" she exclaimed, her breath caught in her throat. She nearly believed the scene to be an accident, whether by carelessness or chance, when the swift flash of greystone captured her eye –

Like a crenel or boulder come alive, the figure moved. A statue with life, masonry with purpose, it sped and hopped with ease, giving no pause to the scene at hand. From under its slate-colored cloak, a glowing white blade appeared. Short at first, the figure ran with it. An assailant – one of the few not claimed by the blast – raised his sword to lash out at the oncoming effigy. In an impossible effort, the figure closed the gap between it and the soldier, its blade extending in length to find the enemy's throat. The fresh corpse hung mid-air while the cloaked mystery rushed past, nary considering the dead man in its wake.

The phenom cleared the barrage of cluttered carriages with ease. A handful of Marlish survivors offered their weapons in protest, a vain attempt to put up a fight. Taresa grimaced, anticipating them to fall by its hand as well.

Sidestep and parry met her expectations, the figure dodging the Marlish, leaving them stunned but untouched.

"My Queen," Everitt cried, shaking himself from the scene. "We've been breached now."

"Yes," Taresa admitted, blankly, "because of her." In a blink, the figure disappeared under a parapet, the shadows masking its path. She tore herself away from the mirage as she looked back to Everitt. Only then did she take note of one's absence: Lady Celia. "Celia?!" Taresa brushed past the knight to inspect the stables. Or rather, the charred remnants of them.

She found no sign of her handmaiden.

"Your Majesty, please!"

She disregarded Everitt's insistence as she raced from stall to stall. She gasped at the sight of mangled flesh in one before noting its long leg and hoof. The next stall bore the fate of another poor mount. She hardly had a chance to inspect a third when Everitt gasped.

"Look!"

The door of the eye of the needle stood unbolted and open. Above the crenels of the wall laid the hillock, where a rider in shamrock-green sped up its incline. Unopposed. Unnerved.

Chapter 25

Stay with me, brothers.

The chair splintered against the charge of a baron, who collapsed away from Dawkin. Dawkin heaved another free chair into the path of an oncoming assailant – this one dressed as a bishop – who stepped to the side, narrowly averting the same fate.

Damn it! he cursed as the man charged. He flung off his clerical robes, which fell behind him as he ran, revealing a suit of white mail. The brilliant sheen nearly distracted Dawkin from the rise and fall of his hilt. Dawkin instinctively lifted his sword to block the anticipated blade.

The weight of a weapon indeed fell upon his. Only, where he expected steel, he found... nothing.

His assailant grimaced as he shoved the might of an unseen weapon down on Dawkin. Dawkin blinked. Had his eyes deceived him?

Marks of blood – from the assailant's last victim – hung in the air above him, suspended, as if foreshadowing his fate.

What is this?

... Glass that cannot shatter...

No, it can't be. 'Tis impossible.

His adversary shoved Dawkin back. He lunged at him, with Dawkin narrowly glancing the translucent blade from piercing his shoulder. The familiar *clang* his sword sang awakened Dawkin from his disbelief.

This is happening, he realized, his consciousness thrust into the present once more as he blocked a cut coming down upon him. His peripheral vision confirmed his fears: the weapons their combatants bore shimmered and shone unlike any metal or material of armament known to man. Like the false bishop, other enemies wielded invisible blades. Still more swung weapons of materials seemingly both familiar and foreign: steel with an unearthly sheen, polished wood bearing ringlets of geometric patterns that appeared as written language, and leaves with the flexibility and strength of leather. From the walls and corners of the hall, the assailants pulled their arms. Where one would expect a solid barrier, enemies dug their fingers and hands into facades that gave way as easily as one dips into water.

As the imposters gathered their weapons and attacked, the rest in the hall scurried, their frantic direction having no rhyme nor reason. Too many had elbowed and crammed toward the entryway; those not trampled made for easy targets, with the assailants' weapons spilling blood and cracking bones in quick succession. The other barons and clergy in the hall not clogging the exit fought back to the best of their abilities, using every bench, candlestick, and free item as weaponry to compensate for their lack of arms.

Pigs to the slaughter. Even as he took down another combatant, the realization waned on him. Whatever warning Cora had imparted on him had come to him too late. *How had she known?* He asked himself for the thousandth time as he fought off another. *Why had the warning been so cryptic? So hidden? So delayed?*

Two barons charged him. One with a blade broad and clear, his also stained with blood. The other wielded a double-headed ax seemingly of wood, which Dawkin knew could cut through him as cleanly as any sawyer's tool. At once, he cleared his head as his training had taught him, bolting toward his latest foes with focus and intent.

Before their clash, the two collapsed at his feet, their faces pained in agony. Their hands fell to their back, signaling wounds to their rear. Instinctively, and without thought, Dawkin extended his sword to the threat behind them –

Only to find Symon in full helm, his visor raised.

"You see me?!" Symon yelled as he brandished a short sword. The unfamiliar blade glowed with a dull green hue, an object no doubt stolen from one of their attackers.

Recognizing his brother's signature look – that squint he had during intense training or battle – he nodded. "Aye!"

"Fall into our circle," he motioned to the stage where the throne had once stood. Dawkin looked to the base of the stairs where the battered chair lay, stunned he had made his way to his brothers so swiftly.

Taking to the stairs two at a time, he ascended the platform. To his left, Ely stood midway up on the steps; he swung a staff at two barons who bore long axes. Voiceless fought among him and Symon, at various sections of the staircase, where atop Gerry stood, unarmed and wide-eyed.

Dawkin fell inside beside his younger brother, who continued to look past him to the carnage before them.

"Gerry, are you hurt?"

"Eh, what?"

"Can you fight?!"

"Aye, yes, I mean."

"Then here." Dawkin offered his sword. Gerry took it, albeit with hesitation.

"What about you?" he squeaked.

Dawkin – his next move lost on even him – looked around, finding the answer in tragedy. To his far-right, a silent knight had fallen to one knee, a spearpoint having found the edge where his gorget and pauldron met. He gripped the spear protruding from his shoulder while his attacker – an imposter disguised as a man of the cloth – put his weight into the weapon. From behind the imposter, an enemy with a halberd closed in.

Eight steps lay between Dawkin and his comrade. Dawkin landed on just one, jumping to the step behind the knelt Voiceless. With momentum on his side, Dawkin leapt over the knight and into the two assailants.

Caught by surprise, the imposters failed to raise their weapons in defense. Dawkin fell into them, the weight of his armor knocking the breath from both men. And himself.

Dawkin rolled off the two, stunned and confused. From outside his line of sight, he heard his name.

"Dawkin!" cried Symon, perhaps, or maybe Ely.

No matter. Dawkin blinked, finding the curve of a blade above him. He spun on his side, the weapon's edge *clanging* on the stone tile beside him. The blade rose again. Dawkin crossed his gauntlets as it fell upon him, the plate bracing the metal.

Whether due to its sharpness or its material, the edge

managed to pierce – however slightly –the thick plate of his gauntlets. The coldness of the blade shocked Dawkin, and yet, his forearms burned with the intensity of a smith's forge. His personage suddenly flushed, he looked up into a face he recognized: High Bishop Perceval. The whole of his visage reflected the man he had known for years, down to the creases he had developed around his eyes in recent years. All his features seemed familiar save one.

His eyes.

At any other time, the detail would have been lost on Dawkin. In the heat of battle, however, he could not avoid it. Blue eyes – of who he did not know – glared back at him, conveying the maniacal intentions of their keeper. The imposter Perceval leaned into his blade, pressing its edge further into Dawkin's flesh. Dawkin ground his teeth, turning to his sides for some reach of salvation.

The assailants he had knocked down had regained their composure, just as the silent knight they had tried to break came down upon them. The Voiceless clapped his steel-clad hands together and swept them overhead, bringing them crashing down on the nearest of his attackers. The other produced a dirk, which he promptly delivered into the side of the knight, its point piercing through the thinnest of mail and plate.

The knight collapsed into the man, flailing about. The first stood to hold the Voiceless in place as his comrade dug the knife deeper and deeper into the doomed guard.

Hardly a moment transpired. A pause. A breath. Yet one of his own fell before Dawkin, signaling a fate he would soon endure.

He stared back at his captor. That face – yes, of Perceval

– glared at him. 'Twas familiar. Not only because it bore the look of the High Bishop: It also carried the reminiscence of another.

The imposter leaned further into his blade. Its edge dug deeper into Dawkin's forearms while simultaneously creeping closer towards his throat.

Those eyes… Wait! No! It's not… It couldn't.

The imposter inched nearer. "That's right, Your Majesty." He grinned as if knowing every word racing through Dawkin's mind. "I know exactly who you are." He stared at Dawkin through the slit of his visor, boring a hole into his soul.

My namesake. Brother Dawkin. From the monastery. But how? Why?

"I know what you and your brothers are," the monk continued. "A scourge to this kingdom. A curse to Marland. Now, your reign ends here."

The searing pain in his arms vanished, as did the pressure. The imposter lifted his blade high, its point aimed at the base of Dawkin's neck. Dawkin crossed his unsteady arms, bracing himself for the attack, perhaps for the last time…

The monk fell back under the tackle of another. The weight off of him, Dawkin shuffled onto his elbows as he struggled to find his footing. The one who rushed Brother Dawkin swept around – the imposter's sword now in his hand – toward the assailants closest to Dawkin, the ones who had felled the silent knight. In quick succession, he thrust his newfound weapon into the weak spots of the first enemy, then the second. An impressive move, as good as any Symon or their best fighters could execute.

Dawkin saw the hand bearing the sword pause before him. A worn appendage. Wrinkled...

Of Lord Artus.

"Grandfather?"

"Come now, lad. Up to the platform." Dawkin hardly had the chance to rise before the elder – with a surge of strength – yanked him to his feet. Dawkin stumbled up the stairs. The remnants of the silent knights allowed him to pass. He hurried up to fall in beside his brother, Gerry, once more. Ely and Symon, seeing their sibling saved, retreated up the steps. Their grandfather joined them from the other side.

"You well?" Symon asked.

"Aye," Dawkin nodded.

"Don't you do that again!" Ely roared.

"I might not have a chance."

Dawkin looked past his brothers. The discord of the attack had peaked. Those allies closest to the assailants had fallen quickly, including many of the Reigning Council. However, Dawkin counted one or two elder barons still moving a limb, desperate to crawl to safety. The others – the few – had sunk back to the fringes of the hall, as timid as beaten dogs.

The imposters, too many to count, coalesced. They came into line with each other, their sights set on the ranks of Voiceless they had thinned. The silent knights, in turn, kept their backs to the Saliswaters. They extended whatever weapons they had: busted chairs, weapons snatched from their attackers, or just their gauntleted hands, all smeared in sweat and blood.

A *creak* interrupted the cautious stalemate. Dawkin

looked up and over the mass to spot the assailants stacking tables and benches before the doors they had just closed.

"It's over," Brother Dawkin boasted as he swept his bishop's robe over his head, revealing a suit of mail beneath. He pointed to the blade in Artus' hand. "I'll be having my sword back now."

"Come and take it!" his lord bellowed, his battle-hardened voice stiffening the necks of all in the hall.

"As you wish," the monk conceded. He ushered his men to the last row of silent knights who stood between them and the Saliswaters.

Dawkin inched closer to his siblings. Gerry, fixated on the enemy, groped for someone to hold onto before finding Symon's forearm.

"Brothers, I'm, I'm..." he started.

"Us too," Symon finished for him.

Ely swung away from the lot of them, facing the enemy. He unclasped his helm, tossing it aside.

"Ely," Dawkin began, seeing his brother exposed, without cover or disguise to mask his identity.

"I gather you know all our secrets." Ely descended the stairs, coming to the middle of the line of the Voiceless. "You think yourselves so damn brilliant. Perhaps you are. But I wonder: How will greater Marland react to you trying to wipe out an entire generation of nobles, let alone their king?"

Brother Dawkin, coming before Ely front and center, smirked. "You must be the snarky one?"

"The one and only."

"Then you may have already gathered the answer. We destroy. We conceal. Then we step into our roles to replace those we've removed.

"Now, I must admit, there are not enough of us to act for all we have slain. Not with this round. And those who witnessed this attack will need to be... convinced... to go along with our ruse. Or risk their memory wiped out for good. Nothing we cannot handle."

"No one will ever believe any one of you to be the king," Ely insisted.

"A bold statement, coming from King Fool," Brother Dawkin snickered. "And that is where you err. We will step into the seat of the Throne. We will reign. Rule. As your personage. Those who doubt us will face the noose. You know a little something of clandestine hangings, now don't you?"

The brothers shared a glance. Even Ely's confidence bristled as he shifted in place.

"Yes, Baron Tristan was one of ours. Like his brother, Sir Ernald. The usurping they started did not end with your abolishment of Har-Kin Boivin. It lives on, with many and more foxes in your den than you could ever know."

"Bastards," Artus seethed. "You bloody bastards." The elder Saliswater tightened his grip on the hilt of his sword. The web of his veins, from his hands to his brow, bulged — the veteran within awakened. The man known only in legend by his moniker, The Gauntlet, returned.

"Nay, we have fathers," the brother admitted. "Well, some of us, I presume." Other imposters in his midst chuckled, inching nearer their intended targets.

"Whoever you serve," Ely started again, "whatever they – or you – stand to gain from this attack, we can provide with an agreement, here and now. My brothers and I will concede what we must, in the name of King Jameson. Enough nobles are present to cast their votes for a treaty, which will stand as legal in the eyes of Mar and men. We can afford a truce for whatever you wish – land in Colinne, ships, gold – without any further bloodshed."

Ely relented. With his pause, the whole of the hall quieted as if to consider his proposal.

"A fine offer," Brother Dawkin finally answered. "But what we want, what we always desire, is not something you're willing to give lightly."

"Which is?" Ely inquired with apprehension.

Brother Dawkin shifted his sights to the wrecked throne chair at his side.

"Your ending."

He raised his foot over it, snapping the armrest in half with his heel.

The Voiceless bent their knees and steadied their fists before them. Ely also fell into a defensive stance, as did Symon and Artus. Dawkin noted Gerry, even for all his distress, fitted his hands tighter around his sword grip, extending its point toward Brother Dawkin.

Brother Dawkin wavered before Ely and his line of silent knights. He bent over to pick the armchair length he had broken. Holding it before him, he swiped at them mockingly, his toy weapon feet from his targets. The Voiceless stood, unflinching, as the imposters before them gathered, closing any remaining gaps between them.

"Make peace with us!" Ely pleaded one last time.

"Nay," Brother Dawkin replied.

"We'll slay the half of you! I swear it!"

"Not bloody likely."

Brother Dawkin cast his armrest aside. His hand now bare, one of his comrades tossed him another arming sword – this one a cobalt-blue metal – which he caught with ease, not even looking in the direction from whence it came. Then he paused, opening his other palm as another of his men handed him a pitcher.

"Enjoy the wine."

The monk lobbed the pitcher over the heads of the Voiceless. It shattered on the platform, spilling its contents on the spot where the chair once sat. Almost instantly, Dawkin weakened. His knees buckled. Nearly swooning, through watery eyes he spotted wisps floating up from the puddle of wine. He pivoted, wanting to yell and wave his kin and knights away from the vapors.

Yet, he could not. For where his speech should have rung came nothing, as his arms disobeyed his intentions to remain at his sides.

Rather than act, the whole of his body relented, leaving him immobile. At a loss to do anything but stare, he turned his eyes to the second, third, and fourth pitchers that took to the air before landing amongst them. Just like the first, the clay containers smashed upon impact, releasing the poison within.

The silent knights dodged the pitchers while their eyes never left the encroaching enemy. Their training served them well; any other men-at-arms would have broken formation. Their discipline, their commitment to keeping their line intact, came at a cost, though. For from their unyielding position, they remained exposed to the tendrils, which rose to pollute their ranks. Those closest stayed in formation as they did their best to lean away. No matter, for they soon showed signs of impairment, what with lowered shoulders and heavy heads.

All the while, Brother Dawkin and his men held back, allowing the toxins to take effect.

Dawkin, for all the fight he could muster, failed in his balance. His palm met the platform. He leaned on it with the last of his strength, his legs having lost the will to carry him.

So this is it? he mused in his haze, the horizon of his fate close at hand. *I fall. My brothers, my grandfather, we end. We. End.*

The scope of his vision contracted. The edges darkened as all in front of him became cast in fog. A curtain fell, then lifted suddenly, as he fought the closing of his eyelids, the coming of eternal sleep.

Thump, thump, thump, thump, thump.

The thundering sounds above, like a herd of horses galloping atop the roof, swept up their collective attention. Dawkin glanced upward, expecting the roof to cave in. Nay, its structure prevailed while the encroaching threat stormed the ears of all in the hall.

Dawkin struggled to right himself. He looked about, finding his siblings attempting to do the same. Gerry collapsed away from Symon onto his left side. Dawkin knelt before him as Symon came along his other side.

Crack, crack, crack.

As his little brother leaned into his shoulder, Dawkin looked up. The section of the roof just above threatened to cave in, the bulge in the ceiling growing with each sharp turbulence.

Brother Dawkin and his cohorts – at last wide-eyed and

off their guard – scrambled as the ceiling fell. Their ranks broke apart with the rain of debris, which swelled to a deluge of wood and sedge. The collapse spread out before them, the shifting materials piling high on a mound bathed in sunlight. A figure landed on the newly-risen peak, cloaked from brow to foot in a flowing slate-colored robe.

All paused before its wake. Some brushed the dirt and dust from their personage. Others simply stood in awe, Dawkin among them. Along with the monk who shared his name.

The hooded figure nary raised its hooded brow when Brother Dawkin, shaking himself from shock, pointed. "You... Betrayer! What are you doing here? You wicked –"

Ghost? Demon? God? Dawkin suspected those terms and more from the monk, whose jaw remained unhinged, his lips parted, ready to grant words to his thoughts. Instead, a gurgling erupted, a slew of slurred speech followed by a trickle of blood.

Brother Dawkin's index finger bent, then his arm lowered before the whole of him dropped to the base of the mound. His body half in shadow, half in the circlet of sunlight from above, the white blade which had claimed him protruded upward, its pulsing glow showing the life it had robbed from its victim.

Those imposters not paralyzed by fear rushed forward, spurred by their martial instinct. As quick as the first of them started, the gray figure stayed ahead of their motion, one flow of momentum at a time.

It flipped from the top of the mound to land in the shadows before the fallen monk. Retrieving the white blade it had thrown, the anomaly suddenly stood awash in light, the sword in its hand radiating bolder and brighter.

Then it moved.

Circles and arcs. Wide in reach. Flashing with fury. The sword seemed to lengthen at all the right moments as the cloaked aberration turned from one set of imposters to another, pivoting only once those before it tumbled.

A few more seasoned assailants approached the hooded one, offering their wary swords and cautious stances. Their vigilance saw the figure answer in turn, first with a pause, followed by bent knees and elbows held close.

From his peripheral vision, Dawkin spotted sets of imposters branching out, sticking to the shadows as they moved to the flanks.

"Brothers, Grandfather –" Dawkin cried.

"I see them," Artus responded first. "Defend the sides and rear of, of that, fighter."

The Voiceless answered the call, spreading their line to cover the cloaked one's most vulnerable points. Artus and his brothers hurried to their ranks to take their place among the silent knights. Dawkin led Gerry to a gap between two Voiceless, one of whom took his beleaguered brother under his shoulder. Gerry leaned into the knight, allowing Dawkin to slip from his embrace to join their hooded guardian.

"Dawkin!" Symon cried, too late.

The cloaked figure merely glanced at Dawkin as he hopped over the bodies of allies and foes. Dawkin joined the side of his new accomplice, his raised spirits tempered by the uncertainty of an unknown.

"Whatever your reason for fighting them, thank Mar you're here," Dawkin said.

The draped one turned – offering a flat, black oval under the hood, its face obscured – nodding in response. It spoke no words, though the radiance from its blade dimmed so that it appeared as ordinary steel.

Their assailants edged closer. Many still bore the familiar faces Dawkin had known all his life. Barons or sons of barons. Bishops and clergy. Knights. From all manner of court sessions and other gatherings. And yet a handful showed the signs of duress, with their garb askew and their grease paint ruined by sweat.

Never take on the horde. Only a few at a time. Or one. Piece by piece, wear down your enemy if no other clear path to victory stands out. His father once told him that. Or perhaps he had read it in the histories of the Century War? No matter. The adage struck him as apt and just, sharpening his focus and setting his resolve. He took in the whole scene before him, noting the close quarters made tighter by fallen enemies and comrades alike, overturned tables and benches, not to mention the debris from the new hole above. He wrapped his gauntleted hand around his blade, preparing to engage the imposters in half-swording.

"What say you?" Dawkin asked of the stranger by his side. "I can take the two in front of me, so long as you don't –"

Interrupting his words, the figure leapt. The blade it bore rose above its head, foreshadowing the strike of steel to come. The imposters raised the tips of their swords and halberds in turn, threatening to impale the hero before its landing. In both awe and worry, Dawkin blitzed forward, hoping his advance would distract one or two of his opponents.

With his first step, the expected and familiar occurred. His calves and thighs contracted. The air rushed through the slit of his visor. He set his sights on the scene beyond the ring of light, to the enemies still hiding in the shadows of the covered hall. His breath held, his other foot ready to bear his weight. With his exhale, his second step took flight.

His third began just like his other two when a change occurred, contrary to all his expectations. His muscles suddenly relieved, weightlessness overtook him. The gust through his visor disappeared. Those in the dimness suddenly found themselves exposed as a brilliance – like something of a second sun – burst, its source emanating from the figure on high.

The assailants raised their forearms and hands to shield their eyes, turning away from the figure as it descended. Dawkin followed their lead, the blinding light invading the opening in his visor. He merely glimpsed the white blade before his eyes pained and instinctively shut. Though he pivoted from the figure, his torso bent *toward* it, as he was somehow pulled inward much like a ship caught in a current.

Crack!

A clap Dawkin could only compare to thunder deafened him. A surge of hot air blew him back while the light blinding him went out. Sailing through the hall, Dawkin opened his eyes midair. He spotted the figure bent on one knee, dimmed blade in one hand, the top part of a broken orb in the other.

A sharp pain jolted up the right side of Dawkin's back as his left shoulder blade collided with a hard surface. Streaks and lines swept before him as he rolled. His head spun. His consciousness became a haze.

Reeling to a stop on his back, Dawkin groaned. He blinked through the throbbing in his head, the aches in his body, managing to turn his head.

The figure straightened. It released the remnants of its orb, which shattered amongst the other fragments of the crystal.

Is that... smoke? Indeed, from the translucent bits, tendrils rose, white wisps not unlike fumes from a fire. Dawkin lifted his head for a better look. A jab shot up his neck. He winced, surrendering to the agony, to rest his head back on the ground. He unclasped the strap of his helm to slide it off. Now free, he gasped.

Dawkin studied the floor with determination. In doing so, his vision began to clear, allowing him to grasp that the tendrils were not from fire. Yes, like smoke, the vapor rose. Yet it also turned and spread, fanning out from the figure like a web emanating from a spider. Those on the floor still rolling and moaning – the imposters, mostly – soon fell silent as the sweeping mist took them.

A current stretched in Dawkin's direction. Against every instinct urging him to remain on the ground, Dawkin fought to his knees, then his feet. He nearly keeled over as he coughed up blood.

With one hand free, the anomaly retrieved another orb from inside its cloak. It approached the barricade the imposters had mounted before the closed doors. Cocking back its arm, Dawkin glimpsed the dark green liquid inside the crystal sphere as the contents swirled, revealing the sparkling translucent bits it held.

In an instant, the figure released its orb. Dawkin barely

had a moment to process the projectile's potential, but in instinct – after seeing the figure pivot and shield itself – he did likewise.

A blast of heat and light washed over Dawkin, who shut his eyes firmly while he lifted his arms before his face. The force of the explosion shoved against all, compelling him to peddle back. By chance, the path behind him remained clear of bodies and debris so that he only sank to one knee while the rest of him remained upright.

The air settled. Dawkin peeked out from under his hands. The once-mighty doors of the hall now stood as two splintered lengths on blemished hinges, while the make-shift rampart had been reduced to blackened debris and falling ash.

The figure – back hunched, knees bent – inspected its slate-colored cloak. Somehow, the unassuming cape and hood had served as protection more resilient than armor against such a formidable discharge. Only the dust on its sleeves and the jostled cowl showed the effects of the blast, leading the anomaly to brush and straighten its covering. In doing so, the rim of its hood drew back, exposing a golden ribbon from underneath. A single curl. So enchanting.

No. It couldn't be...

The hood reclaimed the ringlet as the figure turned back to Dawkin. The cowl framed the abyss beneath it, offering a blackened oval where any would expect to see a face.

No porcelain skin. Nor green eyes. Nor blond strands. Only pitch and emptiness.

Impossible.

Dawkin's lips parted. He knew her name. Didn't he? It managed to evade him, disappearing from his mind and absent from his voice. He reached out to the anomaly, knowing it to be her, even as hood and cloak spun away to flap in the air. In a sprint, the slate-colored hero slipped through the opening and into the shadows.

Dawkin grunted. He bounded from his bent knee onto his two feet; they wobbled beneath him like those of a babe learning how to walk. He forced himself to step, finding his footfalls awkward despite his determination.

"James!" cried Everitt from some corridor beyond the hall. "James! You there?!"

"Aye!" Dawkin finally spoke, his throat burning as he did. His fingers found his neck, allowing him to remember he stood unhelmed.

"You in the Great Hall?"

"Yes, but stay back!" he urged, knowing Everitt would ignore the plea and come anyway. Still, he had to do something to buy time. "There, there is a poison by the hall doors. Vapors. I am fine, and you will be too, so long as we all keep our distance." Dawkin waited. Everitt's steps echoed in response, aligning with his suspicions. He continued to approach, perhaps wanting to move in as close as possible.

Not waiting to see if his Right Captain would heed his warning or not, Dawkin retreated to the stage. He hastened up to the first sibling he found: Ely. His brother, reeling on his back at the base of the staircase, stared up at him with glassy eyes.

"Dawkin," he blinked through tears, "is that you?"

"Aye. What's left of me." Dawkin hoisted his brother to

his feet, who held his palm to the side of his head as he scanned the bodies, both dead and dazed.

"What the bloody hell happened?" Ely pondered.

"Poisoned wine. Potions. Vapors. You name it."

"Dear Mar, why can't these gatherings ever be simple?"

Leave it to Ely to joke at a time like this. Dawkin hardly had the chance to admonish him when a Voiceless stirred, then moaned. Both Ely and Dawkin turned as Symon attempted to lift himself from under a silent knight. They rolled the guard, limp and lifeless, gingerly off their brother.

"He, he saved me," Symon coughed. He sat up, the carnage of the Great Hall coming into focus for him. He groped for his sword, his sight never leaving the imposters scattered before them.

"They're subdued," Dawkin assured him. "For now."

From the sprawled bodies close by, a hand reached for them. Dawkin recoiled, startled, before recognizing the hand.

Artus.

He and his brothers rushed to him. A Voiceless and his attacker had been blown back atop the former king, pinning him down underneath their lifeless bodies. He struggled to lift himself from under their combined weight, managing only to free his arm.

"Are you hurt?" Dawkin arrived first. "Did you break anything?"

"My right side, my ribs, ache," their grandfather grimaced.

Symon grabbed Dawkin by the shoulder to pull him back.

“Help me lift these men off of him. And quickly,” Symon urged.

Dawkin looked Symon up and down. “You’re hardly fit to stand, let alone lift.”

“I’ll manage,” Symon insisted.

“You two want to lend a hand?” Ely asked as he bent to lift one of the bodies by the feet. “Literally, I mean. Dawkin, you grab one of this chap’s arms, Symon the other –”

“James!” their Right Captain called from beyond, his voice louder than before. “James!”

“We have company.” Dawkin looked to the top of the stage.

“Get Gerry up and ready,” Symon nodded. He reached down for the set of arms opposite of the legs Ely held; he ground his teeth, fighting through whatever pain he had. “We’ll tend to Grandfather.”

Dawkin bounded up the steps as his brothers heaved the first body off of Artus. Even before he reached Gerry, he spotted what he knew would be a problem: the curled form of a body, the wrinkled clothes covering him, and the sad mop of hair cupped between two shaking hands. Crippling fear. The kind which had been Gerry’s companion his whole life. Much of the time, it mocked him from the shadows, threatening to come out into the light only at the most inopportune moments.

Now? Dawkin asked, nearly turning away in disgust at the sight of his brother. *You act like this now?*

“Brother!” Dawkin cried, kneeling to rouse him.

Gerry looked up, at first not recognizing his brother. Settling on Dawkin’s steely eyes, he came to, panic washing over his face.

“I saw it. I saw it. Demon. From the ceiling. It fell. From heaven.” Gerry sank before Dawkin’s grip, even as his brother held him firmly. All purpose, along with any hint of vigor, had vanished from him. A shell of a man remained, far from what would pass as a king. “How does a demon come from heaven?”

“Never you mind, you hear?!” Dawkin shook him by the shoulders. “Gerry, you must stand. Rise. Enough of your whimpering!”

“The demon! It flew in. From the sky. The sky!”

Dawkin backhanded Gerry across his mouth. “You’re a king!”

Gerry wept. Dawkin delivered another blow.

“A king!” Dawkin reminded him once more.

Tears soaked Gerry’s face. Dawkin released him, disgusted. As his little brother curled up into a ball, Symon came to his side with Ely close, though he kept his distance.

“What did you do?!” Symon demanded as he cupped Gerry’s head.

“Tried to beat some sense into him,” Dawkin snickered. “It didn’t work.”

“You bastard. You laid a finger on him. You ought to –”

“Brothers!” Ely interrupted. “I hate to spoil the drama, but we still have this to deal with.” He thrust his sword toward the scene before them, which threatened to erupt again. The masses subdued by the blast and ensuing vapors had started to stir, their senses returning as they turned onto their backs or propped themselves upon their haunches. Some heaved or wretched, though Dawkin knew such delays would pass.

The footfalls in the corridor leading to the Great Hall

drew their concern. Dawkin and Ely glanced back at Gerry while he lay in Symon's arms.

"It's still his turn," Symon insisted. "He bears the garb of a king. Even the wounds of a fight, thanks to Dawkin. Help me get him to his feet."

Symon dug his hands under the pit of Gerry's arms, ready to lift him, while his other two brothers stared.

"Well?" Symon asked.

Dawkin closed his eyes. "I invoke the Rule of Mercy."

A sharp pain resonated from his jaw through the whole of his head.

Better expect another one. His suspicions proved correct. Another blow landed upon him, this one to his left cheek.

Though his ears rang, he managed to hear grunts. He forced his eyes open through the blinding pain to find Ely and Symon scuffling.

"He has no right!" Symon cried.

"It's the Law of Terran. We swore to it."

"He broke the law when he drugged me." Symon shoved Ely away. Dawkin peddled back with him, his hands up should Symon redirect his fury. His stronger brother stayed at bay, not wanting to abandon Gerry.

"Your Majesty!" Everitt called. His voice reverberated vehemently, indicating his proximity just outside their confines.

"Dawkin is next to ascend." Ely approached Symon in earnest. "Gerry is, well, Gerry. He cannot rule nor summon in this condition. You must... allow Dawkin the Rule of Mercy."

Symon bent down to inspect his little brother. He wiped

a line of blood from the corner of Gerry's mouth, which stretched down to his chin. "You'll pay for this," Symon promised Dawkin. He turned his back to him as he shielded Gerry. He looked to Ely. "Well, go on. Grab a helm from one of the others. Or two. Nay, three, so we can hide Gerry. No one can see him like this."

"Dawkin..."

The strained voice drew their attention. Propped up against an overturned table rested Artus, who waved Dawkin toward him. Dawkin started for his grandfather, then hesitated. He looked to Symon.

"Go," Symon granted, tempering his anger for a moment.

Dawkin hopped over fallen ally and foe to come to Artus' side.

"What is it?" Dawkin asked, glancing over his shoulder in the direction of the hall doors. "Everitt will be here at any moment."

His breath struck Dawkin; each inhale and exhale deliberate, his effort pained and forced. Sweat beaded his face, glistening in the low light, in contrast to the grime he bore.

"Are you –"

Artus thrust his hand onto Dawkin. He gripped the meat between his neck and shoulder. Dawkin winced though he fought to keep his eyes open.

"Listen," Artus whispered through his teeth. The skin of his face tightened as he locked eyes with Dawkin. "Remember what I taught you in Arcporte while all your brothers were away, frolicking on the Continent."

It pained Dawkin to recall the advice his grandfather

had urged, along with his willingness to take it. *What have I become?* Dawkin had asked himself with every issuance and action he despised. The justification he used – all in the name of Marland – had worn thin by the time his brothers had returned.

For the greater good. That was his mantra. His truth in a sea of disgrace and deceit.

For the greater good. For the greater good. For the greater good...

"You are the true heir."

Dawkin – his internal dialogue broken, his mindfulness returning – stared right back at the Gauntlet. The wise, old patriarch he had none had vanished, replaced by the feared warrior of legend. Right there, capturing his full attention.

"Your father's son. His favorite. And mine. For the sole reason that you can hold this kingdom together. Your brothers have their place, whether they know it or not. Without you, Marland is done for."

"But my brothers... I can't do this alone."

"One throne. One crown. One scepter. *They* can support *you* if you require it. But all the power can only be held by one. A leader."

Artus loosened his grip on Dawkin. He lessened his stare.

"So lead, My King," he pleaded.

He let go of Dawkin.

"James!"

Everitt's cry rang loud and true through the Great Hall. Dawkin rose. He swung around to meet him.

"Sir Everitt!"

Not bothering to glance in the way of his siblings, Dawkin strode up to his Right Captain. Everitt, with what few knights he could muster, surveyed the whole of the gallery. His eyes scrutinized His Majesty with as much intensity until Dawkin gripped his forearm in a soldierly embrace.

“You well?”

“I – yes, I am.”

“And the men? The losses?”

Everitt somehow fell more solemn. “Several. Too many to recollect at this point.” Everitt continued to scan everything. “What in heaven and hell happened? And your armor? Why are you dressed as a Voiceless?”

“A last-minute show of force. Unannounced. It seems such theatrics saved my life.”

“Mar be good.”

A silent knight marched to join Dawkin by his left side. To his right, another Voiceless clanked as he struggled to support a man in helm, partially armored. His brothers’ ruse to hide their identity proved hasty at best. Yet seeing that all stood or laid about preoccupied, it did the trick.

“Your Majesty?” Everitt began. “What is your command?”

Chapter 26

There he goes. Mad.

Symon glanced back in the direction of Arcporte Castle. The salt breeze invaded his visor, its cold telling of the night to come. As the wind whistled through the slits and crevices of his steel, he watched the torches on the rampart light, one by one. All while the topmost windows of the West Tower darkened with the onset of dusk.

Thwack!

He glanced down at his vambrace. The crimson spots looked far less grotesque at sunset. Then again, so did the severed heads, though darkness would have treated them kinder.

As two guards dragged the headless corpse aside, another two struggled with a Lost Soul. Far more squeamish than the first handful, he kicked and wriggled under the firm grips of his captors.

"Mercy! I beg His Majesty, please! Mercy! Mercy!"

A sense of embarrassment blended with pity washed over Symon. *A horrible way to die, really.* Symon looked past the condemned man to the two guards who had removed the headless corpse. As though tossing a sack of grain, they heaved the body into the pit before wiping their hands on their leather-scaled breeches.

Symon couldn't hear the thump of the corpse over the wails of the next convict. Yet, he knew the body had fallen.

He was sure of it. It foreshadowed the next one to come, along with the dozen or so others they still had to finish off before nightfall. Then the oil would be poured, the kindling stacked, as it had gone on for the past several days.

He shook his head at the thought, nearly ignoring the axehead as it rose. *The bloody executioner didn't even bother to wipe the blade. Then again, how could he? He hadn't the time.*

As if awakening from a trance, Symon suddenly found himself on one of the terraced steps which ringed Mar-by-the-Sea Cathedral. How much time had passed? An hour? Mayhaps. The thin stench of ash remained in the air; despite Symon's efforts to stay downwind, the breezes had shifted, as if the air itself wanted to avoid the mass of death their kin had created.

Armor and mail stirred as Ely came up beside him. "You think we're far enough away?"

Symon turned his head. "Whatever do you mean?"

"From, you know."

"I just said I don't."

"Bloody hell, you too?! I swear, am I the only one left with any sense? Me?"

"Ely, say your piece." *Or, as Father would say, "Hold your peace."*

"The, what did Dawkin call it?"

"'Contraband.' And I can hear you." Dawkin glared at them with narrow eyes. "Good thing only the Voiceless are around. Your voice carries, Ely, when you're this nervous."

"Hey, I, I just –"

"Yes, as a matter of fact, we are far enough way." Dawkin held out his right hand. The silent knight nearest him passed him a lit torch, which Dawkin lowered to the ground before him.

The barrels. The pitch-black substance. One of the monks had finally uttered the name. *Seaflame.* That brother, tied and bound, had chewed through his gag and screamed it as they had doused him and the remaining prisoners in...

"Don't –" Symon started.

The wet grass before Dawkin's feet consumed the torch-light faster than any kindling imaginable. Like a crazed serpent, a twisting blazing line raced from their terrace down the rest of the earthen steps. Upon reaching level ground, the curved band of fire straightened as it headed towards the Our Lady of Arc Monastery.

The brick. The mortar. The timber. Gone. Replaced by a white sphere that grew to engulf the monastic grounds.

Symon shielded the slit of his visor. His forearm managed to block the blinding light. The heat proved to be a different story. It washed over his vambrace before flooding in through his visor. His helm filled with what felt like dragon's breath. Indeed, the air inside felt as if it was bubbling on his very pores.

Staggering back from the blast, Symon unlatched his helm. He tossed it aside, liberating his head from the cauldron his covering had become. Though the heat persisted all around him, he gasped for air, hoping against hope for a cool, seaside breeze.

Alas, Mar answered. The swelter subsided. The refreshing wake from the harbor returned, which met the sudden sweat that dripped from every edge of his face.

Symon looked to the monastery. Tongues of orange and

white clung to the few bones of its frame not obliterated. Aside from those remnants, in the absence of the edifice, flames danced, as wild and excited as rabid hunters celebrating their first kill.

Silhouetted before the incendiary glory, Dawkin stood, having not moved from whence he dropped the torch.

"Dawkin," Symon coughed. "Your eyes, you should turn away."

"My vision is fine. The blast did nothing to me."

"Still, it's like staring into the sun."

"It's brilliant. All is right. And that is why..."

"What? Why, what?"

"... It will send a message..."

Within an hour, Symon found himself revisiting that message. Looking up from the rooftop of a tavern on the Curved Wharf, the monastery continued to burn brightly, albeit with less vigor. The once roaring white flames had subdued, taking on an orange glow licking the few remnants of the building's frame. A few tongues had also made their way to the grasses of the grounds not immediately incinerated by the blast. Those outliers made quick work of their victims, marking their newfound conquests with fires of blue and violet.

The variety of hues made a feast for the eyes. A dazzling array of combustion. An enchanting performance of destruction. One could very well overlook how the display marked not creation nor celebration but death.

Footfalls echoing up the stairwell drew cursory glances from Symon and his brothers. Gerry emerged, the steins in his hands clanking together, threatening to slip from his hands. He managed to persevere, resting the four mugs onto the top of a barrel.

"The pub is swarming with talk." Gerry motioned to the fiery hillside with his stein.

Ely glanced at the three remaining mugs. He made no move to grab one. "What'd they say?"

"A great many things. In support, mostly."

"Support?"

"Of the King. They feel his – our – efforts to combat the insurgency sweeping the island is a good start, one which will root out evil..."

Or sow it. Symon stared at the rooftop beneath his feet as Gerry continued. A ruse at listening, for sure. For out of his peripheral vision, he eyed Dawkin.

Their brother brooded in his own way. He resisted the drink as Ely – another oddity – while he focused on the hillside as it burned. He nary glanced elsewhere, nor blinked, or otherwise moved. It was as if he feared the fire would extinguish should he took his eyes from it.

He wants it to burn, Symon knew. Then. Now. Forever. That concentration he bore had persisted ever since he assumed the role of Jameson at Glic Anglisk Castle. Sure, he had taken command and issued directives as any one of them would have. But upon entering the courtyard... Seeing the carnage... The other men-at-arms, on the ramparts, and those felled from the walls. Then the reports, followed by visits, to the surrounding villages, whose tales of tragedy rose into the air as ribbons of smoke. One at first, then several, each slowly crawling against the blue, polluting the sky no matter which direction they swung, as if to taunt them. Come and see. What awaits. For Marland. For King Jameson.

For us.

"Alas."

Gerry stopped himself while Dawkin rose from his seat to grab a stein.

"What do you mean 'alas'?" Ely began.

"You smell that?" Dawkin prodded.

"No."

"I do." Symon wrinkled his nose. He noticed it mere seconds before Dawkin spoke.

Gerry sniffed. "Ashes?"

"The winds shifted. The smell's reached Smallquarter now." Dawkin finally turned his back to the blaze, sauntering in no particular direction as he drank.

"And that means something?" Ely asked.

"Smallquarter," Dawkin said, "is filled with hovels and taverns and houses of pleasure. It's the one place – well, perhaps not the one – let us say it's the *best* place in Arcporte to lose oneself. A man can crawl into a hole there and spend months in his own heaven or hell without ever knowing what's going on in the outside world.

"If any of the Lost Souls evaded us, or if any dared to sympathize with their cause only to shirk from the public upon seeing our justice, the ashes – their scent, their flecks in the air – will make it known no enemy of our kin will escape. We will hunt down every fox, all the devout, and any other who contemplate doing us harm.

"The name Saliswater will become synonymous with unquestioned authority. No more conclaves, with their barons or sons casting shade on our rule. No more questions. No further doubts. The Foxhunter. The Gauntlet. And now, King Jameson – The Sword. All will know the unmerciful strength of our dynasty. Stories of our power will echo from our kingdom to the heavens, to the great Everhall itself. Kin Saliswater. The eternal rulers of Marland."

Dawkin downed the contents of his stein before tossing it from the rooftop, nary a care for how it landed.

"Ashes for ashes," Dawkin muttered as he gazed upon the dying flames on the hillside. "Death for death. As Grandfather and Father taught us. As it should be."

The haunting scent of flame and anguish subsided – or perhaps their tolerance had grown – as another breeze snuck in on them. A chill one, from the harbor, sinking into the depths of their bones. Ely and Gerry pulled the collars of their coats tighter. Even Symon shifted with the cold. Dawkin, his eyes adrift from his brothers while his thoughts wandered, stirred not.

His fire burns from within. His anger. His rage. Propelled by his better judgment, Symon stood. *He must be stopped.*

A hand met his chest. To his surprise, Ely, now on his feet, met him with the softest gaze he had ever witnessed. Not quite hope, nor despair, nor sympathy. A sentiment altogether different. And yet somehow, appropriate.

Symon relented his charge toward Dawkin, taking a step back.

"Do you remember the last quarantine?" Ely asked.

Dawkin turned, narrowing his eyes while his shoulders rose. "The one a few years back?"

"Aye. The second wave of Silver Fever we've known. 'Twas not nearly as bad as the one which left Geremias here bedridden."

"The mage said I developed a resistance from when I

was young," Gerry said, "even if I still bear the scars." The memory of his illness flooded back to him, prompting him to rub his forearms.

"Still, Father ordered the cities to shut their gates. The lockdown sent our economy into a tizzy. Coin fell in value. The price of flour crested. The paupers complained. The barons whined. Even after the fever relented, the threat of usurping continued. If I recall Father's words correctly, the Conclave vowed to call an emergency session."

Dawkin scoffed but offered no words of response, so Ely continued. "You had ascended. Gerry confined himself to Terran just to be safe while Symon made the rounds to check on him regularly. All that left me to my own devices. So I took advantage by partaking of the pleasures – the holes you call them – of Smallquarter."

"Vulgar," Dawkin chastised. "Even for you."

"Tsk, tsk, brother. I wasn't finished. For you see, while I found myself in the alleyways between establishments, I chanced upon a street performance. A troupe had made its way to Arcporte by way of a merchant vessel to set up shop in one of the well-traveled squares. I don't recall the exact narrative of their play, only that it was boisterous and funny and entertaining as all hell.

"Afterward, I approached the manager of the acting troupe. Following a round of drinks for him and his best players, a wave of brilliance overcame me. I plopped all the coins I had right before them and proposed a play of such intrigue, a tapestry of satire, that it would capture the minds of princes and paupers alike."

Dawkin raised a brow. "You? Wrote a play?"

"Well, don't say it like that. The truth of the matter is I

didn't write anything. I merely provided the idea for the story, encouraging the manager and his entertainers to fill in the gaps."

"So, he obliged?"

"The coin helped. After all, what's the point of entering a career in theatre if one cannot exert a bit of influence, at least some control?"

Even in the shadow of darkness, Symon caught sight of Dawkin rolling his eyes.

"So the show went on, as they say. The first performance occurred in the slums of Smallquarter and some other random hovels of Arcporte before moving on to a few other townships in Marland. The acting troupe eventually circled back here where they set sail and were never heard from again."

Ely paused. Dawkin waited for more, along with the rest of them. After a moment, Dawkin raised his hands and shoulders. "That's it?"

"I thought so. Then many months later, when I was in disguise at some random tavern, I overheard a quartermaster and his crew squawking over a play they'd seen in Belgarda. It turns out, my sponsored production had made its way to the Kingdom of Saints."

"Honest?" Gerry piped.

"As veracious as the ash we see falling."

Dawkin continued to feign interest, though, in truth, his mind still seemed elsewhere. Symon, on the other hand, found himself intrigued. 'Twas unlike Ely to spin a yarn of such detail without committing to a point or two.

"Of all the tales to tell," Symon began, "why speak of that one? And why is this the first we're hearing of it?"

“Alas, you pose two important queries, brother. Though the order you present them in is wrong. I must answer the latter first to give you context for the former. For you see, the play I told was all about Father.”

The three of them perked. The hairs on the back of Symon’s neck rose. Dawkin glared bewitchingly at Ely. Even Gerry – not accustomed to confrontation – leaned forward, threatening to pounce onto his feet.

“Before you jump to any conclusions, let me say my piece. The story took place in court and the quarters of counsel. It told of the dealings and drama Father had to deal with to contain the threats of Silver Fever. First, the quarantine. Then, the assignment of mages to the most affected hovels of the island. This was followed by setting prices, appeasing merchants, and, of course, the threats to his very seat on the Throne.

“Of course, in reality, all those events unfolded in the drollest, most boring ways possible. The true story would have lulled the most outspoken babe to sleep. I knew I had to accentuate the plot points as much as possible. Which is what I did on the night I proposed it to the acting troupe. With the help of the tavern’s spirits, I exaggerated Father’s ordeals. One minute, his actions led to tragedy, then the next, satire, and finally, comedy. On and on I went, fabricating more and more, pint after pint... So that by the end, the play presented stood far apart from history. Father – never one to self-promote – emerged the reluctant hero, a ruler who never spared the rod, a monarch a step ahead of all his usurpers...”

Ely stopped. He stared down, finding his pointed gestures and mimicry had led him to the lip of the roof. He balanced himself – one foot on the ledge, the other extending behind him – before hopping back towards the center. He composed himself, taking a moment to straighten the ruffles of his clothing, before resuming his narrative. Only now, with a more somber tone.

"I know you think I acted as Prince Fool, considering the drinking, whoring, and trickery I portrayed. I admit, that... side of me... had its part. No matter. Whatever my intentions that night in the tavern – or those of the acting troupe or of the audiences who went on to see the play – something arose beyond the control of any.

"From what I know, the story of Father evolved. It grew in scope and range, portraying Father as a ruler above every other in merit and ability, one who had been blessed by Mar's grace. By the time the sailors I overheard had seen it, his legend stood as unquestioned. His stellar reputation had seeped into every rank and class of Afarian society, from the lowly paupers of the streets to the proudest royals of the Continent.

"Although I lacked the maturity to see it at the time, in hindsight, the signs of his newfound prestige made themselves known. Perhaps you can remember? Those in Court addressed him with less haste, more reverence. Magistrates reported more merchants paying their tributes on time and fewer quarrels on the streets. Even the Conclave restrained their bickering, with hardly an utterance arising on the supremacy of Kin Saliswater."

"You would lead us to believe your little play had everything to do with cementing Father's legacy?" Dawkin quipped.

"Yes, I would."

“Bullocks.”

“Ever the skeptic,” Ely quipped. “You can believe me.” Ely looked to Dawkin, who shook his head. Next, he glanced at Gerry, who offered a blank stare, before turning to Symon, who likewise knew not what to make of his yarn. Perhaps satisfied by their consideration, he continued. “Or you can write me off, like all of you have when I’ve experienced my highs and lows. Just do this kingdom a favor: don’t lie to yourselves. Whether they started in the highest court or the dankest of gutters, rumors and legends have a power all their own.”

Ely stepped before Dawkin, his eyes piercing the night which had settled between them. “Word of what you did, in the name of King Jameson, will travel near and far tonight. Past the Marlish Sea. Onto the wide Vortriac Ocean. To the shores of Port San-Mont. And all of Afari. Including the courts of every kingdom Father sought to make peace with... You sealed our destiny, brother. By neither chance nor fate, war will be delivered to us, the result of your actions.”

Dawkin stared back, unflinching. “Defend yourself!” Ely snapped. “Do you even care what you’ve done?”

“I care,” Dawkin whispered. “More than you will ever know.”

“Our legacy, the dynasty Father and Grandfather fought so hard to make for, for us, it lies in ruin.” Ely pointed to the monastery, whose inferno had died to mere embers. “There’s your evidence. You – nay, we – will be known for this story, Dawkin. This horror you created.”

Dawkin smirked.

“You think me the jester?” Ely shouted. “What people say about Kin Saliswater will matter.”

Dawkin rose. He set down his stein to stretch. He made his way to the exit, stopping only when Ely cut off his path.

“I wish I had the foresight to know what you would become,” Ely said, offering one last reflection to Dawkin before he tried to escape. “Then I would have emptied the coffers to warn the peoples, to pay for the play of the Monster of Marland.”

Dawkin’s eyes transformed, overwhelmed neither by defensiveness nor rage. Rather, by pity.

“Your point is well-taken. And yet, you miss the most important part. The play – our story – it doesn’t matter how we control the players or how it unfolds onstage.” Dawkin cleared his throat. “What counts is how well we influence the audience.”

The winds shifted. The stench of ash swelled. Symon’s eyes watered. He blinked.

And with that, Dawkin had taken his leave.

Chapter 27

"You need your rest, My Queen. Too much of the night is not good for the child."

Never one to entertain the tales of wives young and old, Taresa nevertheless cocked her head to feign listening. "I'll be in, after a moment," she promised her chambermaid. The woman curtsied to take her leave from the balcony. Taresa sighed, thankful to have another moment to herself, while still altogether anxious for the fire burning before her.

She had directed the attendants to keep the tower unlit. In the presence of such persistent light – one which bespoke of not only crime but the severity of its punishment – it seemed inappropriate to set the candles and torches aflame as though nothing stood amiss.

Hours had passed since her request. The brightest moments of the blaze subsided long ago, the flames threatening to extinguish themselves following their ravenous consumption of the monastery.

Yet, with the wood and vegetation of the grounds having turned to ash, the fire continued. Like ghosts, they appeared as paler versions of their former selves, promising to haunt the rest of the night.

A gentle knock rapped on her door. Taresa sighed. "A moment more."

"Forgive me."

Taresa swung around. Jameson's fist remained curled before the edge of the door as he peeked his head in for a glance.

"Oh," Taresa gasped.

"Your chambermaid said you were still awake."

"I am."

"I startled you." He held himself between the door and its frame, unsure of whether to enter.

"You only disrupted my foolish thoughts."

"Shouldn't you be..." Her husband nodded to the empty bed.

"As should you." Taresa beckoned him from the door before reaching for the flint and candle on the stand by her balcony. With a flick, the wick came to life whilst her husband shuffled to bed.

Jameson sat on the opposite edge, his back to her. She stood on her side of the bed, waiting briefly for him to turn and face her. When he did nothing of the sort, she rounded to approach.

The soft glow accentuated the somber tone he bore. His eyes sunken, his shoulders drooped, he spoke no words. Instead, he allowed his deliberate silence to speak volumes. Taresa turned to the balcony, where the faint light persisted from below. She placed her candle holder on Jameson's nightstand before taking her seat beside him, along with his hand.

"Did your father ever speak of his rule?"

"How so?"

"Of the difficulties he encountered. The weight of the decisions which faced him."

"He was a pragmatic man. He would tell of the edicts he

made, the bickering amongst the nobles he caused, the results of his decisions."

"But never of the toll it took on him?"

"He never shared his feelings about that. Or anything."

Dawkin grunted. "Your father and my father had that in common — most of the time. You see, my father had this reputation of a man unfazed by the Throne. Unmarked by battle. 'The Foxhunter' they called him, a moniker he earned for ousting the spies Kin Foleppi had planted throughout Marland and Greater Afari. And growing up, I believed all the tales about him. How could I not? For whole stretches of my youth, he was gone. Away on some campaign or diplomatic trip, securing the future for Kin Saliswater.

"Then, in the past few years of his reign, he started to... He appeared different. Or maybe I was just beginning to appreciate a side to him that was there all along. He would have these moments, after a long debate with ministers or nobles, when he would tire all of a sudden. The fatigue, or something deeper, would unsettle him. I caught sight of such moments, perhaps a few times, at first not believing what I saw. It was, as if, seeing a man revert to a babe. Or witnessing an elder turn fool in their advanced years. Listen to me. I sound like one myself."

"You don't." Taresa's hand slid from his palm to his forearm, sweeping up and down in a gentle caress.

Dawkin's mind went astray. The hand which comforted him turned from a rich caramel hue to milk-white. Startled, he looked up, finding not Taresa's face but Cora's.

Dawkin withdrew his hand. He shot to his feet, reaching out to the bedpost for support.

"We shouldn't. I'm not the man you think I am."

Perplexed, or hurt, or both, Taresa stood. She inched closer while keeping a respectable distance, careful not to startle him further. She moved within the periphery of is vision. Her hands, with fingers clasped, drifted before her abdomen.

"You hide it well," Taresa stated. "All of you. Or at least you try."

"What?" Dawkin asked.

"The burden. The one you shoulder every moon and sun."

Dawkin ventured to glance upon her. He found Taresa staring back. Not with malice. Nor pity. Nor astonishment. Rather, her eyes presented an offering — an understanding.

"Father did the same. I sensed it, even when he had left a hall or chamber. Servants would scurry, overly concerned by his directives, short and terse as they were. Mother would fret, more than usual, about how I wore my hair or what Ermesinda said or what Nataliya ate. The signs, they haunted that bloody castle. And I hated it. I hated him."

She stepped closer. "Then I saw it. Like you did with yours. Father, he... The Throne took its toll. Yes, he matured along with his reign, and in his rule, the matters which caused him angst in his younger years no longer troubled him in his latter.

"And yet, all that weight. The stress of a hundred-thousand decisions. They tore. They split. Bit by bit. Inflicting wounds so subtle, so deep, he never healed." Taresa paused, looking off to the side as though remembering something long-forgotten. "James, I have a confession."

Tears which never should have been there emanated, from an abyss he had never known of her or expected. "Go on," he urged.

"When we first met, the prospect of coming here, marrying you, it frightened me. Not because of not knowing you. Because of knowing another, who, who would slowly break. And fall. I fear the hopelessness of standing by, of watching it happen, and not being able to do anything about it." She pressed her hands tightly against her abdomen. "For the both of you."

Dawkin – suddenly losing his inhibition – reached out to seize her hands from her. "I won't let that happen. I won't!"

"You alone will be the one ruler the burden will not break?"

Dawkin closed his eyes. *Not one. Terran. My brothers. And I. Four. We will be what others have failed to live up to... We have to... We must.*

Dawkin forced his eyes open. "Yes."

For a moment, if only an instant, he saw it. A glimmer in her eyes. A wellspring of hope.

A distant thunderclap from beyond disturbed their peace. Dawkin squeezed her hands tight as he turned to the balcony. He motioned for Taresa to stay put while he strode outside, drawn to the rising glow suddenly eating away at the night sky.

Smallquarter. A section of structures had erupted in fire, their tongues lashing out at their tightly-packed neighbors, promising to consume them in seconds. Burning bright red – a hue unnatural to any fire he had seen – he knew its source, its meaning.

The threat soon found company to the west, where a line of tenements at the Curved Wharf exploded in a flash of blue-green brilliance. Their proximity to the harbor caused their light to ebb and flow with the onshore breeze, like the bioluminescent tide Dawkin saw every spring.

Randomly, other pockets arose. Some in a furor, no doubt the product of some catalyst the unseen enemy had conjured. Others occurred without haste, perhaps the work of a candle overturned in panic or a torch thrown from a drunk amongst a mob. No matter the particulars. The response to all would be the same.

The magistrates would answer the chaos with soldiers to support them. Crowds would disperse. Martial law would be announced. The reserves called up from the countryside. Along with the men-at-arms from every manor of the island, in answer to the edicts the scribes were drafting at this very moment.

All to meet an enemy, still unknown. Mayhaps one from The Continent. Tosily. Lewmar. Volkmar. Belgarda. All four. Or more.

Taresa came up behind Dawkin. She placed her hand on the small of his back.

"James..." she started.

"War is upon us."

"I know."

"I won't crack. I will not break," Dawkin assured himself as much as he did her.

Taresa held her breath. Along with Dawkin.

"I pray not," she finally answered.

So do I, he thought. *Dear Mar, so do I.*

Afterword

"You had the right of it, Grandfather."

Damn, was his voice always so deep? Colbern asked himself. *Or perhaps he has grown into his role like all of us did before him?*

Colbern studied the War Hall. How it had all changed in a matter of days. The adornments he had come to know in the decades since the Century War had been removed except for one long table with seating for five. All else had been replaced by parchment after parchment showing maps of Afari or potential battle formations for the troops they had amassed. Other tools – a triangular divider, quills, ink wells, wax seals – laid out before them, along with silver trays bearing food and drink aplenty, all suggestive of the long hours their conversation would require.

Beauty was forgone for the practical, leaving utility without apology. The scene reminded Colbern of his younger years when both he and his brother found themselves primed to lead.

"I suppose I did," Colbern answered, moments after the opportunity had passed. His voice carried long and far through the chamber, without furniture or masses to absorb his sound.

"How many this time?" Symon queried.

"Three," Ely snapped before taking a draught from his goblet. "The bloody bastards were entrenched here far too long. One agent had been here for over four years, working first as a baker's assistant before somehow worming his way into the guardhouse as a squire. The little runt was almost knighted, too, before a patrol caught him in the dungeon scouting the tunnels. Only under extreme duress was his ploy uncovered."

Symon shut his eyes and grimaced. "And what of that traitor now?" he seethed.

"Well, like the rest of him, he shat himself when he took to the noose. Struggled for a full minute too."

Colbern turned his lip. He loathed any method of punishment that prolonged the inevitable, with hangings being his least favorite. Berold would have approved, though. *Drat*, he thought. *And if he were here, he would say as much. No matter. It's not his turn. Still, best to keep up appearances.*

"Good riddance," Colbern uttered. "And a display like that sends a message."

Ely raised his goblet to his grandfather in agreement. Colbern returned the gesture, forcing himself to choke down the drink rather than spew it.

"Any idea from whence they came?" Dawkin asked without bothering to turn around. He mulled at the open window, leaning against the pillar as he stared at the harbor below.

Ely shook his head. "Nay. The three captives screamed only a few words to confess their treacherous acts. None spoke of their origins. Mayhaps they grew up in Tosily and were trained to blend into our peoples. Or they could have been recruited from our island and paid handsomely for each year of their ruse. Whatever their way, we'll never know."

Dawkin spun away from the window, grinding his teeth. "Too many secrets! How are we supposed to fight the enemy if we don't even know them?"

Thump-tat-tat-thump. Their signature knock for the day rapped on the door before parting. Gerry entered with scrolls in hand. Forlorn, his eyelids and cheeks hung, speaking volumes of the hour which had passed.

"Brother," Symon began, "is it that bad?"

Gerry passed his scrolls in answer. Still garbed to receive court, he shuffled to the nearest empty chair, dropping his regal circlet as he sat. The ornament clattered onto the table, spinning twice before finally settling down.

Symon unfurled the scrolls, reading through the top one. Ely glanced over his shoulder while Dawkin came aside Symon to snatch the remaining scrolls underneath.

"What news?"

"It says..." Ely trailed off into silence though his lips kept moving as he read. "Truly, am I reading this correctly?"

"Aye," Symon answered ominously.

"Tell me," Colbern insisted.

"Grandfather," Gerry replied low, pinching the bridge of his nose between his thumb and index finger. "It's about us but not to us."

"What is?"

"A Holy Proclamation. From Vloma. A decree with a handful of slanderous points. All against our favor. Part One: Reinterpreting *The Adumbration*. It's a lengthy explanation, but basically, the mages and councilors said the Church just recanted their acceptance that Mar last visited this earth here in Marland. The scroll goes on to state Mar's journey did not end on our island, as previously thought. After careful examination of ancient texts and testimony, a truer version of events points to him concluding his mortal visit not on an *island* but a *peninsula*."

"Blasphemy!" Colbern shouted. "Total blasphemy! And let me guess, that holiest site, this so-called peninsula, is firmly under their control. Port San-Mont, I suppose, right in our own backyard? Or maybe it's the whole sliver of Belgarda? Those self-righteous bastards. Claiming their little land shaped like some serpent could be the last place Mar ever set foot."

"Worse," Dawkin spoke up as he raised his glance from the set of scrolls he held. "The Church went with another site, declaring a new Land of Mar's Ascension: Volkmar."

Colbern gasped. Gerry closed his eyes. Symon crumbled the parchment in his hands.

"Volkmar?" Symon asked.

"You had the right of it, Ely," Dawkin nodded to his brother, who stood opposite of Symon. "And so did you," he added, turning to Symon. "A delegation. A show of force. Though in truth, it seems Volkmar's meeting with Belgarda was more than a diplomacy stunt. Hmmm. Seems their betrayal of us, their newfound alliance, or whatever you want to call it – It all had deep roots, ones planted long before the Lost Souls began their disturbances, and certainly ahead of the attack on Glic Anglisk."

Dawkin rattled on, his words fading into the background, while Colbern considered the depths of the proclamation.

Volkmar. A pagan state of barbarians. With ink and quill, the Church of Mar had baptized a nation of sinners into the blessed. The decree had also damned Marland, which for centuries had acted as the ascension point for the god of Mar. Without the backing of the Church, Marland's historical claim as a holy site solidified its heresy. Monks and bishops working the abbeys and churches of the island would now be forced to turn away the devout, lest they repented their loyalty to Kin Saliswater and swore allegiance to the Devout State of Belgarda over the Kingdom of Marland, praying in the direction of Vloma over Arcporte. While Colbern knew Saliswater could count on the loyalists in the capital and surrounding hamlets, the decision would undoubtedly split the fealties of the countryside, from the Highmoorr Peaks to the Ridge of Tarns to the Farflung Lands.

Colbern leaned on the table. "We can't let word of this get out. Not yet. We must tell our side of the story. Ready the couriers."

"Too late," Gerry said.

"Nonsense. The masses will give consideration to all with the name Saliswater." Colbern reached for the circlet on the table to hand it back to Gerry. "We'll pull the same stunt you and your brothers did. Four acting as one. We'll allow time between each of the public appearances, so if the people talk, we can credit our fastest steads with bringing our dearest King Jameson to all corners of the island."

"Grandfather –" Gerry pleaded.

"Now, now, it will work. And to aid, I will act on your behalf, of course. Why old King Artus still has some leverage to flaunt –"

"Listen!" Gerry roared. He leapt from his seat. "We were the last to know. I don't understand how, but by some trickery and design, the message has already spread."

"Which means one thing," Dawkin added.

"There are more traitors in our midst," Ely concluded. "More foxes in our den. More than we could ever know."

A quiet settled over the War Hall, all while their minds raged with the noise of fear and doubt. None stood more acutely aware of their failures than Colbern, whose head drooped between his shoulders.

Idiots. We were bloody idiots. We believed we expelled the enemy from our island. For over two decades, we lived with this false sense of security, a complacency that left smirks on the faces of our adversaries. But how could we not believe the lie? We lived so carefully. Audemar, ruling unopposed and unaffected as king. His sons – their secret in the dark, with none in the kingdom expressing any hint of suspicion – ascending and descending in rotations, one after another, for years without one falling.

Colbern lifted his eyes. His four grandsons – lost to themselves – remained silent.

This will define them. This challenge. And how they answer.

They need hope.

Colbern cleared his throat. "Your father was half the Continent away when he tasted such treachery for the first time. I suspect you've retained your knowledge of the histories, so repeating them for you now would be a waste of time. I know because I stood before him in a scene not unlike this, much like I do before you now. He sat dejected, with parchment in hand, questioning where it all went wrong."

Colbern sauntered to the pitcher of wine to pour

himself a drink. He cradled the goblet in his hand as he prattled on with his recollection, not sure of how he would end it.

"He prevailed, at least in the day, extinguishing so many of Kin Foleppi that he earned his famous moniker: The Foxcatcher. It's easy to dismiss his efforts in the current moment as failures, but back then, by Mar, did he win the peoples' trust. You'd think your father was Mar reborn the way the common folk and nobles spoke of him. Lords envied his power. Boys ran through the streets and fought over the right of who could pretend to play him. Mothers and fathers named their sons after him. 'Twas an uplifting time."

"Even if it was a façade?" Ely quipped.

Symon slapped his shoulder, chiding him to quiet. Colbern gestured in acceptance, turning to Ely.

"You are right to call out the pretenses of his rule. You must realize, whether true or not, they proved effective. When the Century War came to a close, the Conclave unanimously approved an extension of his rule. Kin Saliswater remained unopposed nearly throughout the remainder of his reign."

"Until he wasn't."

Colbern glanced at Gerry, who had returned to his seat, head raised every so slightly between his sunken shoulders.

"The lie faded, the truth caught up with him. I saw it. I was there when he died."

Dawkin rounded the table to clap his brother on the shoulder. "Aye. As was I. For the first attempt, then the final farewell."

Colbern straightened. "You are sons of King Audemar, early in your reign, learning a valuable lesson: This is what it means to rule. The deception. The weight of power. The fragile peace existing in a world of truth and lies. All of it. It comes with the Throne."

"How did you manage, Grandfather?" Ely asked. "Honestly, you've seen more rule in your life than our father and us put together. What's your secret?"

Dear Mar, would that I could tell you. "Everything you already know. Teachings instilled in you since birth. Always gathering allies at your side, in peace and in war. Building trust by keeping your word. Mercy when unexpected, vengeance when called for... All of it, you know. You only need to see through the conviction of your actions. Rule – unapologetically, with haste – knowing your failures and successes will build, together, your legacy."

"Wise words," Symon acknowledged, folding his arms. "You must have taught Father those same lessons."

"Aye," Colbern admitted.

"'Tis one difference," Gerry said. He rose from his seat, suddenly emboldened by a realization. "Grandfather ruled as one. So did Father. We are four. We needn't do it alone." Gerry pivoted to face Dawkin. "You relieved my rule at Glic Anglisk when... my spirits fell."

"I did."

"Would you do it again?"

Dawkin shifted in place, his eyes darting between Ely, Symon, and his grandfather. They settled back on Gerry, whose own gaze had never strayed.

"Aye," Dawkin confessed.

Gerry turned to Symon. His jaw set, his nostrils flared,

Symon looked to the ground as he approached.

"Brother," Gerry started.

"Yes?" Symon asked.

"In his own way, Dawkin did right by us."

"How can you say that?"

"Because we're still here. No matter our faults, our mistakes, we remain together."

"You think that enough?" Ely pressed.

"Deep down, don't you?"

Ely considered for a moment. "I suppose," he relented.

"Come now, Ely, you can do better than that."

Ely chuckled. "Look at us? Upstaged by a runt."

"Ely," Symon scolded.

Ely extended the palm of his hand. "I jest, I jest. He has the right of it all. He's right, he's right." Ely strode up to Gerry. "We face this together."

Dawkin inched closer, his weariness having faded. "As kings."

"As brothers," Symon added.

"Aye," Dawkin admitted.

Grins ensued. Along with some banter. They later agreed Gerry's truth session could wait until morning. As the evening unfolded, Ely excused himself first. Then Dawkin. Symon and Gerry remained, speaking like lads on the events of court and the tales the captains and the sailors had brought in from the sea. Colbern smirked through it all, grateful for the smaller, everyday moments he could share with his grandsons.

Alas, finally, Symon and Gerry took their leave. The rest of the castle had settled in by then, the echoes familiar throughout the day abating with the passing hours, the

War Hall being no exception. As the wicks burned and the wax melted, Colbern sat back, relishing in the peace of the night.

"You look proud of yourself."

Colbern blinked, annoyed his tranquility had only lasted a moment.

"I thought you had retired," he said, looking over his shoulder.

A familiar face – identical to his own – stared back at him.

"You only wish," his brother, Berold, replied. He patted Colbern on the shoulder as he circled the long table to study its maps and tools.

"How much did you hear?" Colbern gestured to the wall opposite him. Blank and unadorned, with nary a crack distinguishable to the naked eye, not even the four would have ventured to guess it held a hidden door he and his brother had used since their youth.

"Enough. My mind wandered a bit when you drolled on and on with your advice. But my senses returned toward the end."

"Are you admitting I did well, brother?"

"They left united, of their own accord. So don't let the little effort you contributed go straight to your head."

Colbern grinned. "Does that mean you'll finally relent on the boys? Even the smart one?"

Berold huffed as he offered a sharp glance. Colbern shifted before rising, knowing he had crossed a line in provocation.

"The boy needs to be pushed. He's the natural leader of the four. The true king. Like his father was at his age, he's too soft. His edge needs to be honed, sharpened. His strength will come in time."

"You mean his fury."

"Audemar did fine enough with it. He maintained control of his temper – through my instruction – and unleashed his power when necessary. That edge aided him. Made him better." Berold flipped aside a few loose parchments, letting them fall from the table. "You leave *him* to me."

Colbern ground his teeth. Too often, during his ascension as Artus, Berold had flaunted his will. Colbern would learn of his dual use of pressure and brutality, then confront him, demanding he abandon his perilous ways. Berold would promise to ease his clout, only to resume his tactics when the opportunity allowed.

The vicious cycle resulted in a sibling rivalry approaching four scores, one in which Berold's agenda won nearly every time. First, in their shared reign as King Artus, in which Berold's directives always found a way of persisting over Colbern's. Then with their son, Audemar, whom Berold molded into his protégé during the latter years of the Century War.

Now, with their grandsons, with his sights on Dawkin in particular. Berold would ensure he became his father's son, cementing the Saliswater legacy for brutality.

Berold flipped another map, which rolled to the table's edge to fall to the ground.

Colbern glanced at the parchment, which in the dealings of the evening had become stained with wine. Crimson patches dotted the drawings, perhaps serving as Mar's ominous signs of all to come.

The parchment curled as it rolled on the floor. But not before Colbern caught sight of one red-stained land in particular.

Marland.

Colbern turned to Berold, who absentmindedly popped a handful of grapes and nuts into his mouth, oblivious to his brother's judgment.

He corrupted Audemar. He will do so with Dawkin. In light of all that has happened – and so much more we do not know – is that so wrong?

The moral dilemma hardly proved new to him. The memories of his concessions to Berold – allowing him to raise Audemar by his methods – flooded back to him.

He broke their son's kind spirit. He replaced Audemar's openness with cynicism, his grace with vengeance. Then again, so many nobles did the same with their heirs, as did knights with their squires and captains with their sailors. Colbern and Berold had inherited the mantle of kinghood in an era of war, which they, in turn, passed down to Audemar. How else could their son have grown, if not by hardening, to face a lifetime of battles and challenges?

Colbern stood to arch his back. As much as he hated to admit, Berold's way proved right time and again. In the complacency of his youth, he admitted as much, no matter how often he tried to rationalize against it. Now, in the twilight of his years, he came to the same truth once more, this time by way of sagacity and prudence.

He considered his brother for a moment, who tilted the silver platter to admire his reflection.

"Your intentions aside for the moment," Colbern urged. "What do you see in their future?"

Berold smirked. He laid the platter down to snatch one of the wax seals from the table. Then with his other hand, he grabbed a candleholder. He tilted it over the largest unfurled map – an aged painted piece illustrating Marland and the whole of Greater Afari – to pour the melted wax onto the parchment.

"They are four. Four times the brains and brawn Audemar could ever muster. Twice the ability you and I had. One can rule while the other three prepare and plan. Over and over. 'Tis a great advantage possessed by no king or queen on the Continent."

Berold set the candlestick down after having made four blotches of wax, each in separate kingdoms on the mainland. He pressed the bottom of the seal into the nearest spot, leaving a golden four-pointed compass over the land of Tosily.

He went on, imprinting the seal on the kingdoms of Volkmar and the Devout State of Belgarda before pausing over the blotch he had poured on Ibia.

"Empire has never been a choice word in our courts. Our people prefer control over the sea, whose waves and tides remind us it's a waterscape that defies mastery.

"Our kingdom's resources have been pushed to the brink. Fish only feed so many, while wheat and barley stores go empty almost as soon as they can be filled. And that was before the recent chaos set afire parts of the country.

"Colinne remains sparsely colonized, despite its annexation two decades ago. With this new 'threat,' we have the opportunity to convince the Marlish to finally settle in lands not their own. In fact, we'll offer it as an incentive, gifting the bravest knights and the most loyal nobles tracts in honor of their service."

Colbern mulled over the proposition. Similar schemes had been recommended in the past, especially during the height of the Century War. At the time, the kingdom of Colinne had stood in their way, what with their policies on open borders and their multitude of alliances. With those gone, the possibility of success seemed attainable, if only in theory.

"I left you speechless, I say," Berold grinned.

"Will the boys be at an equal loss of words?"

"Perhaps. 'Tis no matter so long as they don't linger in their thoughts, like you do, and act."

As brothers, Colbern thought, remembering the boys' words. *As kings.*

"Relax, little brother." Berold tossed the wax seal up and caught it in his hand. "They are Saliswater. They will prevail."

Yes, they will. But at what cost?

The End

www.ingramcontent.com/pod-product-compliance
Lightning Source LLC
LaVergne TN
LVHW012338100826
845148LV00018B/2704

* 9 7 8 1 7 3 7 1 2 9 0 1 1 *